THE HONEY BUBBLE

THE HONEY BUBBLE

A NOVEL

GEORGE D. PUTNAM

Writers Advantage

New York Lincoln Shanghai

The Honey Bubble

All Rights Reserved © 2002 by George Putnam

Writers Advantage
an imprint of iUniverse, Inc.

For information address:
iUniverse
2021 Pine Lake Road, Suite 100
Lincoln, NE 68512
www.iuniverse.com

ISBN: 0-595-25275-3 (Pbk)
ISBN: 0-595-65064-3 (Cloth)

Printed in the United States of America

~ ONE ~

Curly Peetz couldn't afford a drink that night. Kenny had given him a free one, but it got stale long before Curly finished it. A fresh drink would have occupied his mouth—the lazy way he took a sip every five minutes or so and swooshed it around a good minute like a pretentious wine taster before swallowing—and therefore he might not have talked on and on until Kenny couldn't stand it anymore. When the breaking point finally came, Kenny angrily phoned another bar owner down the street to help him set up the murder of the man he held responsible for his own desperate, fragile existence. Other than that, it was a normal night at Kenny's.

The drink's only ingredients were blueberry-flavored brandy and 7-Up, in a tall glass with lots of ice. Curly, who was homeless, called it a Blue Seven. He used to brag that he'd invented the Blue Seven, but the guys he bragged to about it hated fruity drinks as much as they hated teetotalers. When Kenny made it, the drink effervesced with lively invitation to Curly's hungry eyes and dry mouth. He imagined its red straws holding up a high diving board from which he could jump into the ice-cold clear blue below and get transported to a paradise of sweet tranquility. But since then, the drink had become flat and pasty, like liquid floor wax.

Kenny's regulars that night, all four of them, had already gone home. They, too, could no longer tolerate Curly's unceasing blather. Kenny stayed open anyway. You never know, he told himself nightly, when a new customer might come in and become a regular. Meanwhile, he cursed his utilities for costing him more than he was taking in.

Tall, lanky, and pigeon-toed, Kenny Grimmet had thin hair and a needle nose. He was forty-five. The way he rested his hands on his hips with

1

his thumbs pointed forward and fingers pointed backward made him look like an ostrich. He walked like one, too. His black eyes showed a crude intelligence. Chain-smoking had stained his teeth, and tar-strength coffee he drank throughout the day made them even darker. The only exercise he got came from chronic complaining. His vile breath could move objects.

The threadbare carpet in his bar smelled like old gym shoes. Its tomb-like atmosphere was broken only by metallic groans from an ancient ice machine coughing out ice cubes at regular intervals. Dust as thick as a dime covered everything. Drinks thrown violently at wood-panel walls over the years had left pockmarks that you couldn't tell from moon maps. None of his stools matched. The closet-size bathrooms were Curly's responsibility; for cleaning them daily, he got a Blue Seven and a package of beer nuts. This wasn't bad, as his food of choice outside Kenny's was cherry Pop Tarts and grape soda, and Gummy Bears for dessert.

Because Curly looked at his Blue Seven when he talked, he could not see the fixed grimace on Kenny's face. What he said in a grating monotone didn't amount to anything Kenny didn't already know anyway. It was like having to endure a home video so god-awful that it gagged the family dog. The highlights were that his single mom died when he was little, then an eccentric aunt raised him while she worked at Cooper's Drug Store until getting fired for stealing a carton of non-filtered Camels, then she slept with every barfly in Hillside Park for twenty bucks a pop, and eventually no one ever saw her again. As Curly said all this, Kenny's bored eyes followed an intrepid cockroach skittering across a cocktail napkin, the only movement in the bar.

"Just before my crazy aunt, though," said Curly, "when I was eleven, uh, maybe twelve, no, prolly when I was twelve, no maybe eleven…well anyways, I moved in with my grandmother." An irony in the recollection privately amused him. "And boy, was *that* a disaster."

Usually you could ignore Curly, like you ignore politicians at fundraisers when all you want is the food there. He rarely talked anyway. Mostly he just stared ahead like a bored squirrel in a cage. But tonight he was antsy. Kenny couldn't have cared whether Curly was antsy or brain dead, but his ability to tune him out was weakening with every dreadful minute.

"What a disgrace," said Kenny.

Curly thought this was a sympathetic response to the wretched lows of the lifestory he was reciting. But it was actually Kenny's reaction to how miserable being in the same room with Curly was.

"She was really a great old lady," continued Curly. "Except her feet stunk bad, really bad. She'd sit there watching TV with them bare feet of hers on this little stool about so high, front of her lazy chair. Her head'd be back and her mouth'd be open and she'd be snoring till, like, three or four in the morning. Then she'd wake up and her throat'd sound like Drano, you know, breaking up some backed-up drain, you know?" He tried to mimic the sound of running water. "The stool had these two little soft spots where she put her heels on. I'll never forget how them feet stunk up the whole trailer, kind of like, I dunno, musty or something—"

Kenny slapped the bar. "What a *disgrace!*" he said, louder than the last time. His tone expressed hopeless, exhausted resignation.

Curly showed worried confusion. "What's the matter?"

Kenny dropped his head dejectedly and let it hang as far as it would go without breaking off from his shoulders.

"I'm serious, Kenny. What's the matter?"

"What's the matter is Thursday nights, anybody gets a paycheck's out *spending* it. But no. No, *here* I'm running a *morgue.*"

Curly sounded wounded. "It's not my fault nobody comes in."

"Yeah, yeah, just order up, will you? Maybe I can make a nickel 'fore the night's over."

"I can't order up. I'm broke."

"Ah *Christ,*" said Kenny. "I just meant *hurry it up.*"

Curly was vexed. "You mean you want me to leave?"

"Just forget it," grumbled Kenny. He folded his arms in a gesture of resolve not to let Curly get deeper under his skin.

Curly was hurt. His self-esteem was already so low that he took every bad thing that happened this side of the Rockies as a personal rebuke, even earthquakes. "You *could* tell me what's bothering you."

"I just did," shouted Kenny.

At forty-three and a frail five-eight, Curly had sad brown eyes, big ears, fleshy lips and a narrow chin. When he stared at you with interminable curiosity, as he often did, you'd think he was analyzing your thoughts, as if collecting information with which to connive something out of you. But that would have required strategic thinking, and Curly was too simple for that. To most people, the only vibe he gave off was indifference. His abundant hair, with its messy bangs and unruly curls, gave him a youthful look, even though he moved with the bone-tired manner of a slump-shouldered field hand. Barroom brawls had knocked out his front teeth and flattened his nose into the shape of a coconut macaroon. He hadn't fought in years, but not because he'd become a coward. He stopped because his record was "0" and fill-in-the-blank. The irony was that he'd never *started* fights. He'd just tried to break them up, and when he tried too hard the fighters turned him into a punching bag.

Without sounding confrontational, Curly said, "Hey, Kenny, if you don't want my business I'll go to Marty's."

Kenny scoffed: "*You'll* go to Marty's?"

"Yeah, I'll go to Marty's."

"You're not going to Marty's. You know why?"

Curly sighed. "Here we go."

"That's right, 'here we go.' Marty wouldn't let you through his frigging *door*, that's why, and that's why *I'm* stuck with you."

Curly knew Kenny was right, that Marty would never let a stinko like him in his club. If Curly had anywhere to go, he would've left just to show Kenny he was tired of all the insults. Instead, he just shrugged and sipped his warm Blue Seven.

Kenny pounded the bar. "*Damn* these whiners preaching about drinking being bad for you! When I grew up, *everybody* drank, and everybody had a good *time* drinking. Now you've got to get religion, you've got to eat vegetables and stuff, and *I'm* going *broke* because of it."

Now Curly felt bad for Kenny. Kenny was just trying to make a living, he thought. "You're all right," Curly said with a grin.

"Go to hell," snapped Kenny. He ran his fingers through his hair and paced the length of his bar, and then said, mostly to himself, "The hell with this. I'm calling Cammy once and for all." He approached the phone next to his cobwebby cash register and picked up the receiver.

"How come you're calling Cammy?" said Curly.

"Shut up," said Kenny.

Kenny dialed Cammy's number. Curly shrugged helplessly and continued sipping his warm Blue Seven.

~ ~

Cammy's was a mile-and-a-half from Kenny's on the ground floor of a two-story brick building on the north side of Hector Street, a commercial artery that bisected Hillside Park in the northeastern-most section of Los Angeles. Half its storefronts advertised products in Spanish. Boarded-up windows on abandoned businesses were as common as cracked sidewalks and sagging fences around empty lots. Community leaders avoided the gentrification bug like a bastard child.

The town had four bars: Kenny's, Cammy's, Marty's, and the Sonoma Inn, also called Dom's, which also had a restaurant. Marty's outdid the other three combined. While Kenny's and Cammy's customers at any given time could fit into the front seat of a beer truck, and Dom's did a tad better, Marty's drew big-spenders from surrounding communities and pockets of Hillside Park.

Cammy Waller was fifty-one, five-six, and barrel-thick from eating bar snacks and microwaveable hot dogs. He had empty brown eyes, rubbery jowls, and thick hair that he kept groomed with enough gel to make a truck skid. On first impression, you might listen to him attentively because he was blessed with a deep voice that sounded like a lyrical tuba, and he spoke slowly, as if words came only after thoughtful deliberation. Within seconds, however, you realized he was a colossal bore for whom creative thought required a translator.

When Cammy bought his bar fifteen years earlier, after moving from Ohio, where he'd been a machinist, he named it "Camille's Corner," even though it wasn't on a corner. He also liked "Camille's *Cozy* Corner." Chronically indecisive, he dropped the "Camille" and called it "The Cozy Corner." But fear that people might be confused when trying to find a bar with "corner" in its name that wasn't on a corner forced him to change it to "Cozy Camille's." Then someone told him that "cozy" was a sissy word for a bar where workingmen drank. He tried "Camille's," but that sounded like a woman's dress store. So he settled on "The Knothole," but it never stuck.

The night Kenny phoned him to plan murder, Cammy had one customer, a seventy-year-old retired furniture mover and full-time drunk named Earl Zell. Earl looked like Frankenstein and was about as articulate. When nursing his ninth brandy-water, he got a sudden warning from a convulsing stomach, which prompted him to stand on wobbly legs, lurch forward, and cover his mouth as if holding back bile.

"No, please don't throw up in here, Earl," said Cammy.

Soon Earl took his hands from his mouth, sighed with relief, then gingerly sat back down.

"All right," said Cammy. "False alarm."

Earl looked at him with a punishing stare. "What 'throw up?'"

"Like you did last night," said Cammy.

"I din' puke lass night," said Earl.

"Yes you did, Earl. I ought to know. I had to clean it up."

"I din' puke lass night, I said."

"You sat right there and threw up, Earl. Now I think you should leave before you do it again."

"*You* leave."

Cammy chuckled. "Earl, I *own* this place."

"Big deal. All you got's welfare cases coming in."

"Now, why do you have to talk like that? My goodness. I didn't say anything against you, just your drinking. Your drinking tonight, I mean."

"Kenny'd let me in," said Earl. "I could go to Kenny's. I would, too, 'cept he waters his liquor down. Why should I pay for watered-down liquor? I'm not paying for watered-down liquor. My money's as good as the next fella's. Money doesn't grow on trees, you know. My money's as good as the next fella's."

Cammy tried to sound stern. "Earl, you've got that same look in your eyes you had last night just before you threw up, that scary look. Now I'm politely asking you to leave."

"No, I said. Marge isn't off yet and the bus stopped running."

"Then wait outside. I'll stay out there with you. You can't beat that. It's a nice warm July night out there and I'll wait right alongside you. If there's any trouble, we'll duck right back in again."

Earl hadn't heard. He was staring at Cammy as if planning revenge. Then he heaved up his last few meals. His stomach contents spread over Cammy's bar like an oil slick on a lake. Earl grinned, wiped his mouth with his sleeve, then belched. It was louder than an assault rifle. With mock sincerity, he said, "Musta been sumpin I ate." He took his change and staggered out.

Cammy just stared at the mess. Then came Kenny's call. Cammy answered brusquely. "The Knothole!"

Kenny could tell Cammy was irked. They weren't bosom buddies, but occasionally when Cammy closed up early he would visit Kenny to commiserate about the paucity of their customers. Though they competed for the few drinkers left who couldn't get into Marty's or didn't like the family-friendly atmosphere of Dom's, their alignment against Marty for having all the four-star customers bonded them like POW's.

"It's Kenny," he said. "You sound as pissed as me."

"Well Earl just threw up again," said Cammy.

"I hate that guy." Kenny stretched the phone cord outside Curly's hearing range and spoke quietly. "Are you alone?"

"I am now."

"'Cause I want to talk and talk serious, if you know what I mean."

Cammy shook his head. "You work hard, you put in long hours, you expect some reward at the end of the day, but instead you get throw-up. It's just laying there, Kenny. It's disgusting. It's all over my clean bar."

"Cammy, I'm talking about what we talked about numerous times, how to get out of this rut. You know what I mean?"

"Not really."

"*Think*, Cammy."

"Uh, oh, now I know. You mean killing Marty."

"Now you're cooking with gas."

"So this is really it? It's finally time?"

"Why not?" said Kenny. "We're on our last legs here."

"Well, you knew just when to call, Kenny. If you could see what I've got to clean up here—and for what? I bet I didn't take in forty dollars since lunch."

"Tell me about it," said Kenny. "The way things are going, the pressure where my next buck's coming from, I swear I'm going to die in a *week*. Not manner-of-speaking, not 'in-other-words,' but *die,* six feet under, a box covered with dirt, worms and everything."

"I've never heard you so pessimistic."

"That's *optimistic,*" snapped Kenny. "Work's the salvation of the soul. You heard that, right?"

"You bet," said Cammy. "I read the Bible, so…"

"I *want* to work. I *need* to work. But I got no damn customers. How am I supposed to work?"

"I know what you're saying, Kenny. A man needs to work to feel important in today's society, so…"

"So come on over and we'll talk about it."

"Are you alone?"

"No. I got the whole crowd from Dodger Stadium in here. Of *course* I'm alone. Except Curly, but I'll run him off when you get here."

"Well give me a minute." Cammy hung up, then stared at the vomit again. He decided to leave it. This was unusual, as he always kept a clean bar. He locked up and went to his car, a banged-up Ford Escort, which he'd moved earlier from his parking lot in the vandal-roving alley out back to Hector Street, where it would be safer. He didn't start the car right away. The night was quiet and lifeless.

"Am I really going to talk to Kenny about murdering somebody?" he said. "Somebody rich, with good looks, charm, a wealthy wife, a beautiful mistress, stuff I wouldn't know what to do with if I had it?"

Cammy had a tendency to say yes so as not to hurt people's feelings. But now, thinking about Earl Zell's vomit, and then thinking about *more* vomit the *next* time Earl got drunk, Cammy thought his impulse to say yes may have served him well for once. He'd been so depressed anyway. He'd done nothing with his life. In quiet reflection, he'd lament, "This is as good as it's going to get."

Well, maybe not after tonight. He started his car and drove down the street to Kenny's.

~ ~

Kenny's had twelve stools. Two bare fluorescent bulbs on a low, square-tiled ceiling provided the only light, and one of them flickered. A pool table no one used because its felt top was torn and frayed became one big rectangular ashtray. When Cammy entered, stale air from windows hammered shut and nicotine-stained carpets made him cover his nose and breathe through his mouth.

Curly, still perched on a stool in the middle, heard the door open and turned around. "Hey, Cammy," he said.

"What's doing, Curly," said Cammy.

"Nothing much," said Curly. "I was just telling Kenny about my crazy aunt and he gets all worked up and everything. Man, if you don't talk to him, he gets grouchy. If you talk to him, he gets grouchy. I can't win with that guy, you know, Cammy? Hey, when did you get the glasses?"

"Couple days ago," said Cammy. "Thanks for noticing."

Curly studied him. "They make you look like one of them arithmetic teachers at some college somewhere."

If anyone else had told Cammy that he looked like a professor, he might have glowed; in his own mind, he looked like a giant pinto bean. But from Curly it meant nothing. He breathed through his nose and tried not to flinch at the odors. "Kenny taking a whiz?"

"Yeah," said Curly. "He's in the head."

Cammy was ambivalent about Kenny. On one hand, when Kenny set his sarcasm aside, the two could talk about their common rut in a way that made Cammy think they were friends. On the other hand, Kenny had to dominate every discussion and win every argument. Cammy had felt so clobbered by him that he'd thought he was back home getting reamed out by his dictatorial mother. She had niggled him into proper conduct with humiliating anger without ever having said one good thing about him. Even in her grave she disapproved of him, mostly because he never married. Forget that his wooden lumpiness made women scatter; Mom thought Cammy should have college-educated beauties falling all over him.

Kenny exited the restroom zipping up his fly. "Hiya, Cammy."

"What's doing, Kenny?"

Kenny moved behind his bar and lit a cigarette. "Take off, Curly," he said. "Me and Cammy are going to talk."

This surprised Curly, as he always closed up with Kenny, except the nights he spent with his chubby girlfriend, Bernice. "But I didn't finish my drink yet, Kenny. Can I at least have a paper cup to put it in?"

"This ain't Starbucks."

Cammy interjected, "Why don't you let him finish his drink?"

Kenny thought about it. "Yeah okay," he said begrudgingly.

"Thanks, Cammy," said Curly. "I really appreciate it, Kenny."

Kenny leaned close to Cammy and started to speak quietly, but stopped when he felt Curly's intruding ears. "Damn it, Curly."

"I'm not listening," said Curly. "Really, I'm just thinking to myself."

Kenny slapped the bar. "All right, take your drink but bring the god-damn glass back tomorrow."

Curly scooted off his stool and headed for the door before Kenny changed his mind and made him leave the glass. "See you guys."

"See you, Curly," said Cammy.

After Curly left, Kenny let out a long sigh. "I can't stand it anymore, Cammy. You know that? It's past the point, I swear."

"What is?"

"*This*," said Kenny. "This crap, what I called you for."

"Oh yeah," said Cammy. "Say, have you got a spare beer?"

Kenny nodded. Cammy went behind the bar and got a longneck Bud. He preferred bourbon but didn't want to pour it in a glass with diseased microbes on the rim. At his own bar, glasses were clean and everything worked. Each night he wiped his bar down with white vinegar and in the morning oiled it with lemon-scented polish. He cleaned every bottle with Windex, chose metal pourers over cheaper, plastic ones because metal ones shined when clean and plastic ones didn't, and he arranged each bottle so that its pourer faced the same direction as the other pourers. Mirrors and glass shelves sparkled. Every hour, with or without customers, he changed the dishwater and disinfectant rinse in his sinks. He used scouring pads to remove mucous, lipstick, and finger smudges from his drinking glasses. He never served a drink in a glass he wouldn't drink from himself. Do onto others, his mother always said.

Cammy returned to his stool. "How do we do this?"

"Same as we always talked about," said Kenny. "Shoot him when he's done banging Rachel, put the blame on her." Each Monday, Marty's bodyguard, Cedar Roach, drove him to the bank to withdraw a hundred grand for cashing personal and payroll checks during the week, and then to Rachel Ellis' house, where they made love. The trysts were called "Monday Nooners." If you didn't know about them, you hadn't been around Hillside Park long.

Kenny spread his palms as if showcasing a banner headline: "Get this: 'Mistress Kills Rich Lover When He Wouldn't Leave His Wife.' Is that a headline or what? Who's not going to believe *that*?"

"But everyone knows Marty and Rachel love each other."

"So *what*?"

"No, I'm just saying they get along better than anybody I've ever heard of before. And they're not even married, so…"

"Horse shit," said Kenny. "They scrap just like me and Judy did. But so what? Things change with women, especially mistresses. They feel cheated, used, then comes them claws where they want to rip your eyes out. Judy saw me checking out this Oriental chick walking in front of our car once when we were at a stop light and I tell you the shit she yelled at me—whoa, burned my ears."

Cammy grinned. "Made a sailor blush, huh?"

He was already irritating Kenny. Anyone talking to Cammy had to keep him focused. Cammy knew it, too. He wondered if his mind meandered because of an involuntary obsession with his mother, as if he were seeking her approval by trying too hard to say something smart when all he needed to do was not say anything stupid.

"We're not talking about how Marty and Rachel get along, okay Cammy?"

"No, I know. It's just I know *my* parents wanted to kill each other half the time. You know something? My father got rid of his guns just so he wouldn't shoot my mother when they got in fights."

"Let's stay on track."

Cammy sipped his bear. "Yeah, okay."

"Rachel's *got* to be thinking Marty's never going to leave his wife."

"You would think so."

"Absolutely, that's our angle. Plus she's getting up there. Maybe she wants a kid some day. Nature's not going to wait forever, you know. What is she, forties now?"

"But she's still a goddess. I saw her a couple months ago at Ralphs. She was in shorts. Oh, those legs. Oh, my."

"Cammy, we're not here to talk about Rachel Ellis."

"No, no, I'm with you on this. I'm with you all the way."

"Ba-*doop*," said Kenny. "That's the blue-ribbon answer. I want to go while the getting's hot. I want to do this Monday."

"You want to do this Monday?"

"Yep. Strike fast, hit a home run, the works. With Marty dead, his club closed, you and me, we get a stampede of new business from all his old customers. I'll bet you we can't serve 'em fast enough."

"All right," said Cammy. "Monday it is." He tried to conceal half-heartedness, but didn't succeed.

"You really mean it, Cammy? 'Cause we're not challenging Marty to a game of pick-up sticks and whoever wins gets his customers. This is some serious shit we're getting into here."

"I know, Kenny."

"Good. Then let's go see Dom."

Cammy was surprised. "Dom?"

"Yeah, what's wrong with that?"

Dom made Cammy queasy. "What are we going to see Dom for?"

"Cammy, how many times did we talk about this? If you and me pulled this off without him he'd go right to the cops."

"No, yeah," said Cammy.

Kenny got animated. "Somebody runs in, 'Dom, guess who got killed? Marty! Rachel shot him dead.' No *way* Dom buys *that*, Cammy. First thing going through his mind's: 'Bullshit, Kenny and Cammy were up to something.' That's what Dom's going to think the second he hears what we did."

"Yeah, okay," said Cammy. "When?"

"When what?"

"You said 'let's go see Dom.' When?"

"Now, what do you think? Halloween? No, we'll catch him before he shuts down."

"No, yeah," said Cammy. "Sure."

Kenny started his closing chores and Cammy finished his beer. Soon, Kenny stopped and looked askance at him.

"What's the matter?" said Cammy.

"When'd you get glasses?"

"Couple days ago."

"Yeah well they make you look older."

~ TWO ~

The first-time visitor was astonished to see how busy Marty's was on a late Thursday night. Half the customers were dancing wildly to a cover band that played hard-driving, upbeat songs. The visitor, Mike Shihadeh, was fifty, handsome, and educated. He came to see if Marty wanted to sell his club. Marty's lawyer, Lou Carini, had set up an informal meeting; Marty often got inquires from buyers looking for a moneymaker. Mike owned liquor stores in Pasadena and Monrovia, but he wanted a nightclub. When a liquor salesman told him about Marty's, he came to see what the hubbub was about. Announcing himself to the bartender, Mike had to shout to be heard. When the bartender said he'd get Marty, Mike turned and surveyed the club.

The Main Room had a two-story ceiling. Circular, linen-topped tables with bentwood chairs surrounded a dance floor. Seating was also available on high chairs at ornately painted cherry-wood counters on the walls. If you didn't want conversation drowned out by the noise, you could go to the East Room or West Room, neither of which had music, just conversation. The three rooms connected through an arched passageway lined with countless photos of Marty and his customers. Each room had its own bartenders and cocktail waitresses. They all wore red vests, white shirts, and bow ties.

Mike noted that the club catered to merrymakers more than to serious drinkers. Attire ranged from casual to fashionable. He had expected subdued lighting. Instead, the club was festively lit. Spanish lanterns diffused peach-colored light in sunburst fashion on glossy, white-brick walls. Ivy plants exfoliated from hand-painted clay vases in wrought-iron wall-baskets. At twelve feet up, the walls disappeared behind short, sloping fake eaves covered with mission tiles. Above the tiles, the walls curved into a flat-black ceiling with no fixtures or lights on it. The effect was of being in a big open room with the night sky above you. The club's centerpiece was a water fountain of mosaic tiles lit by submerged floodlights. The lanterns, plants, brick walls, eaves and black ceiling simulated an evening in a stately courtyard amid green gardens and quietly running water.

Marty was thanking customers for their patronage. With an infectious grin and sparkling eyes, he patted shoulders as he moved from table to table. "Glad you came, hope you're having fun," he said. He wore a light sport coat over a cotton shirt with corduroy trousers and calfskin loafers. He was sixty-four, five-eleven, and had a medium build and straight shoulders. His receding hair was white and wavy. He had lateral wrinkles in his round forehead and a bulbous nose that dwarfed a small mouth until he grinned, at which point his smile got big and toothy. Saggy bags under his brown eyes reflected the long, tireless hours he put in seven days a week.

The bartender got Marty's attention and indicated Mike. The two men met with cordial smiles, then went to Marty's office, a photo-lined room in a hallway off the Main Room. Marty closed the door and went around his desk while Mike sat in a chair that faced the desk. The pulsating live music could be felt through the office walls.

"Mr. Bagliamente," said Mike. "Your nightclub is charming and elegant and lively." Marty thanked him, and two minutes of small talk followed. Mike impressed Marty as being an easy-going and smart opportunist. "Do you not wish to move to a better location?"

"Why should I?" said Marty. "When customers like you as much as you like them, geography's not an issue."

"But in America they say location is everything."

"And as you can see, that applies here."

Mike laughed.

"When I opened this place, Hillside Park was clean and safe. There was family entertainment all over the place. It was very satisfying. But it changed and I didn't. So from where I'm sitting, looking over my customers, everything's the same, because it comes down to people. I agreed to meet you as a professional courtesy, but I won't sell."

"Let me say only that you have not heard my offer. I would not change anything. I would not tamper with your success."

"It doesn't matter," said Marty. "In terms of location, there are three other clubs within a mile or so of me you could check out."

"Would it benefit me to inquire of their owners?"

Marty didn't want to talk against his competitors. "Why not? At the end of Hector Street that way's a place called Kenny's. In between us is one called Cammy's, though out front it says 'the Knothole.' Just off Hector Street, in the other direction, there's a bar-restaurant called the Sonoma Inn, but everyone calls it 'Dom's.'"

Mike felt that Marty was being less than direct about the value of his competition. "Do you mind telling me why you won't sell?"

"My family's been in this business three generations. It's all I know."

"But you can be tempted at least to consider an offer."

"Temptation's attractive, sure, but so's resisting it. A friend of mine says I need to be spiritual. She may be right, I don't know. But I do know my club binds me to my ancestors and something about that touches the soul. I wouldn't be here if food didn't bring them together in the first place. They met at a picnic in Italy. The story goes, my grandfather said, 'Rosa, I like-ah-you cannoli,' and Rosa said, 'Augusto, I like-ah-you osso buco,' then Augusto slip-ah the pepperoni to Rosa, and a bigga baby boy come, and they live-ah-happily ever after."

Mike laughed. He understood why Marty's customers liked him.

"I've been telling that since I could walk. They eventually emigrated and opened a diner in Cleveland. The 'bigga baby' was my dad. He took it over and I grew up in it. Before most boys shave I was a busboy, chef's assistant, waiter, and what I liked most, a greeter. So there you go, Mike."

Mike grinned. "You are as stubborn as me."

"That's probably true. My grandfather used to sit with his customers with something from the kitchen for them to sample. Right there, that was the bond. My dad did the same thing with his. It personalized the business. That's how I run mine."

"But where is the restaurant?" asked Mike.

Marty thought about how to answer. It was a touchy subject. He and his wife, Gloria, had a son, Paul, who grew up in Marty's just as Marty had grown up in his family's Cleveland restaurant. Employees and customers alike became extended family to the little boy. One night in his twentieth year while a pre-med student at U.S.C., Paul took a date to dinner and a movie, dropped her off at her home, and went to Marty's to hang with his father. Later, when he left, a stolen pickup truck screaming west just north of Hector Street ran a stop sign and rammed Paul's car into a utility pole. He died instantly. Awakened residents saw the driver view up close what he'd done, then tear back into the truck and screech away. His legs were rubbery. They got his plate number. The truck had been sold days before from a dealership a few miles south, on North Figueroa Street in Highland Park. But Marty skipped over all this. "The Main Room *was* a restaurant. What's out there now is the same as when we opened, except for the dance floor. We put that in when I refused to re-open after I closed up for my son's funeral. I just lost the desire and energy to supervise the kitchen."

"I am sorry for the loss of your son," said Mike.

Marty nodded acknowledgment. "Memories of him here—jamming his toy in our old pasta machine, stealing mints from the hostess—they're all I have. Some things you can't sell." He didn't add that the loss of his son and getting no vengeance from his death was made worse by his wife's holding him responsible. A drunk had killed her only child, and she'd lumped that anonymous killer in with all drunks and spread the blame to all bar owners. Marty and Gloria stayed married but were never intimate again. Shortly before all that, Marty had hired Rachel Ellis, then twenty-one, as a weekend bartender. She'd been working at Dom's, but Marty's had better tips, better clientele, year-end bonuses, and a superior boss. In the wake of his son's death and his wife's subsequent remoteness, Marty found solace in Rachel. They'd been lovers since. Marty even bought her a house near his club.

Mike stood and extended his hand. "I am glad to have had the opportunity to talk to you, Mr. Bagliamente. If there is any change, please contact me. I would like to do business with you."

Marty shook his hand. "Glad you came by, Mike."

They walked to the rear exit. A valet fetched Mike's car. Marty's valets wore uniforms and worked under bright lights he had had installed to insure his customers' safety and to keep vandals away.

"I noticed your drinks are inexpensive," said Mike.

"That was the silver lining to tearing out the kitchen. I ended up with so much storage space that I could buy loads of wholesale liquor at big savings."

"Which you passed on to your customers," said Mike.

Marty nodded. "My competitors were overjoyed."

Mike grinned, then drove off. Marty returned to the club. He had an unpleasant task ahead. He needed to tell his chauffeur, bodyguard and bouncer that he was going to cut back his hours. If there was one thing he know about Cedar Roach, it was that he did not like change.

~ ~

When Cammy finished his beer, Kenny had emptied the cash register into a paper bag and hidden it beneath the bar. He grabbed his keys, turned off the lights and headed out with Cammy at his side.

"I can't believe we're finally going to do this," said Cammy.

"Should've done it years ago. Nobody's been screwed like us, the way that wop prick rakes in all the dough with that greasy smile of his. Upside, the whole world knows about him and Rachel, even his own wife. You hear about that all the time, mistresses going over the top. I'm telling you, this is one sure angle."

"Yeah," said Cammy.

They walked to Cammy's car in front. There was ample parking after dark because nothing was open except the four bars, and they hardly looked inviting. Neither Kenny's nor Cammy's had windows, outside lights, or barkers promising a good time inside. Dom's was behind his street-fronted parking lot and a canopy that extended from his entrance. Marty's entrance was in the rear alley. As Kenny locked his door, the black stillness of the night was broken by the distant sound of a man cursing in Spanish. Where the street crossed railroad tracks two hundred yards away, they saw that a bum carrying an open beer bottle had fallen, risen awkwardly, and cursed at losing his balance. All they could make out was his stumbling silhouette against a faraway porch light on a ramshackle house behind high weeds.

Kenny said, "'He yours or mine?"

Cammy laughed emptily. How could he laugh with sincerity at such a depraved symbol of his rut? The bleakness reminded him of how crappy Hillside Park was, especially for meeting women. During the day, auto and pedestrian traffic busied the street like an ant farm, but in the wee hours it became a cemetery. Most of its stores closed by six, its supermarket by ten. An all-night coffee shop was set so far back in a drab mini-mall that it couldn't be seen from the street, so no one traveling by didn't know about it. Besides, as all-night coffee shops went, it had all the warmth of an ice floe.

Cammy and Kenny got in the car. Kenny, lighting a cigarette, said, "The thing we've got to keep in mind here's to not get emotional. That's when you make mistakes."

Cammy looked at Kenny. "You never killed anybody before, right?"

"Eh, maybe once," said Kenny. "I didn't stick around to find out. No, this asshole one night's hitting on Judy when me and her were at some dive back when I was still painting houses, and right there, not three stools down, he's tickling her ear, blowing in it and shit. So I go to my car, I get this wrench out—big plumber's wrench, weighs like three pounds—and man I hammered that son-of-a-bitch lover-boy in the head. Judy's screaming, blood's flying all over the place. I'm not saying he died, but I guarantee he woke up thinking a tank ran over him."

"So nothing like what we're going to talk to Dom about?"

"Not really. See, Cammy, wars generally come down to the haves versus the have-nots. Marty's getting all the business and he's not giving anything back. He thinks since he's king of the jungle he can spray piss all over the rest of us. And he doesn't even *live* here. At least us and Dom, we live here. We need movie theaters back, decent restaurants, places where people can have a drink afterwards in quiet, not all that noise like Marty's got. Me, I'd get a sense of community going here again so we can all share the wealth."

"Knock on wood," said Cammy. But he didn't buy a word of it. Kenny was selfish and contemptuous of everyone. If Kenny could get away with it, he'd run down pedestrians just for the fun of it. Cammy drove toward Dom's.

"Marty's got his club and he's got Rachel," said Kenny. "But what's anyone else here got? Birdseed, that's what, no chance of making inroads into anything. You got locusts eating this town alive and nobody's doing anything about it. That's where we come in, Cammy. We can turn things around soon as we get rid of Marty."

"Kenny, did you ever have sex with her?"

Christ, thought Kenny, this dumb bastard couldn't keep his mind on track if it was made of train wheels. "*Who*, Cammy?"

"Rachel."

"C'mon," said Kenny. "Let's keep focused here."

"No really," said Cammy earnestly. "Did you ever sleep with her?"

Kenny put on a nonchalant air, puffed on his cigarette, and waited until he exhaled before answering. "Yeah once."

Cammy brightened. "No."

"Me and Judy weren't getting along so good this night I ran into her at Dom's. She was still drinking back then, back when she was kind of heavy. I guess her and Marty were having some kind of beef. So I laid the old sob story on her, how I've got to whack the weenie since Judy's not fulfilling her wifely duties and all. Next thing I know she's out in my car, back seat, ba-*doop*, right in Dom's parking lot."

Cammy hit his steering wheel. "My, my, heaven on earth." He couldn't erase a smile. "Did you pay her?"

"I know she had that rep, but I never paid for it with her or any other girl."

"Give me one night with Rachel," said Cammy, glancing heavenward. "Then you could kill me. I'd die smiling. You know something? I wonder why Marty doesn't marry her. I know *I* wouldn't let another man anywhere near her if she was mine."

Kenny tossed his cigarette out the window. "Cammy, we've got to present our case to Dom, not that he won't go for it if it's not all spit and polish. So enough about Rachel. And another thing. I want to cop Marty's check-cashing money, too—shoot his ass *and* get that money. That's a hundred grand the three of us can fix our places up with."

"Geez Louise," said Cammy.

"'Cause right now they're like cancer wards, our places. People want to see stuff going *on* when they come in a bar. They want action, entertainment, thrills. They don't want to see the likes of Curly Peetz or Earl Zell sitting around like corpses with vultures circling all around 'em."

"A third of a hundred grand? Whew."

"That's a pot of gold," said Kenny. "We'll need it. We need to hook his customers in before they go someplace else. We need to spruce our places up. People like places that look inviting."

Cammy turned into Dom's parking lot. The Sonoma Inn was two short blocks south of Hector and Sonoma, the town's busiest intersection and the most concentrated commercial district. It gave Dom a lunchtime crowd of merchants and employees who enjoyed his homemade Italian spicy-sausage soup, which he served free in cups with garlic bread and with no limit on refills. Everyone loved the soup, even people who couldn't stand Dom's noisy bar customers. Dom also benefited from being near freeways leading to Pasadena to the east and Glendale and Burbank to the west.

"Dom don't think much of you, you know that, don't you, Cammy?" said Kenny.

"Yeah, I know." He shut off his motor. "But you know something, Kenny? I don't really care if he likes me or not."

"Yeah, it's not like him and me are going to go get an ice cream together, either. But when we start gussying up this old town, we'll all get along better. At least we won't have no more money worries."

"I think so, too. Thirty-three grand, depending on how it's split up, that's a lot of money, so…"

Cammy parked near the canopy leading to Dom's entrance. No one was around. The faint sound of a siren was so far away that they couldn't tell if it came from downtown or from one of the freeways.

"I'll do the talking," said Kenny.

"I know," said Cammy.

~ THREE ~

Dominick Catina was at his cash register trying to ring up a beer for an orange-haired, tattooed hustler in oversized jeans who looked about nineteen. Dom, who always whistled "Jimmy Cracked Corn," was sixty-six, a stout five-nine, had a plump face, and was bald with gray hair on the sides of his head. He had very bad eyes. His bifocals looked like welders' goggles.

People liked Dom because he appreciated their business. If anything, he was too personal. He'd rant about his ne'er-do-well son, his rotten son-in-law, and spoiled grandkids. But he stopped just before getting tiresome. His place was clean, his employees efficient. The restaurant had Victorian-style booths. Background music was easy listening. The food was average. Salads were crisp. Virtually all of his restaurant business came from repeat customers. They got big servings and were gone by ten p.m. Unlike Kenny and Cammy, Dom had employees do all his work. The only time he mixed drinks was at night, when he could also do his books. But pulling double-duty taxed his eyes. He zeroed in so close to the paperwork that it looked as though his nose were screwed into the top of his bar.

Nobody in Hillside Park hated Marty more than Dominick Catina. The reason was that Marty believed his son's killer had come from Dom's, and had taken it out on Dom. Cops had interviewed Dom's patrons and employees about who might have driven a pickup that night *and* come from his bar, but no one had. Dom had denied responsibility by saying that nobody would have stolen a vehicle and *then* come into his bar. Someone would have stolen a vehicle, then gone *joy riding*. But no one in

Dom's that night had gotten drunk and stolen a pickup. The police had confirmed this.

Marty's logic for indirectly blaming Dom was threefold. One, Dom's was the only bar east of the accident. Two, driving west from it on Hector Street, you could drift right at a fork and be on the street the drunk driver took. Three, Dom used to serve customers until they fell down drunk, but the day after the accident he eighty-sixed anyone even halfway to tipsy. Marty declared that this change of policy had sprung from guilt. Despite the improvability of his charge, Marty punished Dom by barring Dom's customers from his own club and eighty-sixing his own if they patronized Dom's. Hidden spotters reinforced this. The effect was a permanent reduction of Dom's nighttime business.

When Kenny and Cammy entered the Sonoma Inn, they saw Dom trying to discern the keys on his cash register through his bifocals. He tilted his head back to see through the bottom half of them. The effort forced his mouth open like a goldfish at feeding time. By squinting hard, he could not see that the orange-haired hustler had snatched bills from the register when it opened.

Kenny and Cammy, whose entry went undetected, watched the hustler give himself a silent, giddy thumbs-up.

"Put 'em back, asshole!" shouted Kenny.

The hustler froze. His reaction to getting caught red-handed approximated being stabbed. Dom, turning to see who'd spoken, lowered his head to look through the upper half of his bifocals, saw Kenny and Cammy, then looked through the lower half to see what had made Kenny shout. Then he took the bills back from the hustler and barked, "Scram!"

The hustler walked with measured steps past Kenny and Cammy until he reached the door, then sprinted into the night.

"We just saved your profits," said Kenny.

"My profits are fine," said Dom. "What do you guys want?"

Cammy grinned. "Working hard or hardly working?"

Dom hated Cammy's overreaching attempts at friendliness, so he ignored his comment. The older Dom got, the less he could tolerate fools, unless they were customers. Cammy wasn't surprised that he was getting the silent treatment. Dom knew Kenny and Cammy hadn't come to organize a chapter of the Audubon Society. Kenny had been trying to convince him and Cammy that Rachel was the way to destroy Marty. They never disagreed; they just didn't know how. Then he got the idea to kill Marty and blame it on Rachel, but they first had to start rumors that she was getting tired of promises Marty made to leave his wife.

"Start talking," said Dom.

Kenny and Cammy sat on adjacent stools. Dom's had eight. The back bar, all glass shelves at a mirrored-wall, was lit by fluorescent lamps under blue lenses to get a luminous marine effect.

"We figure it's time to improve the bar business for us little guys here," said Kenny.

"Just say it straight out," said Dom.

Before Kenny could respond, Cammy invoked a sympathetic tone. "It's okay, Dom," he said. "We know your history with Marty."

Dom put his finger in Cammy's face. "Don't try to handle me."

Kenny glanced coldly at Cammy for speaking up. It was obvious to Dom that the two had discussed protocol before entering.

"What have you done so far?" Dom said to Kenny.

"What we've done so far is come here. We just feel the time's right, right here and now, all engines full steam ahead."

"I'm not whacking anybody," said Dom. "Marty could be a nine-foot purple giant with a neon sign saying 'whack me' and I still couldn't see him."

"We know your eyes are bad," said Cammy.

Dom gave Cammy another disapproving look, but Kenny took his attention back by saying, "No, we'll do the whacking, Dom, me and Cammy. 'Far as you, you put it out Marty and Rachel had a big dog fight, say a week or so ago—you just heard, something like that."

"Rumors, my specialty," said Dom.

"'Rachel's tired of being alone,' 'Rachel feels used after all these years,' phrases like that," said Kenny. "Just let those float around. Just say you heard this and that then change the subject."

"I'll figure it out," said Dom. He gathered his paperwork as if he knew he wouldn't be getting back to it for another day. "You two showing up like this—if somebody was here there could be questions later."

"Nobody was in here, were they?" said Kenny. "Just that thieving kid."

"Just don't get sloppy. No phone calls either. They check that."

"Yeah well just give us *some* credit," said Kenny. "We took the first step. We took the initiative here."

"Keep something in mind," said Dom. "With me, I hate that son of a bitch Marty with a passion. But you guys, it's your livelihood."

"So you're better than us, is that it?" said Kenny.

"I didn't say that."

"Sure sounded like it to me."

"That's 'cause you're paranoid."

"Just 'cause you say it don't make it true. You said you don't need this like me and Cammy, I'm just saying explain that."

Dom raised his voice: "My family's comfortable and *I'm* not crawling up walls. Is that enough of an explanation?"

"Just say we're assholes, why don't you?" said Kenny. "No, pound for pound you're just the best ever, aren't you?"

Cammy grinned. "You guys. Never a dull moment."

Kenny reached for a cigarette.

"No smoking," said Dom.

"It's after two," said Kenny. "Who's coming in, the governor?"

"Both of you, please," said Cammy. "Let's just be friendly, okay?"

Nobody responded. Dom took off his glasses and rubbed his eyes. Kenny lit his cigarette and made a show of inspecting Dom's array of drinking glasses behind his bar. Cammy tapped his fingers.

~ ~

Last call had just been made at Marty's. Scores of customers were leaving and others were on their final drink, all under the scrutiny of Cedar Roach. Marty's eyes found Cedar's, he indicated the water fountain, and they met there. Marty could have waited until closing to talk with Cedar, but Cedar lived by self-imposed time constraints, one of which was getting home right after work. There, after relations with his live-in mate, a teenage Mexican girl, he listened until four in the morning to an all-night radio show about paranormal phenomena, his big interest along with biographies of great men.

Cedar was in a three-button jacket over shirt and tie. At six-three and two-forty, with thick arms and chest, he projected an image of mystery and fear. He looked younger than his forty-four years. He had smooth, clear skin, straight teeth, big lips and a narrow nose. His blond hair was combed back tightly so that it looked like a shower cap. He lifted weights in a bedroom-turned-gym at his Eagle Rock duplex and jogged before work. He didn't smoke or drink. As a kid, Cedar developed a theory that there were only two kinds of people, weak and strong. Every year when Daylight Saving Time began or ended, he knew which classmates and teachers were weak. They were the ones who showed up late the day after clocks turned forward and early when they turned back. But Cedar was punctual every day. He was no goody two-shoes, just disciplined. He hated people with vices.

His rigid work habits had appealed to Marty when they'd met. Marty had gone to a private investigator to help find the drunk who'd killed his son after the L.A.P.D. stopped investigating. The P.I. had a young trainee, Cedar, who, because of attitudinal problems, couldn't cut it in the Glendale Police Department. The P.I. came up empty, but Marty was impressed with Cedar's attention to detail. He'd grown up in Hillside Park and knew all the punks. Thinking this would be an asset when dealing with bar owners growing bitter over being crowded out by his club, Marty offered Cedar job security and more money if he'd be his bouncer, bodyguard, and chauffeur. Now, twenty years later, Marty had to tell Cedar that his routine would change. That was like telling Major League Baseball to make its players wear skirts.

When Cedar and Marty met at the fountain, Marty didn't speak right away. They often went whole nights without conferring. What then, thought Cedar, made Marty call a conference only to delay it?

"You want to take Mondays off?" said Marty. "Say till six?"

Cedar raised his eyebrows. "I don't understand."

"My sister's kid, Joey. He just turned eighteen and she's been bugging me to find him a job. She thinks he's going to be a Peter Pan if he doesn't spread his wings soon. I thought I'd start him off driving for me."

This insulted and disappointed Cedar, but he concealed his reaction. "Like you don't do enough for your sister."

Marty grinned. "Freda's not selfish, just neurotic."

"There's a difference?" said Cedar.

"Now you sound like Rachel. Everything's got two meanings."

"Nobody ever said Rachel doesn't know what's going on," said Cedar with a measure of respect.

Marty nodded. "Freda wants an answer this Sunday. We're having cake for the kid. I don't need indigestion before I even sit down to dinner."

"You always said Joey wasn't too smart," said Cedar.

"What do I know? He's never had a break, no father, no guidance. I guess he can't stay interested in any one thing."

"Maybe he's got Attention Deficit Disorder." Cedar's belief in the paranormal made him theorize that human behavior was affected by radio signals from an energy source in space known as Cygnus A.

"What makes you say that?" asked Marty.

"This town. Chemicals in the air."

"My understanding, he hardly goes anywhere."

"There's chemicals in the home too," said Cedar. "Carpets, drapes, radiation emission from appliances, cleaning compounds. He could have Multiple Chemical Sensitivity from it. That affects your immune system, your emotional state too. It can cause anxiety disorders."

When Cedar expressed his theories and beliefs, Marty always played the wide-eyed, closed-mouth, hands-in-his-lap student to Cedar's revered Professor from Egghead U. But tonight he pressed him because the subject was his only nephew. "I think Joey's problems stem from a lack of ambition."

Cedar responded quickly. "An amalgam of sensitivities can result in trauma to the individual."

"*Chemicals* can ruin ambition?" asked Marty.

"It's called depression."

"I'm not going to tell Freda to put him on medication."

"No, that's more chemicals."

Marty never knew how to tell Cedar without hurting his feelings that he thought his theories were garbage. "All I'm talking about is starting him off one day. After a while he'll have a résumé out of it then maybe he could work for a limousine service till he finds something he likes."

"Are you going to give him a piece?" asked Cedar.

It was a logical question. Cedar never strayed far from Marty, as too many people knew Marty carried wads of cash. He'd been assaulted twice with intent to rob before Cedar intervened, once in the Main Room and once in the parking lot. Cedar had sent the attackers to the hospital. The money Marty carried was for cashing checks, which drew in customers, especially on paydays. Once they got money in their hands, they stuck around and spent it. Marty also handed out loans on the spot. He never asked for interest and never recorded the loans. But if a loan was not repaid, Cedar was dispatched to collect, unless Marty thought the individual in arrears couldn't repay, usually due to misfortune; in this case, Marty dissolved the loan. But when someone could repay but didn't, word reached Cedar through people wanting to stay in Marty's favor, and Cedar went out to settle the matter with his fists.

Marty trusted Cedar—crazy theories aside—shared business ideas with him, and talked to him about Rachel, a former high school classmate of Cedar's. This gave Cedar power other employees didn't have, so they kept their distance. They also viewed him as a sadist because of how he treated unruly customers once he got them in the parking lot. He wasn't content to slap them around and send them to bed without the Disney Channel. He wanted to inflict pain.

"I'm not giving Joey a piece," said Marty. "He'd shoot his foot. No, it'll be all right." This last sentence was Marty's way of signaling that he was finished with a conversation.

"Are you sure you want Joey starting out on the S-L?"

Marty nodded. "It's just to the bank and Rachel's and back. What's that, four, five miles round trip? It should go all right."

"The S-L's a powerful car."

"I got him a bike once, he never even used it. I offered to buy him a car when he got his driver's license, but he said no. Besides, I'm right there next to him. And don't worry. I won't trim your pay. Come in at six. That way you get most of the day off."

"Sure, I understand," said Cedar.

Marty looked over his customers without speaking. This was always a sign that he was getting reflective. "I'd like to start Joey off here," he said. "If I had my druthers, anyway." Cedar knew Marty was thinking that his club would die when he died. It saddened Marty to envision such an outcome to the years of hard work he'd put into his business. Yet there was no one in his family to take over. His wife hated the bar, his sister was unstable, and his nephew was a loser. "But Freda and Gloria would sooner shoot me than get Joey started here," added Marty. "They despise drinkers. I'm getting too old to argue with them anymore. Whatever they want, they get."

Cedar avoided Marty's eyes. He said, "John Stuart Mill wrote that the most important thing women have to do is to stir up the zeal of women themselves."

He threw quotes at Marty and others all the time. Marty rarely figured out what relevance they had to a given discussion, so he usually nodded perfunctorily. "Joey could make a lot of money here, taking over one day," he said. He paused as if lost in thought, and then snapped back. "But if Freda wants him to be a doctor, a lawyer, a scholar, whatever, even a toaster repairman, that's what I'll help him be. If she wants him to sell maps to movie stars' homes, I'll buy a basket for his bike with a little bell on it."

"All the money you could give him to do whatever he wants and he sits idle," said Cedar. "Complacency is the deacon of the devil."

"If it doesn't work out, if he runs over somebody, if he's bored, we'll just go back to how it is now. Appreciate your cooperation, Cedar."

Marty patted Cedar on his shoulder and moved on. Cedar returned to gazing at customers. For the moment, he didn't want to think about Marty's replacing him one day a week as driver-bodyguard. His first impression, though, was one of encroachment on his territory, his duties, his very relationship with Marty. Ever the analytical, methodical thinker, he tried to suppress his emotional response. For the time being, he would watch for troublemakers among the departing customers. There were always a few who balked at being told they had fifteen minutes to finish their drink. But they didn't balk long, not with Cedar Roach in their faces.

~ ~

Kenny finally broke the awkward silence at Dom's. "What're we on here, a death watch?" he said. "C'mon, guys."

"Yes," said Cammy. "Time's a wasting."

"Yeah," said Kenny. "We've got business to talk about." Dom put his glasses back on. Cammy tried to look alert. Kenny looked at Dom. "You got to start the rumors tomorrow. We're doing it Monday."

"*This* Monday?" said Dom.

"No, a year from Monday. And we're copping his check-cashing money too."

"That's a little greedy," said Dom.

"It's *very* greedy," said Kenny. "But we need to fix our places up or else this whole idea's a waste of time."

"It's like an added bonus," said Cammy. "It's between thirty-three and thirty-four grand apiece."

"That's a plum, Dom," said Kenny. "I want to bring dancing in my place, like Marty's got. You know them big round lights in the middle of the ceiling with them little square mirrors on them that rotate? People like that when they're dancing. All I need's a band—get the word out there's a new nightclub in town, ba-*doop*. Get the younger crowd in, forget the Metamucil crowd—bunch of tightwads with fixed incomes and all. I can charge a cover charge, jack up prices, just start wheel-barreling in the dough. I can't wait."

"Big plans, you two," said Dom. He didn't believe Kenny could be successful at anything that required hard work and finesse.

Kenny turned to Cammy. "How about you?"

"Well, I'm interested in hiring a bartender so I could take a little time off, maybe meet someone I can marry."

"There goes your dough," said Kenny. "'How fat's your wallet, sir?' Naw, you're better off going to Vegas and getting hookers."

"Well that's not me," said Cammy. "If I could really afford it, I'd like to hire stand-up comics. They probably cost a lot but I wouldn't have to charge as much as those comedy clubs on Sunset Boulevard charge."

"That's stupid," said Kenny. "There's nobody left around here even speaks enough English to *get* jokes. You're going to hire *messican* comics talking about beans and farts? That'll get laughs."

"There's comedy clubs in L.A. and Pasadena," Dom said to Kenny. "Why not one in between?"

Silence followed. It appeared to Dom that Kenny, outnumbered in support for Cammy's idea, didn't know how to save face. The silence allowed Cammy to gloat privately that he'd had the good sense not to reveal a different reason for wanting time off, one he knew they'd ridicule. It was that he loved long, uninterrupted bowel movements. His mother had made a ritual of hers by taking coffee and cigarettes and reading material into her bathroom for an eternity. But for Cammy, relishing a lavish bowel movement in the comfort of his home meant waiting until he closed his bar in the early morning. He moved his bowels at work when he had to, of course, but that meant hurrying, worrying about germs on the toilet set, the smell others left in the bathroom, people coming in, leaving the bar untended, etc.

"Okay," said Kenny. "I spend my share on dancing, Cammy gets comics, Dom, how about that laser surgery for your fucking eyes they got now?"

Dom snapped: "My prostate's bad too but I'm not letting some quack stick a knife in my nuts and I'm not letting another one burn holes in my eyes."

"You're really keeping up with the times," said Kenny. "Hey, we'll need a gun. I'm not using mine."

"I'll get you one," said Dom. "But you're picking it up."

"I'll come get it," said Cammy. "After all, it's just a hop, skip and a jump."

"Sunday night," said Dom to Cammy. Then he looked at Kenny, "Now what about this Nazi?"

"Cedar?" said Kenny.

"Yeah. Him and Marty are like Fred and Ginger."

"Marty's not going to be screwing Cedar next Monday Nooner," said Kenny.

"I *know*. But he's going to be right outside."

Kenny grinned wickedly. "And that's going to be a beaut, him waiting out there like that. 'Can't interrupt the lovebirds.' No, no. Wouldn't you love to see him squirm in that car instead of going inside and looking like a fool for interrupting them two?"

Dom grinned at Kenny's scenario. This made Cammy's skin tingle, just like when his mother berated him for stupidity. His impulse, then as now, was to retreat. But now, with much at stake, he had to confront his fears.

"Fellas," said Cammy. "I'm not getting something here."

"There's a bulletin for you," said Kenny.

Cammy said timidly, "Well…isn't Rachel, uh, I mean don't you think she'll call the cops?"

"What?" said Kenny.

Cammy's heart sank. "Well yes. Cedar will see her running around like a chicken with its head cut off. Won't he? I mean he's not going to be sitting in Marty's car after she sees what we've done."

Kenny and Dom shared exasperated expressions. Cammy didn't know why. "Cammy," said Kenny, "it's a murder-*suicide*. Where's your head at? Cops come in, they see Marty's brains blown out, they see Rachel shot through *her* head, they see a gun on the floor with her prints on it, they put it all together—the mistress, the cheating husband—I explained all this not twenty minutes ago."

"Not the suicide part."

"Did I *need* to? Did you think we were going to shoot Marty in a blaze of bullets then wave hello to Rachel 'how-ya-doing beautiful' on our way out?"

To no one in particular, Dom said, "The mind reels."

"Easy, Dom," said Kenny. "So he got his wires crossed."

"With him it's an acquired characteristic."

Cammy got off his stool and walked in circles with his eyes on the floor. How could I have been so off? he asked himself.

"Anyway," said Kenny. "By the time Cedar gets the nerve to go in after knocking prolly a hundred times on Rachel's door, we're back at work, and Marty and Rachel are getting stiffer by the minute, right guys?"

Dom nodded. Cammy nodded, too, but without looking at the other two. Kenny got off his stool. "Cammy will get the gun Sunday. Right, Dom? You'll be ready for him?"

Dom nodded, then looked at Cammy. "Show up like you're giving me a ride home. Wait outside and I'll bring it when I lock up."

"Okay, Dom," said Cammy. "Sure thing."

"We're all set then," said Kenny. He tugged Cammy's sleeve, and they walked out of the building without speaking. Only when they reached Cammy's car did Kenny speak. "What were you *thinking* back there?"

Cammy didn't answer. He went to the driver's side of his car and focused on unlocking the door. Kenny took a drag on his cigarette before mashing it on the ground and speaking to Cammy over the roof of the car. "Something like this, there's no room for not thinking. We got one shot to do it right or we're dead, all three of us."

Cammy opened his car, got in, and unlocked the door for Kenny. Kenny sat in the passenger seat. He knew Cammy felt bad about his mistake, and he didn't want to rub it in. "We better get some relief for when this goes down."

Cammy's voice was low. "Yeah."

"I'll get Curly. Couple bucks, he'll do anything."

"I'll get Leon," said Cammy.

They drove back to Kenny's in silence. Cammy was rattled that Rachel was going to have to die. Kenny looked the window out at Hector Street. He waned to browbeat Cammy, but what was the use? There were things about him you had to accept if he was going to be your friend. One was his being a step behind everyone else. When they reached their destination, Kenny got out of the car and held the door open.

"Next few days, *think*, Cammy. After that no one will care."

Cammy nodded.

"It don't take an intellectual to pull this off. It's more like just following procedure. We come up with a plan, we follow it, it gets done. End of story."

"Yeah, I know," said Cammy.

"Somebody like Marty, *he's* some intellectual? My ass. There's *nobody* like that in Hillside Park. Marty may *think* he is, Cedar may think *he* is, but they're all just like us except for they got a few breaks. Besides, what's an intellectual anyway? I'll tell you what an intellectual is. Some guy thinks if you put a monkey in a room with a typewriter, one day he'll write some Shakespeare book or something. *That's* an intellectual. Well what's that tell you right there, Cammy? Don't that say it all?"

Kenny closed the door and walked away. Cammy drove home. He didn't know why he should listen to Kenny anyway. Kenny wasn't a businessman and he was a lousy bar owner. He hadn't even earned the right to own one. He'd just gotten lucky. Twelve years ago when Kenny's beer-guzzling, aspirin-popping, Nyquil-swilling, broomstick-skinny wife, Judy, took off with a loud-mouth, redneck letter carrier and, soon after, ran Kenny's one credit card over the top, Kenny had been painting houses for a living. But the fumes got to his head. Once after a long day of mixing paint, climbing ladders, sanding walls, and washing brushes, he'd tried to take his socks off without taking off his shoes first. "That's it," he'd said. "Wife's gone, got no money, hell with it." About that time, the previous owner of Kenny's croaked, and the owner's widow, a coarse, gruff-voiced woman named Hazel, shut the bar down before deciding later to fix it up and sell it. She didn't want to deal with drunks the way her husband had, nor did she need the money; she owned a busy towing service. Grief over her husband's death had made her re-evaluate things. She'd told friends: "Hillside Park was such a nice place to grow up and raise kids in. Now look at it." Hazel was addressing not only the dreadful truth about the town but, more specifically, the eroding quality of her husband's patrons. They were no longer working men who'd wind down during happy-hour before going home to be husbands and fathers. They'd become dispir-ited loners who'd made the bar their home at the expense of their fami-lies. Back then the bar was called "Bill's Place." Hazel had hired Kenny to paint the building inside and out. But during the job, he'd gotten smitten with the idea of owning a nightclub. So he shacked up with Hazel, twenty-four years his senior, for the sole purpose of screwing her out of the bar. He'd told her he'd saved money as a house painter, which was a lie, and that he was thinking of buying the bar. Fine, she'd said, but they argued incessantly about the price. Hazel finally reopened

Bill's Place and, as a compromise to Kenny until they reached agreement, hired him to run it. Soon, however, she choked to death on a shrimp burrito, and Kenny ended up owning the bar by default. He'd phonied-up a document on Hazel's stationery as the only evidence of a transaction between them, and that sufficed for the title transfer.

Since then, he'd run the bar's original customers out by dint of his charming personality, which was exacerbated by drinking binges. Lately, however, he'd slowed his drinking to the point of abstinence; he needed a clear head to figure a way out of his rut. But to people who knew Kenny, the abstinence was only temporary. When he ended it, watch out.

All this was on Cammy's mind when he pulled in front of his apartment building half-a-mile from Kenny's and shut off his engine. He checked up and down the street for danger before getting out of his car. That's all I need, he thought: to get killed by some gang driving by. It had happened to one of his customers when he'd gone to get a sandwich from the coffee shop at Hector and Sonoma. Rival gangs decided to shoot it out without regard to who came between them. Cammy's customer took a bullet through his head, and ended up on life support for three months before they took him off a respirator. On the other hand, thought Cammy, getting shot by unknown persons would be a good way to end my misery. Better if it was Kenny, though.

~ FOUR ~

Marty went to his office to call Rachel Ellis while Cedar oversaw closing-up procedures. She answered groggily. "It's late, Marty."

"I caught you asleep," he said.

"Forget it. I had to get up to answer the phone anyway."

Marty laughed. "So what'd you do today?"

"Bought a new dress."

"Can't wait to see it. Were you dreaming about me?"

"I don't know, I was asleep," said Rachel.

Marty laughed again. "Sorry about the late hour. I had to talk to Cedar."

"And you're still breathing."

"No, he didn't have a problem with it."

"You never know about guys like that."

"What do you mean, 'guys like that?'"

"Loners," said Rachel. "He was a loner in high school and he's still one."

"Rumor has it he's shacking up."

This didn't surprise Rachel. "Ten bucks says she's just a sex-bag."

"Sounds like male-bashing."

"I'm just saying he can't connect with other human beings."

"I'm sure there's worse to say about a person."

"Don't you like how he drops hints he's this profound thinker?—then when you want more he gives you this back-off look. First defense for your typical crackpot."

Marty laughed. "I like how you see things. You make me think. My God, you were such a wise investment. I'd be an empty man if it weren't for you."

When Marty hired Rachel, she was five-seven, effortlessly thin, with a slender neck, narrow shoulders, elegantly slim arms and long shapely legs. Her black hair was straight, her eyes flashy blue. She never wore makeup or dressed in anything other than shirt, pants, and whatever footwear was handy when she woke up in the morning. But Marty detected in her a desire to refine herself.

Rachel's father, a small-time roofing contractor, had raised her. Along with his two employees in Pancho Villa mustaches, he always smelled like oily tar; you didn't want to light a match around him. Every night the trio hit the bars in Hillside Park until they were kicked out for rowdiness. By the time her father got home, drunk and stumbling, Rachel was asleep. And because he got up early, they went days without seeing each other. They lived in an old apartment building on Sonoma Boulevard next to a tire store whose owner kept a Doberman chained up in the back. They had no laundry facilities, no air conditioning, not even on-site parking.

Rachel went to the same high school as Cedar Roach. She'd slept around since her teens, done drugs, and gotten into trouble. With a fake i.d., she got into the same bars her father went to, one being Bill's Place, the bar Kenny took over. Her father went there after work one night when she was shouting profanities at an ex-boyfriend while others frothed at her braless boobs flopping under a loose T-shirt. After thrusting her middle finger in her ex-lover's face, she drunkenly fell off her stool and landed on her back. Her father dragged her out by her hair and beat her up in the parking lot.

"Let me tell you something else about Cedar," said Rachel.

"What?"

"I just know he's resenting you right now. I just feel it."

"How do you know that? And what's to resent?"

"He's got father issues to work out."

"So?"

"So you're his surrogate."

"His father was a drunken history professor. I run a night club."

"He was weak and he had no sense of responsibility. Cedar's *obsessed* with responsibility, and you just took some of it away."

"It's a couple measly hours."

"I'm telling you, Marty, those Flash Gordon ideas are his *drug*."

"So what? If it makes him happy—"

"That's not the point, Marty. He's capable of conjuring up scenarios that can backfire on *you*. And something else he resents—his father was charming, but *he's* a total washout. That's another thing he needs to blame someone else for—just watch."

Marty had learned long ago not to question Rachel's judgments about people, unless he just wanted to have fun listening to her defend them. Time and again she saw aspects of behavior in others that Marty never saw, or that he saw but didn't heed as warnings of unpredictability. Early in their relationship, Rachel thought she'd cultivate her ability to read people by majoring in psychology, but after a half-hearted attempt to get through Pasadena City College, she dropped out and went to a bartending school near Atwater Village instead. When she turned twenty-one, Dom hired her for his night shift and, sure enough, with her sterling beauty and easy way with men, she increased his business overnight. She would have applied at Marty's at the time, but Marty's had some class, and she didn't feel, with her rough edges, that she could cut it there.

Guys used to hit on her at Dom's, and the successful ones were not disappointed. But before long they'd fight over her. The fights upset diners. Dom didn't know what to do. If he'd fired her, he would've lost the extra business she'd brought in. If not, he'd lose restaurant customers. One night when he'd kept her over to discuss the matter, they ended up sleeping together, then again over a holiday weekend when his family was away. But when Dom got protective of her, Rachel sensed that her employment with him was doomed. So, armed with a little experience, she went to Marty and asked for a job.

Marty saw in her a vulnerable woman waiting to be nurtured into a sophisticate, like his wife, a banker's daughter. He liked the challenge. And it didn't hurt business to hire a pretty, come-hither bartender. All he'd asked was that she ease her Belle Starr side. When she put on a red vest, white shirt, bow tie and makeup, she looked like a movie star.

"Now it's my turn to tell you something," said Marty. "If Cedar's taking father issues out on me, he's stupid."

"It's not intelligence. It's denial."

"Your favorite word."

"It's a little overused, I'll give you that."

"Besides, what's so bad about obsession? *I'm* obsessed with you."

Rachel couldn't help but grin. "You're just saying that because you woke me up."

"Right, it has nothing whatsoever to do with wanting to drive over there and burying my tired old bones in your arms and not wake up for a month."

"Won't see *me* waving a stop sign."

"So, are you going to wear that new dress tomorrow night?"

"Marty, let me go back to sleep or I'll look like shit."

"That'll be the day. Promise I'll be in your dreams?"

"Ooh, the pressure, the pressure," said Rachel. "Good night."

Marty said good night. Time with Rachel was wonderful. Time with Gloria wasn't. She had hip-replacement surgery recently, and the recovery made her complain incessantly around Marty. Rachel never took Marty for granted. From the beginning, she found him to be patient, wise, caring, humorous and shrewd. She watched him make customers feel important by listening and responding with concern to their interests and worries. She knew he was developing an interest in her, too. Carefully watching how he greeted customers and showed appreciation for their patronage, Rachel noted what kind of women caught his fancy. Some were swooned by his fascination with their intelligence, whereas the guys she'd grown up with were intimidated by a woman's intelligence. She never met Marty's wife; Gloria had stopped visiting Marty's long before Rachel was hired.

Eight months after Marty hired Rachel, his son was killed. When they became lovers, she stopped seeing other men. He refused to let her work again; he didn't want their affair to affect his relations with other employees. He bought her a house on Golding Circle, a winding road in the hills above his club, gave her credit cards for anything she wanted, and encouraged her to shed boorish behavior she'd absorbed from her father. She went to A.A., but it wasn't easy, and she continued to drink. They fought frequently over it. But in her late-twenties she got sober and went on a program of diet and exercise, including four mornings a week at the gym.

Marty respected Rachel's fierce refusal to let him win arguments just because he supported her. And she knew that without him she would have ended up a barfly like other girls she'd grown up with, tossed from man to man and bar to bar until they ended up as fixtures in dives like Kenny's. While she retained a quick temper and often used harsh candor, Rachel never reverted to her self-destructive ways. Her beauty and figure continued to hold Marty spellbound, though she was growing critical of her looks. Seeing signs of crows' feet and a double chin, she abandoned hope of getting her pencil-thin waist back. It was taking more exercise and fewer calories to look good, but she was content to know that she was still the apple of Marty's eye.

Marty rose from his desk, locked the door of his club, said goodnight to Cedar, and drove home. The door he locked was steel-plated, double-bolted and identical to another door twelve feet away. The second door was to the storage room, which everyone called the "Kitchen," because that's what it was before Marty converted it into his private office and storage area. The Kitchen consisted of two parts. The first was filled with bar supplies and ceiling-high shelves lined with a pack rat's trove of junk that included plumbing fixtures, tools, and boxes of old receipts. The other part was an inner sanctum that consisted of bed, bathroom and kitchenette. Marty napped there and spent nights when he was too tired to drive home. The storage room was always locked from the inside with a dead bolt, on the outside with a lock key, dead bolt and alarm key. No deliveries were made without Marty personally unlocking the door and supervising. Only Rachel had extra keys.

The Ft. Knox security was to protect Marty's inventory and floor safe, which contained his bank draw for cashing checks. It also contained personal inventory documenting his relationship with Rachel Ellis.

~ ~

Cammy couldn't get to sleep that night when he got home. After moving his bowels, he went through the same routine as always when he couldn't sleep. He showered, donned his jammies, made popcorn with melted butter, sat in his favorite chair, tucked his slippered feet under his chubby legs, leaned back, and turned on an old movie. Throughout the movie, however, a question nagged him: Why am I going to help kill two people who love each other? He couldn't think of a good answer.

~ ~

Kenny had no problem going to sleep. It took eight minutes, including time to masturbate. He knew he had irritated Cammy and Dom with his abrasive personality. He also knew that no matter how much money he put into his bar, he probably would never make a good living. He wasn't likeable enough to run a successful operation. But he still needed to bust out of his rut, and whacking Marty was the way. He saw all kinds of problems with an increase in business. He'd have to hire help, a clean-up crew, maybe an accountant, and, sure enough, they'd be pains-in-the-balls. He'd have to work the same hours he was putting in now, just because he couldn't trust his help not to steal from him and not to slack off when he wasn't around. Nobody's competent nowadays. And, bottom line, he didn't care if he got caught. Maybe it will make the six o'clock news and Judy will see it, he thought. She's probably shacking up with some jerk, probably that same idiot redneck letter carrier. She'll know I went out doing what nobody could tell me *not* to, which is getting my way. And if she never hears about me again, so what? Screw her, just like she did me. Yes, just wiping a successful guy like Marty off the planet was satisfaction in itself. Kenny always hated guys who breezed through life getting whatever they wanted.

~ ~

Dom went right to sleep. He had no anxiety about Marty and Rachel getting killed because he didn't have to do it. Rachel was beautiful and sexy, to be sure, and the memory of those nights with her was still vivid. On the other hand, she had quit working for him and had gone to Marty's instead. That made Dom look bad, and it cost him business she'd brought in. So she had to pay. There could be fallout if something went wrong, but Dom wanted Marty dead at all costs, even if Marty never knew it was Dom who was taking vengeance out on him. I'm Italian, Dom thought. Vendetta is an Italian word. And that's how it should be.

~ ~

Cedar got home at two-twenty, banged the girl staying with him, and then got up and listened to talk radio for ninety minutes. One thing about Cedar: he liked to think there was a scientific reason for every thing and a human motive behind every action. This was why he enjoyed being a bouncer at Marty's; it gave him ten to twelve hours a day just to *think*. These thoughts led to elaborate theories for why this and that happened. Sometimes he'd share his theories with his live-in mate, a sixteen-year-old named Helen Hernandez. Helen knew enough English just to get by. Cedar had taken her in because she was a virgin, and all he wanted was quick and easy sex, i.e., no foreplay or condoms. The only times he expressed his theories to her were post-coital, when he was free of stress and staring at his bedroom ceiling as she lay beside him. That she nodded acknowledgement at his astrophysical ramblings was enough for him to keep talking, even though all she responded to was the self-congratulatory tone in his voice for his brilliant observations.

Cedar's belief that behavior was affected by radio waves from the expanding universe led him to create an acronym: S.L.A.P.P.E.R., for Static Linear Accelerator of Protons Propelled by Energy Release. The energy came from particle interaction among galactic clusters. He introduced this to Helen one night after sex.

"All living beings," he'd said, "are connected to a supreme directive set down when earth was created. I call it 'The Great Directive.' It's great because order comes from it, and order is good. What's bad is that Slapper disrupts the structural components of this directive."

Helen had no idea what he was talking about but she didn't want him to know. "Why for joo ess important?" she said.

"Because Slapper's got zillions of hyper-charged neurons per micro-inch. That's what makes it electrostatic. But it's mobile too. It dances around the planet like a marble bounces around an empty bathtub."

Helen searched for a question that sounded intelligent. "Ess big, Slapper?"

"I can't say for sure. But I know it's a preserved, vertical force-field. I suspect it looks like a bolt of lightning."

"How many year since you know Slapper?"

"Lots."

"How it works?" asked Helen.

"It disrupts our synaptic strands, the oscillating frequencies that bond us to the Great Directive. Yours are different from mine and mine are different from yours, but the frequencies that keep them operating are the same. That's where Slapper comes in. When it's in proximity to us, it alters these frequencies. We can't stop it. Nothing can. If it enters us, I think it comes through the parietal bones, which make up the cranium of our skulls."

Despite not knowing synapses from syrup, Helen expressed awe. "Slapper have mush power."

"Yes, it does. When our synaptic activity is disrupted, we lose control over thought and actions. Sometimes Slapper disrupts us only temporarily, but it can determine our destiny. That's what happened to Hitler, Charles Manson, the Clintons, people like that."

Cedar theorized that the atmosphere was not what scientists said it was. He accepted that when compressed, it had the thickness of a dime and that it carpeted the planet. But when not compressed, it was just like the air we breathe; i.e., made up of allotropes you can't see or feel. He dismissed that it was formed from gases as earth cooled over the millennia; nothing you could put your hand through with no resistance could protect such a gigantic and complex system of living organisms from as powerful a force as the sun.

Instead, he believed that the "atmosphere" was created by extraterrestrials to preserve the planet the same way you use plastic wrap to preserve meats and vegetables. It was obvious that if extraterrestrials cared about life on earth, they wanted to protect it from the sun. The other planets, barren as they were, either lost or never had this layer. This is what made Earth special. This was Cedar's proof of extraterrestrials.

The destruction of an uncharted sun four billion years ago created such energy that billions of Slappers were released. Some were still shooting through the heavens and some collided with other stars. But one headed to earth. Cedar was certain that a hole in the ozone layer acted as a portal for Slapper. Once through, it had so much energy that it journeyed haphazardly on earth's surface like a top and disrupted synaptic activity along the way.

Cedar didn't tell anyone about his Slapper theory, except for Helen, whom he thought had the brains of a chicken. He didn't care much about her anyway, at least out of bed—chubby, pimples, flat nose, droopy eyes, a gopher chin—but she never refused him sex. She got wet fast, moaned when he finished, and uttered sweet nothings when he rolled off. For sex and household chores, including cooking, Helen got two hundred cash a week. It was fine with her because Cedar was gone most of the time.

After making love to Helen, Cedar's routine was to go to his living room and sit in his favorite chair with the radio on. Between commercials, he would read from an extensive library he'd inherited from his father and which he added to when he read a good book review in the *L.A. Times*. Tonight, however, he kept the radio volume low because he needed to think. He needed to find an ulterior motive that would explain why Marty bumped him from chauffeuring duties in favor of his loser bastard nephew Joey. Cedar couldn't come up with a motive right away. But he always knew that if he thought long and hard about it, he'd find answers.

When he finally trotted off to bed, he woke Helen up for more sex. She obliged him, and he went to sleep immediately after finishing a minute-and-a-half later. His unquenchable appetite for sex and the speedy way he gratified it didn't offend Helen; she didn't know any better. He never said anything affectionate, but the way he grunted satisfaction and squeezed her with his big strong arms at the end made her feel wanted and needed, which no one else ever had. This was what Cedar had ascertained when he picked her off the street in the first place.

~ FIVE ~

The next day, Friday, was chipper for Kenny. Whacking Marty was the biggest thing he'd ever do in his miserable life, he kept telling himself. He opened at six as usual, stocked his beer case, and then sat on a stool and smoked a cigarette. A few minutes later, Curly entered and said hello. He did not expect a hello in return, as Kenny wasn't one to greet him. But this morning he did.

"Hey, Curl," said Kenny.

Curly was surprised. "You musta got lucky last night," he said. Curly was kidding, of course, because Kenny didn't stand a chance with women. If he'd gotten lucky, it probably would have been with a sheep, and even then he'd have to have drugged the animal.

Curly proudly showed Kenny the glass he'd taken out of the bar last night. "See?" he said. "Brought it back just like you said to."

"Put it on the bar."

Curly did as told and then went to the back room, filled a bucket with hot water, got Ajax and a sponge, and walked to the bathrooms to start scrubbing. Kenny stopped him on the way. "I need you to fill in for me Monday a couple hours."

"Sure, Kenny," said Curly. "Glad to."

"I've got to go to the D.M.V., wait in line with all the retards and perverts," said Kenny. "Eleven to two, something like that, coupla hours."

Curly nodded, then continued to the restrooms. Kenny smoked away. He liked a few cigarettes before his morning coffee. When Curly returned, he asked, "Hey, Kenny, did Bernice call?"

Bernice Horl was Curly's girlfriend, a forty-two year old blimp who rarely left her house. She thought Curly was sweet and lovable, which wasn't untrue, but the real reason she liked him was that no other man in the known world would sleep with her. Bernice was also sweet and lovable, but she weighed as much as a cow and, because her head was huge with lots of angles, she looked like Jack Palance in *Shane*. She would call Curly at Kenny's, the only place to reach him, and Curly would go visit her afterward. They'd eat dinner, watch videos, and he'd spend the night. The next morning when he left, Bernice would reward him with two twenty-dollar bills. She also let him shower at her place. Actually, she *begged* him to, because he smelled like garbage. Bernice had been asking Curly to move in with her. Morals, he said, prevented him from doing so. What he really meant, but wouldn't say because it sounded hokey, was that the thought of living with a woman and not paying the bills made him feel unmanly. Bernice argued that a trust fund she lived on was more than adequate to cover his meager needs. But it didn't matter. Despite happily accepting free drinks at Kenny's, Curly always said that mooching just wasn't in him.

Kenny hated Bernice. When Curly visited her, Kenny was robbed of a target to ridicule. Plus Curly was getting laid and he wasn't. So when Curly asked about Bernice, Kenny exploded. "*She didn't call, Curly!* She'd have to take *donuts* out of her mouth to use the phone."

"You shouldn't talk about Bernice like that," said Curly.

"I'll talk about her any way I want to."

"Just 'cause she's a little heavy."

"'A little heavy,' my ass. She's as big as a dump truck."

Curly pouted. "Don't talk about her like that, okay?"

Kenny put his thumb in his mouth and cried like a baby who'd just stepped on a mousetrap.

"Stop it, Kenny," said Curly. "That's really mean, okay?"

Kenny kept up the ridicule.

"That's not funny, Kenny."

Kenny took his thumb from his mouth. "She's the only girl I know of that thinks a romantic evening out's going to the *supermarket*."

"Her doctor says she's got medical problems."

"*Every* fatso's got medical problems. Let me tell you something, Curly. Bernice isn't just fat, *she's ugly*. Spit goes down her chin. And you know *why* she's ugly? 'Cause her folks should've committed *suicide* instead of screwing the night they conceived her."

"I can't believe how mean you are."

"When something's true it's not mean, it's a *fact*, like a chair or something. Christ, you remind me of Judy, how she'd keep jabbing at me and jabbing at me till I finally lied and admitted there was some sinister meaning behind every thing I said, like I couldn't have an innocent thought without some hidden agenda. Then I'd have to say anything, *any stupid thing* just to shut her up, and she'd *still* get pissed off and *still* keep jabbing at me. So it didn't make any difference *what* I said. Christ, how I ever stayed married to her 'long as I did's beyond me."

"When did Bernice ever hurt you?" asked Curly.

"*I was talking about Judy!*"

"Yeah, but Bernice is a nice person."

"She's a *dick,*" said Kenny.

Curly returned the cleaning supplies, then sat in a booth with his legs stretched out and his head against the wall. Kenny lit another cigarette and waited for customers. After his first drag, he looked away from Curly and said loudly, "I *was* in a good mood before the village idiot opened his yap."

Curly just shrugged.

~ ~

Cammy, as always, opened his bar at five minutes to six. He immediately smelled Earl Zell's vomit. He'd forgotten about it. Nor had he any desire to clean it up now. All he wanted was to get back home and sleep.

When he cut a lemon to make twists for drinks, his fingers were shaking. He put the knife down and looked in the mirror. His face was white. My God, he thought, how can I get through the day? How can I get through the weekend? I can't kill Rachel Ellis, that's all there is to it.

He finally broke down and cleaned up the vomit. He hoped the smell would be gone before his first customer came in. It was usually an old guy from Boston named Leon O'Connor, who looked like Mickey Rooney and wore a beret. When seventy-two year old Leon did come in at six-fifteen, Cammy had set up his bar for the day: fresh coffee, fruit cut for drinks, radio on, bathrooms cleaned and air conditioner on low. Cammy asked Leon if he'd cover for him a few hours. Leon said yes, and Cammy drove home to sleep. On the way, he kept saying to himself, "I can't, I can't, I can't."

When Dom arrived at work just before noon, his day bartender, Charlie, who'd been a bartender for forty years, had four customers. They were talking about whether the Dodgers would make the playoffs. Charlie was the kind of bartender owners loved; once his shift ended, he set up the house with the tips he'd gotten. This pleased customers and increased business.

Dom made sure his kitchen help had set out cups for his spicy-sausage soup around a big tureen on a table between the bar and the restaurant. His wife made the sausage at home, his chef prepared the soup each night before leaving, and Dom put the final touches of herbs in before closing. By lunchtime the next day, the soup had simmered for hours. When everything at the soup table looked ready, Dom sidled up to Charlie and spoke casually.

"I found out Marty and Rachel are splitting up," said Dom.

"Where'd you hear that?" said a surprised Charlie.

"I don't know, somebody," said Dom. "They've been scrapping for weeks."

"After all these years. Maybe you could take her back on nights, Dom. Bet she still turns heads."

"She wouldn't stick around Hillside Park," said Dom. "You know how vindictive Marty is."

"Depends on who's running out on who," said Charlie.

"Maybe, but I didn't hear any specifics."

"Yeah," said Charlie. "I'll tell the wife. That's news."

~ ~

Kenny had an okay morning that day. His early crowd of unemployables had left by eleven-thirty, and his lunchtime folk—from businesses within walking distance who drank their lunch, and then after work attended court-ordered rehab meetings—left by one-twenty. When the last one left, Kenny sat on a stool and put his head on the bar. Daily, except weekends, he could count on a good two hours of mid-day sleep. An electronic bell on his front door awakened him when someone entered. Curly had restocked the beer case, straightened stools, and collected drinking glasses. So when Kenny napped, Curly did the same.

~ ~

Soon Cammy was sick to his stomach. He'd returned to take over from Leon just before noon after getting three hours of sleep at home. Since then, he had a few customers but couldn't talk to them, couldn't gather his thoughts for anything other than salutations. Worry about the plan to murder two people had been crippling him since Kenny put its details forth the previous night. By three o'clock that afternoon, his stomach hurt. Probably nerves, he thought. That's all I need, diarrhea. I'll never get through this. The last time he felt so nervous was when he prepared himself to eighty-six permanently a big-spending customer four years earlier. The guy had gotten into a fight with his wife at their apartment when both were wretchedly drunk. That particular fight, like the ones they'd had at Cammy's every time they drank together, wasn't unusual, except that the wife didn't survive it. Her husband said she'd slipped and cracked her head open on the kitchen floor. The cops said he'd pushed her so hard that she fell and cracked her head open. After interviewing the couple's friends and neighbors, only to learn that they fought like savages regularly, the D.A. had to let the husband go because it could not be determined if the wife slipped or was pushed. Cammy knew the guy was headed to his bar that night to celebrate his freedom. He also knew in his gut that the man had killed his wife. Thus, the whole day he was queasy and pale with nervousness. When the guy finally came in, Cammy mustered courage and told him his business was no longer welcome. The guy left, but not with threatening to come back with a gun. For four days, Cammy couldn't eat without indigestion and he couldn't sleep. Then word came that the man had put a bullet through his head. His friends said he was depressed because he missed fighting with his wife. But for those four days, Cammy was a wreck. Now he was just as much a wreck.

When his last customer left, Cammy called Kenny. He could not conceal urgency in his voice. "Kenny, I can't do this."

"Do what?" said Kenny.

"I can't go through with this."

"Our plans? Why, what's the matter?"

"It's just plain wrong. I know when something's wrong and this is wrong. I can't do it."

"Can't do *what*?" said Kenny.

"I can't go through with it. It's just plain wrong."

Kenny panicked. "What changed? What the hell happened?"

"Nothing, I just don't like the thought of killing Rachel."

Kenny cupped the mouthpiece and turned to Curly. "Curly! Beat it!"

Curly woke up groggily. "Wa-what?"

Kenny barked, "I got an important call here."

"I don't want to go now," said Curly.

"Take off or you're canned!"

Curly usually could tell if Kenny was fired up or just letting off steam. Seeing that this was a volcanic eruption, he scooted out the front door. Kenny returned to the phone and realized that Cammy had continued talking.

"…and my stomach's in knots," said Cammy.

"Snap out of it, will you?" said Kenny. "You're acting like a pussy."

"I don't care. I don't want her getting killed."

"I don't either, but we can't whack Marty without whacking her too. Use your brain, Cammy."

"I haven't stopped using it. I'm using it so much I can't work. I can't function. I hurt all over, Kenny"

"Cammy, this thing—we can't go soft, we can't take any prisoners. Rachel's part of the equation, like it or not."

"But she's innocent. Marty's lived his life but Rachel's got hers all ahead of her."

"So *what*? There's a price to pay for anything worth having. Rachel's the price we're paying. There's no other way."

"You in particular," said Cammy. "You've been intimate with her. How can you think of murdering someone you've been intimate with?"

"I was just funning with you about that. I never slept with Rachel."

Cammy took a breath. "You didn't?"

"No, you think she'd sleep with a slob like me?"

"Then what'd you tell me you did for?"

"I just *told* you—I was having a little fun."

"You call killing an innocent woman *fun*?" said Cammy.

"No, Cammy, damn it. The funning was me teasing you a little. It's got nothing to do with killing her."

"Fun. It's all a lot of fun to you, isn't it, Kenny?"

"Oh get off it. What are you, a priest or something all of a sudden? Some naïve little kid? We all talked about numerous times, plenty of times."

"If you lied to me about that you can lie to me about anything."

"Stop it," shouted Kenny.

"*Now* how do I know what you've got planned? How do I know you're not going to rub me out and take it all yourself, the money?"

"Cammy, you're going off your rocker. What's gotten into you?"

"I've never lied to you, Kenny, never."

Kenny screamed: "You better get your bearings straight 'cause we're going through with this. It's not like we're going to drive a couple planes into some building, Cammy. We talked about this a long time. Was that just bullshit from you or what? Now I'm going to hang up and you're going to have a glass of water and sit down and quit worrying. This is a chance of a lifetime. You've got to do it or you'll end up like Earl or Curly or that stupid old Leon O'Connor and all the other losers around here! If you back out, if you don't call me back and say you're with me on this, I swear I'll kill you!" He violently hung up.

Cammy hated being lied to and taken advantage of, even though it happened all the time. He thought about the phone call. His night crowd would be in soon, working stiffs ready to throw back drinks and have a good time, and if he was going to do anything about his predicament, he had to do it now.

Therefore, he did what his situation called for. He phoned the scariest man in Hillside Park.

~ SIX ~

Marty's started filling up early. Fridays were especially busy because Marty had to prepare for being out from six-thirty to nine, when he and Rachel went to dinner. Until six, he worked with his bar manager, Gino Cardona, to restock his four bar stations, two in the Main Room, one apiece in the West and East Rooms. He went in and out of his storage room, locking and unlocking it each time, and then, when finished, he showered in his office and put on fresh clothes. At five each day, Cedar ate at home with Helen before banging her and returning to work promptly at six.

A few minutes before five, Cammy called Marty's. Cedar knew something was amiss when Gino, always friendly and business-like, approached him with a curious grin. Gino was gay and open about it. Cedar had a problem with gays.

"Cedar, get this," said Gino. "First there was the Magna Carta, then there was the Declaration of Independence, now there's a phone call for you." Gino was referring to the fact that no one ever called Cedar at work. Cedar forbade it. He told Helen not to because he didn't want it known he was shacking up. Cedar thought the call might be about his mother. She was senile and in a rest home. He hadn't visited her in years. Maybe she died, he thought. If so, thank God, as she'd be out of her misery.

Cedar didn't acknowledge the humor with which Gino informed him that he had a call waiting for him. He merely went to the phone at the bar in the Main Room, picked up the receiver, and said, "This is Cedar."

"Cedar, this is Cammy."

Of all people, thought Cedar. "What do you want?"

"I have to talk to you," said Cammy. "It's extremely urgent."

"What's extremely urgent?"

"Uh, I'm kind of nervous right now."

"I don't care about your problems."

"No, it's not mine, actually. In fact, I'm trying to stop a problem from happening, bigger than you can imagine, so…"

Cedar grew impatient. "What is it?"

"I can't talk on the phone about it. It's not appropriate. Some things you just can't talk on the phone about. Cedar, I'm pleading with you. For once in all the time we've known each other, can you please help me out? You're the only one I can think of unless I go to the police."

Cedar considered himself as bright as anyone, certainly anyone in Hillside Park, so when a zero like Cammy said he had something worthy of calling the cops about but instead deferred to him, he showed interest. "All right, talk."

"Will you just meet me?" said Cammy. "Can you get away for a few minutes? It'll only take a minute, I promise."

"This had better be good," said Cedar.

Cammy already started feeling relief. "You'll be glad I told you, I promise with all my heart. Can you meet me in my parking lot? I'll go wait out there right now to save you some time, I mean so you don't have to get out of your car or park or anything, anything time-consuming."

"All right," said Cedar. He hung up. As he headed out, he passed Marty. "See you after my break," he said.

"Have a good dinner," answered Marty.

Marty was holding a bottle of Jim Beam and bundles of cocktail napkins. As he watched Cedar leave, he thought he'd heard a dismissive tone in his voice. It made him think that Rachel was right, that now, half-a-day later, Cedar may have had a delayed reaction to hearing that his Monday driving gig was being taken over by someone else. Marty wondered if he should make Cedar explain his terse goodbye. But soon Cedar was gone, and Marty still had work to do if he was going to shower and pick up Rachel on time.

~ ~

Curly stayed banished outside Kenny's long after Kenny slammed his phone receiver down on Cammy. He would have gone back in but he didn't know if the coast was clear. So, instead, he watched cars go by on Hector Street. Occasionally a motorist waved to him. Many residents knew Curly from his years of roaming the streets. Curly waved back, but with little enthusiasm. Something had been bothering him. Last night, after Kenny's anger-inspired phone call to Cammy, Curly went looking for a place to finish his Blue Seven and to sleep for the night. He'd settled for the recess of the entrance to the drug store his crazy aunt worked at for years, Cooper's, across from Marty's. But soon he'd seen Cammy's car go by with Kenny as a passenger. Curly was curious to know where these two competitors were going, as they weren't known to chum around together. So he walked east on Hector Street. When he reached Sonoma Boulevard, he looked south and saw that Cammy had parked at Dom's. By the time Cammy and Kenny exited Dom's, Curly had stepped out of view until they drove off. He'd heard Kenny tell Cammy that if they weren't careful someone was going to die. Now, half a day later and again ejected from Kenny's over another angry phone call, this one also to Cammy, Curly was sure that he and Kenny, and now Dom, were planning something ominous. He was dying to tell Bernice about it.

Bernice Horl lived in a three-bedroom, hilltop house in Eagle Rock. It had belonged to her parents. Her father, Budd, a life insurance executive, started an annuity fund for Bernice when she was born. He was fifty-eight at the time, his wife, Doris, forty-five. Budd and Doris wanted security for Bernice, an only child, because they were pretty sure that by the time she started out on her own, they would be dead from old age. They were right about being dead when she reached college, only it wasn't from old age. Late one night on the San Diego Freeway, a wrong-way driver killed them in a head-on collision as they returned home from a dinner party in La Jolla. The endowment, in addition to her parents' estate, which included stocks and real estate, ensured that Bernice would never have to work. But losing her parents had sent her into an emotional plunge that avoided rock bottom only through the prolonged intervention of prescribed tranquilizers. She was insecure to begin with because she'd never been asked out and was certain she would remain single. She wasn't hideous or grotesque, but her face and figure should have been given to a very large man. By fifteen, she was a thick-framed, five-foot-eleven colossus with tree-trunk legs and Popeye arms. She had a five o'clock shadow that you could see at eight in the morning. When her hair was short, her head looked like a box a new basketball comes in. Her chin evoked pugnacity. Her forehead protruded like a greenhouse window in a suburban home. By twenty, when she'd reached six-two and three hundred pounds, her doughy face had grown around her features as if they'd been pushed in by brute force. Despite her Paul Bunyon size, she wasn't masculine. She could sit with the poise of a charm school graduate and walk like a princess. Her voice was soft and lilting. When she finally weaned herself off medication, she used junk food to cope with depression. The more weight she gained, the less she felt like leaving her house, so she sent out for groceries and meals. She settled in at three-ninety. Her Eagle Rock property was maintained by an elderly Mexican gardener who Bernice had invited to live in her guest house after his wife died of breast cancer. A cleaning lady came in, and a business manager did her finances. Bernice spent lots of time on the phone and had company over, including Rachel Ellis, her best friend going back to high school. Bernice and Curly met nine years earlier, after her gardener bought bags of grass seed from Nick's Hardware on Hector Street and Curly, who'd been sleeping in the alley behind Nick's, offered to help load them in the gardener's car.

"It's not like I got anything else to do," Curley had said at the time. "I just feel like putting the old muscles to work."

The gardener said okay, and later that day he introduced Curly to Bernice when they seeded her lawns. She felt a low-grade chemistry with the callow, timid, skeletal, floppy-haired man-child. Their rambling banter had a self-perpetuating rhythm that delighted Bernice. His odor and missing teeth were turnoffs, but she liked that he stood there and talked to her as if it were the natural thing to do. The natural thing other men did was run as if escaping tear gas. It was about the same for Curly; he'd talk to anyone who'd talk to him, but most people wouldn't just because of his appearance.

Bernice made extravagant dinners for Curly, whom she contacted by calling Kenny's, and he came over and they had fun and good conversation. Then one day, Eddie dropped dead, and Bernice called Curly to be consoled. He came over, and they ended up in bed, and that fused them. But even though they'd been lovers for nine years and she gave Curly forty dollars each morning after they made love the night before, Curly was still shy about inviting himself over. It was better that she called first; that way no one could say he was taking advantage of her.

Curly was pretty sure Bernice would call by the end of the day. She always gave him an hour to get to her house on foot, and, being somewhat meticulous, she factored in the transit time and the time he needed to shower and change clothes before they sat down to dinner. Curly was eager to get back inside Kenny's in case Bernice called. Not only did he want to see her again, but the story about Kenny and Cammy visiting Dom late at night was eating at him, and he wanted her opinion on what he might have meant.

~ ~

The narrow alley behind Cammy's was bumpy from prehistoric potholes. Its loose gravel and worn asphalt made a crunchy sound under the slow-moving wheels of Cedar's Jeep Cherokee. Shards of broken glass from shattered wine and beer bottles lined the alley like so many sequins. On one side of the alley, behind buildings that faced Hector Street, were parking spots and closed-in storage areas. Each had a dumpster with lids misshapen from overuse. Barred windows over blackened or newspaper-covered panes were everywhere, along with urine-stained walls, gated doors with chain locks, and alarm-bell boxes topped by pigeon droppings. Gang graffiti was everywhere. The other side of the alley was lined with an array of fences behind homes. Some were chain-link, some wood panels hammered onto cross beams, some sagging brick walls, and one an abandoned automobile wedged between a garage and a tool shed that looked like an outhouse.

When Cedar turned into Cammy's parking lot, he saw Cammy standing worriedly on a concrete stoop at the door of his rear entrance. A low-hanging, cone-shaped, metal-shaded night light at the end of a long-stemmed wall-bracket was pointed down so that it looked like a dunce cap descending onto Cammy's head.

Cammy stepped off the stoop and approached the Cherokee after Cedar stopped the vehicle and looked at Cammy from his driver's seat. Cammy was jittery, his face ashen, his eyes with deep circles under them. He rocked back and forth as if to maintain equilibrium against the threat of passing out from an amalgam of fear and sleep deprivation.

"Thanks for coming," said Cammy. "I really appreciate it." He ran his hand through his hair and wiped his dry mouth with his fingers. "You might not believe this, but every word's true. I hope you don't get too excited because there's plenty of time to stop it. That's why I called you now, because nothing's been done yet. It's all in the planning stages, so…"

Cedar sighed. "Say what you have to say, Cammy."

Cammy stepped back as if creating distance between himself and Cedar's potential arm's-length reach. "I'll just say it right out, okay Cedar? There's a plan to kill Marty this Monday."

Cedar's long-practiced, self-sculpted impenetrability had just met an Olympian challenge. His jaw dropped and his big lips parted. He always knew he might have to take a bullet for Marty, but he never imagined he'd hear of a deliberate plan to kill him, especially from a dumpy dork.

"When'd all this happen?" said Cedar.

"Last night."

"Who's doing it?"

"Kenny."

"Who else?"

"Actually, and I was kind of hoodwinked into it, Cedar, but uh, me. But that's why I called you. I sort of went along until I heard—"

Despite the distance Cammy had created between them, Cedar grabbed Cammy by his throat and pulled him close. Cammy's eyes widened and his legs collapsed. To keep from falling he held onto to Cedar's arm like a bat hangs from a tree limb.

"Does anybody else know about this?" said Cedar.

Cammy nodded and gagged for air at the same time.

"Who?" barked Cedar.

Cammy was near terror. Cedar let him go, and he dropped to his knees. "Dorn," he said, lowering his head in shame.

"Competition's too tough?" said Cedar. "Is that why?"

Cammy nodded without looking up.

"It was Kenny's idea, wasn't it?" said Cedar.

Cammy nodded.

"Vine-ripened cowards," said Cedar. He got out of his car, stood over the prostrate Cammy like an executioner on a caffeine binge and jerked him up until their eyes met. "You and I are going to talk tonight and you're not going to say a word to anybody about this. Understand?"

Cammy nodded.

"Especially that rat Kenny," said Cedar.

"I know," said Cammy, close to tears.

Cedar let him go with a shove. Cammy planted his palms in the ground to keep from falling on his back. He looked at Cedar with a trembling body.

"You still live on Mesa?" said Cedar.

"Yes, number six. It's the one with the porch light on. It's in the rear on the second floor."

"I'll be there at two forty-five sharp. Now get back in there and go to work."

Cedar got into his car and drove off. His tires spit gravel all over Cammy. Cammy wasn't sure what had just happened. He knew he was still alive. He had not heard "You have the right to remain silent." He wasn't wearing an orange jumpsuit with stenciled numbers on the back. But he also knew there was something oddly comforting in Cedar's order to get back in the bar and go to work. It made him glad he'd revealed the murder plan. Cedar was going to handle Kenny, thought Cammy. He's just taken it out of my hands and he's going to get tough with Kenny so I don't have to.

Cammy stood up and wiped dirt from his hands. He could work the rest of the day without further discomfort. In fact, when he thought about it, he got almost giddy. This so-called murder-suicide was not going to happen. No, there would be some other way to make his life better, a way that did not depend on a criminal act.

Earl Zell, who'd arrived when Cammy was outside, was waiting for him. "Cammy, what do I gotta do to get some service here?" he growled. "I gotta ring a dinner bell or something?"

"I'm right here, Earl," said Cammy, moving behind his bar with friendly animation.

"I could've been a robber," said Earl. "I could've took all your money out."

"You're too good a man for that." He was already fixing Earl a brandy and water. He placed it on a cocktail napkin. "First one's on me," he said.

Earl raised the glass and smiled gratefully. "Whatever's your pleasure, m'lord."

As Earl tasted his first drink of the day, Cammy turned from him and grinned broadly. He was elated at having had the guts to face Cedar Roach and unload the pressure of the plan to murder.

~ SEVEN ~

Kenny smoked cigarettes and paced his bar like a madman. "I'm going to kill him," he said of Cammy. "You can't trust morons." He picked a margarita glass from his back bar and threw it across the room. It shattered. He wanted to phone Cammy and call him names, but he remembered that his angry ultimatum included Cammy calling *him,* and he didn't want to grovel by calling first.

Outside, Curly was still waiting for Kenny to cool off before he went back in. Then he saw a BMW pull up and disgorge the well-dressed Mike Shihadeh, who was following up to his visit with Marty by checking out the other bars. Mike locked his car with his remote while studying the surrounding area. Curly didn't think Mike looked too impressed with what he saw. There was a barber shop next to Kenny's with a locked gate over the open door and a window in front that had finger smudges on it. The barber was sound asleep on one of his two chairs. On the other side of Kenny's was a Laundromat with young Hispanic mothers washing clothes while trying to keep their young children close by, lest they run out and into the street. Someone had overloaded a washer, from which suds and water had spilled onto the floor into little pools. Wet footprints from the barefooted children covered the rest of the floor. Mike nodded a greeting to Curly on his way into Kenny's. Curly smiled back.

Any well-dressed stranger to come into Kenny's always made Kenny think it was an undercover guy from the Vice. His reaction to seeing Mike was, "Shit, they're busting me again." He wouldn't put it past the Vice to camouflage one of its own in GQ attire. But when he noted Mike's expensive suit, his regal carriage, olive skin, and big honker, how he looked like

66

those slick guys on some Arab TV station talking about raising oil prices against heathen America, he thought, "This guy ain't the Vice. All that's missing is the towel on his head."

"Howdy," said Kenny. "What can I get you?"

"A Coke, please," said Mike.

Mike's Middle-Eastern accent confirmed that he wasn't a cop. Kenny fixed him a coke. Mike looked at the filth in the bar, including the margarita glass in pieces on the floor, and tried not to reveal his disgust. "Mike Shihadeh."

"Kenny Grimmet, nice to meet you."

"I'm surveying night clubs here for business opportunities, Mr. Grimmet." He didn't want to say more. He'd come to learn what he could about Marty's through its competitors, if indeed he had any, and if not, why. But since seeing the squalor in Kenny's, Mike regretted coming in.

"Looking to buy?" asked Kenny. He'd never thought of selling. He wouldn't get anything for his bar and didn't know what to do if he sold it anyway. But the idea that he might own something of value intrigued him.

"It depends," said Mike. "I went to one down the street last night. It made me wonder if this isn't a lucrative market."

Kenny thought fast. "The Knothole. Yeah, we draw from the same resources. Give people what they want, they come in."

"I was talking about Marty's," said Mike.

Kenny acted remiss. "Oh well, yeah, that's been here awhile."

"Does the Knothole do a business similar to Marty's?"

"Not really," said Kenny, sensing his credibility eroding. "But the owner and me, we sorta been thinking about merging."

Mike wanted to leave without appearing uninterested. He needed to stall. "If you merged, would the operation be here or at the other location?"

"We're just in the talking stages right now," said Kenny.

Mike handed Kenny a business card. "Call when you decide, Mr. Grimmet. What do I owe you?"

"Dollar," said Kenny.

Mike left a dollar and change and said goodbye. Kenny was disappointed in himself for not exploiting Mike's interest in his bar. "Up your ass, Omar," he said after Mike left. Then he got an idea: Mike had given him a pretext for calling Cammy. He phoned. One ring, two rings, no answer. Cammy knew it was Kenny; Kenny couldn't let things go.

After Cammy's phone rang several times, Earl Zell looked up from his drink. "How come you're lettin' it ring like that?"

"I just am," said Cammy.

Kenny knew after five rings that Cammy was not going to answer. He hung up. So that's how he wants to play, he thought. He broke another margarita glass, which left him with one. He called again. Ring, ring. Now Cammy knew for sure it was Kenny.

After more unanswered rings, Earl said, "Cammy, that's driving me crazy. Can't you answer it anyhow?"

Cammy thought he'd better answer or Kenny would call every five minutes. He picked up the receiver. "The Knothole," he said.

"It's Kenny, I got a heads-up for you."

Cammy was guarded. "What heads-up?"

"Some rich towel-head's checking things out," said Kenny. "He's looking to buy a bar. He's probably coming there to see if you want to sell yours."

This was the last thing Cammy cared about. "Thanks," he said flatly.

"Don't you believe me?" said Kenny.

"Of course I do," said Cammy. "Why, *you* wouldn't lie to *me*."

This ticked off Kenny. "Cammy, you're a part of this. I need you. For God sakes, think of the positives, thirty-three grand in your hands by Monday afternoon. You've never had that much money."

"This is not the best time to discuss it."

"Okay, so you're not alone," said Kenny. "Is that it? Was that just a code phrase you used there on me?"

"Affirmative," said Cammy.

"Like they're going to think that's not weird," said Kenny. "What geniuses you got there? Earl? Watch him puke again. Look, I'll make it easy for you. I'm going to say something and you say yes or no, okay?"

"I believe I can abide by that," said Cammy.

"All right," said Kenny. "Here goes: 'I, Camille Waller, will reconsider what I said to Kenneth Grimmet last time we spoke on the phone together.' Just *reconsider*. Nothing final. You say yes or no, but before that think about a new car, comics up the ass, people standing in line to get in your bar. And the women, Cammy, they see you rolling in the dough, big nightclub owner, you can take your pick, they'll be all over you. Okay? One two three, *go*."

Cammy thought a yes would keep Kenny at abeyance and not violate his promise to Cedar. "Yes," he said.

Kenny was relieved. "That's the best news I heard since they invented tit implants. We'll talk later on, okay?"

"Yes," said Cammy, and they hung up.

Kenny prided himself on being a persuasive talker. "I could sell flies to a pig rancher. Next time I'll get Cammy alone, there's no way he can back out." He lit a cigarette, put his hands on his hips the funny way he did, and grinned. He even made a vow: next customer in gets a free drink, I don't care who it is. If it's Dracula and he wants a Bloody Mary out of my own blood, I'll give him a double. Soon two local house painters, Mexicans in their thirties, wearing painters' pants and caps, strolled in and sat at the bar. They weren't regulars, but if their job site was close to Kenny's, they came to Kenny's. If it was closer to Cammy's, they went to Cammy's. One bar they didn't go to, however, was Dom's. Dom once hired them through a contractor to paint his house, and as they were finishing he called his wife and told her to offer them cold beers. She did, the painters accepted, and then Dom went home and feigned outrage that they'd pilfered his private stock of beer. When they told him his wife had offered the beers, Dom called them liars on top of thieves and threatened to sue their contractor for breach of implied trust. Dom knew the contractor didn't have insurance against a lawsuit. The contractor balked, so Dom got his lawyer involved. The contractor, worried about a license revocation, offered Dom the cost of the work his painters did if he called off his lawyer. Dom agreed. The contractor knew he'd been had. His painters said they'd kick Dom's ass if they saw him again.

Kenny, giddy over Cammy's capitulation, said cheerfully, "Afternoon, *mi amigos.*" He rubbed his palms together. "Friday, huh?" he said. "Best day of the week. Payday, right? What can I get you fine gentlemen? Coupla brewskees?"

The painters nodded. As Kenny grabbed two Buds, he thought he'd tell a joke. "You guys know how Cinderella died?"

The painters looked at him blankly.

"At midnight her Tampax turned into a pumpkin," said Kenny, laughing.

The painters didn't understand. Kenny put their beers on cocktail napkins beside chilled glasses. "Three fifty," he said.

As they reached for their wallets, Kenny said to himself: "Why should I give these cheap bastards free drinks? They've never tipped me once."

~ ~

Cedar was rattled after his back-alley meeting with Cammy. One of his favorite quotes was from Hannibal: "To be defeated is pardonable; to be surprised is not." What Cammy had just told him surprised *and* shocked Cedar. But instead of feeling guilty of being unaware of the plot to murder Marty, he took refuge in his belief that other forces were at work. If Cedar thought long and hard, he would have a new theory that would blame Marty for putting his own life in peril rather than blaming himself for dereliction in protecting him. Cedar believed that until the time came for people to surrender to powers greater than their own, they had to monitor their actions in accordance with civility and order as defined by Aristotle's writings on virtue and

Thomas Jefferson's writings on how men should govern themselves. But now Cedar thought it was time to reconsider all this.

As long as he'd known Marty, Cedar never looked at him as anything but a winner. To his employees, customers, and community leaders, Marty was king. Awards for excellence from civic and business groups testified to that. You could see them on display in the passageways connecting the West and East Rooms to his Main Room, along with photos of him standing beside local mayors, elected and honorary, from all over the county. Marty had been chosen Grand Marshal several times by businesses, schools, churches, and merchants in Hillside Park for their holiday parades. Residents with relatives from out of state took them to Marty's. Marty and his wife were honorees for their work in local and citywide charities. If any person owned the soul of Hillside Park, it was Marty. Car dealerships had come and gone, fancy restaurants had bitten the dust, national corporations had sent marketing teams to test if a franchise could survive in the densely populated town, yet only a few greasy spoons lasted. But Marty's not only lasted, it thrived, and its success was due to its owner's commitment to excellence.

Now, however, after hearing that Marty was targeted to die, Cedar saw his boss as anything but a winner. He saw him as a victim. Marty had called the shots for so long that his sovereignty was a given, yet soon he could be snuffed out like a bug. Winners didn't let others get the best of them; they were never passive. Even in death, they went out fighting. The Kennedys could have been heroes, but they let themselves get killed. Reagan let himself get shot, but he didn't die from it. Victims were unaware of people ostensibly close to them who had sinister motives. Cedar found it difficult to justify these two images, winner and victim, in one man. By what force of nature could a man so totally in control of his life and the lives of others suddenly lose it all? To explain this, Cedar had to find evidence in something higher. His conclusion was that Slapper had reached Hillside Park and caused misfires in the synapses of Kenny Grimmet, Camille Waller, or Dominick Catina, or all three, and the result had brought out their evil. The opposite of order was evil, and Slapper shattered order. Cedar felt bad about this changed view of Marty, but he couldn't help what had happened. So let it be written, so let it be done. The limits that had confined Cedar's behavior up until then now had been dissolved. He sensed, but didn't know yet, that he was being called upon to alter history.

During dinner, he did not talk to Helen. Nor was there a hint that they would have sex afterward. Helen had no idea what was wrong, but she could read his moods. He sat at the dinner table and ate with the somber focus a death row convict gives his last meal. Helen didn't like the snub.

Cedar had always gotten home between six and seven minutes past five; tonight it was closer to twenty. Helen was afraid to ask what had caused the delay. At five-thirty, when they normally headed to the bedroom, not a word had come from Cedar. Usually he'd talk about a cosmic theory he had been developing and how it related to Marty's. On smoggy days, for example, he tended to see a change in customers. It was never overt, nor could you measure it with any device. But if you looked hard at the same ones who came in every day, you could see they dragged on smoggy days. Conversely, on clear days, they had a little more bounce in their walk. Helen believed these observations, and Cedar liked informing her of them. But today, she wondered if his silence and indifference to sex were related to his tardiness. Did he have sex with another girl before he got here?

Finally she said in a worried voice, "Why you for late today?"

Cedar held up his palm straight up for two full seconds, and then resumed dinner as if she'd said nothing. Helen slammed her fork and spoon on her plate, abruptly pushed her chair back, and carried her utensils to the sink in a show of pique. This took Cedar from his contemplative mood. He kicked his own chair out, approached and pointed his finger at her. "This is not about you, so shut up."

"How come joo dun wan no sex weh me?" asked Helen. "Joo haff a gurfren I dun know about?"

Cedar raised his hand sharply. Helen flinched like a dog about to be beaten. He had seen this reaction in his mother, when his father beat her. But he didn't know this about Helen, that she'd been abused. No wonder; he never asked her anything about herself. All he'd done was lecture her.

When Helen realized that Cedar was not going to strike her, she cried. Cedar couldn't stand to see a woman crying; it was like pictures of starving children or mutilated animals. Yet he felt responsible. He could not turn away or offer comfort, because between her tears and his attempt to comprehend the arrival of Slapper in Hillside Park, he was near paralysis.

Helen rested her head on his chest at his stood in front of her. Her hair was still wet from the shower she'd taken in accordance to his demand that she always be clean for sex. She put her arms around his chest and pulled him close. Soon he put his arms around her, too. She looked into his eyes and said, "Les go may loff."

"I'm sorry," said Cedar. "It must have been my synapses. There's evidence of an episode of negative energy in town."

Helen's voice was gentle and sincere. "I dun care. I yes wan for joo to may loff to me."

She wiped her tears away, took his hand, and led him to their bedroom.

~ EIGHT ~

Marty and Rachel dined at Mama Funelli's, a family-owned restaurant on Colorado Boulevard at the eastern boundary of Glendale. It had bare concrete floors, checkered tablecloths, green walls decorated with drawings of Italian herbs and spices, and balls of provolone in plastic netting hanging from lattice woodwork over the cashier's counter.

Marty liked Mama Funelli's because its food was authentic, like his grandfather's. The Friday special was osso buco. He ordered it, along with a salad, minestrone, two glasses of Chianti, and for dessert, espresso and Italian cheesecake. Rachel ordered pasta with marinara sauce. Marty liked the restaurant so much that he donated his club for its employees to celebrate each Christmas. He sealed off the West Room and provided an open bar. In return, though not as a quid pro quo—he insisted on paying his own way—they were given a table isolated with movable partitions to ensure quiet during their meal. He ordered flowers each Friday to adorn the private spot.

Marty and Rachel entered at seven o'clock to lively greetings from the hostess and food servers. They loved him for his big tips and generosity at Christmas. The founder's daughter, Anna, an effusive, rotund woman in her sixties, called out Marty's name. "I wanted to show you my new grandson," she said. "Isn't he adorable?" She thrust a photo of a newborn in front of them.

Rachel smiled at the photo. "He's darling."

"That's a handsome young man, Anna," said Marty.

Anna beamed. "I'm so proud."

"What's his name?" said Rachel.

"Anthony Joseph," said Anna.

"That's a strong name," said Marty.

"Thank you," said Anna. "Enjoy your dinner. I just wanted to show you Anthony's picture. I'm so proud."

When Anna left, Marty whispered. "Anthony's a mutt."

Rachel laughed guardedly. "Shame on you."

"Compared to my boy?" said Marty. "My boy made the Gerber baby look like a wino."

Rachel laughed again, this time less guardedly. She and Marty reached their table. "The flowers are lovely," she said as he pulled out her chair.

"So are you," said Marty. "If I didn't tell you before."

"I can't remember when you didn't."

Marty put his napkin in his lap. "I'm getting forgetful."

"No you're not. Something else is on your mind. What is it?"

"Things," said Marty. "I don't know what."

"Did something happen at work today?"

"Work's fine," said Marty.

"At home?"

"Ditto there," said Marty. "Gloria ordered a washer and dryer. Avocado color. I would've ordered white."

"You're upset she didn't ask you first."

"That would've surprised me, not upset me. No, our home's her castle. She can do whatever she wants with it."

"Then what's bothering you?"

The waiter brought Chianti for Marty and iced tea and a menu for Rachel, and left. "It might be Joey," said Marty as he picked up his wine.

"He's on your mind, you mean?" said Rachel.

Marty nodded. "I've been thinking about Paul since my sister asked me to help him find a job."

"Wait," said Rachel. "Who's on your mind? Paul or Joey?"

"Both," said Marty. "One reminds me of the other."

In a gesture of embarrassed forgetfulness, Rachel put her hand to her forehead. "My God," she said. "You should've said something. The anniversary, it's just around the corner."

"I didn't want to spoil your night," said Marty.

"It's your night too."

"I guess." He sipped his wine. "Twenty years, four days from now." He kept his eyes on the table in silence, then said wanly, "I don't know. I just don't know, Rachel. It just seems to come up."

Rachel took his hand. "That Joey reminds you of Paul?"

"Yeah. How, I don't know. They're so different. Paul knew what he wanted and went for it. This Joey's a car without gas, the way he mopes around. I'm afraid he's going to turn out like Cammy Waller. One day he's just going to die, and where his death certificate says 'cause of death,' the doctor's going to write 'boring.'"

"He's probably a nice young man."

"I think he donated his brain to science and threw ambition in to sweeten the deal. And I'm sure he only had half a brain to begin with."

"You're putting expectations on him that Paul never got to fulfill," said Rachel. "You and Gloria raised this child to be a good son, to be a doctor, and he was headed there when, God rest his soul, some asshole took his life. But what's Joey had? A nutty mother and no father. You ought to have compassion for the boy."

Marty looked away. Rachel saw him digging deeper into his thoughts. She glanced at her menu while keeping an eye on him.

"I see Paul in his eyes," said Marty. "Like a ghost from the dead. Joey's got this way of looking around the dinner table, certain expressions he's got. It's making Sunday dinners creepy, I'll tell you that. I think Gloria sees it too. Not all the time, just sometimes. But enough, just enough where it matters."

"Have you talked to Freda about this?"

"Not a chance," said Marty. "She'd start thinking about Joey's father, then she'd cry. Gloria would too. No wonder I put in all the hours I do.

Who wants to be around that all the time? No, I can't talk to Freda about it. It's too personal, too sensitive."

"Maybe she's feeling separation from Joey. He's got to leave home some day."

"No question, that's part of it."

Rachel tried to steer the conversation from emotion. "Now you've got me curious what he looks like," she said.

"You'd see Paul in him," said Marty, "the way you pick up on stuff."

"So he's a handsome kid."

Marty nodded provisionally. "Put him in a suit, straighten his shoulders, tell him try not to look so uninspired, yes, he'd be handsome. But he needs backbone. A man without backbone's no man. He stays a kid, and nobody takes kids seriously, not like a man with backbone."

"Confidence, you mean," said Rachel.

"Whatever his screwy mother's been tearing down in him since he stopped peeing in his diapers, yeah, whatever you want to call that. Can you believe Freda and I came from the same parents? Take away her Prozac and she'd be wandering the streets like Curly."

Marty paused to sip his wine. Rachel watched his eyes. "You want Joey to learn how to run the club, don't you, Marty?"

"I'd love him to. He'd probably like it. It's a man's job, don't you think? Handling all those drinkers?"

"A woman could do it, but yes, I understand," said Rachel. "She'd have to be strong. She couldn't back off. But a woman could do it."

"Still, it's out of the question. Getting permission from Freda? I'd rather cut my throat. It doesn't matter I've supported her like a welfare queen. No, just the thought of precious little Joey being anywhere near all that booze…"

"Marty, some things have changed since then. A lot of people don't drink like they used to, they're more responsible now, with designated drivers and all that. And bar owners are more watchful about that, too, thank God."

"Drunks are still killing people on the road," said Marty. "To this day I worry one of my customers is driving an unguided missile home. And there's the bigger truth, Rachel. I've been a terrible husband. I may come home every night, I may escort Gloria to various functions for the sake of appearances, I may go to church with her, give her nice gifts and whatnot, but I'm in no position to open old wounds. Twenty years, there's still festering. You don't lose your only kid and have your wife blame you for it the rest of your life and think you can ask a favor when you know she won't do it no matter what. No, I've got to respect her wishes."

Rachel looked away and didn't say anything.

"What's the matter?" asked Marty.

"I feel I'm on the outside looking in," said Rachel. "All this talk about Joey, you and Gloria, your sister—I've got no say."

"Are you kidding?" said Marty with an endearing grin. "One, I know you care, and two, you're the center of my life."

He squeezed Rachel's hand. She put her other hand on top of Marty's, and they shared an affectionate look.

～～

The Sonoma Inn was busy that night but not hectic, which was fine with Dom. He was preoccupied over worry that the rumor he'd started about Marty and Rachel having a stormy relationship had not come back to him, boomerang-style, to confirm that it had legs. He worried, too, that Kenny might suspect he never started it in the first place. Like everyone else, Dom hated the thought of answering to Kenny. You couldn't engage him; you had to battle him.

Dom had done well with rumors. When he started in the business, he and a partner named Glen owned a restaurant in San Gabriel that became profitable soon after it opened. In no time, however, Dom wanted it all for himself. But Glen wouldn't sell his half, so Dom set out to destroy him. He told Glen's wife, Sally, that Glen was having an affair, which was true. The news devastated Sally. Without saying who told her, she confronted Glen, who admitted the truth, apologized, and dutifully ended the affair. But Dom told Sally that Glen did *not* end it and, indeed, was pursuing women right and left. The marriage suffered more. Glen turned to drinking. One night Dom urged Sally to see him at his bar, ostensibly to give her evidence of Glen's cheating. But the real reason was that he wanted to sleep with her. In her vulnerable state compounded by drinks, she'd be a pushover. As it turned out, when Sally arrived, one of Dom's big-spending drunks came on to her before she even sat down. Dom didn't know what to do: eighty-six a good customer or risk losing Sally. The dilemma vanished when the drunk put his hands on her and she rebuffed him. The drunk retaliated by smashing a glass in her face. It required fifty-six stitches. Dom later talked Sally into telling a divorce lawyer that Glen had been abusing her and to use the facial injury as evidence of this, and that he, Dom, would swear that he had seen Glen, not the drunk, inflict the injuries. Sally agreed. It worked. Glen, by then a despondent, fall-down drunk, could not prove he did not abuse his wife, and couldn't care either way how the charge played out. The settlement forced him to sell his half of the business to Dom. Dom later had an affair with Sally, and then dumped her when his wife got suspicious.

This was on Dom's mind when he felt it was time to tell Kenny that the rumor seemed to fail. His office was a small and windowless cubicle just off the hallway between the waiting area and his seldom-used banquet room. It had a plain gray desk and squeaky swivel chair, a well-used sofa, two metal cabinets, and a small table radio Dom kept on for local news. He removed from the top drawer a well-worn book of personal phone numbers and cocked his head back to look through the lower half of his bifocals until he could read the alphabetical tabs on the pages. He opened the "B" tab to get the number for Bill's Place, even though Bill's Place had become Kenny's.

There was a time when Dom knew the bar's number from memory. Dom and Bill were friends, and they talked all the time on the phone. Dom and Kenny were not friends. Dom didn't even consider themsleves colleagues. Kenny was no more a bar owner than he was a Rhodes scholar. A bar owner ran a respectable business, had the social skills of a press agent, brought friendly conversation to customers, and, more than anything, advanced the whole *concept* of neighborhood bars. God knows they deserved it. They used to be where Americana happened, thought Dom. They defined Americana. Neighborhood bars were where you kept in touch with friends, where you watched the World Series, where you took your son on his twenty-first birthday. There wasn't a bar owner alive who didn't know the following to be true: a woman alone in a bar after eleven p.m. was there for one reason, to hook up with a strange man. But these days, Dom knew, with public drinking frowned on, any such woman was looking to get *killed*. Any woman who went to Kenny's would be killed all right, but not by a psycho masquerading as a lonely man; she'd be killed by vermin, the non-human kind. Dom always felt that these traditions for running a good bar eluded Kenny.

"It's Dom," he said after Kenny answered the phone. "How's it going?"

"It's okay," Kenny said. He turned away from his customers, seven in all, and spoke quietly into the receiver. "Why, what's up with you?"

"Did you hear anything about Marty and Rachel?" asked Dom.

"Like what?"

"Like a rumor, what do you think?"

"Take it easy," snapped Kenny. "No, I didn't hear anything. Why, didn't you start one like I said to?"

"Of course. That's why I'm asking."

"Well I didn't hear anything."

"Me either," said Dom. "It's looking like no one cares. What if we're just jerking ourselves off here? Who really cares if him and Rachel split up?"

"If no one cares, no one cares," said Kenny. "You can't force 'em to."

"That's what I thought," said Dom. "Did Cammy hear anything?"

"How do I know?" said Kenny. "We weren't supposed to communicate, remember? That was *your* brilliant idea. Who'd you tell anyway?"

"Charlie," said Dom.

"He's got a big mouth," said Kenny. "Maybe give it time."

"It looks like it's not going to circulate," said Dom.

"Dom, I keep telling you. If it don't, it *don't*."

"What're you arguing with me for?"

"Because you're acting like a pussy. Just look at what me and Cammy are doing then look at what *you're* supposed to do, and you tell me if you deserve a third of the booty. You couldn't even start a simple rumor. That was your job and *you blew it*."

"Did you want me to hand out fliers?"

"Just take responsibility for once." Kenny hung up, turned around and put on a cheerful face. "How's it going, guys?" he said to his customers. "Anybody need a refill?" Two customers did. Kenny refreshed their drinks, over-charging them in the process and saying thanks for their tips.

Dom hung up his phone, took his bifocals off, dropped his head and rubbed his tired eyes. "Asshole," he said of Kenny.

One of his secret pleasures was imagining Cedar Roach squeezing Kenny's neck until Kenny's eyes burst. Dom knew that Cedar hated Kenny. Whenever Cedar's name came up at Kenny's, Kenny would say "Commander Cedar and his intergalactic voyages," and his customers would laugh. Dom put his glasses back on and looked at his watch. Nine-ten, it said. He sighed, and then opened his bottom drawer and moved papers around in it. Under them lay two loaded guns. He palmed one and thought: I'll give this one to Cammy and shoot Kenny with the other. I would like that very much.

~~

Cammy had a good night. The towel-head Kenny phoned him about never showed, which was one less thing to worry about before getting ready to meet Cedar later on. He was prepared to accept whatever Cedar had up his sleeve to deal with Kenny. By ten o'clock, he ordered pizza for his customers. They were ordering drinks, tipping heavily, and having a good time. Cammy was so content that he didn't think once about moving his bowels.

~ NINE ~

Marty's had a typical Friday night. The band kept customers dancing at full throttle. Every chair in the East and West rooms was taken. Cocktail waitresses hopped around tables like kangaroos. Cedar watched it all. Nothing about his demeanor of vigilance was unusual, but inside brewed a caldron of emotions. He unobtrusively strolled into a room and stepped back from the crowd to study individuals for caustic behavior. Seeing nothing to flag, he moved to the next room and looked there. Tonight he hoped to find an obstreperous drunk to smack around, for only by beating up some deliriously happy sauce-head could he purge his anxiety over the conversation he'd had with Marty. He had four hours before Marty's closed. He knew his stability was loosening.

"I am a ticking bomb," he thought.

He took comfort in believing that Slapper, like a zapping tentacle from a celestial cyclone, had indeed found Hillside Park and was short-circuiting synapses in people everywhere. He said to himself, "I, Cedar Conrad Roach, have been granted the sole privilege of seeing this strange behavior unfold. Ergo, it is a moral imperative for *me* to act upon whatever conclusions *I* draw from the unfolding."

He felt good about this rationale, so good that he expanded his concerns. For years, he had been wondering why violence was commonplace in America. Why didn't angry people settle their differences neatly and privately like they used to, when you called a guy a son-of-a-bitch and were done with it? You considered the source, you turned the other cheek, you brought a lawsuit. But lately, if an individual did you wrong, you came back with an arsenal and killed him and everybody else in the way, then aced yourself before the police got you—all within camera range. Why did revenge killings have to be public spectacles that took innocent lives? Why did aggrieved persons have to scream out to be heard? Where was it all heading? The closest Cedar came to an answer was that the increasing size of the hole in the ozone layer had let in more slappers, which meant more messed-up synapses and more evil. He could not embrace this explanation fully, however, because it suggested that slappers stayed only in the United States, which was unique for the violence that concerned him. The Slapper he imagined encountered no boundaries in its travels around the planet.

As these thoughts occupied him, Cedar saw a man in his late-twenties with an earring and a buzz cut sitting at the bar in the Main Room and talking to an attractive woman on the next stool. Each had a drink. Buzz Cut wore an open-collar shirt, an unbuttoned dinner jacket, dress pants and loafers. The woman wore a mini skirt that exposed ample thighs right up to her crotch, a blouse tighter than skin on a grape, high heels, and enough dangling jewelry to disrupt radio signals. From the flirtatious way they leaned into each other, Cedar figured that before long one would follow the other home.

But a vulture on the other side of the woman was interfering. He was thirty-two, six feet, slender-framed, wearing a golf shirt, snug blue jeans and new sneakers. He had the determined look of a guy who had just been dumped by his girlfriend and had challenged himself to replace her with flair and speed. Maybe the combo would work another time and place, but, as far as Buzz Cut was concerned, it was not going to work tonight. With Vulture's predatory eyes on the woman, he kept lobbing what he thought were witty comments into their conversation. Buzz Cut gave him a warning look.

Cedar allowed himself to see the imminent confrontation between Buzz Cut and Vulture as a diversion from graver matters. He gave the situation sixty seconds to combust. As the bouncer who answered to no one as long as his enforcement tactics did not result in a lawsuit, Cedar could have been a benevolent cop or a belligerent cop. Tonight he did not feel so benevolent.

Buzz Cut and Vulture started throwing insults, and then Buzz Cut jabbed his finger in Vulture's puffed-out chest. The latter pushed the finger away. Buzz Cut punched Vulture, who reeled with his arms flailing. People shrieked and ran. The woman skirted off. The bartender reached out to grab either man. Upon seeing the approaching Cedar, however, the bartender backed off, just like you avoid falling boulders on Pacific Coast Highway.

Cedar grabbed Buzz Cut by the coat and jerked him around to face the exit, clutched the back of his pants, lifted him off his feet, pointed him forward like a battering ram, and carried him through the parting crowd.

"What are you doing?" Buzz Cut yelled. "*He* started it!"

The bartender ran ahead to open the door for Cedar. Outside, in view of two parking valets, Cedar dropped Buzz Cut to the ground. "Come back and you'll be charged with trespassing," he said.

A valet whistled to two guards for them to keep rubber-neckers away until Cedar took care of business. The valet stood by the door to the club so no one came out. The other approached a booth where car keys were kept. Inside were switches for outside lights. The valet turned off all but one halogen lamp atop a pole. This hid the action under the canopy from the alley.

When Buzz Cut stood up to protest being manhandled, Cedar punched him in the nose with a jack-hammer fist. His knuckles felt the man's nasal bone snap. Buzz Cut staggered, and then gained awkward equilibrium by planting his feet wide apart. He covered his nose with both hands. He saw blood on his fingers. "You *ass*hole!" he screamed.

He threw a punch at Cedar, but Cedar pulled back and, with his left fist, hit the side of Buzz Cut's face with the full power of his bulging arm. Buzz Cut's head almost came off. This time he lost his legs and fell on his side.

Cedar told the valets to get Buzz Cut's car. When they did, he re-entered the club to take care of Vulture. Cedar's reputation for strong-arm tactics was legendary. To those not yet in a state of inebriation wherein they believed they were invincible, the legend was enough to keep them in line. But after too many drinks, these same guys were ready to kick the Terminator's ass. Vulture was one of these. He had been warned by the bartender to get out while the getting was good, but he rejected the advice. Instead, upon seeing the returning Cedar, he rolled up his sleeves.

Marty arrived the same time that Cedar returned from the parking lot. "You've had too much to drink, pal," Marty said to Vulture.

Vulture pushed Marty aside. That was all Marty needed. He whispered to Cedar, "I don't want the coroner showing up," which was permission to knock this guy silly without killing him.

Cedar nodded, then faced Vulture. Vulture swung, Cedar ducked, and Vulture lost his balance. Cedar picked him up by locking his arms and skirting him outside. There, the valets once again prepared to keep the ensuing scuffle private. Cedar let Vulture take another swing, but he missed and fell on all fours. Cedar hit Vulture's lower back with his fist. Vulture yelped. Cedar stepped back and waited to see what Vulture did next. The wobbly man lumbered into a standing position, and then tried to tackle Cedar by barreling through him. Cedar stepped aside and kneed him in his head. Vulture fell again. Still thinking he could mount an assault, Vulture rolled to a squatting position, then sprang from it and, leading with his head, tried to take Cedar down with his arms. This time Cedar entwined his fingers on both hands and brought them down on Vulture's head like an anvil. Vulture went limp, landed face-first on the pavement, and remained motionless for fifteen seconds. When he came to, he rolled over and looked at Cedar.

"I'm coming back with a gun," said Vulture.

Cedar raised his size-thirteen shoe and stomped Vulture's right hand with his heel on the man's knuckles. Vulture yelped again. Cedar grabbed the man's hair and held it firm while ramming his knee into Vulture's face until it looked like pizza. "Can you hear me?" he said.

A dazed Vulture mumbled in the affirmative.

"If you come back it'll be the last thing you ever do," said Cedar. "Now be smart and go get help."

As the valet rushed to find Vulture's car, Cedar straightened his tie and re-entered the club, on the way rubbing his knuckles, which had gotten a nice workout. He felt better now. He could concentrate on how to deal with Cammy and Kenny in a few hours.

~ ~

Cammy was out the front door of his bar at two-oh-six and home three minutes later. He opened a window in the front room of his small upstairs apartment and another in the kitchen to air out the place. He had a satisfactory bowel movement, lit a candle to cover the smell, brushed his teeth, changed his socks, and put on slippers. Until Cedar arrived, he sat in his favorite chair and read the only magazine he ever subscribed to, *Reader's Digest*, a continuous subscription his mother started for him when he graduated from high school. That and a used car were his graduation gifts. He'd saved every issue.

~ ~

Kenny's last customer left a few minutes past two. He didn't feel like going home. He wanted a drink, but knew if he had one it would lead to another, and then heaven help him. Then something happened that made him believe in God for all of twenty seconds. A strange woman rushed in. She was attractive and had a nice figure—probably a nurse getting off a late shift. She wore those heavy, flat-heeled white shoes.

Kenny thought: how perfect, she's coming in alone, probably wants some action, here I am, no one around, maybe I can score. Then he realized that she was distraught and out of breath. She pointed in a direction roughly south on Hector Street and yelled, "Call the police! A man's on the sidewalk standing right there in the open masturbating!"

Hillside Park was not the Vatican, thought Kenny. He didn't want to scare the woman off or act blasé, but he couldn't think of what to say. Finally he said, "When'd you see this, ma'am?"

"About a minute ago," she said. "I've been waiting for Triple A. I just started running. This is the only place I found open."

"So a few minutes?" said Kenny.

"Yes, why? What's that got to do with it? There's a pervert out there masturbating right in the open!"

"Well—"

"Well *what*?" she screamed. "Aren't you going to call the police?"

"Well, no, actually."

"Why not?" she shouted. "What's the matter with you? Why are you just standing there? Why aren't you calling the police?"

"'Cause it's been three or four minutes, lady."

"So *what*?" she said. "What's that got to do with it?"

"He's probably finished by now," said Kenny.

The woman was horrified at Kenny's response. She left in a huff.

"Blew it," said Kenny, then closed up his bar.

~ ~

Marty and Cedar closed up on time and without further incident. Earlier Marty had talked to his valets about Buzz Cut and Vulture. The savagery of their beatings concerned him. He wondered if Rachel wasn't right about Cedar getting close to the edge. He decided to confront him as he was moseying into the Main Room. Marty joined him by the water fountain. Cedar positioned his feet at shoulders width and crossed his hands in front like he'd seen secret service agents do when he was a kid. They talked over the din of laughter and raucous chatter from all three rooms.

"How's it going?" asked Marty.

"Okay," said Cedar without taking his eyes from the customers.

"Have you given any more thought to Monday?"

"Joey taking over?" asked Cedar. "No. It's a done deal."

"Are you sure about that?" asked Marty.

"Yes."

"You don't have to jump up and down like a monkey."

"I'm not a jump-up-and-down guy," said Cedar.

"I know, but I don't think you mean it," said Marty.

Cedar gave a quick look around the room, then faced Marty. "Listen to what Tennyson wrote," he said. "'My life has crept so long on a broken wing, thro' cells of madness, haunts of horror and fear, that I come to be grateful at last for a little thing.'"

"What are you talking about?" said Marty.

"You want me to repeat it?"

"Just tell me what 'thing' you're so grateful for," said Marty.

"This job," said Cedar.

"That's like me being grateful somebody invented cars," said Marty. "You've had this job twenty years."

"That doesn't mean I lack gratitude."

Cedar's tone was flat and even, like narration on a documentary about dung flies. Marty thought it was patronizing. "It's pretty clear you're bothered by this," he said.

"I'm not bothered by this," said Cedar calmly. The way he ended each comment with emphasis irked Marty. Rachel once told him that when Cedar was being petulant, he employed a tactic called passive hostility. Marty did not like passive hostility.

"Cedar," said Marty. "We've been together too long for you to hold back. So let me give you an out. If it really bothers you, I'll find something else for the kid to do."

Cedar faced Marty again. "Did I say anything negative about him that didn't reference my concern about your safety?"

"No, I don't think so," said Marty.

Confident that he'd made his point, Cedar turned back to look over the crowd. This fueled Marty's annoyance. He felt like screaming at Cedar, but he'd never screamed at an employee in front of others; any dressing-down was done in his office. Marty knew whatever more he said was going to sound petty, so he decided this was one battle he did not have to win. He turned away and mingled with customers the rest of the night.

Cedar thought: that's another sign that Marty's hit bottom. Winners don't back away from a confrontation just because it might get nasty. Then a thunderbolt of enlightenment struck him. It made his view of Marty suddenly crystallize into a cleansing, revelatory truth. "That's it," Cedar said to himself. "*Slapper* made Marty cut back my hours. All *I* did was react."

This was what Cedar had sought, this revelation, his defining role in the next phase of Hillside Park's history. It was taking shape like a form coming out of the darkness, the whole clarifying process now jump-started by his encounter with Marty. "I didn't see it coming because I was blinded by admiration for the man," he thought. "He's been the main force in my adult life. I've been his protector. It wasn't my job to analyze him, just people and situations near him. But now I see the truth. Marty's time is up and Cammy brought me in to close the deal. Marty all but told me so just now with the wedge he put between us, his nephew. It was subtle, but it worked. Slapper told him to push me back, to sever all ties that bind."

Cedar finally felt liberated. By closing time, he had reached a state of peacefulness that was visible in his demeanor. Marty thought at first that Cedar was trying too hard to compensate for their earlier awkward conversation. But he knew Cedar better than that. If Cedar didn't like you, he wasn't one to rosy things up. What, then, wondered Marty, had happened to Cedar?

As one of the valets turned off the lights over the parking lots and darkness enveloped the alley, Marty took out his alarm key and lock key and, while securing the back entrance, nodded goodnight to Cedar. Cedar returned the gesture, then left for his Cherokee. Marty handed each valet a hundred-dollar bill. This was his custom on Fridays, a tip on top of a paycheck on top of tips they earned.

Cedar calculated that he had thirty-seven minutes to go home and tell Helen he was going out for a little while. He wasn't sure what he was going to say to Cammy. He just knew it would come, like words came to Moses after visiting the burning bush.

~~

Helen was so used to Cedar waking her for sex when he got home after work that she woke up with the regularity of a rooster at dawn. Each night, as he meticulously placed his coat, shirt and pants on hangers, she rolled on her back and started to moan and purr and caress her breasts and simulate masturbation to feign arousal for his pre-sex enjoyment. He did not want anything coming out of her mouth except sounds of pleasure; they could always talk after sex. She couldn't ask how his day went, how he was feeling, or whom he favored in the next presidential election. Tonight, however, when Cedar got home and Helen woke up, he did not remove his clothes. Instead, he sat on the side of the bed.

"I've got to straighten out a situation," said Cedar. "I'll be back in an hour. He kissed her forehead and whispered, "Don't worry, you're my only sweetheart. *Mi novia.*"

This placated Helen. She watched Cedar don his freshly laundered jogging sweats and sneakers, go to the bathroom, wash his hands, brush his teeth, and leave.

On his way to his car, Cedar had three things in mind: 1) How to kill Marty; 2) How to get what he was entitled to after twenty years of dedicated service; 3) How to leave Hillside Park without a trace.

~ TEN ~

At two forty-three, Cedar reached Cammy's apartment building. Except for barking dogs, the neighborhood was quiet. A concrete walkway lined with withering geraniums led to two adjacent apartments on the first floor. Screens on the windows were ripped. The walkway went around the building to a wooden staircase whose handrails were wrapped with carpet fragments to protect residents from splinters. Cedar walked up the staircase to the second floor. He didn't have to guess which apartment was Cammy's. In the rear of the building, an empty water bottle next to a front door gave it away: it had a sandwich baggie over its opening and was secured with a rubber band. Heaven forbid a reusable bottle would collect a falling leaf. Cedar knocked. He heard a click-thoop of a recliner chair inside.

"Hi, Cedar," whispered Cammy as he opened the door. "Thanks for coming."

Cedar entered. Cammy indicated a short sofa under plastic covers. Bookcases filled with trinkets were on either side. "Can I get you anything?" said Cammy. "Pound cake? I can heat it in the microwave. I've got beer, wine."

"No," said Cedar.

Cammy sat in his recliner and leaned forward. "I don't know what got into me, Cedar. Sometimes I feel like I'm just waiting to die. It's a real pain, a physical pain, I mean. I get so depressed I eat junk food, then I get cramps and gas and I can't sleep. So when Kenny called it was one of those deals where you don't really think, or you try to hide what you're hearing and you just go along hoping you'll be better off when it's over. That's what happened to me, Cedar. Well thank God nothing happened. I couldn't live with myself otherwise."

As Cammy talked, Cedar noted the room. A TV so old it had knobs on it sat atop a portable table next to a pre-war wall furnace. Wall furnaces that old usually had charred grillwork where the heat exits. But the cover on Cammy's shined like a new refrigerator. The room was impeccably clean. The kitchen doorway had stiff-bristle floor mats on both sides. The armrests on his recliner were covered with plastic. Next to it, a Pembroke table had a reading lamp on top and room left over for a remote control and a TV Guide, which was weighted open with a water glass on a rubber coaster. Cammy had drawn red circles around movies listed in the Guide he wanted to see.

A wall featured two pictures of his mother, one in a studio setting, the other with her sitting next to Cammy on a two-seater with his arm around her. He was thinner then, his hair blacker, his mug happier. His mother seemed worrisome, stern, and skittish, like Norman Bates. In the solo picture, she projected a self-conscious majesty that probably worked for Cammy and no one else. In the other one, she smiled, but it looked accidental, as if she'd been caught reacting to an impish son when decorum called for a more stoic pose.

A short hallway had a linen closet on one side and a showcase bedroom on the other. In between was a bathroom with pine-scented candles inside, glossy-blue walls, and a shower curtain with bunnies on it.

"Have you talked to Kenny since this afternoon?" asked Cedar.

"Yes, but I didn't tell him anything," said Cammy. "He called me, he wanted to see if I was still interested. I told him what you told me to say but I didn't say anything else. There's no way he knew I was fibbing."

"How'd this start?" said Cedar.

"Well the plan—the details—they told me I should've figured it out but I didn't. It sort of went over my head. The plan was, is, to kill Marty and Rachel to make it look like a murder-suicide, to make it look like she was—"

Cammy kept talking but Cedar stopped listening. Rachel's name shook him. His reaction came from a history with her that started in high school. He was mysterious back then, too, and girls in the student body found it attractive. Some flirted with him, but he showed no interest; they thought he was stuck up. But Rachel, ever daring and defiant, sought him out, and they had three sexual encounters over six days in her apartment when her father was out carousing.

Neither she nor Cedar ever told Marty.

In her wild years, Rachel loved sex, the naughtier the better, and being the only girl in a big school to bed down with the brawny and sullen Cedar Roach, a dapper dresser to boot, gave her an added charge when they finally got together. She changed his life. The hungry, animalistic way she kissed and nibbled him from head to toe after ripping off his clothes and straddling him until his head exploded with orgasmic pleasure was to be a once-in-a-life experience for him. Cedar sensed it the first time. He wanted to ask why he was so lucky, why, with every other guy in high school lusting after her, she'd chosen him. But fear that she might say he was merely sport kept him from asking. He suspected it was because she was as different from the other girls as he was from the guys: girls hated her because she was promiscuous, and guys hated him because he could break their necks. They all suspected that Rachel, with her outstanding looks and crude upbringing, would end up either dead at an early age from hard living or hooked up with an older man whose wisdom made guys her age look pathetically immature.

After their three times in bed, Cedar used to lie awake at night wondering if they would get together again, and if so whether he should initiate it. But he was too worried she'd say no, and then he'd have to hurt her. He would see her between classes, always with different guys. If Rachel was anything, she was affectionate, even if only for the duration of a relationship. Cedar wanted to make eye contact with her as they crossed in hallways, so she could see longing in his face, but she always looked away. When she did see him, she smiled as if he were just a one-time friend. This made him cringe. How can she be so cold? he'd wondered. Did she plan it that way?—flirt with a guy, let him have her full and raw, then leave him hanging? If so, she was a sexual genius.

Rachel never stayed with one guy long, not until Marty. In the years since, when Cedar saw her around town, and occasionally when she greeted Marty for their Monday Nooners, or the few times she closed the club when Marty was ill, he got knots in his stomach. She'd smile blithely at him, just like in high school after their flings. He'd smiled back, but without warmth. He *wished* he could smile back with great enthusiasm and affection, but her neglect of him was a stone in his shoe. Privately, she would always be Cedar's own Marilyn Monroe. He ached to be in Marty's shoes. He imagined visiting her on Golding Circle and having marathon sex, giving her rousing orgasms to the point where she would beg him to come back, and eventually she would never let him go.

"…so that's when I said what I did," said Cammy.

"To Kenny," said Cedar.

"Yes, just before I called you," said Cammy. "So even though he knows I'm still in on it he's probably wondering what's on my mind on account of my reservations. You know Kenny, a million questions."

"Does Dom know?" asked Cedar.

"*I* didn't tell him. I couldn't harm Rachel. She's—"

"Tell me about the plan," said Cedar.

"Well…I'm supposed to pick a gun up from Dom Sunday night—he can't drive, you know, because of his eyes—and Kenny and I were going to shoot Marty and Rachel Monday before he goes back to his club."

"What's Dom's part?" asked Cedar.

"He was supposed to start rumors about Rachel getting sick and tired of Marty's promises to leave his wife. That would be this morning, starting the rumors I mean, yesterday I mean, because it's Saturday already. Kenny thought that would plant thoughts in people's minds—"

"Cammy, listen to me," said Cedar.

Cammy stopped talking, sat back and put his hands on the armrests with a show of dutiful attentiveness.

"What do you think Rachel does all day?" asked Cedar.

"I never thought about it," said Cammy. "I don't know."

"You think she waits in that old house for Marty to come over Mondays and have sex with her? No. She's involved with him and other businessmen in an illegal fund worth millions of dollars. It's designed to keep black males in their own neighborhoods so they don't rape and pillage the rest of Los Angeles. The fund hires undercover agents to supply them with drugs and weapons. It's been going on for years."

Cammy's eyes widened.

"Politicians all the way up know about it," said Cedar. "No Beverly Hills couple wants to worry about their daughter getting caught in gang warfare on her way to grammar school. Once in a while an A.C.L.U. lawyer, some journalist, some do-gooder hears about it, next thing you know he's dead in a freak accident."

"My Lord," said Cammy. It was barely audible. "What has this world come to."

"Rachel couriers for them," said Cedar. "She hits contributors from San Marino to Torrence, charms them over lattes and croissants. She's got it down pat."

"This is the Rachel Ellis we all know?" said Cammy.

Cedar nodded. "It's racism, fear of what barbarians would do to innocent Angelenos if they weren't drugged half the time and killing each other the other half."

Cammy kept shaking his head. "I can't believe what I'm hearing."

"You could check it out," said Cedar. He meant this as a dare.

Cammy held up his palms. "Oh no," he said. "No. No, see my mom always told me there's sheeps in wolves' clothing but there's wolves in sheep's clothing too, the ones you never hear about. I always thought Marty and Rachel were nice people. How can they sleep at night?"

"It's an ugly world," said Cedar. "But you can change it, Cammy. You three need to go through with your plan."

It took Cammy five seconds to understand what Cedar said. He was going to speak, but Cedar cut him off.

"You know why Marty guards the Kitchen? It's full of illegal weapons. They're all confiscated from busts. They're never used in prosecutions. Police call him before they go out to ransack these gang beehives and he unlocks the back door and gives them whatever firepower they want—the kind ballistics can't match with police-issue weapons. They kill with impunity. Marty likes it."

"I forgot what 'impunity' means," said Cammy.

"They get away with it," said Cedar.

"You know something? You're talking about vigilantes," said Cammy. "That's wrong. That tears at the whole fabric of our society and—"

Cedar interrupted. "Do you have nieces or nephews?"

"My brother in Ohio's got two kids." He pushed himself out of the chair and took a wallet-size photo of a boy and girl from the middle shelf of a bookcase. "I send them money for their birthdays and Christmases, what little I can." He showed Cedar the pictures. "My nephew beat me at chess. He was five at the time."

"Imagine some rat killing them during a burglary when he's looking for money to feed his habit."

Cammy pulled back the pictures. "Cut that out."

"Now imagine that rat traced back to Marty and Rachel."

"This just makes me sick," said Cammy. He returned to his recliner.

"You have to execute them," said Cedar.

"Wait a minute, Cedar. Why are you putting it all on me? I couldn't do anything like that."

"You're cool-headed," said Cedar. "Dom's blind and Kenny's crazy. A man who can't control his mouth can't control his actions."

"Well why don't you?" asked Cammy, more out of curiosity than as a challenge. "I wouldn't tell anybody. You can trust me, Cedar. Ask my customers, I'm trustworthy."

"No, Cammy, you're in."

Cedar abruptly stood up. Cammy was scared.

"We're not done talking yet," said Cammy.

"Yes we are. I'll call you at five-fifteen tomorrow afternoon," said Cedar. "Tell me then if you're in or not."

Cammy rose from his recliner. "What if I say no?"

"Cammy, do you have any idea what those kids wake up to every day? No father, crime right outside the door, hopelessness on every corner, no one saying 'that's wrong' to them. Every election, white Angelenos vote down bonds for better schools, libraries, more police, anything to improve life down there. You think your life is bad, Cammy? Those kids don't stand a chance. And that's before Marty and Rachel get to them. Are you part of it?"

"Of course not," said Cammy.

"Then listen: the only way for evil to triumph is for good men to look the other way."

"I know," said Cammy. "I read the Bible."

"That's not from the Bible," said Cedar.

"It isn't?" said Cammy.

"If you look the other way, if you ignore evil deeds, you're as guilty as the people who commit them, in this case Marty and Rachel."

"You're right," said Cammy. "You just opened my eyes. I'll help. I'm in for the good fight."

"Then tomorrow night, two-forty five, here, the three of us will go over the layout of her house."

"What three?"

"Call Kenny, tell him you slept on it, you feel better about going forward with the plan," said Cedar. "Don't say anything else."

"But he'll ask all kinds of questions why I changed my mind in the first place," said Cammy.

"Tell him just what he needs to know," said Cedar.

"What about you being with us on it?"

"I'll tell him."

"*Before* tomorrow night?" asked Cammy. "Are you leaving that up to me? He won't believe me. He'll think I'm screwy. Nobody would ever believe you're going to help kill Marty Bagliamente."

"I'll tell him," said Cedar. He patted Cammy on the shoulder. "You'll do fine. You're a good man and this is for the public good."

Cammy bit his lower lip to keep from letting emotion overcome him. He always treated Cedar with an adoring respect, and Cedar never exploited it. But tonight Cedar knew praise would go a long way; Cammy carried his need for praise like a nationalist carries a flag.

"Count on me, Cedar. We'll change this city. I'm glad we're on the same team now."

Cedar nodded, then turned and left. Cammy returned to his chair and plopped down. "I still can't believe it," he lamented.

~ ELEVEN ~

Marty got home at two-forty. Surface streets at two in the morning provided clear sailing from Hector Street to Sonoma Boulevard to Colorado Boulevard to Verdugo to Chevy Chase Canyon Drive. His house was on a winding, hillside street a quarter-mile south of a private country club. Houses were large, two-story, Spanish style, expensive, and little changed in the four decades he and Gloria lived there. His curved, red-brick driveway had a steep grade from the street to the elevated house. Under the shadow of two huge trees, the front yard sloped down with terraced, plant-filled brick potters on one level alternating with cobblestone walkways between wrought-iron benches and planters on the next. The walkways connected with each other via a brick stairway with iron handrails from the street to the front porch. At night, floodlights mounted on trees lighted the whole area.

The house opened to a polished-marble foyer whose austere décor made it feel like a vestibule in a church not big on ostentation. Its only features were an arched mirror and busts of Mozart and Verdi on pedestals. A cast-bronze chandelier brightened the foyer like a skylight. The foyer opened on the right to a step-down, high-ceiling living room in eighteenth century Venetian motif with a green-marble fireplace and a bronze-based marble coffee table surrounded by four nineteenth century Italian chairs. A Kirman rug covered the center of the floor to a high arched front window. At the window, artful floor vases were arranged so that plants of varying heights and fullness got the morning sun. From their Cleveland home, Gloria had brought a floral-print sofa and round table for a Tiffany lamp. To the left was a dining room with flat-pink silk curtains around gray-papered walls, interrupted twice by modern paintings in matching black-wood frames. Four canister lamps hanging on wire-thin cords over the center of the room kept soft light aimed on a glass-covered table.

Gloria always kept the Tiffany lamp on for Marty when he was working at night. He used to tell her not to waste the electricity, but she persisted. Keeping it on was a habit that started when their son was a teenager and he stayed out too late. Gloria used to sit at the living room window and worry about him. Her only companion was the Tiffany lamp. When Paul finally came home, Gloria went back to her bedroom before he discovered that his tardiness had caused her lost sleep and worry. This habit of vigilance, born from loneliness and worry, did not end when Paul started college and it did not end after his death. Gloria would get out of bed during fitful sleeps and journey down to the living room to sit by the big window. She knew, of course, that Paul would never be coming back, but this did not stop her from waiting as if he *were* coming back. She liked being alone in the quiet. It kept his memory alive.

Marty entered his house, turned off the lamp, and walked to his bedroom at the end of the second-floor hallway. Gloria's bedroom was at the other end with its door closed. She had her own bathroom; Marty used the one in the hallway. He closed his bedroom door and turned on the light. As he removed his shoes, he saw that Gloria had placed an unsealed birthday card on his dresser with a Post-it note saying "sign this." The card read: "To Joey, our loving nephew, on his eighteenth birthday."

Marty knew why Gloria hadn't waited for the morning to hand the card to him. They hadn't been speaking. Earlier in the week, she had called him at work to ask if he could pick up a suit she'd bought for Joey by phone from a men's store on Glendale Boulevard; she couldn't drive to pick it up herself because of her hip surgery. The problem was the abrupt and demanding tone she used before Marty even knew why she'd called him. He didn't say no because of her harsh tone; he didn't say no at all. He merely asked if his sister Freda could pick it up, as she had more time than he had. But Gloria mistook his suggestion as a refusal. This misinterpretation prompted her to complain about his time at the club, a tiresome and decades-old complaint. Marty knew, even as she nagged him, that the real reason for her outburst was the approaching anniversary of their son's death. Every year it was painful: buying flowers, going to the cemetery, arranging for a special mass, reliving that horrible night when the police phoned to say that Paul had been killed on a lousy street so close to the club she hated. In fact, she would assert, if Marty hadn't owned the club, Paul would never have been there after his date that night and therefore would not have been in the path of a drunk driver. He would have been safe at home where he should have been.

Marty hated Gloria's mind-numbing complaints about him and his club. He wanted to scream that he, too, relived that painful night every year, and that he, too, felt terrible and depressed on his way to the cemetery and during mass and on the way home to a house that should have been filled with a grown son, daughter-in-law and spirited grandchildren. Why couldn't Gloria share her feelings with him instead of using them as weapons to punish him for something he didn't do? But he did not want to deepen her ill feelings with countercharges, so he just listened until she exhausted herself and eventually hung up on him.

Marty signed the card, "Love, Uncle Marty," and put it back in the envelope for Gloria to seal. He looked at photos of his son on top of the dresser. Some had Gloria in them. She was a beautiful woman back then. It wasn't only her angelic features and the elegant grace with which she carried herself. It was a thoughtful and generous soul whose kindness made Marty feel that he couldn't have found a better woman to marry. And what a terrific son they'd had, and what great friends they'd made in California because of Gloria, and how selfless she was to befriend his head-case sister, Freda.

Marty continued to stare at old pictures of Gloria and wondered how things had gone so wrong between them. Maybe if he had sought therapy he could have learned what part he had contributed to the breakdown of his marriage. He knew it had started long before his son died; Paul's death just put a stake through the heart of the marriage. Gloria deserved more of me than I gave her, he thought. But the club needed my hands-on involvement. I had to welcome customers, keep employees in line, and the restaurant—my God, that was a full-time job even *without* the bar. Why couldn't she understand that? Or did I just prefer the club to nights at home with Gloria and little Paulie? Am I lying to myself all these years later? Was it my selfishness that ruined my marriage?

Marty didn't have answers and he was weary from seeking them and he was tired of punishing himself for having a mistress and then he was just plain tired. He finished undressing, went to the bathroom, brushed his teeth, washed his face, turned out the lights and went to bed. His last thought before falling asleep was whether he should take the opportunity of his nephew's birthday dinner to show his gratitude to Gloria for sticking by him all these years, maybe with flowers. No, he thought, that would take away from Joey's birthday celebration.

~ ~

Cedar had another stop to make on his way home from Cammy's. It was to a small house on Vista Madera, which ran parallel to Hector Street on the other side of the alley behind Marty's, Kenny's and Cammy's. It was busy enough to have a bus line, though with fewer and less frequent stops than the buses made on Hector Street. It was mostly residential, but small businesses clustered on every major intersection.

The house he drove to was owned by an old reverend who ran his church via the mail. Before getting into the religion business, he was a drunk at Kenny's when it was still called "Bill's Place." The drunk crossed the street one night after it closed, and a car hit him and broke his legs, after which he became born-again. Since then, with social security and disability payments, donations from church members, and monthly rent paid by a tenant for a rear bedroom with its own entrance, the minister just made ends meet. Cedar knew all this because the minister's son was his friend growing up. The renter, however, was Kenny Grimmet.

At three-ten, Cedar parked in front of the house. It was set back behind a wooden fence around the front yard. He walked to the entrance to Kenny's room on the side. No lights were on. A chain-link fence separated the house from an auto-repair shop next door with junkers in the back and stacks of used batteries along the wall. Security lights were mounted all around the shop. The house had a deep back yard with four citrus trees and old lawn furniture with grass growing up around the legs. A row of cypress trees kept the back yard quiet from traffic in the alley.

Cedar gently tried the door to Kenny's room. It was locked. He kicked it loose with the flat of his foot. It popped open with a bang.

"What the—" said Kenny.

Light from the repair shop helped Cedar to ascertain Kenny's whereabouts in the small room. A terrified Kenny sat up on a flat mattress. Cedar put his hands around Kenny's neck. "You-son-of-a-bitch-Kenny!" he said.

Kenny grabbed Cedar's wrists, but Cedar wouldn't let go. He lifted Kenny by his neck and threw him on the floor. He closed the door, found a light switch, and turned it on. Kenny flinched from the light. He was naked from the waist down and sitting with his legs bent and both hands on the floor to hold himself up. His t-shirt had wet semen in the front.

The room smelled like *Eau de Ashtray*. Kenny threw a shoe at Cedar, not to inflict injury but to show outrage at the galling intrusion. Cedar deflected the shoe. It hit a wall poster of a sexy pitch-woman for Black Velvet whiskey. The poster moved enough to hang off-center. Its frame outlined layers of nicotine deposited over the years. The dark-brown veneer covered every stationary thing in the room, including the other walls, ceiling, doors, dresser and roll-down window shades brittle enough to crack if you sneezed. You could probably get through the nicotine with a putty knife.

A tall dresser had soiled shirts and pants lain over its open drawers with the knobs broken off. Piles of clothes on the floor of an open closet spilled onto a carpet, whose original color was impossible to detect. The bathroom walls were the same ugly brown as the rest of the room. Cigarettes left on top of the dresser and bathroom counters had burned ash-trails to the edges. Two coffee cans, one by the bed and one by the toilet, were filled with cigarette butts.

"What the hell are you doing here, asshole?" barked Kenny. "This is breaking and entering."

"Not murder, though," said Cedar.

Kenny pulled his stained-yellow sheet over himself and scooted back onto the mattress. "What're you talking about?" he asked.

"Cammy told me everything."

Kenny's face turned white. "That prick."

"Don't worry," said Cedar. "He's in. You're lucky he told me."

"Yeah, I feel real lucky."

"Rachel keeps a nine millimeter Walther under her bed," said Cedar. "Marty's orders. You'd have both been shot dead."

Kenny showed the same delayed confusion Cammy had shown twenty minutes earlier. "What's all this about? You trying to help or what?"

"I'll help you set it up, but you and Cammy are going to pull it off."

"What the hell are *you* interested for?" said Kenny. "This is bullshit."

"Just do what I say," said Cedar.

Kenny could neither hide his intrigue nor appreciate it without a cigarette. He reached for a pack and a lighter on the floor.

"Don't smoke around me," said Cedar.

Kenny held the cigarettes and lighter in his lap. "What do you mean 'Cammy's in?'" he said. "He *already* said he's in."

"I told him to say that," said Cedar. "I had to give him a pep talk. So don't ruin it. Get it through your thick skull, Kenny—hear him out and do what he says."

"*He's* in charge now?" said Kenny. "Great—*you* get involved and the cream goes straight to the top. Are you trying to tell me *you* want Marty dead? You expect me to believe that?"

Cedar took two short threatening steps forward.

"Okay, okay!" said Kenny, raising his hands protectively. "Don't get so lathered-up, man."

Cedar held his tongue. It was a tactic he knew would prompt Kenny to think aloud.

"Look, man," said Kenny. "Curly was pissing me off the other night with that diarrhea-of-the-mouth he gets once in a while, so I called Cammy to blow off some steam. That's all it was, man. But he signs on right away, so we take it to Dom a couple minutes later and *he's* on board too but—but what the hell, that don't mean it was going to happen. It was just talk, you know? I mean, yeah, maybe it would've, maybe it wouldn't have—I don't know. Now *you* come all in here all hot and bothered—what do I know, man? What do I know what's going on?"

"Know this," said Cedar. "Get cute and it's all over for you."

"Yeah, yeah. Look, I've got a right to know what you want out of this."

"No you don't."

"Don't pull that arrogant crap on me, Cedar. I know you too long. I'm smelling a set-up here."

"I don't sell anybody down the river," said Cedar.

Kenny looked for a sign that more was coming, but nothing came.

"Yeah," said Kenny with sudden, naked resignation. "I guess you don't." He ran his fingers through his hair. "Then get out of here so's I can at least have a smoke, will you? A man's got to have one vice."

Cedar gave Kenny a long look, then turned and moved for the door.

Kenny said, "You telling me that's all you came over for, to tell me to go along with Cammy? This is all bullshit."

Cedar turned and took another threatening step forward.

"All right, *all right!*" said Kenny, this time pulling his legs close as if expecting to get kicked. "What about Dom? You gonna do your angel-in-the-night routine on him, too?"

"Dom doesn't need a pep talk."

"You've got to give me *something*, Cedar. It feels like I'm having a dream here, a nightmare. *You and Marty?*"

"It's personal," said Cedar.

"Murder's pretty personal, I'll give you that. All's I can say's the old wop must've pulled a fast one on you for you to throw away what you got invested in him after all this time."

Cedar opened the door and left.

Kenny lit a cigarette. While exhaling, he smiled. "What do you know," he said. "Big bad Cedar Roach is going to help whack moneybags. Sweet Jesus, ain't life interesting."

~ ~

Cedar drove home. He took Sonoma to Eagle Rock Boulevard to Colorado Boulevard. The streets were dead except for bakery, produce, and dairy trucks. No buses, taxis, pedestrians, cyclists, nothing, just gray street lamps against a black, warm night sky. He thought about calling Helen from a payphone to say he was en route. Show her some consideration, he thought. She's a good girl, asks little, gives a lot, puts up with even more. But he didn't phone her. It would have been a meaningless gesture. Real men didn't waste their time on meaningless gestures, he thought.

He pulled into his duplex just off of Colorado Boulevard, on a quiet, two-lane side street not far from where Curly's girlfriend, Bernice Horl, lived. The neighbors had jasmine on the other side of the fence separating the properties. Cedar loved the smell. He closed the door on his Cherokee and stood a moment to inhale the fragrance. It wasn't as strong as when the jasmine bloomed in the spring, but now, in the wee hours, with no noisy kids around, no smelly cars driving by, no TV's blaring from their neighbors' windows to distract a tranquil mood, the jasmine was just as nice as when it was in full bloom.

He entered his bedroom, took off his clothes, lay next to Helen and folded his hands over his chest. She put her hand on his stomach and moved it gently toward his groin the way he liked, but he brushed her away.

"Not tonight," he said staring at the ceiling.

"Why not?" she asked quietly.

Cedar's response was terse. "I don't want to talk."

Helen withdrew her hand and stared at the ceiling with Cedar. On occasions, all post-coital, when he shared his latest metaphysical theory with her, he spoke without the brusque authority he used at other times. It was as if he wanted to hear how his new theory sounded for the first time but also to bestow on an attentive listener his unique and profound view of the universe. During these times, Helen detected pride in his voice, the kind that came from discovery after scholarly research guided by noble purpose. But tonight, Cedar's voice was filled with sad resignation. Helen didn't know he was talking to his creator. When finished, he rolled on his side with his back to her and said nothing more. Helen wondered if he would ever tell her what he was thinking.

~ ~

Kenny tried so hard to fathom what had compelled Cedar to turn against Marty that he couldn't sleep. At four o'clock, he phoned Cammy. Cammy bolted up to turn on his bedroom light. "Hello?" he said, thinking it was the wrong number.

"It's Kenny."

"Kenny, it's late. Do you know what time it is?

"I heard you and Cedar had a little talk."

"Cedar?" Cammy said weakly. "Well where'd you get that?"

"He just told me," said Kenny. "What'd you talk about?"

"When did he talk—"

"It doesn't matter *when*! Now what'd you talk about?"

Cammy spoke guardedly. "Well he was wondering, just making sure I was feeling okay."

"Cammy, he either threatened you or he upped the ante. What was it?"

"I don't know what you mean," said Cammy.

"You're not clever enough to do this to me," shouted Kenny. "I know you didn't change your mind by yourself."

Cammy looked for an out. "Can't this wail till tonight?"

"What the hell's 'tonight?'"

"We're getting together here, at my place, after we all close up."

"Who?" asked Kenny. "You and me?"

"No, the three of us. At two forty-five sharp. Didn't Cedar tell you?"

Kenny did not want to appear ignorant of something as important as a scheduled meeting that included him. "I'm not interested in details like times and all that," he said. "Listen, Cammy. I'm not a fool! You must've shit in your pants when you found out he wants a piece of this. *I* did. Cedar Roach don't come in telling you he's going to help murder a guy like Marty Bagliamente and all you say is 'okay, next topic.' I thought I was having a nightmare. How'd you even *tell* him about it in the first place?"

Cammy kept his voice steady. "I really need to sleep."

"Hey! This was *my* idea and now *you* two are running the show? Cut me out like I'm some, some *fifth wheel*?"

Cammy liked hearing that he was co-runner of the show and that his new partner, Cedar, was such an intimidating force, especially to a know-it-all like Kenny. It gave him pluck. "Nobody's saying you didn't come up with it, Kenny. But Cedar's in charge now and I'm doing what he told me, because you know why? Because he's Cedar Roach, that's why."

"We'll just see who's boss. *Maybe* I'll show up tonight. It depends *on how I feel!*" Kenny slammed down his receiver, then lit a cigarette and inhaled like a vacuum cleaner on overdrive.

When Cammy hung up, he didn't feel bad. In fact, he enjoyed holding his own with Kenny. It was time the tables were turned. But any pleasure he got from sticking it to Kenny was doused by what Cedar had told him about Marty and Rachel. Cammy often wondered why inner cities never got any better. Weren't Civil Rights laws passed when he was in his teens? It made sense that rich white people would try to confine the urban poor. Nor was he worrying about what to do next; he could leave that up to Cedar, a natural leader, because with Kenny and Dom calling the shots, the whole thing would have been a disaster. No, his worry was more personal. It was about how clever Marty and Rachel were to mask their evil ways.

"Why didn't I see it?" he asked himself.

Cammy always respected Marty and Rachel. He had praised them to others. No one was more loved in Hillside Park than Marty. No one ran a better nightclub. No one was more generous to needy people. And Rachel, with her magnetism and beauty, was so classy. But their cleverness to deceive, and the absence of it in himself, gnawed at Cammy as he looked into the mirror opposite his bed. His eyes had dark sagging bags under them. His jowls, heavy and bloated, made his mouth look small and hard, like a hole in a tree, as if it belonged to an old man who'd forgotten how to laugh.

Look at that ugly face, he thought, how dull and forgettable its. No wonder I'm so blind to what's beneath appearances. Nobody shows me any attention so I don't show them any. I turn them off so they turn me off. He remembered how his mother screamed at the frequency of his missing the obvious: "Are you wearing blinders *and* earplugs?" she'd yell a dozen times a day. "People think you're *stupid*!"

And now it's come back to haunt him, he thought. He turned off the light and put his head on the pillow. He pulled a sheet up to his shoulders, then cried. If there's a mistake on Monday and I get killed, who's going to care? My customers will just go somewhere else and after a few days they won't think of me or my bar anymore. Who's going to notify my brother and niece and nephew? And what are they going to say when they find out? One rotten bar on a rotten street doesn't open its doors anymore, and that's all there is to it. And what if it all works out and I get some money to fix up my bar and get new business? Is my life really going to change? Are people going to treat me any better? Kenny won't. Dom won't. Earl Zell won't, and he's just a drunk. When you're so low that even a drunk won't look up to you, why do you want to go on living?

"How come I can't be just a little bit happy?" he said. He half-expected an answer; when self-pity drives one to tears, someone somewhere has got to be listening, he thought. He rolled back on his side, pulled another tissue from the box on his bedside table, squeezed it into a little ball and kept dabbing at tears. His last thought before falling asleep was: At least I'm not a scumbag. I'm a decent person. Marty and Rachel are the scumbags.

~ ~

Kenny was perturbed throughout the day. He kept slapping his bar and cursing. This slowly drove out his customers. Curly slept during their exodus. Kenny was dying to tell Dom that the great, ominous Cedar Roach had entered their scheme—a shocking turn of events—but he held back because telling Dom would be conceding that he'd lost control of the operation.

Kenny and Cammy and Dom had talked for years about destroying Marty's juggernaut business. Ideas included hiding drugs in his club and then tipping off the cops, sprinkling poison in ice bins in hopes that nauseous customers would sue Marty into bankruptcy, and even torching his building to make it look like arson to collect insurance. The latter was the easiest to execute, but it lacked credibility, as Marty would never intentionally destroy his club. No, the way to get rid of Marty's was to get rid of Marty.

Kenny finally came up with an idea that obsessed him for its cleverness: exploit Marty's affair with Rachel by making her jealous. Find a woman with a sultry voice to phone Rachel's house and ask for Marty, then hang up when Rachel wanted to know who was calling. This would provoke her legendary temper and cause her to confront Marty, and his resulting emasculation among employees and customers would render him unable to manage the club. Even Cammy laughed off the idea. Dom got angry over it. But Kenny went forward. He held auditions for women to see whose voice was the sultriest by having them rehearse dialogue he wrote. But when he offered only fifty bucks—this, after exhaustive auditions—the would-be actresses walked away.

Tales of Rachel's temper used to reverberate throughout the bars. One was her reaction to the money Harper's Funeral Home, a family-run business in Eagle Rock, had charged her to bury her father. At his death from alcohol poisoning when Rachel was still drinking, she discovered he'd left no will or insurance, nor was his roofing business worth a dime. Rachel had screamed profanities at the elderly, dignified Jules Harper, the home's owner-director, accused him of being a parasite, and of having no ancestry that walked on two legs. She knocked over candles in her father's viewing room and threatened to come back armed. The last part never happened, but it became folklore anyway. Though Marty paid for the burial—Jules Harper had handled his son's funeral with taste and dignity—Rachel nonetheless returned after her father's interment and gave Harper another tongue-lashing that, according to a grieving family that witnessed it, went on for twenty minutes. Jules Harper needed medication to calm down afterward.

All this was on Kenny's mind when his phone rang. It was Bernice calling for Curly. Bernice despised Kenny for ridiculing her boyfriend. "May I speak to Curly, please," she asked with warp-speed iciness.

Kenny dropped the receiver. "It's the whale," he said to Curly.

Bernice heard this, which is what Kenny wanted. Curly shook himself from his nap and picked up the receiver. "Hey, Bee. How ya' doing?"

"Always a little bit better when I hear your voice," said Bernice.

Curly blushed. Bernice spoke with breathy coyness. "And how are you today?" she said.

"Okay," said Curly. "I slept good last night. Guess what. Kenny asked me to work a couple hours Monday. So I'll have extra money next week."

"That's then, handsome," said Bernice. "What are you doing now?"

"Taking it easy," said Curly. "Just me and Kenny here."

"Do you want to visit me?" she asked. "I would really like it. I made corn muffins. If you leave now they'll be warm when you get here."

"Sure, Bee, I'd love to," said Curly.

"All right, sweetie," said Bernice. "I'll be waiting."

Curly hung up. He couldn't wipe the anticipatory smile from his face, even when he saw that Kenny was ready to insult him: "Let me ask you something, Curly. When you're crawling all over that big fat carcass of hers, do you ever tell her you love her?"

"Me and Bee like each other," said Curly. "I don't know why that bugs you so much."

"It doesn't," said Kenny. "I think it's just *swell.*"

Curly headed for the door. Kenny had to get in one last dig. "Why don't you marry her for all that money she's got? You're not going to get rich off the forty bucks she gives you to dip your wick." Curly ignored him. "Keep banging her and she'll be a *sperm* whale 'stead of a regular one."

Curly left without saying good-bye. Kenny regretted teasing him. He blamed it on his anxiety over tonight's meeting. It was a good time to call Dom. Dom was in his office.

"Are you sitting down?" said Kenny.

"Yeah, why?" said Dom.

"Well, guess who's taking over?"

"Taking over what?"

"What do you think? Disneyland?"

Dom barked. "Just tell me."

"Our thing, that's what."

"With Marty?"

"Ba-*doop*."

"What do you mean 'guess who's taking over?'" asked Dom.

"Guess who wants Marty dead and he's putting his neck on the line to get it done," said Kenny.

"*Just say it!*"

"Cedar," said Kenny. A pause followed. "Sure as shit," he added.

"You are kidding me?" asked Dom.

"Could I have made that up?"

"You're telling me Cedar's in this with us?" said Dom.

"Straight from the horse's mouth."

"How the hell'd *he* find out?"

"Cammy told him."

"That idiot," said Dom.

"He got scared about Rachel being hit so he called him, and lo and behold Benedict Arnold's going to the front lines with us."

"We can't trust this guy," said Dom.

"Do we got a choice?" said Kenny.

"What's his part in it?"

"I'll get that tonight. We're meeting on it."

"Does he know I'm involved?" asked Dom.

"Far as I know he knows everything," said Kenny.

"Sounds like an inside job."

"What do you mean?"

"He's going to be driving Marty, he's going to be right there."

"That's what it looks like to me too," said Kenny.

"And you're going *along* with it?"

"For the ride so far. We'll see what happens. Maybe it's legit. Maybe Cedar's tired of taking orders."

"It's hard to believe, that's for sure. Maybe he wants to whack Marty then raid whatever's in the Kitchen."

"He could've raided that place any time."

"Marty probably tried to screw him out of a percentage. We better get off the phone. Am I still supposed to give you guys a gun tomorrow night?"

"I'll find out all that," said Kenny.

"Cedar's got an arsenal. You guys don't need mine anymore."

"I said I'll let you know. Listen, whatever Cedar wants, Cedar gets. That guy's got a fuse shorter than my dick."

"You let me know 'soon as you can," said Dom.

Kenny hung up without saying goodbye. He was relaxed after sharing the news. The rest of the day and night, he kept his eyes on the clock. As closing approached, he went to the bathroom with great frequency. Dom also felt less worry. Like Kenny, he believed Cedar's participation was a godsend; Cedar was the ultimate go-to guy. That's why Marty kept him close to his vest. Give Cedar a job to do, it gets done.

In no time, Dom was whistling "Jimmy Cracked Corn."

~~

All four bars closed at two that night. Cammy went straight home, prepared a tray of mixed nuts, drinking glasses with lemon wedges in them, and put out napkins and a pitcher of ice water. He lit candles for the bathroom, kept the lights on in the kitchen, and dimmed the lamp next to his recliner chair.

Kenny went home and smoked cigarettes. He lay on his bed with one hand behind his head and the other on his penis. He couldn't think of anything to do until it was time to leave for Cammy's.

Dom got one of his customers to drive him home. He lived near North Figueroa Street and Colorado Boulevard. On the way he savored what was going to happen on Monday. He wished Marty's dying breath would find their eyes locked so that Dom could say: "I just might go put the moves on the grieving widow." This thought stayed with Dom until he was dropped off.

Cedar had vigorous sex with Helen. She was so glad his appetite had returned that when he said he had to go out awhile she didn't ask where.

~ TWELVE ~

A few hours earlier, Curly Peetz and Bernice Horl had eaten dinner, watched a video, made love and fallen asleep; the routine was always the same when Curly visited. But tonight the dynamics were off. Two nights earlier, Curly's restlessness had driven Kenny to act on a long-festering desire to plan murder. Tonight, it drove the usually calm Bernice to tears.

Nothing made Bernice feel more like a homemaker than when she cooked all day for Curly, set the china out and, finally, dressed up for him. Upon arriving, he showered, and while he put on clothes she had washed from his previous visit, she put the dinner on the table. Her dining room was a mix of dark woods and green-gray wall-covering between drapes covering two French windows. The centerpiece of an oval mahogany table and chairs was a silver crystal candelabra holding eight candles.

After praising the feast before him, Curly said reflectively: "You know what I was thinking today about?"

"Me, I hope," said Bernice.

"I always do that," he said with a grin. "No, I mean something sort of out there, y'know, sort of weird."

"You've got me intrigued."

"I was thinking, wouldn't it be cool if we could talk to plants?"

"You were thinking that?" Bernice asked while buttering her roll.

"'Cause then, like, all we'd have to do is say 'g'morning, bud,' and they'd grow from, like, happiness. Wouldn't that be cool?"

"It would be wonderful," she said. "They'd be like little children."

Curly was glad she liked their banter. But then, with no warning, he unloaded. "I was wondering, Bee. I think something's in the air."

"What do you mean? Good or bad?" said Bernice.

"Definitely bad."

"Why? What happened?"

"Well the other night Kenny was really out of sorts and—"

Bernice frowned. "I don't want to hear about that creep."

"You don't?" Curly asked.

Bernice detected disappointment. "All right, go ahead."

"It's sort of about him and Cammy," said Curly.

"Ugh, a double-dose."

"Dom Catina too."

"*Oh please*," said Bernice.

"Well, maybe it's nothing." From her reaction, Curly decided to change the subject. "I sure like hot showers here, especially after the long walk up."

"You could shower ten times a day here if you wanted," said Bernice. "I'm not going to run out of hot water."

Curly answered quietly with his head down, "I know."

"Why don't you just stay here?" said Bernice.

This made Curly frown.

"You know I get tired of asking," she added.

"It's just, you're such a good person and I haven't done anything good in my life and, it's like, in a way, I mean when you think about it, you shouldn't have to suffer just 'cause we might live together one day."

"Curly, I may be the only person in the world who knows you're not stupid. You're too decent to *fake* being anything you're not. But somewhere along the way you threw in the towel, and that's fine with me if it works for you, because I don't want to be judgmental. But unless you've got another girlfriend, it's ridiculous for you to be homeless when you could be sharing everything I have here and pleasing me at the same time."

"I don't have one, Bee. I don't want another girlfriend either."

"Then what is it?" she asked.

Curly couldn't face her.

Bernice sighed without revealing her disappointment at his refusal to answer. "Okay, Curly. Just tell me what you wanted to say and get it out of the way."

Curly squirmed. "Well I'm not really sure, 'cept Kenny was all mad the other night. Usually he's gotta be drunk before he's like that."

"He wasn't mad at you?" asked Bernice.

"I don't think so," said Curly. "No, I was just telling him about my grandmother, you know, when we lived in Pomona and San Bernardino and Fontana…uh, no. It was Pomona *then* Fontana *then* San—"

"I don't care where, Curly," said Bernice. "Just tell me what he did."

"Well he says 'the hell with it, I'm calling Cammy,' then he calls Cammy and then he starts whispering so's I can't hear, but then a couple minutes later Cammy shows up and Kenny kicks me out so's I can't hear what they're talking about either. See, this is all 'cause he's not making any money, how he's fed up with his business—like calling Cammy's gonna change all that. So then, I'm sitting in front of Cooper's—this is maybe ten minutes later—and I see 'em driving up Hector Street, the two of 'em. Bee, in all the time I knew them I never saw them go anywheres together."

"Where'd they go?"

"Well, that's just it. I go up to Sonoma and Hector and I see Cammy's car at Dom's, parked, you know. Bee, they were talking at Dom's."

"Is that all?"

"Well no, 'cause then I seen 'em coming out. Now, what would them three guys be talking about when what prolly got 'em together in the first place was Kenny saying how disgusted he was with his place and how he was going to call Cammy and do something about it?"

"Curly, believe it or not I don't think about those guys."

"Yeah, but what about Marty?"

"What about him?"

"Well I thought maybe it's them three against him sorta, kinda of. Oh, I forgot to tell you something I left out about it. When Kenny and Cammy came out of Dom's, Kenny said how they gotta be real careful or someone can die, something like that, 'someone can get killed,' I think he said."

Bernice put her utensils down. "I don't care about Kenny and Cammy and Dominick. I care about us. Now, have you finished?"

"I guess."

"Am I supposed to do something about it or what?"

"I guess not," he said wanly.

Bernice took a long breath, after which they resumed eating. "Will you tell me what you're worried about between us? Because it sounds fatalistic, and I've never known you to be fatalistic."

"I just don't want to hurt you, Bee," he said.

"It's not your nature to hurt anyone. Nothing bad's going to happen to you. So what if you haven't done missionary work or started charities or things like that? You haven't killed anybody. You're not a thief. You're not a rapist. To me you're considerate and thoughtful and I know you care about me, and that's all *I* care about."

Curly felt chastised. "All's I can say is, I really do care about you."

"And?"

"And that's why I can't move in with you."

Bernice started to cry with enough power to make her body tremble. "I can't keep waiting for a man to show me he *really* loves me."

When Curly saw her tears he started to cry, too. When Bernice saw this, she was doubly confused. She scooted her chair out and went into the hall bathroom and closed the door. Curly followed. He heard her crying and sniffling.

"Bernice?" he said to the door.

She didn't answer.

"Do you want me to leave?" he asked.

She didn't answer.

Curly turned away from the bathroom door and started to leave. He wanted to run and never come back. But he heard a faint "No." He turned back. Bernice had opened the bathroom door. Her eyes were red. She had a balled-up tissue in her hand. She forced a smile that didn't last long. Curly extended his arms, and they hugged. Bernice towered over him. He could have been hugging a gasoline pump.

Bernice finally said, "Ice cream and strawberries for dessert?"

"My favorite," said Curly.

They returned to the dining room and resumed dinner in silence.

"Sorry I got emotional," she said. "Sometimes a little cry helps."

"Yeah, makes ya' feel better," he said.

"My mother always used to say people who love each other should leave their problems at the bedroom door."

Curly didn't know what she meant.

"Not take them in the bedroom," she explained.

Curly still wasn't quite sure what she meant.

"They shouldn't let their squabbles interfere with *making love.*"

"Oh," said Curly. "Yeah, right."

Bernice took her plate and Curly's to the kitchen. Curly went to the living room and put a videocassette in the VCR. He turned down the lights and sat on the sofa. A breeze tickled window curtains on its way through the room. Despite their disagreement, Curly didn't feel the night would be any different from the others he spent with Bernice. She entered with two bowls of chocolate ice cream topped with strawberries. She handed Curly his with half-a-bow, as if pretending to be an eager-to-please servant, then made a whirl of her body to sit beside him. Curly was pleased that she smiled. He saw it as an attempt to put their recurring argument aside in order to enjoy the rest of the night. He kissed her on her cheek.

"Thank you, Curly," said Bernice. Then she snuggled next to him.

They quietly watched the movie Bernice had rented.

～～

Forty-four minutes after the bars closed, Cedar reached Cammy's apartment building after parking two short blocks away. A lone pedestrian was coming from the other direction. It was Kenny. He was smoking. "How's it going," he said in a seemingly casual voice.

"All right," said Cedar.

"Funny how this town doesn't seem so shitty when it's asleep, huh?"

"They're all that way," said Cedar dismissively. He did not want to engage Kenny in conversation unrelated to the reason they were gathering. Although he wasn't sure what to say to him and Cammy, his purpose was to inspire them. He would have called the purpose a "pep talk," but he did not see himself as a cheerleader. Cheerleading required animation and vigor.

Half a minute later, they were at Cammy's apartment. Having heard them walk up the outside stairs, Cammy swung open his door as they knocked.

"Hiya, fellas," he said.

Cedar entered. Kenny ground his cigarette out next to the welcome mat. Cammy glanced disapprovingly at the mashed butt, then looked at Kenny, but Kenny had already reached the mixed nuts Cammy had put out and was shoveling them into his mouth. Cammy went inside and indicated where they should sit. "I thought you could take the chair," he said to Cedar.

Cedar sat in the recliner. Kenny sat in the sofa and grabbed a second handful of nuts. Cammy filled the three glasses with ice water. "I got some refreshments here," he said proudly.

Kenny put more nuts in his mouth then grabbed another handful. While chewing the first handful, he shook the rest like dice at a craps table. "This is like one of them classic summit meetings," he said, as if trying to overcome nervousness. "Like when Churchill met Hilter and Mussolini."

"It was Truman and Stalin," said Cedar.

Kenny shrugged. "Yeah well…"

Cammy sat next to Kenny. "I had a busy day today," he said. He'd hoped to initiate small talk, but it didn't work.

Cedar said: "Thomas Jefferson wrote that the most effectual means of being secure against pain is to retire within ourselves and to suffice for our own happiness. He knew humans deserved to be happy. He studied treatises on happiness before he wrote the Declaration of Independence. But the problem with his notion is its implication that happiness exists absent conflict, yet conflict is as natural as life itself. It is the intrusion of one being onto another. A fish gets eaten by a bigger fish, a bigger fish eats that one, and so on. That's the cycle of life: conflict and resolution. The idea is to find happiness within that cycle. This is what we're going to talk about."

"I like being reduced to a guppy," said Kenny. He'd intended to bring levity into the room, but Cedar wasn't amused.

"Nobody likes a wise ass," said Cedar. "Don't interrupt again."

Kenny put more nuts in his mouth. "Yeah, okay." Then he took another handful and shook them while chewing. Cammy wondered if Kenny was going to eat all the nuts. They cost him almost seven dollars.

Cedar continued. "You two have a natural right to be happy."

"So you're saying what we're doing here's okay," said Kenny.

"It's in accordance with nature," said Cedar.

"So I could kill anybody I want," posed Kenny. "I could kill *you* and it'd be okay."

"You would need a purpose," asked Cedar.

"Say I don't like your looks," said Kenny.

"In nature it's done for survival," said Cedar.

"So if you come up with a good-enough reason, you can whack anybody. Is that right?" said Kenny. "Is that what you're saying?"

"With a caveat," said Cedar. "To thine ownself be true."

"Let's try again," said Kenny. "If I'm barely surviving I can whack a guy making more money than me as long as I'm being truthful about it."

"We're not going to justify the rectitude of the conflict between you two and Marty," said Cedar. "We're here to discuss the logistics of resolving it."

"What's that supposed to mean?" said Kenny.

"It means that from here on out you don't question why you're doing this. You accept that it's a natural consequence of wanting happiness. And you accept it by repeating from here on out: 'it's kill or be killed.'"

The room went silent for fifteen seconds. Cammy looked at the floor and nervously scratched his thighs. Kenny stopped eating nuts.

"One more thing," said Cedar. 'Nothing is more hateful to wisdom than too much cunning.' Do you know what that means?"

Kenny said, "Why can't you just speak plain English?"

"It means your boldness to execute this plan will help you elude investigators. They will accept at face value what they see at the crime scene."

"A murder-suicide you mean," said Kenny.

Cedar nodded. Kenny turned to Cammy and boasted, "Told ja'."

"But all that changes if you get cocky," said Cedar.

"*Me?*" laughed Kenny. "Perish the thought. Look, I'm okay with all this, except I've got to know what you told Cammy to change his mind."

Cedar glanced away as if put out, then answered. "What do you think Rachel does all day?"

Kenny got sarcastic. "Oh, any *number* of things."

Cedar repeated what he'd told Cammy about Marty and Rachel. This surprised Cammy; he was under the impression that what Cedar told him was confidential.

When Cedar finished, Kenny showed no surprise. "I didn't know Marty did that," he said. "But I knew it went on. So what, though? Who wants spodas taking over the city?"

"What's a spoda?" said Cammy.

"They're spoda be white but they're not," said Kenny. He looked at Cedar. "Everybody knows rich people run the world."

"Well excuse me for being outraged," Cammy said to Kenny.

"Let me tell you something, Cammy," said Kenny. "They don't *have* to get doped up and they don't *have* to blow each other away. If I brought a homo in here and told you 'give it to him up his exhaust pipe,' would you?"

"I won't dignify that with an answer," said Cammy.

"Well you just did," said Kenny. He turned to Cedar. "So far I don't know anything I didn't know before tonight, so do you got any ideas on how we actually put bullets in these two on Monday?"

Cedar started to answer, but Cammy interrupted. "Kenny, don't you care that Marty buys off the cops but we get busted whenever the Vice feels like it?"

Kenny was exasperated. "Cammy, none of it's going to matter in about thirty-six hours, ba-*doop*! Cedar, tell Cammy it's not going to matter."

Cedar leapt up and put his face in Kenny's. "I'm tired of your sarcasm."

"Wow! What'd *I* say?"

"We're talking about two lives here," said Cedar.

"I know that, man," said Kenny.

"Then act like it," said Cedar. "Now are you going to keep your mouth shut about what I just told you or do I have to cut your tongue out?"

"Yeah, yeah, yeah, just don't blow a gasket, all right?" said Kenny.

Cedar backslapped Kenny. Kenny *and* Cammy were stunned at this.

"I can take all the drunks and heathens in Marty's day after day," said Cedar. "But two minutes with you and I'm ready to kill."

"That's *your* problem," said Kenny. "We don't have to talk after this any more. Is that okay with your conflict-resolution *bullshit* ass?"

Cedar threatened another backhand. Kenny flinched, and Cedar returned to the recliner. "I'm not going to be driving Marty on Monday," he said. "He's breaking in his nephew to do it."

"That can't happen!" said Kenny. "*Nothing* out of the ordinary can."

"He's going to bring it up at his family dinner tomorrow," said Cedar. "That's all the substantiation we need that Marty initiated the switch and that it had nothing to do with what you guys planned."

"Who's all that at his family dinner?" said Kenny. "Him and his wife and that ugly sister of his?"

"And his nephew," said Cedar. "You two are going to drive in separate cars to Vista Madera and Arrow. The apartments there have cars out front most of the day, so two more won't be noticed. Park at twelve-twenty-two, then walk across the street to that little meat market. I'll pick you up there, in the parking lot. Got that?"

"Twelve-twenty-two," said Cammy.

"What about getting in and out of Rachel's house?" said Kenny.

"And what about Marty's nephew?" said Cammy. "If he's sitting in the driveway, how are we supposed to get around him?"

"You're not going to," said Cedar. "I'll drop you off behind her house. You'll go through to her back yard. An old lady who's deaf lives behind her. She's got a dog that barks, but it always barks, so nobody's going to notice."

"Does it bite?" said Kenny.

"It's fenced in," said Cedar. "Go to the rear fence. It's made of one-by-sixes. When Rachel goes to the gym that morning, I'll loosen the slats in it. All you have to do is tap them and they'll fall. Her bedroom is next to her driveway. Go through the window of the *other* one. I'll have it and the screen unlocked."

"How are you going to get in?" asked Cammy.

"I have a key," said Cedar. "That's all for now. I'll tell you the rest in the car when I pick you up Monday."

"You're kidding," said Kenny. "That's all we get now?"

"If you think too much about it beforehand you'll make mistakes," said Cedar. "Bring a weapon and gloves. You'll be back at work by one."

"Look, you don't get to keep it all in your head," said Kenny. "What about the check-cashing money? It's going to be with that nephew, right? So how are we supposed to get in the car to get it?"

Cedar rose and headed for the door. Kenny stood up to complain. "Who do you think you are, man? This is some serious shit we're doing here. We could go away for life, even get the chair if we screw up. Now we find out we don't even get to know what do to until *you* feel like telling us?"

Cedar turned back abruptly, but Cammy rose and stood between them. "Fellas," said Cammy, "let's be friends, all right?"

"Twelve-twenty-two," said Cedar, then left.

When the sounds of Cedar's steps down the outside stairwell faded, Kenny said, "What an asshole that guy is. What was all that shit about, those stupid quotes? I really like being talked to like I'm a moron."

"Just trust him," said Cammy. "I know I do."

Kenny lit a cigarette.

"Please don't smoke in here," said Cammy.

Kenny ignored the request. "I tell you," he said. "This town's too small for me and Cedar."

"What are we going to do?" said Cammy.

"I don't know. I know we can't say no to the trail boss, damnit."

"Am I still supposed to go get a gun from Dom tomorrow night?"

"Cammy, do I know? He said bring a gun, bring a gun."

"And gloves," said Cammy.

"I'm not getting any gloves," said Kenny.

"I have an extra pair," said Cammy.

"What the hell do you use gloves for *here*?"

"Washing dishes," said Cammy.

"Figures," said Kenny, moving to the door.

"Wait," said Cammy. "Who's going to do the actual…"

Kenny turned back. "We know Cedar's not and we know Dom's not."

"I suppose," said Cammy.

"Look, Cammy, we're at the end of our ropes. Everything depends on us pulling this off, so we've just got to hope Cedar knows what he's doing."

"I suppose," said Cammy.

"Make sure you get that gun from Dom," said Kenny.

"Okay," said Cammy. "Thanks for coming over."

"Yeah," said Kenny, opening the door and leaving.

Cammy locked the doors, got a can of deodorant from under his kitchen sink and sprayed the room to cover the cigarette smoke.

~ ~

By eleven o'clock that night, Curly and Bernice had finished watching their movie and made love. Her bed was a double king. She never wanted such a large bed, but it belonged to her parents and she used to sleep with them when she had nightmares as a little girl. As it turned out, the extra room gave Bernice and Curly more space for sexual playfulness.

But tonight the sex was subdued, almost therapeutic. No fanfare, no bells and whistles, no William Tell overture. Neither Curly nor Bernice planned it this way. It was if, by invoking her mother's aphorism about keeping your troubles out of the bedroom, Bernice had set the tone for an act of love to follow rather than Curly putting on a three-ring display of cocksmanship.

When it was over, Curly took her hand. "Bee, you're the only person that treats me with any respect."

"I have a secret for you," said Bernice. "You're the only man I ever loved. And even if another man loved me, he wouldn't be as gentle as you."

Curly was embarrassed. "Come on."

"It's true, Curly. I'm saying I love you." She kissed his forehead. "I'm saying I'm in love with you." She cupped his cheeks and turned his face to meet hers. "Can you tell me you believe me?"

"You want me to tell you I love you?" said Curly.

"Only if you really feel it," said Bernice. "I don't want you to lie."

"I don't lie."

"Tell me what you feel about me when we make love."

"It feels really good, Bee." He looked away. "I remember once in grammar school one day, me and some other kids were having recess way out behind these buildings. It was like a park, grass and trees and stuff. A perfect day, I remember, totally quiet, clear sky and all, y'know. We were just laying on our backs, arms and legs all out and stuff, and somebody said— no, it was me—I said there'd have to be an atomic bomb go off to make me move a muscle and the other guys said the same thing. It's like we were paralyzed, like we were on drugs, but this was long before drugs."

"A natural feeling."

"Yeah, totally natural," said Curly. "Like lazy and dreamy and stuff. I'll never forget that day. Isn't that weird, Bee? Like, nothing really happened, but I just remember feeling so perfect just laying there."

"Life-changing," said Bernice.

"Yeah, that's what I'm trying to say. You're always putting it better than me, y'know? It's like I get the thought and you find the right words."

"What about that day?" asked Bernice.

"Well, it's just that the only thing better than that day's when I'm here and we just made love."

Bernice guided his face into her breasts and pressed it there. "Curly, if that's your way of saying you love me, I'll take it. I want to make you feel this way the rest of your life."

She felt his body relax, as if he'd gotten a weight off his chest. But then she felt a tear fall onto her breast. He really loves me, she thought, and he's not afraid to cry about it. She said a silent prayer of thanks. If she had turned her eyes down, however, she would not have seen in Curly's face the look of beatification she assumed was there. She would have seen his fear of losing her.

Later, when Curly fell asleep, Bernice eased out of bed, put on her robe, closed the bedroom door, and went into her living room. She sat in the dark and called Rachel, who answered on the first ring.

"It's me," said Bernice. "Do you have a minute?"

"Yes," said Rachel. "Is everything all right?"

"I've got good news and bad news," said Bernice.

"Give me the good first," said Rachel.

"Well, he finally told me he loved me."

"After all this time."

"Can you believe it?" said Bernice. "You should have seen him, Rachel. He was crying. It was so sweet."

"What's the bad?" said Rachel. "He wants a dowry?"

"He still won't move in with me," said Bernice.

"Surprise."

"It's all I want. Is that so much to ask? What am I doing wrong?"

"Curly's a funny guy," said Rachel.

"He was telling me he's never done anything good in his life, that's why he prefers being homeless. What kind of thinking is that? It's like moving in with me is worse than, I don't know, boot camp or something. I couldn't have made it any easier for him. I almost begged. What more could he want? Do you think he's confused?"

"Oh-no-not-at-all," said Rachel.

Bernice laughed. "I meant do you think he *knows* he's confused?"

"If he doesn't, don't tell him. Any man who's content to live on forty dollars a week he gets for sleeping with his girlfriend is onto something."

Bernice laughed louder. "What's worse, I don't even know what he does with it. If I didn't buy him clothes he'd have to walk around naked."

"Nice image," said Rachel.

"Could you talk to him?"

"You don't want me talking to him, Bee. I never got Marty to move in with me so how can I talk a man I don't know into moving in with you?"

"But Marty's married. I'm all Curly has."

"Not really," said Rachel.

This startled Bernice. "What do you mean?"

"It sounds like he's obligated to someone or something, a principle, a cause, a belief," said Rachel. "And you're second."

This made sense to Bernice. "Can't you give me any advice?"

"I don't think so. Marty and I used to fight about it all the time. We never had any energy left over for understanding each other. So I finally gave up and we've gotten along better ever since."

"So I shouldn't say anything anymore?" asked Bernice.

"I don't know, Bee," said Rachel. "I think something about you makes him feel unworthy, or at least uncomfortable."

"Except after we make love," said Bernice. "He compared it to going to heaven."

"They're all like that till football comes on."

"Oh, something else, why I really called this late. Curly thinks Kenny and Cammy and Dominick are conspiring against Marty. I'm not sure what for. He heard them talking outside the Sonoma Inn after it closed the other night. They were saying someone was going to get killed. Does this mean anything to you? Supposedly they're all mad at Marty for monopolizing the bar business. You don't think they might try something, do you?"

Rachel answered assuredly. "If Curly heard correctly maybe something is up. I'll call Cedar Roach and tell him."

"Why not the cops?" asked Bernice.

"Cedar can handle it," said Rachel.

"But the police ought to get involved," said Bernice.

"Marty pays Cedar a lot of money so he doesn't have to get the police involved with his business."

"Why don't you tell Marty yourself?" asked Bernice.

"He's got too many worries right now," said Rachel. "He's taking it out on me, but I let him vent."

"I wish Curly would vent. Then I'd know what's on his mind."

"It'll work out, Bee."

"Well anyway, don't tell anybody where you heard it. If something's really up, I don't want Curly in jeopardy."

"I won't," said Rachel.

"Thanks. 'Night, Rache."

They hung up. Bernice crawled back into bed and snuggled close to Curly. She put her huge arms and massive legs around him gently, so as not to kill him. Then she kissed him once behind his ear before falling asleep.

~ ~

A bad dream woke Rachel up that night. In it, a car on a deserted mountain road was moving sideways toward a cliff as if pulled there with chains. A storm made whatever was pulling it impossible to see. Rachel was in the back seat. She kept yelling to the driver, an indiscernible figure, to do something. The driver either could not hear or chose to ignore her. She couldn't get out of the car and she couldn't reach the brakes. She banged on the windows and kicked the doors, but escape was futile. Just as she looked through the car's window and saw certain death below, she woke up with a gasp. Soon she settled down and drifted back to sleep. It wasn't until she woke up later and went to the kitchen to brew coffee that she recalled the dream. Then it hit her. "Loss of control," she said as its details came back to her. She related the loss of control to what Bernice told her Curly had heard.

~ THIRTEEN ~

Rachel believed in dream analysis. Your body tells you things, she often said. She made a mental note to contact Cedar. She wasn't worried about calling him, as they had a common interest in protecting Marty. Plus, she thought, he ought to get a charge out of hearing from me after all these years. Though she remembered her flings with him, they were not distinctive. He was in quick and out quick, just like the others. He was big and strong and hard all over and had powerful thrusts, but knowing how to please a partner wasn't in him. Of all the guys she was with, only Marty knew how to make love. He spent more time on a single caress than others took for the whole sex act.

She put on her workout clothes and drove to the gym. She liked to get there when it opened at five o'clock. Too many guys tried to hit on her, so she got there before most of them did. By ten, she had returned, eaten breakfast, read the *L.A. Times*, done light gardening, showered and dressed in a sleeveless blouse, shorts, and leather sandals. She went to a book of phone numbers and found Cedar's. Marty had insisted she have it, along with Gino Cardona's, his bar manager. His edict, in the event that something happened to him, was for Gino and Cedar to shut down the club and hand over their keys to Gloria.

Cedar was working out when Rachel phoned. The bedroom he had converted into a gym had a wall-to-wall floor mat. One side was all mirrors. A TV and VCR sat on a shelf opposite a stair-climbing machine. He exercised to taped episodes of Andy Griffith and Jeopardy! before running two miles on Colorado Boulevard. His regimen took an hour: forty minutes of weight-training and twenty on the climber. He did not like to be interrupted, but when Helen knocked on his door and said that a Rachel Ellis was calling, he nearly had a heart attack.

When Helen saw his reaction, she said, "Why she call you for?"

Cedar wiped sweat from his forehead with a hand towel. "It's my boss's girlfriend," he said. "I'll need privacy."

Helen grudgingly went into the kitchen. Cedar picked up the phone in his living room. He could not imagine what Rachel wanted. Even thinking about it forced him to disconnect from all other matters. "Hello?" he said.

Rachel wedged the receiver between her jaw and shoulder so her hands were free to apply lotion on her arms and legs. Her hair was wet from the shower; she'd blow-dry it after the call. She did not expect it to last long. She was phoning to get information, not share memories. From her recollection of Cedar and everything she'd heard about his volatility, she was wary of mentioning the rumor, but nothing made her think he was disloyal to Marty. She was cordial. "It's been a long time, Cedar. How are you?"

Cedar was astonished at the power she still had over him. He could see her straddling him with her brazenly confident smile and penetrating blue eyes fixed on his escalating excitement. They said, "Go for it, Cedar, this is the best you'll ever have," just before he spasmed with pleasure.

"It has been a long time," he said. Vanished from his control were the menace, the mystery, the edgy voice, all mannerisms he'd perfected to protect against small talk and annoying, inquisitive minds. "How are you?"

"I'm fine," she said. "You?"

"I'm getting by," said Cedar. "I'm surprised. What's this all about?"

Rachel wanted to ask who had answered his phone; it would have been fun to tell Marty that Cedar had a gal living with him. But she didn't want to explain how she knew. "I wanted to get your thoughts on a rumor I heard."

"Okay," said Cedar.

"What do you make of Kenny and Cammy and Dom getting together against Marty?"

This surprised Cedar, but not enough to dislodge his attention to Rachel. "You're talking about three big-league losers. Where'd you hear it?"

Rachel was guarded. "I don't want to say."

"It would get me close to the source," said Cedar.

She knew he was right. "Curly Peetz. He heard them talking in Dom's parking lot the other night. I guess that's where he slept that night."

"Do you know who he told?"

"I don't know that he told anyone," said Rachel.

"Except whoever told you," said Cedar.

She affected a comically sly tone. "The vodka I swam in all those years may have drowned out a few memory cells."

"Funny how it's *selective* memory cells," said Cedar, advancing his own brand of comic slyness. "I'll check it out, be happy to." He did not want the conversation to end. "How should I contact you if I hear anything?"

He's on the hunt, thought Rachel. She wanted to say, "Call Western Union, Bub." Instead, she said with a pleasant tone, "*My* phone works."

"A phone call it will be." He'd put out of his mind that she'd be dead soon. "Rachel?"

Here comes his big move, she thought.

"I'd like to see you again," he said.

Rachel did not want to encourage him. "That's sweet."

"I can't get over you." Cedar couldn't believe what was coming out of his mouth. A lifetime of cold, calculated thinking was just vanquished by bubbling sentiment, yet he couldn't stop. "Do you know how hard it is to listen to Marty talk about you and pretend I'm not interested? There's no one like you, Rachel. I can't say I wish we never got together, but I'm a failed man because of it. No one could ever do for me what you did. You set me adrift in a sea without ports."

"Poetic leanings," she said. "Is that a new side?"

"I'm full of surprises," said Cedar. "Rachel, you were a narcotic to me."

The depth of his feelings surprised her. "I don't know what to say, Cedar."

"Don't say anything. I just had to get it off my chest."

"I'm a big believer in that," said Rachel.

Cedar chuckled.

"What's so funny?" she said.

"Marty says that's the bane of your conversations."

"You'd think he'd get it one of these days," said Rachel.

"You know how thick men are."

"We're all imperfect. Maybe we'll talk more when you get back to me."

"I'm glad you called, even if it was over a nuisance rumor," he said. "I'm going to hang up now before I say anything else embarrassing."

"There's a saying in A.A., Cedar: 'You're as sick as your secrets.'"

"Thoughtful," he said. "But I don't drink."

She wanted to say that his cosmic theories were the same kind of addiction. Instead, she said, "I meant I should have called long before this. I used to be a man-eater and I suppose I left a few corpses along the way."

"You have your aphorism, I have mine."

"I bet I'm going to hear it."

"Don't worry, it's positive," said Cedar. "'No secret lives without guilt.'"

"Meaning?" asked Rachel.

"Meaning act on it, purge the guilt."

"We're probably in the same neighborhood on that."

"Does that mean we can meet for coffee? I'd love to talk to you."

"Time sure changes people," said Rachel. "The Cedar Roach I knew stayed closed up like a clam."

"That Cedar Roach was scared. He felt like teacher's pet where teacher took her clothes off for him. I don't mean to sound tawdry—I respect you and how you've changed. But every time I think about you I'm right back in my senior year and you've just walked up to me outside Mr. Hoffman's math class and asked if I wanted to come over to your apartment that night."

"Ah, Mr. Hoffman," she said.

"So, you remember."

"Some things the vodka left alone."

Cedar was feeling more confident. "I'd like to hear those memories some time, see if history's changed them."

"And who's going to judge if it has?" she asked.

"We'll hold court," said Cedar. "May the best person win. What do you say?"

Rachel had finished moistening her arms and legs and was screwing the cap on the lotion bottle. "I think we should keep this on a business level."

Cedar felt a rejection looming. "Sure. I'll call you."

"Thanks, Cedar. I enjoyed talking to you again."

"Same here. Bye, Rachel."

They hung up. Rachel felt uneasy. Nothing Cedar said could erase her suspicion that he was a loner with crazy ideas; that he still held a torch for her was evidence of that. She went to her bathroom to blow dry her hair.

Cedar felt good after telling Rachel his feelings, and he was narcissistic enough to believe she enjoyed hearing them. But he also heard "no sale" to his reunion invitation. Just as he wondered if he could win her over with greater effort, Helen stepped in and reacted to telltale signs in his eyes.

"Joo lie jour boss' girlfrien'?" she said in a confrontational tone.

"I told you there's no one else, so quit asking," he said.

Helen had doused his lustful thoughts. He left for his run. He no sooner got into a rhythm that he thought about what he'd said to Rachel. Now it embarrassed him. She was probably laughing at him. That's all right, he thought. She'll be dead tomorrow. Nor did he worry about the rumor. Yes, it was coincidental that Curly had overheard Kenny and Cammy—well, maybe not so coincidental. After all, slappers work in mysterious ways. He was convinced, especially after Rachel phoned, that Slapper was spreading its electromagnetic frenzy all over the city. Nothing else could explain the behavior of all involved, even himself, how he'd gone from worshiping Marty to seeing him as a powerless victim who was going to die real soon.

None of it mattered anyway, because once Marty was out of the way, Cedar would be long gone. And he knew where he'd go. He'd thought about it for years: pull a Ted Kaczynski—hole-up in the middle of nowhere and enjoy nature as God intended. To hell with computers, DVD's, wireless gadgets—all that stuff that Cedar thought took people away from each other and polluted their minds. Where Kaczynski erred was telling the world what he thought of it in that rambling manifesto he mailed to newspapers. He should have kept his mouth shut, gotten a more comfortable cabin, and taken it easy for ten or so years. Then he could have returned to civilization. If when he returned, civilization had become more hospitable than when he left it, fine—stay and mix. If it had become more hostile, go back to isolation.

Cedar's theory of Slapper did not include an abuse of nature. If Slapper had a purpose, it was to punish mankind for abusing nature. Because whoever put the protective layer around the planet wanted the planet to stay pristine, and if they ever came back to monitor its progress, Cedar wanted to be far away from their wrath. He'd be with bears and lions and the crisp, deep greenery, and at night he'd lie under black skies with a billion stars he could practically touch. No man-made sounds. He'd be at one with God.

Then another thought came to him. What if Kenny and Cammy killed only Marty? With him dead and Rachel spared, her financial resources would end. Could he exploit that? But the deeper he got into these lurid thoughts, the more he felt that she would reject him, even in her post-Marty life. That she'd made rapturous love to him in high school then cast him aside when she had nothing to lose but now might reject him when the rest of her life and very survivability were at stake made him want to punish her. Still, he could not shake the remotest possibility that, should her life be spared, Rachel could be available for the taking. She might go with him to the wilderness, just the two of them in a cabin with no phone, no television, nothing but nature outside and a warm bed inside.

~ FOURTEEN ~

For his first day of work as a part-time chauffeur, Joey Bagliamente walked to Marty's from the home he shared with his mother, Freda. It was a small, three-bedroom house four residential blocks south of Hector Street. Freda had lived there since she moved to California with her parents. They paid her rent until she got a degree in education and found a teaching job, whereupon she paid her own bills and, soon after, bought the house. She'd been with the Los Angeles Unified School District ever since. Her income was enough to live comfortably in Hillside Park but not enough to buy a house in a better part of the city.

At school, Joey was a minority in the Hispanic and Asian student body. Freda wanted to send him to a private school, but as a loyal member of the teacher's union she did not want to look like a hypocrite. He rarely ventured out of Hillside Park anyway; all he needed was within a seven-mile radius.

Joey was a skinny five-foot-eight. He had thick, moppy dark-brown hair, skin pure as a vanilla shake, and puppy-like black eyes that, together with a natural shyness, made him look disarmingly innocent. His cheeks were red. His jaw-line tapered to a soft, curved chin. Like his uncle, he had a wide, stubby nose, the only thing that kept him from looking like a pretty girl. He didn't smile much. He wasn't unhappy, just unresponsive, as if his thoughts were elsewhere. Nor was he impolite. When you conversed with him, you wanted to knock on his skull and ask if anyone was home. His mother used to think he was dim-witted, but his grades proved otherwise.

Freda also thought, because Joey hadn't brought home girls, that he might be gay. It wasn't until she mercilessly interrogated his teachers that she found out he liked girls. The problem was that he looked like a younger brother to the ones he asked out. Nor was he assertive. He'd asked one of the girls to the senior prom and she'd said yes, but only to spite her estranged boyfriend. When Joey found out, he told her she should get back with her boyfriend if she wanted. She did, and he ended up seeing a movie alone that night.

When Marty announced at last night's family dinner that he wanted Joey to drive for him, Gloria and Freda knew it was more a favor to Joey than a necessity for Marty. They had no idea how much cash he took from the bank each week, nor did they believe he needed protection. They thought Cedar, as bodyguard and chauffeur, was Marty's vanity.

Joey entered Marty's from the alley, went down the hallway, and knocked on the outer office door. "Come in, Joey," yelled Marty. He was finishing his weekly bank deposit of customers' checks when Joey entered. Marty grinned as if he hadn't seen him in months, walked around his desk to shake hands and slapped him on the back. "Have a seat, I'm almost done."

Joey sat. Marty returned to his chair. "Look at all this," he said. "Just to keep my customers happy. If I don't cash their checks, they'll go to a bank and spend their money somewhere else. First rule of business: take care of business. You know what that means, Joey?"

"I'm not sure," said Joey.

"You take care of business by taking care of customers."

"Oh."

"That's what my dad taught me and that's what his dad taught him. Can I get you anything? A Coke? Shirley Temple?"

"No thanks," said Joey. He took in all details of Marty's office. The walls were covered with photos too personal for public display. Most were of Rachel. Joey knew about her from vicious comments made by his mother and his Aunt Gloria, though they never made them in Marty's presence. He'd seen the pictures before, but this time he studied them. What a babe, he thought.

He wondered if he would see Rachel when he dropped Marty off at her house on the way back from the bank. He knew about the Monday Nooners. Gloria had learned of them and the Friday dinners at Mama Funelli's, when a woman Marty permanently eighty-sixed from his club for drinking too much ended up a regular at Dom's and told him everything she knew about Marty and Rachel. Dom encouraged her to call Marty's wife and tell it all, and she did. The result was further distance between Marty and Gloria.

When Marty saw Joey looking at Rachel's pictures, he erased all doubt that Joey had no interest in girls. It wasn't that his eyes got big or that he licked his lips or that smoke came out of his ears. He showed no expression whatsoever, just a fixated study of each picture. Marty examined his nephew the way a photographer examines a subject. It was as if he'd never really considered the boy in person before. At family dinners there was never time; Marty always wanted to get back to his club where questions of infidelity did not loom over him like pointed guns. And the creative energy it took to maintain conversation that didn't involve his club or Rachel kept his mind too active to think about Joey as anything other than another diner at the family table. He saw that Joey's collar, though buttoned to the top, was loose around his thin, feminine neck. His silky skin was glossy, his eyelashes long, his eyes clear, his gaze absorptive. He could be my grandson, thought Marty: he has Paul's features. The big difference was that Paul was gregarious; he would flash his confident grin and shake hands with self-assurance and warmth. Joey was a hermit.

Marty didn't blame Joey for his shyness. He blamed his mother. After moving to California, Freda Bagliamente had taken up so many different lifestyles and political causes that, Marty believed, she never kept one identity long enough for her own son to know her. She'd been a flower child, radical feminist, religious revivalist, psychic advisor, mystical ecologist, Taoist, an animal-rights nut, a lactation advocate and an organic-foods expert, not to mention an insufferable and incessant dieter. She had pursued each of these causes with vigor and determination.

Marty regretted never taking the time to be a surrogate father to Joey, just as he regretted not trying harder to save his marriage. He knew he'd take these regrets to his grave. But he also felt he'd provided well for his family, no small chore considering that he didn't go to college and never had to be a puppet for anyone. He was his own man and proud of it. He wished he could impart his life's experiences to his young nephew. When he tried before, Joey's mother got in the way. She never saw Marty as anything but a saloon keeper, this despite his giving her a hefty monthly check to supplement her own income from the day Joey was born.

"You know who that is?" said Marty, indicating Rachel's pictures.

"I'm pretty sure."

"Well," said Marty, "you know what you know."

He waited for a response, but Joey was silent. Joey sensed that his uncle wanted to converse, but he'd come to work; it never occurred to him there was going to be anything social about it.

Marty sat back. "Joey, a man makes mistakes in his life, he has to live with them. He doesn't blame others. You stand tall and you say 'this is what I am, this is what I've done,' and you take on the world. That's how a man lives his life. If he hasn't hurt too many people along the way and he's done well for himself, he'll die a proud man but still a humbled man, because there will always be greatness around him, right up to the end. You always try to do good, and if that's how your life goes, you'll never want for more. And if you share with others less fortunate what you've earned on your own, then you can say you've done your ancestors and your family well. I'll say just one more thing because we've got to get going, and that's this: never let anyone tell you what you can or can't do. You do what you think is right for yourself and for your family."

"I know, Uncle Marty." His voice was low-keyed, his tone appreciative.

"Because your mom grew up when it was just the opposite: 'if it feels right, go for it.' Joey, thinking and feeling are two different things. When you know the difference, you'll be on the right track."

Joey nodded with a polite grin. "I know, Uncle Marty."

"I decided last night this is a good place to learn about human nature. Your mom and aunt don't want you hanging around here. If they yank you out, I can't do anything about it. But I'm going to try to keep you here as long as I can. And you know why?"

"No," said Joey.

"I want you to see what happens to people when they drink, how they lose I.Q. points but at the same time loosen up and get friendly. Somewhere in there there's a balance. I wish I could calculate it, but I don't know how. I just know stress is bad, bad for the body and bad for the mind. A drink or two helps take it away, and people need that, they need to relax and have a good time. But too much of it's bad because you lose all perspective. I love seeing people having a good time. It's in my blood, I hope it's in yours too."

"I'll stay if you want," said Joey.

"Good. When we get back, you just hang around."

"Okay, Uncle Marty."

Marty took a set of keys from his pocket and handed them to Joey. "Think you can drive my car?"

"I drive Mom's," said Joey.

"It's out back. I already told the attendant to point it out to you. Give me five minutes, okay Joey?"

"Okay, Uncle Marty."

Joey left the office while Marty finished his paperwork. Minutes later, he pulled up to the Hillside Park branch of Bank of America in a mini-mall at the intersection of Hector Street and Sonoma Boulevard. Marty exited his Mercedes carrying a well-used, plain canvas bag containing his deposit and went inside to the merchants' window. Joey looked out the window of the expensive car and watched people going in and out of stores. He half-thought they would look at him, a young kid driving a six-figure car, but no one did. Maybe Mom should've gotten me one of those chauffeur's caps you see on TV, he thought. Marty returned a few minutes later and directed Joey to head east on Hector Street to Golding Circle. On the way, they passed Marty's. It was nothing to look at, just a plain, two-story brick building between a used-furniture shop and a pet store. Over plain double doors that did not open from the outside without a key, a neon sign said "Marty's," and on the right door a notice that said "Free Parking in Rear."

"Let me ask you something, Joey," said Marty. "You think I should do something about the front of my bar?"

Joey shrugged. "Like what?"

"I don't know," said Marty. "It's not like I'm hurting for business, but I wonder if dressing up the front would help out."

"Help out how?"

Marty thought it was a stupid question. "I don't know," he said with a disappointing tone.

Joey tried to divine what his uncle was thinking. But Marty was staring out the window without focusing on any one thing.

Soon Joey reached Golding Circle. Marty said to turn right. Joey turned onto the narrow, two-lane road with single-story houses and small businesses on each side of the street. He stopped when it intersected Vista Madera. After cross traffic passed, he continued. A half-mile in, the street's grade increased, and the Mercedes kicked into second gear. No other cars were on the road. The noise of Hector Street and Vista Madera vanished behind them. Soon only houses lined the streets. They were packed close together on narrow parcels.

"I always thought the top of this hill should have a lovers' lookout, a place for young kids to go on first dates, you know?" said Marty. "Instead of all these unsightly houses."

Marty waited for a response, but Joey said nothing. He was merely staring ahead. Great conversational skills, thought Marty. "Two more streets, then three houses in on the right," he said.

Joey drove at fifteen miles an hour to negotiate the winding road.

"There," said Marty. "Pull in the driveway."

Joey did as told. When he was in the driveway he turned off the motor.

"Joey, I have a girlfriend," said Marty. "She's a good woman, no matter what anyone else says."

Joey stared at Marty without comment. He was surprised at how shabby Rachel's house was. Why didn't Marty buy her one that reflected his own taste and wealth? The drab, box-like building was set back on a lot with no shrubbery or trees. Its walls were a dull beige, its trim a faded white. Two aluminum windows with fake shutters faced the street. The porch was a concrete slab from the door to the driveway. A rain-bird sprinkler weighted down with a cinderblock kept the lawn green in the center and brown at the corners. Unlike the other houses, Rachel's had no bars on its windows.

Marty opened his canvas bag and counted twenty one-hundred-dollar bills. He folded ten in half and put them in his pocket, then closed the bag and put it on the floor in front of him. "You know what you've got to do, right, Joey?"

"Keep my eyes open?"

"Right," said Marty. "That's all you've got to do."

"What if somebody comes?"

"Run. It's not worth your life."

Marty handed Joey the other hundred-dollar bills. "Give me these when I get back."

Joey took the bills. "This is a thousand dollars, Uncle Marty."

"Yep," said Marty. He got out of the car, closed the door, and looked back at Joey through the open window. "How's your mom, Joey? She seemed all right last night but I can't always tell with her."

Joey did not want to hurt Marty's feelings by reminding him of the low regard his mother held him in, so he shrugged.

"That's what I thought," said Marty. "She doesn't like what I do but she doesn't mind taking my money."

Joey, trying to mirror Marty's ironic tone, grinned. "Women," he said. "All the same, right Uncle Marty?"

Marty wanted to laugh at Joey's naiveté. "You're a good kid, Joey. Are you going to be okay here?"

"Yeah," said Joey. "I brought something to keep me busy."

Marty looked over the car's interior but saw nothing that would confirm this. He decided not to ask for an explanation, then walked to Rachel's front door.

Joey said to himself, "Go get 'em, Uncle Marty!"

Marty knocked on Rachel's front door. Rachel opened it. She wore a sexy robe. She greeted him with a kiss, then stepped aside for him to enter. Normally when she greeted Marty for Monday Nooners, she stayed out of view so that Cedar wouldn't see her in a robe. But today she was curious what Joey looked like. She'd fixed herself up with makeup and jewelry. Her loosely tied, knee-length robe showed off her shapely legs. She wore silk slippers. Joey liked her fluid moves.

"That's the kid, huh?" said Rachel.

"Yeah," said Marty. "Freda's kid."

Rachel locked the door behind them. The living room was like a cheap motel. It had a long, flat-cushion sofa that was old but not worn. A plain, wood coffee table was in front. The room had two matching barrel chairs. The walls were clean and bare. Three round tables—one for each chair, another next to the sofa—all had plants on them. They gave the room its only life. Each table had photos of Marty and Rachel on it. As they headed for the bedroom, Marty unbuckled his belt and Rachel loosened the tie on her robe. When they got there, Marty put the ten hundred-dollar bills on a dresser and grinned. "This is to keep you exclusive to me," he said.

"Nature's taking care of that," said Rachel. "Look at me. Sagging boobs, my ass looks like a grocery bag…"

"You look better than ever," said Marty.

They embraced, then continued to remove their clothes.

Joey rested his elbow on the window frame of the driver's side and casually looked around the car. He reached for the canvas money pouch and got big-eyed at the cash inside. He folded it closed and returned it to the floor, then took from his left pants pocket a fresh bulb of garlic. From his right front pocket he took a toothbrush tube that had a paring knife in it wrapped with a moistened paper towel. From his rear left pocket he took out a cutting board custom-cut to the size of a deck of cards.

He sniffed the garlic. "Mama *mia*," he said. He smacked his lips, then peeled the garlic with a sculptor's care and precision.

~ ~

Cammy left his apartment for his rendezvous with Cedar and Kenny. He was a wreck. He had cried intermittently throughout the night. It wasn't that he lacked resolve to do murder, it was that his life had reached the point where only a criminal act could revive it. At three o'clock that morning he had gotten out of bed, knelt, and prayed for strength to do the right thing by removing two evil people from the planet. He had to check himself, however, because he found himself praying to his mother instead of God.

"Not you, Mother," he'd said. "Besides, I'm mad at you. I wouldn't even be in this predicament if you didn't keep yelling at me so much. I'd have self-confidence and cleverness and whatever else successful people have. Anyway, I'm not talking to you. I'm talking to God." Then he continued his prayer.

When he went back to bed and still couldn't sleep, he got a wild idea. He took paper and pen to his kitchen table and wrote a letter to the *Los Angeles Times*. He outlined what Cedar told him about Marty and Rachel and the illegal weapons in the Kitchen. If the letter were made public, which could happen only if he died during the crime, his act would be vindicated, even if it meant that the police would call it an execution rather than a murder-suicide. If he did not die and the act was successful, he could still send the letter later, only he would sign it "a concerned citizen" to preserve his anonymity. But for the time being, the mere act of writing the letter would help to lessen his anxiety.

He placed the sealed letter on top of his dresser and wrote on the envelope "in the event of my death." When he returned to bed, he went to sleep. He woke up at the usual time, drove to his bar, and asked Leon O'Connor to take over. Leon, as always, was happy to. They were friends.

Leon used to be a regular at Kenny's and a semi-regular at Cammy's. Years earlier, Leon went to Cammy's one day looking for sympathetic company after he'd had a nasty fight with his wife. His daughter, who was living in Minnesota, had left her husband and needed to move in with Leon and his wife, which was fine with them. But they were shocked that she had gained fifty pounds and had let her once-fashionable hair turn gray and ragged, this for a forty-one-year-old woman who used to be thin and attractive. Though Leon got used to his daughter's bloated figure and Pete Rose hair, his wife was not so accepting. She chided her daughter for letting herself go and attacked Leon for not supporting her against their daughter. Listening patiently to a morose and confused Leon, Cammy had used soft-voiced diplomacy to express his view that found valid arguments in Leon's position *and* his wife's. Leon felt better because he was allowed to pour out his feelings without being criticized the way his wife had criticized him—with an acid tongue that called into question his intellect, character, and manhood.

But when Leon had *another* fight with his wife over the *same* issue the *next* day, instead of going to Cammy's again for fear of being overbearing, he went to Kenny's for sympathy. He'd barely finished telling Kenny what the problem was when Kenny butted in. "Fifty *pounds?*" he said. "Gray *hair?* She's probably a *dyke!* Kick her fat ass out the door!"

Whereupon Leon told Kenny to go to hell, and Kenny yelled, "*You* go to hell. You're an asshole, just like everybody else from Massachusetts."

Since then, Leon O'Connor had become Cammy's best customer.

Cammy told Leon he'd be back around one o'clock, then he looked over his bar as if he were saying goodbye to an old friend. Even though it was going bust, Cammy loved his bar. It was his home. He'd made countless friends there. Some had moved away, some stopped coming in because they quit drinking, still others died of old age. But they all liked Cammy and his bar. Each time he heard an entering customer say, "Hey, Cammy, how's it going?" he felt he added something to that customer's life, even if only a minor diversion from the drudgery of the day.

He returned home for a little sleep but didn't get much. He went to the storage bin in his garage, found a second set of rubber gloves, and laid them out on the kitchen table with the pair he used for washing dishes, next to the gun he'd gotten from Dom the previous night. After placing the gloves and gun on his kitchen table, Cammy shaved and showered and ate buttered English muffins, two soft-boiled eggs, and three gingersnaps for dessert. When he was ready to leave, he put the gloves and gun in a paper bag, then looked over his apartment the same way he'd looked over his bar. He had a more personal reaction this time. Its furnishings had come from his childhood home, what was left after he and his brother sold off their mother's furniture when she died. It wasn't much—tables, bookcases, a dresser, lamps and pictures—but for fifty-one years it was part of his life and the last connection to his mother.

He stood in the doorway and wondered if he should prepare for never returning, short of the letter to the newspaper he'd written last night. Then he went to the kitchen to make sure no food was left out and that he had dumped the wastebasket. Yes, it was as clean as a surgical suite. He closed the door, went to his car and drove to Vista Madera and Arrow.

~ ~

Cammy and Kenny met outside their cars on Arrow Avenue, a narrow side street that connected Hector Street with Vista Madera. Cammy was still locking his car door when he said, without looking up, "I need you to do something before we do this."

Kenny blew out a sigh of irritation. "What *now?*"

"I need you to ask me a question. I heard something once, it helped me out a lot. It's a tale, sort of a parable. Guess who told me?"

Kenny had no patience. "Christ, Cammy, I don't know."

"Earl, when he was still working," said Cammy.

Kenny scoffed. "Great. Barfs all over and *you* get wisdom from him."

"I said when he was still working," said Cammy.

"He's *always* been a drunk," said Kenny. "Just say it, will you?"

"Okay," said Cammy.

He and Kenny moved to the sidewalk. Cammy stopped and faced Kenny. Kenny wouldn't look at Cammy when he told his tale, but he listened. "These two cowboys, Jim and Bob, they're being chased by bloodthirsty Indians across the plains of the Dakotas and the Indians are closing in and it looks really bad. So Jim looks over and yells, 'Hey, Bob. We gonna make it?' And Bob says, '*We got to.*' See Kenny, he didn't say, 'Well I *hope* so,' or 'I *think* so,' or 'maybe if we try really hard, we will.' It was nothing like that. No, Bob says, 'We got to.' That's it. That's all he said. You get it, Kenny? You get the point?"

Kenny grimaced. "I don't know what the hell you're talking about."

"No see, it's all attitude," said Cammy. "The way Bob answered, there was no escape valve, no options, no way to make it without just plain, 'We got to.' That's a great answer, Kenny. Don't you think it inspired Jim?"

The sidewalk was lined with trees close to the curb and hedges on the other side. Kenny had to step around an Hispanic boy on his knees, in shorts with no shirt or shoes on, who was trying to align the chain on his bicycle with the teeth on its sprocket. "So what do you want from me?" he said.

"Well, can you just be Jim?"

"Just be Jim."

"Yes, just ask me if this is going to work out, just ask me if what we're doing here is going to work out."

Kenny was exasperated. "Cammy, is this going to work out?"

"It's got to," said Cammy. He looked for a reaction in Kenny. When he didn't get one, he said, "Well?"

They had reached the corner. Cammy would not cross the street without getting a satisfactory response from Kenny. "Well?" he said emphatically.

"You know how dumb you are?" said Kenny. "'*We* got to.' '*We*,' Cammy, '*we*.' *That's* what the guy said. '*We* got to.' Not, '*it's* got to.' '*It*' is not even a person. Your whole point was just lost. '*It*' can't be inspired. You just lost your whole point, you know that?"

Cammy was embarrassed. He saw a darkly prophetic meaning in his failed attempt to motivate Kenny and himself.

Before Cammy knew it, Kenny was already across the street. Cammy waited until a bus passed, then joined him at the meat market.

~ ~

Cedar had been watching the clock for an hour. After his workout, he started a long-delayed project that he knew would take most of the afternoon. It involved bolting bookcases to the building-long wall shared by him and tenants on the other side of his duplex, a quiet young Persian family. The father worked at a produce company and the mother stayed home with her children. Cedar had lined the wall with high bookcases and filled them with hardcover books, mostly history and biographies, so that the density would act as insulation against noise from the neighbors. But he never bolted the bookcases to the wall for earthquake-safety.

The day Joey Bagliamente replaced him as Marty's driver turned out to be a good day to begin the project. One, he now had time and, two, hammering starter nails and drilling into wall studs would make continuous noise for the neighbors. Thus, he could account for his whereabouts during the killings if

Helen continued the drilling and hammering while he shuttled Kenny and Cammy to and from the execution site.

It took over an hour to unload the books and pull the bookcases from the walls to locate the studs. Helen swept and cleaned behind them as Cedar packed books. He had timed the project so that he could begin hammering and drilling the same time he knew Marty, a creature of habit, left with Joey to go to the bank and then onto Rachel's for their tryst.

Cedar showed Helen how to drill. At seventeen minutes after twelve, he told her he was going to Nick's Hardware for more materials and that she should continue the work in his absence. She was happy to. He drove to the meat market where Cammy and Kenny were waiting.

~ ~

Marty and Rachel made love, the same as always, with a little kissing, a little teasing, and then Marty climbing on top and thrusting for as long as he could hold out, until Rachel started her assent to orgasm, at which point he pumped faster. Today she put turbo energy into satisfying Marty to take his mind off of the anniversary of his son's death. The closer he got to climaxing, the more she encouraged him to ride her like a rodeo star.

"Oh, Marty," she moaned. "Oh, Marty, my God, Marty," and so forth.

~ ~

Joey, still in Marty's Mercedes, was slicing garlic cloves on his cutting board while whistling "Questo O Quelia" from *Rigoletto*. He'd developed a love of opera from his Aunt Gloria, who always put operas on for family gatherings at the Bagliamente house in Glendale. The garlic slices were so thin that they were almost transparent. Joey sniffed the aroma bursting from them and exhaled with a heavenly expression on his face.

~ ~

Cedar pulled his Jeep Cherokee up to the meat market parking lot, where Cammy and Kenny were waiting. Kenny got in the passenger seat; Cammy took the rear. Cedar turned back onto Vista Madera, headed into the hills for Rachel's house and started talking. "Let me see the gun," he said.

Cammy opened the bag, and Cedar saw that the gun was a thirty-eight with a two-inch barrel and that it was loaded.

"Kenny," said Cedar. "You go through the unlocked window in the guest bedroom. It's the one with the shades up. Close it behind you quietly. Guns are loud."

"I'm doing the shooting?" said Kenny.

"Yes," said Cedar. "Cammy, stand outside the window. As soon as you hear the gun go off a second time, open it. It will save Kenny time when he comes back. Kenny, shoot Marty once in his chest. Get close. Rachel's left-handed, so shoot her in the left side of her head, just above her temple, then put the gun in her left hand, then reach between the mattresses and take her own gun out and bring it with you. It's loaded, so watch it."

"How do you know it's there?" asked Kenny.

"I bought it for her. Don't ask questions. I'll tell you what you need to know."

"Excuse *me*," said Kenny.

"They're making love now," said Cedar. "They stay in bed thirty minutes and talk. But don't let that fool you. Do this quick and get out of there. I'm going to drive around and be back where I left you off. This whole operation must not take more than ninety seconds. Have you got that? Ninety seconds. Get in, do it, get out."

"Yeah," said Kenny.

"Yes," said Cammy.

Cedar was two streets from Golding Circle and facing a red light. He looked at Kenny and said, "Don't be cute."

"What's that supposed to mean?" said Kenny.

"Don't watch," said Cedar.

"Oh, now you think I'm a pervert?" said Kenny.

"Put the gloves on now," said Cedar. "Both of you."

Cammy took the gloves out of the bag, handed one pair to Kenny, and put the other on himself. As Kenny donned the gloves, he said, "Thinks I'm a pervert."

"Shut up and listen, Kenny," said Cedar. "Rachel will get out of bed after they're finished to fix up her hair and makeup and put her jewelry back on before she gets back in bed with him. You shoot—"

"How do you know all that?" asked Kenny.

The interruptions made Cedar bite his lip. Nonetheless, he answered calmly. "I've known Marty a long time. Things come out after a while."

"Just curious," said Kenny.

"Shoot them before she gets back in bed," said Cedar. "Don't make it look like she shot him *in* bed. According to our scenario, she'd get out of bed, get her gun, shoot him and then turn it on herself. In fact, she'd shoot him twice, such would be the ferocity of her anger and frustration. So shoot him twice. We want the police thinking this is a crime of passion between a married man and his mistress. Cammy, don't do anything until you hear *three* shots, not two."

"Three, okay," said Cammy.

"Now repeat what you two are going to do."

Kenny spoke first. "We go to the window without the shade, we open it, I go in…hey, wait…where's their bedroom?"

"Left of the one you'll be in," said Cedar. "Don't be too cautious. Walk right in with your gun pointed, step forward and shoot him twice in his chest. One or two seconds will pass before Rachel comprehends what's happened, whereas you'll have the advantage because you know what's next. The *left* side of her head. Keep the gun perpendicular to her head."

"I got it," said Kenny.

"If she's looking at you, what side is her left?" asked Cedar.

"Same as my right," said Kenny.

"Correct," said Cedar. "Then what?"

"I put the gun in her left hand, I take the one out of her mattresses and go back to the window in the other room."

"Between her mattresses," said Cedar.

"Right, between 'em," said Kenny.

"And the window he goes back to is the one I will have opened for him," said Cammy.

"Correct," said Cedar. "Go back the way you came, through her back yard and out to the street where I'll be waiting. Speed and precision."

"What if something goes wrong?" said Cammy.

"You've got one chance to get it right," said Cedar. "Get it right."

Cedar reached Golding Circle, turned right and headed to Rachel's.

"How do we get Marty's money?" said Kenny.

"You're not going to get that money," said Cedar.

"Oh great," said Kenny.

Cedar grabbed Kenny by his collar. "You want to spew sarcasm or you want to listen?" he said.

"Get your hands off me and I'll listen," said Kenny.

"Whoa boy," said Cammy.

Cedar let go. He was at the point on Golding Circle where the grade increased. "If this works," he said, "you'll have Marty's customers for the taking. That ought to be enough if you change the way you run your bars."

"The deal was we get that cash," said Kenny.

"Do we really need it, Kenny?" asked Cammy. "Listen to what he's saying. We don't really need it."

Kenny ignored Cammy. "What if that nephew of his hears the shots? What if he panics? Say he runs off or something. That'd leave the money in Marty's car for us to take, right?"

Cedar briefly stopped at a three-way stop sign, then continued on. He raised his voice. "If you take the money, the police will investigate a robbery-homicide instead of a murder-suicide. You want that played out?"

"I want the cash we were supposed to get," said Kenny. "You knew about it when you came on board, man."

"You can't always get what you want," said Cedar.

"This is a great time for fairy tales," said Kenny.

Cedar turned left off of Golding Circle for another winding road that ran almost parallel to it.

"Man, this pisses me off," said Kenny. "You're a back-stabbing asshole, you know that, Cedar?"

Cammy raised his voice. "Kenny, there's no time to fight over it."

Cedar stopped in front of a small house on the passenger side of his Cherokee. He pointed between the house and the one next to it. "Go through there," he said. "When you come back, the last one out must pull up those slats and push the nails back in so they'll stay up. I'll be back in ninety seconds. Ninety seconds. Now get out and 'let slip the dogs of war.'"

Cammy lifted the gun over the front-seat headrest and held it out for Kenny. Kenny took it, sneered at Cedar, then opened the door and stepped out of the car. Cammy was already out. As Cedar pulled away, he was confident he hadn't been seen by nearby residents. No cars drove by and no pedestrians were out.

~ ~

Marty and Rachel finished making love. Marty rolled on his back and sighed from exhaustion. "That was great," he said through heavy breathing.

"Me too," said Rachel. She kissed his cheek, affectionately held his hand a moment, then got out of bed, put her robe on, and sat on a wrought-iron chair at a dark-wood antique vanity desk. With her back to Marty, she faced three oval mirrors configured to show multiple angles of her face. They were connected with hinge-brackets that held fluorescent tubes for maximum lighting. "How was the family last night?" she said, combing her hair back into place.

"Same," said Marty, slowly catching his breath. "Gloria got Joey a nice suit for his birthday, dark blue. He liked it."

"How was she?" asked Rachel, reaching for her earrings.

"Cranky," said Marty. "Hates using a cane."

The bedroom was cozily decorated. On a Victorian mahogany chest of drawers with clear-glass knobs, Rachel kept hand-painted ceramic houses, the kind you see on Christmas cards meant to evoke quaint New England villages carpeted with snow. The walls and ceiling were light tan, the floor-trim and wall-trim burgundy. A two-tone mauve, hand-woven rug covered most of the hardwood floor. Thick white curtains had splotches of burgundy and gray scattered throughout its pattern. Framed pictures of Marty and Rachel were on the walls. Each side of the bed had its own chest table and antique lamp. The one closest to the window had a telephone and answering machine on it. A carved-maple hope chest sat under the window.

The wall opposite the window had plain-wood shelves that held a stereo system, books, and bouquets of dried flowers bursting from eclectic vases. On a shelf next to her senior yearbook picture was a hand-painted porcelain incense-burner Rachel got when she and a bunch of kids from high school drove down to Ports O' Call one day to buy marijuana paraphernalia. Though she'd given up pot when she quit drinking, she still lit incense, especially when Marty visited during slow nights at his bar. Between the shelves and her desk was a French ladder-back armchair with a cushion seat. Marty had draped his clothes and underwear across the back of it and put his shoes and socks beside it.

"Sometimes those things take a long time to heal," said Rachel.

"Especially when you're older," said Marty.

"Will you stop with that 'older' business?" said Rachel good-naturedly while glancing at Marty at the reflection of the center mirror. "Look at you. You've got your health, lots of money, a million friends…"

"I suppose," said Marty while wiping his brow.

Rachel took a tissue and leaned into the mirrors to remove lipstick that had smeared when she kissed Marty, then applied a fresh coat.

~ ~

Kenny and Cammy walked between the two houses Cedar had pointed out. Without slowing or breaking stride, Kenny grabbed Cammy roughly by the shoulder. "Change of plans," he said. "You're doing the whacking."

Cammy glared at Kenny. "*You* are," he said in a whisper.

"No way," said Kenny. "The deal's off 'cause of what just happened. We're doing things *my* way now."

"Kenny—"

"We're reversing roles, nothing else is different. You heard what to do. Take this and do it." Kenny handed the gun to Cammy. "Take it, I said!"

Cammy would not take the gun.

"Then the whole thing's off, 'cause I can turn right around and walk back to my car and not give a shit *what* the rest of you do."

"You're not backing out because of Cedar," said Cammy. "You're just a coward."

"Think what you want," said Kenny.

They had stopped walking. An old basset hound with gray around its mouth barked at the two men. Cammy could see Rachel's house over the backyard fence in front of them. He looked back at the street to see that Cedar had pulled away, then looked back at Kenny again. "If he finds out we didn't do this, you know what he'll do?"

"What, kill us?" said Kenny. "Why would he do that? Let's just call the whole thing off. Without that money what's the point anyway?"

Cammy angrily took the gun from Kenny and walked to the fence separating the two properties. He pushed two long wood slats nailed to support beams. Both fell. He went through the opening. Kenny followed.

They saw two bedroom windows at the rear of Rachel's house, saw that one had closed curtains behind it and the other didn't. They moved to the latter and saw that the latch was not secured and that the screen was open.

Kenny whispered, "Hurry up."

Cammy raised the window and clumsily crawled through. Kenny quietly pushed the window closed.

~ ~

Rachel, puckering her lips to spread the lipstick evenly, thought she heard a sound from the other bedroom. But she dismissed it and continued putting on makeup.

~ ~

Kenny turned away from the window and looked out at Rachel's back yard to make sure he and Cammy weren't seen going through the fence. Cammy got his bearings in the bedroom. He was shaking as if standing in an arctic blizzard. The room was empty save for a queen-size bed, neatly made, and a table next to it. Nothing covered the hardwood floor or the walls. An open closet door revealed nothing but a few hangers inside. His first thought was that the empty room confirmed what Cedar had said about Rachel, that she was a phony, that her house itself was probably a front for nefarious activities. Who lives in a small house and keeps one of the bedrooms empty? he asked himself. She doesn't even use it for storage? Was the house a secret meeting place for the slimy people she and Marty consorted with?

Cammy shook himself from these concerns and moved cautiously to the hallway in front of him. With the gun at his side, he listened for sounds from the next bedroom.

~ ~

Rachel, still at her desk, was using another tissue, this one dipped in cold cream, to remove smudged mascara. She leaned close to the center mirror.

"When you think about it, Marty, Gloria's a saint, the way she puts up with us." She dipped another part of the tissue in more cold cream and tended to the other side of her face. "Maybe some day I could meet her. Wouldn't that be a riot, Marty? After all these years, Gloria and I meet? What would I say, I wonder." She moved closer to see if she'd gotten all the mascara off. "Wouldn't that be a riot? For the life of me, I wouldn't know what to say. 'Hello' works, I suppose." Expecting an answer from Marty, she raised her eyes to see his reflection in the center mirror. "She'd probably tell me to go to hell," said Rachel. "Who would blame her?"

A smidgen of mascara remained in the inside corner of Rachel's left eye. She moved in closer to wipe it away. "You have nothing to say, Marty?" She turned and looked at him for three long seconds. "Marty?" she said.

~ ~

Joey, still whistling an Italian aria, took an empty baby food jar from his right pants pocket and unscrewed the lid. He gently placed the slices of garlic inside, one at a time, with the care you'd use when unwrapping a razor blade while jogging.

~ ~

Cammy was inches from Rachel's bedroom. He kept his back flat against the wall next to the doorway, took a deep breath, and prepared to whirl into the bedroom with the gun aimed at Marty.

"Marty!" said Rachel.

Marty's eyes were closed and he lay motionless. Rachel jumped from her desk and felt his wrist. "No, Marty," she said. "No, *no.*"

She picked up the receiver on the bedside table and punched nine-one-one. "Don't let him die, *please* don't let him die," she said.

Cammy heard all this. His eyes jumped like a wild man's. Was this a joke? Did those guys pull a fast one? He heard Rachel scream.

"Come quick, 9225 Golding Circle in Hillside Park," she said. "A man's not breathing, he's not moving, he's got no pulse. You've got to hurry!"

~ FIFTEEN ~

Cedar had circled two short blocks twice and returned to where he had dropped off Kenny and Cammy sixty-eight seconds earlier. He stopped in the middle of the street with his motor idling. Between the two houses he saw that Cammy and Kenny had removed the designated fence slats. In eighteen seconds, according to his math, they would return to his car.

Kenny, standing guard, grimaced in anticipation of loud, frightening gunshots. He counted to himself.

Cammy put the gun under his belt, then retreated to the other bedroom, where he saw Kenny's back through the window.

At the same time, Rachel ran through her living room to the front door.

Joey had just secured the lid on the jar of garlic slices. He intended to use them later for dinner. He liked to drop sliced garlic into hot olive oil, add crushed red pepper, salt, dried basil and oregano, tomatoes, red wine, let it cook for thirty minutes, then pour it over steaming pasta. There was nothing like it in the world.

Still whistling, he returned his paring knife to its container, pocketed it and the cutting board, rested his left arm on the open window and waited for Marty to return. He no sooner put his head back than he saw the front door to the house burst open and a distraught Rachel emerge with a horrified look on her face.

Joey sat up straight like a shot. Rachel ran to the Mercedes and shouted through the driver's side window. "Marty's not breathing," she said. "Come help me."

Something happened to Joey that had never happened to him: the world stopped, like a wide-screen movie jammed on a single frame. Looming right before him like a venerated monument was a sight he'd never seen in the flesh. Rachel's robe had opened down to its terrycloth belt to reveal not six inches from his big, frozen eyes her full naked breasts. Joey was agog at the sight. He had not heard what she'd said about Marty.

Cammy, who thought Rachel was still in the house, opened the window in the other bedroom. Kenny looked at him with gripping puzzlement. "What're you *doing*?" he said.

Cammy lifted one leg through the window. "Marty's dead," he whispered.

"What do you mean he's dead?" said Kenny. "I didn't hear anything."

Cammy struggled to get through the window. "No, he had a heart attack. Let's get out of here."

"What do you mean he's dead?" said Kenny. He stood before Cammy to block his exit from the window. "He's not dead. He's sleeping or something. Get back in there."

"Let *go*!" said Cammy. "I heard her call an ambulance. *Move*, Kenny."

"You're just chickening out."

"I know what I heard," said Cammy. "Now let's go. We got what we wanted."

"I'm not going anywhere," said Kenny. "I want that money."

Kenny pushed Cammy back until their locked arms. Contorted halfway in and out of the window like a pretzel, Cammy grunted for strength to pull an arm free and push down on Kenny's shoulder. "She's going to hear us!" he said.

Kenny let go and fell backward on the ground. Cammy climbed out of the window. "Look for yourself if you don't believe me," he said. "I'm leaving."

Kenny grabbed Cammy. "Not till we find out what happened."

Sixty-four seconds had passed since Cedar returned. He risked drawing attention if he stayed in the middle of the street much longer.

When Rachel saw that Joey was paralyzed by what she thought was her shocking announcement, she slapped him on his cheek. "Did you hear me?" she said. "Snap out of it. I need you. Come on!"

She ran back into her house. Joey collected himself and followed her. He found her standing in the living room with her face in her hands and nodding toward her bedroom.

"Hurry!" she screamed. "Tell me it's not true. *Tell me he's not dead!*"

Joey, white-faced, moved cautiously in the direction Rachel nodded.

Cammy and Kenny heard Rachel through the open window.

"They're both in the house," whispered Kenny. "That means the money's out there unguarded. Let's get it."

"No," whispered Cammy. "Cedar's waiting."

"No, this is *perfect*," said Kenny. "We get the money without *killing* anybody."

Kenny had no time for Cammy's indecision. He ran low to the ground behind Rachel's windows and on to the driveway. Cammy didn't know what to do. He feared angering Cedar but worried that Kenny might screw up. He ran to the opening in the backyard fence.

Cedar had counted three-plus minutes of waiting. They could have killed Marty and Rachel *and* still had time left over to cook an egg, he thought. He slammed his steering wheel. "Incompetents," he said. He sped away without breaking traction.

Joey stood in the entrance to Rachel's bedroom and stared at his uncle. He saw Marty's peaceful eyes, open mouth, head tilted to the side. An irony hit Joey. For the first time in his life and within seconds of each other, he'd been in the presence of a beautiful woman's magnificent naked breasts and in the presence of a human corpse. But not just any corpse: Uncle Marty was the closest thing he'd had to a father.

Cammy ran to the street behind Rachel's. He looked up and down the street, but saw no Cherokee.

Rachel bolted into her bedroom. Seeing Joey standing still, she shoved him aside and shouted, with her voice cracking, "Do something or get out of the way."

She moved to her closet and turned on a light inside. Joey did not resist the shove. He felt deadened anyway. Memories came in flickers. All the colorful stories of Grandpa Frank and Great Grandpa Augusto were from Uncle Marty. At family dinners, he especially admired how skillfully Uncle Marty deflected with gentle humor his mother's endless carping about how unfairly life had treated her. He knew beneath his uncle's easy-going exterior was a desire to stab Freda with his fork between salad bites for her constant complaining, yet there was also the self-restraint to maintain relations with her. By observing how his uncle coped with the implacable Freda, Joey learned a valuable lesson: you can be cool or you can be a jerk. To him, that was life's big lesson, courtesy of Uncle Marty.

Rachel removed a skirt and blouse from hangers in her closet and draped them over one arm, then reached to the floor for a pair of shoes. "Get his clothes, will you?" she said. "Marty was a proud man. You want him going out buck naked in front of some dopey paramedics thinking he's just another stiff?" She stepped away from her closet and saw that Joey had not moved. "*Do* something!" she said.

Joey hadn't heard her. Instead, he stared with a distant look in his eyes and spoke with sadness. "All my life Uncle Marty's had that club."

"Well he doesn't anymore," said Rachel. "Now hurry, nine-one-one's on the way."

She took bra and panties from the top drawer of her chest of drawers and draped them over the blouse and skirt already on her arm.

Cammy had returned from the street to find Kenny returning to Rachel's back yard with Marty's money pouch. He grabbed Cammy's shirtsleeve.

"It's all *here*," whispered Cammy.

"Cedar's not there," said Cammy.

"He'll be there," said Kenny. "He's got to wait for us."

"No, he's gone," said Cammy. "We took too long."

"We'll just *wait* for him," said Kenny.

Cammy pushed Kenny's hand away. "We can't wait," he said. "The ambulance will be here with a siren on, then the neighbors are going to come out and see us. They're going to *see* us, Kenny! The cops'll ask around—they always do. The neighbors'll see us!"

"Then we'll *drive* out of here. The keys are in the ignition."

"Marty's car?" said Cammy. "Then they'll *know* we were here."

"Here doing *what*, Cammy? Trying to kill a man's already dead? We'll *ditch* the car. C'mon!"

Kenny ran to Marty's car and jumped into the driver's seat. Half a step behind, Cammy took the passenger seat.

When Rachel saw that Joey was still paralyzed, she shook him with both hands. "Get with it, kid!"

Joey finally collected himself. "What can I do?"

"Help me dress him," said Rachel. "His wife doesn't need to know how he died. Get his clothes over there."

Rachel stiffened at hearing a noise outside.

"No," she said aloud but to herself.

Joey heard her exclamation. He watched her reaction to the noise. Her eyes reflected the dawning realization of insult added to tragedy, as if her expression said: "It can't be happening but it is."

Her eyes darted to the other bedroom. Then she registered the sound she'd heard just after she and Marty finished making love. The sound now had meaning. Putting these elements together, Rachel ran into her living room. Joey followed. She opened her front door and saw the Mercedes racing out of the driveway. "Damn!" she shouted.

"What."

"I told him this would happen," Rachel said in a tone of sad, unwished-for vindication.

"Told him what would happen?" said Joey.

Not yet knowing what Rachel was looking at, Joey peered around her and saw the Mercedes burning rubber out of the driveway. "They're stealing Uncle Marty's car!" he said.

"Those *bastards*!" said Rachel.

Cammy, breathing heavily, covered his ears at the sound of the burning tires. "We're supposed to be inconspicuous!" he shouted at Kenny.

Kenny was too exhilarated to be admonished. "Screws him to death!" he said. "Can you believe it, Cammy? *I* can't. She *screws* him to death! Cammy, we got everything we wanted. No downside! This is like a goddamn miracle. I've *never* been lucky. *This* is lucky."

Kenny was speeding down the winding road. Cammy braced himself with one hand on the armrest and the other gripping his seatbelt's shoulder strap. "You're going too fast," he said.

"Talk about Easy Street," said Kenny. "Hey Judy, *up yours*, bitch! You could've had a piece of this!"

"You're going to get us killed," said Cammy.

Kenny hit the brakes to avoid a car backing out of a driveway, swerved to miss it, then slammed on the accelerator again. The torque snapped Cammy's head back.

Kenny's tone was like a child's glee. "Jeez, this thing's got power."

"Well just don't crash," said Cammy.

~ ~

Joey was still standing in the doorway of the house when Rachel brushed by him on her way back to her bedroom. Why didn't I take the keys out? he asked himself. My first day and I lose his money *and* his car.

Rachel returned carrying her purse, keys, shoes, bra and panties, and from her clenched teeth hung her blouse and skirt. "You-drive-I've-got-to-change," she said, nodding for Joey to follow her outside and around her house.

"Where are we going?" he asked.

"We're getting that money back," said Rachel. She tossed her keys to Joey and ran to an old Corolla at the end of her driveway. The car needed body work and tires. Joey ran alongside her until they reached the car. She moved to the passenger side, Joey to the driver's.

"What about Uncle Marty?" he said.

Rachel didn't like stupid questions, and her facial expression conveyed that. She juggled her clothes to free a hand and opened her door. Joey unlocked the driver's side door, got in, reached over and unlocked the passenger door. Rachel sat in the front passenger seat and arranged the clothes in her lap to put them on in the right order.

"I warned him about carrying all that money around," she said.

Joey put the car in reverse. Rachel lowered her face into her hands. Through sobs and sniffles, she cried, "My dear baby, my dear, dear baby." Tears ran through her trembling fingers and onto her robe. "What am I going to do?" she said to no one. "You're so innocent, you're so innocent."

Joey wanted to comfort her, but he felt like a stranger. Instead, he concentrated on backing out of the long driveway. He looked over his shoulder and pressed the accelerator gently. The car began to roll out.

Rachel raised her head and wiped her cheeks: "The idea's to *catch* them."

Her tone startled Joey. "I know," he said.

"Then step on it!" she said.

Joey pushed down harder on the accelerator.

~ ~

Kenny was stopped at a red light on Vista Madera. An Hispanic woman was pushing a baby carriage across the intersection and making sure her other two children stayed apace with her. Two teenage boys rode bikes on the crosswalk on the other side of the intersection.

"Stop bugging me, Cammy," Kenny said. "It was a clean getaway."

"I'm talking about the ninety seconds he worked out for us," said Cammy. "He had it all worked out and we blew it."

"Blew *what?*" Kenny held up the money pouch. "Is *this* blowing it?"

"We've still got to face Cedar," said Cammy.

"Hey, screw him."

"Kenny, we had a plan."

"What'd Cedar ever do for me?"

"That doesn't matter. We had a plan. We have to stick to it."

"*Screw* him and *you too* if you can't see the beauty here. Cedar can shit beer-bottles for all I care. It's *over*. We *won*. We got all the marbles. Cedar's got nothing and on top of that he's out of a job."

"We stole a car. That's against the law," said Cammy.

"Only if we get caught."

"So get rid of it."

"I know what I'm doing," said Kenny, tapping the steering wheel before the light changed to green. Cammy couldn't stop squirming.

~ ~

Joey was driving down Golding Circle faster than he wanted to, but Rachel kept prodding him to hurry. When he slowed for a stop sign at the three-way intersection, she yelled, "*Just go through it.*"

He did as ordered. "I ran a stop sign!" he said. His frightened eyes were locked on the rear-view mirror.

Rachel slid down in her seat so as not to be seen through the windows as she put her panties on under her robe, then her skirt. "Christ," she said. "He's a Boy Scout."

"No I'm not," said Joey. He awkwardly negotiated a blind curve in the road. "But Uncle Marty told me the money's not worth my life."

"Well it *is*," said Rachel.

Golding Circle straightened out, widened into four lanes, and headed south to Vista Madera a mile-and-a-half ahead. Joey saw that the

Mercedes had pulled through the green light and was seconds away from Hector Street.

"Catch them," said Rachel.

"If I go any faster—" Joey cut himself off. He had turned to Rachel to protest her backseat driving when he saw that she had pulled her arms from her robe, leaned forward to let it fall behind her, and was wiggling free from it. She had nothing on from the waist up. Joey gulped and gasped at seeing more female flesh in person than he'd ever seen.

"Watch out!" screamed Rachel, pointing as she donned her bra.

Joey had drifted into opposing traffic and was headed for a collision with a bread truck. He froze. Rachel jerked the steering wheel half-a-turn until her car re-entered its own lane. The bread truck driver hit his horn.

"Thieving sons of bitches," said Rachel.

Joey was completely disoriented after seeing Rachel's breasts. *She got naked right in front of me*, he said to himself. He wondered why he was so lucky to have this gift thrust upon him. The first time, she probably didn't know her robe was open. But now, sitting right next to me, she drops her robe without a care in the world! Maybe the rumors were true, he reasoned, that she was just a cheap prostitute back then, that she screwed every guy in Hillside Park, and Uncle Marty was so messed up from his kid dying that he fell in love with her regardless of her reputation. No, it can't be. Uncle Marty's not like—*wasn't* like that. But why else would this totally beautiful babe let me see her tits sitting right next to her? *Oh man!*

"Who?" said Joey, vaguely hearing the last thing Rachel said.

She had fastened her bra, put her blouse on, and sat up in her seat. "Them," she said pointing to Kenny and Cammy.

"You know them?" he asked.

"Never mind," said Rachel. "It's nothing you need to know about."

"Hey, I'm family," said Joey. "It's my mom's fault I didn't spend more time with Uncle Marty."

"Make excuses," said Rachel. "Let me tell you something, kid. Excuses are like assholes. Everybody's got one and they all stink."

"I'm just saying my mom didn't want me around all the liquor and cigarette smoke and drunks."

"You tell your tight-ass mother Marty ran a respectable business. He gave his customers a good drink at a fair price and he made sure they always had a good time."

"I didn't say it's wrong or anything," said Joey.

Rachel finished buttoning her blouse, then reached down to fetch her shoes from the floor. "Then the one day his bodyguard's not with him, two vultures rip him off," she said. "They couldn't carry Marty's underwear."

"So you *do* know them," said Joey.

"They've been jealous of Marty for years."

Joey raced to make the green light. He was doing fifty-two in a twenty-five mile zone. "Who's 'they?'" he said with his eyes aimed forward.

"Couple of bar owners," said Rachel.

"Kenny's and The Knothole you mean?" asked Joey.

Rachel was trying not to cry again. Joey could tell that if she tried to speak, her voice would crack. He knew about holding in emotions. Being raised by a mother who got distraught over every little thing had taught him that if he remained silent at such times, Freda would go into blue moods that lasted for days. If he forced her to talk, her blue moods were sometimes very brief or averted altogether.

Joey used this on Rachel. "They'd rip off Uncle Marty?" he asked.

"Kenny would steal from the homeless."

Joey felt privately triumphant. Maybe they *are* all the same, he thought. The light at Vista Madera turned red. A car in front of Joey and another in the next lane slowed to stop, so he went around the slower one and through the light. As he looked out for cops, he faced Hector Street. All its lanes were clogged with cars going through the intersection.

"Don't slow down," said Rachel. She pointed left. "I think I know where they're going."

Joey winced as if preparing to crash, then, with a pounding heart, turned sharply from Golding onto Hector Street. The Corolla pulled in front of an on-coming car, which it missed by a split-second, then tail-spun until Joey steadied it in the center-left, eastbound lane. Seeing the Mercedes two lights ahead, he sped up and maneuvered between slower cars in both lanes. "What if we catch them?" he asked.

Rachel didn't answer. Joey saw that she'd taken a gun from her purse. It was the one Cedar had bought for her at Marty's request.

"What's that for?" said Joey. It was another first for him, a gun up close that didn't belong to a cop or security guard.

"If you think I'm letting two worms take your uncle's money when he can't get it back himself, then you're not a Bagliamente. Now catch those bastards or get out and I will."

"No, I will," said Joey. He honked for cars to get out of his way.

~ ~

Kenny was halfway through Hillside Park. He had hit every red light on Hector Street, which agitated Cammy further. "Ditch this car, will you!"

"After we stop at Dom's," said Kenny.

"We *can't*. They'll see the car. They'll know who it belongs to."

"Too bad," said Kenny. "Dom's keeping the money in case we get stopped. I'm not getting stopped with a hundred grand on me. I'll give it to Dom then ditch this thing in Compton. That's where they all end up anyway."

"No, we'll never get back in time," said Cammy. "Ditch it on one of these side streets. Besides, we'll get killed in Compton."

"Look who's talking, you with your bleeding heart over them spodas. You know what nobody ever taught you, Cammy?—quit while you're ahead." Kenny looked in his rear-view mirror. "Hey, what's this?"

Cammy turned and saw Rachel's Corolla driving behind them.

"Is that who I think it is?" said Kenny.

"Where?" said Cammy.

"The passenger, right behind us," said Kenny.

"It's Rachel," said Cammy after craning his neck to look behind. "*Now what do we do?* She's hooked in to the L.A.P.D. We're *dead*!"

~ ~

While the chase on Hector Street continued, Cedar drove near Rachel's house until he felt it was safe to return to where he'd dropped off Kenny and Cammy. He was ninety-percent convinced that they'd carried out the deed; all Kenny had to do was shoot two people confined in one room, and he had the advantage of surprise. There was always room for error, but Cedar knew Kenny wasn't stupid or slow-thinking like Cammy; he could improvise. But getting out cleanly would be troublesome, which is why Cedar worried when Kenny and Cammy failed to rendezvous with him. He kept his mind busy by praying. While asking for forgiveness, he reminded his Maker that, as creator of the universe and all elements therein, He bore responsibility for unleashing Slapper on Hillside Park.

"The greedy motives of three hapless souls were emboldened by an irresistible force of nature, Lord, a power superceded only by Your justness. One of these souls sought my help. I believe he was guided to do this by a spark of goodness and virtue in his soul. So what was I to do? Thomas Jefferson said when evil breaks out into overt acts against peace and order, it is time for rightful citizens to intervene. I pray that on Judgment Day, You will rule that my intervention was correct, because without it these two incompetents could have caused a bloodbath."

He returned to the street where he'd dropped off Kenny and Cammy. The fence between Rachel's back yard and the house behind it still had two slats removed and lying on the ground. Those incompetents never came back, he thought. He took a chance and drove around the block to Rachel's house. When he got there he was confused: the Mercedes was gone, Rachel's car was gone, and her front door was wide open. He thought about running inside for a look, but a distant siren changed his mind. He drove off.

~ ~

Joey was unable to pull alongside the Mercedes; it went too fast and he lacked the boldness needed to force it off the road. He watched Kenny turn right onto Sonoma Boulevard. Just after Joey made the same turn, he and Rachel saw the Mercedes enter Dom's parking lot. Seven cars were parked near the entrance. Kenny took the next available space. Seconds later, Joey parked opposite on the other side. Traffic was heavy on Sonoma Boulevard, but no one noted the speed with which both cars tore into the parking lot. Nor were any pedestrians around to see Rachel get out of her car and head for the Mercedes with her gun at her side. Joey also got out but waited for the determined Rachel to make the next move.

When Kenny saw Rachel angrily approaching the Mercedes, he closed the windows, locked the doors, and stuffed Marty's money pouch in his pants. "You should've shot her on general principles," he told Cammy.

Rachel stepped to the closed passenger window, pointed her gun at Cammy and shouted, "Get out!"

"No, stay put," Kenny said to Cammy.

"You're nuts," said Cammy. He opened the door, stepped out, and raised his hands in surrender.

Rachel directed Joey to go to the driver's side of the car, then said, "Give him the money, Kenny."

Kenny got out of the car, pushed Joey as if he were a nuisance, then said to Rachel in a conciliatory tone: "Look, we just saw a car with the keys in it and took it. Is it yours? I don't know. Take it back if you want. We didn't hurt it or anything."

"Give the money to the kid," said Rachel. "I'm trained to use this gun."

Kenny turned to Cammy. "Annie Oakley here," he said. He took the pouch from his pants and tossed it to Joey. Joey took it, looked inside, and nodded to Rachel that all the money seemed to be there.

"Get out of my sight," Rachel said to Kenny and Cammy.

Cammy gratefully stepped away. Kenny reluctantly did the same. Rachel took her purse from her car, put the gun in it, and whispered to Joey. "Take my car and get out of here."

"What do I do with this?" said Joey of the money pouch.

"Give it to your aunt."

Rachel walked to the driver's side of the Mercedes, then, realizing that Joey hadn't moved, walked back to him, "What's the matter?"

Joey whispered, "Aren't you going to call the cops?"

"I got what I wanted," she said.

She entered Marty's car.

"What about me?" shouted Joey.

"Get out of here!" she said. She got in her car and drove away.

Joey thought Kenny and Cammy might attack him. But they just stood there like the idiots he'd been told they were. If anything, they looked overwhelmed by what had happened. Joey got in Rachel's car and drove off.

"Shit!" said Kenny. "I wanted that!"

Cammy was breathing as if he'd run a marathon. "We're ruined," he said. "One call from her and we're as good as dead. She's in with the cops."

Kenny angrily faced Cammy. "Didn't she just walk away?"

"Yeah, but so what?"

"So she doesn't give a shit about calling the cops."

"How do you know?"

"Somebody *that* connected does *not* want attention. Not only that, but maybe the cops don't want any attention from her going to *them* either. Tell me, do you got to be told *when* to think?"

"You think so?" said Cammy. "I mean, you think that's what just happened?"

"Cammy, she just walked away from two guys she had every right to shoot dead and call the cops about."

"Maybe you're right."

"Besides, she's got to know we were up to something. Tell me that's not proof Cedar was right about her and Marty."

"Cedar sure knows what he's talking about."

"Damn, we had a hundred grand right in our grasp," said Kenny. "C'mon, let's tell Dom."

They entered The Sonoma Inn. Dom's cashier-hostess was seating people. Dom, who had reached for two menus after seeing two figures enter, lowered his head to see who they were through the upper section of his bifocals. Recognizing them, he indicated for them to follow him to his office.

~~

Rachel drove to Marty's. She parked behind, went inside and found Gino Cardona, the bar manager. She took him aside in the Main Room. He knew something was wrong. Rachel hadn't been in Marty's for months, and even then it was just to pick him up for a private black-tie event downtown. Before that, Gino couldn't remember the last time Rachel had come around.

"Bad news," said Rachel. "Marty just had a heart attack. He's dead."

Gino closed his eyes in silent prayer. "My God," he whispered.

"You know his standing order," said Rachel.

"Close up and throw the key away, you mean."

Rachel nodded. Gino's eyes were teary, like hers. "Does Gloria know?"

She shook her head. "Paramedics are probably just getting there now."

"This was at your place?" said Gino.

Rachel nodded.

"Let me call Cedar," he said, moving for a phone behind the bar.

"He knows," said Rachel.

Gino returned to his stool. "Then where is he?"

Rachel didn't answer. She wasn't even sure that Cedar knew. But she suspected it.

"Did you call him?" asked Gino. "How do you know he knows?"

"Could I be alone please?" she asked with a hint of impatience.

"Of course, Rachel," said Gino. "You want to use his hallway office?"

"Thank you."

"I'll unlock it," said Gino.

"Thanks," she said.

Gino put his arms around her. "You have my condolences."

"Thanks, Gino. I'm sorry for you, too."

As they moved for the rear-entrance hallway, Gino took keys from his pocket. "It's going to be one sad day here," he said. He unlocked Marty's hallway office door.

Rachel went inside, closed the door, put her head on his desk, and wept. She wanted a drink but fought the temptation.

~~

Dom and Kenny and Cammy entered Dom's office. Dom closed the door behind them and told them to sit. He sat behind his desk, then turned off his table radio. "What happened?" he said.

"Marty's ticker gave out," said Cammy, snapping his fingers. "Just like that."

"What do you mean 'his ticker gave out?'" asked Dom.

"He had a heart attack," said Kenny.

Dom snapped. "Knock off the attitude, Kenny. I'm just hearing about this. You shot him, he had a heart attack. Which is it?"

"We *didn't* shoot him," said Kenny.

"I never got the chance," said Cammy. "Not only that, but we had to steal his car to get out of there. Kenny doesn't care, but to me that's grand theft. We could lose our liquor licenses."

"Wait a minute, wait a minute," said Dom. "Slow down." He looked at Kenny. "You went there to kill this prick and he had a heart attack instead?"

"Are your ears as bad as yours eyes?" said Kenny. "We went there to kill him and he had a heart attack. Want us to say it twenty more times? Cammy's right, it's like God did our work for us. Right there, right that instant, ba-*doop*, deader than a dog."

"You're kidding," said Dom.

"But look," said Cammy. "We took his car. *We took his car.*"

Dom shouted, "Cammy! Grand theft's better than murder. You're not going to get corn-holed in the joint for stealing a car and they can't nail you for murder if you didn't kill anybody. Even my fucking grandkids know that. Now where's the money?"

"They took it back," said Kenny.

"*Who* took it back?" asked Dom.

"Rachel and that kid, Marty's nephew, some dope 'was driving for Cedar today," said Kenny. "They followed us here just now, right outside."

Dom massaged his temples. "Are you telling me nobody did anything wrong here except take Marty's wheels?"

"That's *right*," said Kenny. "*He* gets dead and *we* get his customers. Only difference is now we don't have that money to fix our places up with."

"And you just gave Marty's car up to that whore?" asked Dom.

"Yeah, just now," said Kenny. "She follows us, she pulls a gun on us, she takes the car back and the money, then she's off like the Long Ranger."

"*Lone* Ranger," said Cammy.

A pounding on Dom's door startled them. It was Cedar. He walked in, looked at Kenny and Cammy and immediately determined that they had not done what they were supposed to have done; he saw no dread in their faces. He closed the door, then lifted Kenny off his chair by his collar. "You want to tell me what happened?" he said.

"Calm down, Sparky," said Kenny.

Cammy stood up and said, "We didn't have to shoot anybody, Cedar. We were that close, too—*that* close—when we heard Rachel call nine-one-one, you know why?"

Cedar didn't have the patience to ask why.

Kenny, understanding this, blurted out: "Marty had a heart attack right after banging Rachel—lights out, bing, just like that, ba-*doop*, ba-*doop*."

Cedar studied Kenny's eyes long enough to know he was telling the truth. It made sense. Marty never exercised, he'd been under stress, and Rachel could have put him through the ringer before he finished with her. He processed the ramifications of this, then said, "Where's Rachel?"

"Just left," said Kenny. "'All the commotion, we didn't get out fast enough for you so we took Marty's wheels, his money, too. Next thing you know, Rachel follows us here. That gun you said she had? She pulled it on us, just now, outside, she got his car back, then she split."

"What about the driver?" asked Cedar.

"He took Rachel's car," said Kenny.

"The money?" asked Cedar.

"She made us give it to the kid," said Kenny.

Cedar hit Kenny in the chin. Kenny staggered, then fell against the wall and slid involuntarily into a sitting position on the floor.

"That's for stealing the car," said Cedar. Then he grabbed Cammy by his collar and squeezed until it tightened. "And you let him."

He did not wait for Cammy to answer. He pushed him roughly. Cammy fell back into his seat. Cedar turned and looked at each man, including Dom, with contempt, then opened the door and left.

Kenny rubbed his chin. "I hate that guy," he said. "I like how he assumes it's *me* 'stole the car."

"You want my advice?" asked Dom. "Forget about the money and forget about him."

"Sure," said Kenny. "*Your* place don't need fixing up. It's me and Cammy 'need work on our places, so it's not your problem, is it, Dom?"

"Lay off me, Kenny," said Dom.

"Yeah, just screw over Kenny and Cammy, right Dom?" shouted Kenny. "Dom just got his main competition eliminated, so he's happy, right?"

"Dom didn't say that," said Cammy.

Kenny started to stand. Cammy held out his hand to help, but Kenny batted it away. "All's I know is I *want* that money," he said. "It could take forever to build up new business."

"Then *get* it," Dom barked. "Just get out of here. We've got nothing left to talk about anymore. It's mission accomplished and every man for himself. And if you *don't* get out of here I'll have you *thrown* out."

Kenny got to his feet. He was stunned. "I'm speechless," he said.

"That's *another* miracle today," said Dom. He glared at Kenny through the top of his bifocals. "We're going back to how it was. I run my place, you guys run yours." He looked at Cammy. "Where's my gun?"

Cammy handed him the gun. Dom put it away.

"Right back the way it was, huh Dom?" said Kenny. "Me and Cammy plan this thing, *you* jump on like some leech, then when it don't turn out like it's supposed to, no sweat off *your* balls, right?"

"It *did* turn out like it was supposed to," said Dom.

"No thanks to you," said Kenny.

"I *was* prepared to go down with you guys if it went south," said Dom. "So don't tell me no sweat off my balls. You got ten seconds."

Kenny was defiant. "I'm not walking back to my car."

"Take a bus," said Dom. "One, two, three, four—"

"Okay, okay," said Kenny. "I hope your eyes get cancer." He opened the door, kicked it hard against the hallway wall, and stormed out. Cammy followed him through the waiting area and outside. They were so consumed by the events that neither man blinked from the bright sun after stepping from Dom's darkened bar.

"Talk about ingratitude," said Cammy.

"Dom's *always* been like that, the cheap wop," said Kenny. He made a fist and bit his knuckles. "Ten minutes ago we had a hundred grand in our mitts, now we've got to wait for the bus like a couple of losers."

"What about the money?"

"*You* figure it out," said Kenny. "I'm sick of taking the lead."

Kenny ran across the street to the other side of Sonoma Boulevard for the bus stop, in the process dodging motorists and flipping them off when they cursed at him.

Cammy waited for the signal, then crossed. The bus bench was full of Kenny's favorite people: non-whites. He started to ask for information about the bus route and schedule but couldn't bring himself to do so. Instead he looked up at a sign posted high up on a traffic-light pole for what he needed. While reading it, he reached into his pocket for change and shouted above the din of traffic noise to no one in particular: "What the hell's it cost to ride the goddamn bus?"

~ ~

Cedar hated not knowing what had happened in Rachel's house. Even more, he hated having to ask two morons what had happened. Someone was going to pay for this, but first he needed to find Rachel. As he got in his car, he tried to ascertain the odds of Marty dying from natural causes seconds before he was to have been shot to death. Of course it was impossible. But the drama of the timing convinced him that Slapper had become humanized, calculating; had become his friend, maybe even his savior. Perhaps instead of zigzagging all over the planet, it had stayed in Hillside Park. And maybe, just maybe, it was communicating with him directly.

First, Slapper had selected Cammy to tell him about the murder plan when he could have told anyone else or told no one at all. Then it had authorized him, Cedar, to commandeer the plan. And then, to prove that his tactics were correct, it had rewarded him by causing Marty's natural death instead of a bloody one that police might have traced back to him. How could events be interpreted any other way? he asked.

He drove to Marty's. The Mercedes was there. Customers were driving away, some of whom normally spent hours in the club before leaving. They know, he thought. He parked and went inside. Marty's hallway office was closed. Cedar opened it without knocking. Rachel was behind Marty's desk. Her makeup was smeared, her eyes watery, her skin ashen, her fingers shaking. She'd just lifted her head from the desk, had the phone receiver in her hand, and was about to punch a number when she looked at the entering Cedar and put the receiver down.

"I just heard," said Cedar, closing the door behind him. "I'm sorry."

"Surprised it wasn't from a gun?" she asked.

"I don't know what you mean," said Cedar, sitting in front of her.

Rachel wiped her eyes. "I called you yesterday morning to look into a rumor and you never—"

"I was about to," he said.

"To report what?" she said. "The sun came out?"

"You don't get to smart-mouth me, Rachel."

"Marty cut back your responsibilities and you retaliated. They couldn't have done what they tried without help. They were there trying to kill him."

"And you too," said Cedar. Rachel just looked at him. "A murder-suicide," he said. "The spurned mistress."

Rachel looked away with incredulity. "Jesus, what small minds can conjure up." She looked back at Cedar. "And you didn't try to stop them."

"I gave Marty over half my life, Rachel. I would have taken a bullet for him. But he got sloppy and complacent. That I found intolerable."

"So this was all about you," she said.

Cedar stiffened. Rachel knew he hated criticism.

"When did you find out all this?" she said.

"After you called me," said Cedar. "Cammy gave it up voluntarily, Kenny, involuntarily. Dom was out of the loop on the execution phase."

"Were you going to stop them? Or was it outside your job description?"

"How precipitant could I have been without knowing when they planned to do it?"

"I see," said Rachel. "You found out *what* they were going to do but you missed *when* they were going to do it. Talk about sloppy and complacent. And you probably think you're an honorable man."

Cedar stiffened again. "Does it matter what led up to today, Rachel? I've got a news flash for you: Sugar Daddy died of natural causes."

"Lucky for you guys, huh?" she said.

"You know they'll profit from what happened. They think dressing up their bars will attract new customers. That's why they wanted his money."

"I'm done talking with you, Cedar."

"Yes," he said. "You're upset, you're probably already feeling alone."

"Don't you dare attempt to analyze me," said Rachel. "That's all you take comfort in, the ridiculous conclusions you draw. You're just like every addict, only it's not a substance you're addicted to, it's scenarios you create in your mind that justify everything you want to do. 'The stars told me to.' Cedar, you've been in your own little world your whole life. But just don't bring me into it, because I find it pathetic."

Cedar wanted to smack her. Nobody ever talked to him like that. But he saw that by weeping and not flashing her allure, Rachel looked so damaged that her only hope lay in being rescued, and that was his job.

"Rachel, with your talents and beauty you could have gone right to the top. That's what I admired about Marty—that he kept you. I thought I was above envy, but I wasn't. He could have his money, his power, his business acumen, that killer smile, that charisma, all that. But whatever he had to get you, that's what I would have taken from him. And I would have given anything for it."

"Your dreams are part of your pathology," said Rachel.

"So let's agree my timing's off. But you've just been marooned and I'm offering you a new life. Whatever he gave you, I can give you more, because I wouldn't share my affections with another woman or a business."

"You really want to give me something, Cedar? Give me privacy."

"What for?" he said.

"Right now, a phone call," said Rachel.

"Who would *you* call?" said Cedar.

"Somebody I care about," said Rachel. "Somebody I don't want to have to read about Marty in the obituaries."

"Since when did you care about anybody but Daddy Warbucks? You've got nothing now, no one."

"Let me set you straight," said Rachel. "When Marty and I met, he needed someone like me and I needed someone like him. That's all it was. Since then, the relationship was based on my appreciation for all he'd done for me."

"So love had nothing to do with it," said Cedar.

"There's only one kind of love." She looked away and spoke with a suddenly distant, quiet tone. "All the others are ephemeral."

"What's that supposed to mean?" asked Cedar.

"You wouldn't understand. Cedar, you're just a messed-up loner. And instead of recognizing the need to deprogram yourself through counseling, which is what *humility* is supposed to bring about, you construct these walls around you, only they're really mirrors. They force you to see what you are, which is disillusioned, but you're more comfortable being barricaded by them than you are in tearing them down, because then you'd have to go through life naked and unprotected like the rest of us. You'd have to show your flaws. Well let me bring you down from whatever planet you're orbiting. You're not going to touch me. You're sick, and I'm sure you were in on whatever those three stooges tried to pull off today. And one more thing. I'm going to tell you what no one's ever had the courage to, including Marty. You're a damn fool."

Cedar was furious. He snatched Rachel's purse from atop the desk. Before she could protest, he opened it and looked inside. He ignored her gun and a half-ounce can of pepper spray; instead, he rummaged through crevices and side pockets. Not finding what he was looking for, he dropped the purse on the chair next to him, out of her reach, and said, "Stand up."

Rachel remained seated. Cedar walked around the desk and forcefully lifted her from the chair.

"Get your hands off me," she said.

Cedar felt the pockets on her skirt and blouse. She didn't have the strength to resist. He reached between her legs to feel if she'd hidden anything in her panties. She pushed him, but he finished before she could impede his effort.

"Sit down," he demanded.

Rachel obeyed. Cedar moved back to his chair and faced her. He spoke as if pitching a business proposition. His tone suggested he would not accept its rejection. "Every Monday since I worked for Marty, I drove him to the bank, then your place, then back to the club. Each time he gave you ten bills, then took ten more out before we got back to his bar. And that doesn't count other times you got together."

"The other ten's a surprise to me," said Rachel.

"You want to piss me off, Rachel? Because that second thousand put away has to be a million by now, unaccounted for and tax-free. Gloria gets his estate and his club, but that stash isn't part of it. Now, I know it's in the Kitchen and you do too. So you're going to get in there and help me find it."

"So that's what this is about," said Rachel. "Find it yourself."

"I can't," said Cedar. "I don't have keys for the Kitchen. You do. And don't lie."

"I don't have any either," she said.

"Not on you, unless you put them where the sun don't shine," he said. "Maybe I should check there."

"I said I don't have them."

Cedar shouted. "He banged you in there plenty of times, and you didn't come in through the hallway to get in."

"I don't have them, I said. The only ones I ever used were the ones Marty carried. If he needed me to get in here, he left them for me at the house. And quit saying he 'banged' me. It's called making love."

"Yeah, sanitize it," he said.

"When a man's wife won't give him sex because of sustained grief over the worst tragedy any parent can suffer, he has to get it somewhere else."

"Some sustained grief," scoffed Cedar. "Twenty years."

"Damn you!" said Rachel.

"You want to talk about *me* being a fool? His kid marries a utility pole and twenty years later he's still whimpering about it. Get over it."

Rachel had to bite her tongue not to insult him further. Instead, she said, "Marty never told me where the money was, just that he'd take care of me."

"Never told you? Was he going to tell you from the grave? He made the mortgage payments on that house, and your car's not worth stealing. So whatever you've done with a grand a week the last twenty years is your business. Maybe you saved it, I don't know. But the rest, what's in the Kitchen, we're finding it together. And if I don't get it, I will plug up the only way you've got of making a living. Now, you can help me get that money and leave town with me, and you'll do all right. That will be your reward. If you help me and don't go with me, fine. Get another Sugar Daddy. But if you don't help me, I'll kill you. It's me or death."

He stood up and moved for the door but kept his eyes on Rachel.

"You can call the cops," he continued. "But I don't have the slightest idea what you'd tell them. I don't believe heart attacks are illegal. If they were you'd be charged with murder." He smirked. "That's quite a notch for your résumé, screwing a man to death. It's almost tempting." He opened the door. "I expect an answer by dusk."

Cedar left without closing the door. Rachel swiveled the chair around so she wouldn't be seen by employees passing by. But she no sooner made the turn than Cedar re-entered, went to a wall opposite the desk, and yanked the phone jack out from the wall. "Make your 'private' call somewhere else," he said. "We're closed, by order of the late Martin Bagliamente."

Cedar waited for Rachel to leave. She rose from her chair, walked around the desk to pick up her purse, then headed for the door.

Cedar stepped in her path and showed his palm. "His car keys."

Rachel hesitated.

Cedar said, "You can walk home. It'll give you time to think about your options."

She gave him Marty's car keys.

"And remember," he said. "Dusk."

Rachel left.

~ SIXTEEN ~

The news spread like a firestorm. Every phone call started with "D'you hear about Marty?" Merchants feared that with Marty's well-lit and guarded parking lot gone, nighttime vandalism would increase. The owner of the drug store across the street, Sam Cooper, was called at home by one of his employees, Meg Szymczak. Bed-ridden at age eighty-seven, he sadly recalled how he and his long-dead wife had dined at Marty's all the time when it was a restaurant. Anna, from Mama Funelli's, clutched her chest when recalling that only three nights before she had shown Marty a picture of her newest grandson. The owner of Nick's Hardware was heartsick. He and Marty had been good friends, even though Nick was a church-goer who disapproved of bars. When Marty needed a replacement part for his club, he walked to Nick's, and he ended up chatting with Nick and his employees often up to an hour. The service station owner where Marty had his cars gassed, lubed and oiled said, "A chapter in this town's history has just closed."

Dom was the first to break the news. After Kenny and Cammy left him to catch a bus, Dom told Charlie, his daytime bartender, and Charlie called his wife, a secretary-bookkeeper for a family-owned plumbing business in Hillside Park who knew as many residents as anyone. Even though she was, by association with Dom, an enemy of Marty's, she kept relations with him and Gloria by exchanging Christmas cards with Gloria every year.

~ ~

Joey had driven to a residential area two blocks from his house. He didn't want to go home for fear that the bastards who took his uncle's car might come looking for him there. He could see them torturing his mother until she said where the pouch was, even though she wouldn't know what they were talking about. The safest place for the money was on his person. So, with the terrycloth belt from Rachel's robe, Joey tied the pouch around his stomach under his shirt. It made him look bulky, but getting caught with the money was better than having his house ravaged and his mother possibly hurt.

Joey wanted to get the money to his aunt, as Rachel told him to, but he had no desire to tell her that her husband was dead. He wouldn't know what to say if she asked how he knew about it. Another reason he didn't want to talk to his mother or aunt this soon was that he knew *exactly* what they'd say: "Joseph, you're the man of the family now." He didn't want to be the man of the family. How could he be the man of the family while still living under his mother's rule? Besides, she had the emotional stability of Mike Tyson.

All Joey could think about was Rachel. "Did she show me her tits accidentally?" he said aloud. "Did she even care I saw them? What if it's just a matter of not being modest? If is it, maybe I could see them again."

Then his conscience kicked in. "Here Uncle Marty drops dead and all I can think about is his girlfriend's tits," he said. "I'm sick!" In a display of self-punishment, he banged the steering wheel. But when he finished, he thought about Rachel again. He wondered if she would have taken off her robe in front of anybody else. Probably not. But then, why him? Maybe she just felt comfortable with him. That was probably it. Yeah, no big psychological explanation, really. But still, could it happen again? Was she sending him a message that what was good for his uncle was sort of okay with him, too? And if by some miracle he could sleep with her, would that be incest? No, not for him, just for her. Wait, *would* it be incest for her? He wasn't sure. No, incest was when you slept with your own family. Whew, good. He got that out of his mind.

He put the car in gear and went looking for her. He drove by her house. Paramedics were there. A few neighbors stood around and watched. When he saw a gurney wheeled into the house with its straps dangling, the ones that would secure his uncle's body for transport, Joey berated himself for his preoccupation with Rachel. Deep down he knew he should have called his mother and told her about her own brother. The problem was that he didn't have any change for the phone. He had a hundred thousand dollars in cash, but no quarters.

He drove to a mall in the center of town, a block west of Marty's. It had thirty-some stores, including the video store from which he rented movies. He could borrow a quarter from the guys there and use a payphone outside Ralphs, the cornerstone on the mall, to call his mother at work. He drove east on Golding Circle to Arrow, which would take him to the mall, but first he drove by Marty's. There he saw his uncle's Mercedes. He also saw Cedar coming out from the rear entrance.

"That's whose job I just took," he said to himself. "I don't think he wants to see me right now." Joey drove on to the mall.

～～

Cedar drove to Rachel's house. He needed to get in and find the alarm key to the Kitchen before Rachel returned. Whereas Marty, Rachel, Cedar, and Gino all had keys to the club, only Marty and Rachel had the Kitchen key *and* the alarm key. The only time Marty set the alarm was when he closed the club for the night. When it was open, no one needed access to the Kitchen, because Marty did the stocking.

When Marty occasionally opened up to Cedar, he used to reveal things he otherwise kept private. One was his Monday Nooners. He'd talked about them not as chest-thumping adventures but as something close to sacred. He never got specific; he revealed enough for Cedar to get a sense of the routine, part of which was that just before getting undressed, Marty put his change, keys, and jewelry in a crystal tray on Rachel's vanity desk.

When thirty-some minutes of after-glow in bed ended, he changed the order: he got dressed first and *then* retrieved the tray's contents. His club keys were on a ring. They included one for the entrance, one for his hall-way office, one for the Kitchen, and one for the alarm to the whole club. The latter was stubby, shiny, and tubular. The four-key ring never left his possession.

The Monday Nooners were on Cedar's mind. He knew that if Marty's heart attack came before he got dressed, his keys might still be on Rachel's desk. If it came after he got dressed, the keys could be on his person. Or in both cases, even amid the confusion of a sudden fatal heart attack, Rachel could have had the presence of mind to take Marty's key ring for safekeeping.

The ideal situation for Cedar was to find *both* sets of keys, Rachel's and Marty's. If both had been murdered as planned, he could've gotten into the Kitchen without the alarm going off, because the alarm would not be set. But he would still need a key. Without a key, he would have to remove one of the doors from its moorings. It would be worth the work, of course, because only three people in the world knew about the money Marty stashed for Rachel in there, and two of them would be dead. But with Marty dead and Rachel alive, he worried that she had the same idea about the hidden money that he had. Only it would be much easier for her, because she had all the keys. Cedar did not like the disadvantage this gave him.

When he parked in front of Rachel's house, two attendants from Harper's Funeral Home were loading Marty's body into their van. A few neighbors stood outside to watch with detached curiosity. That's some grand exit for a man who kept Hillside Park on the map, thought Cedar: a siren pulls a bunch of slugs away from their daytime soap operas so they can watch him being gurneyed off to his final resting place.

Cedar waited until the attendants left before he entered Rachel's house. By then all was quiet. First he locked the window and screen in the spare bedroom he'd opened earlier, then secured the slats in the fence through

which Kenny and Cammy had passed. When he entered Rachel's bedroom, a thought crossed his mind, the same one that crossed Cammy's
when he realized that the guest bedroom was empty except for a bed.

That thought was that no one lives here.

Earlier that morning, when Cedar sneaked in the house to unlatch the
screen and unlock the window in the spare bedroom, he had bypassed
Rachel's bedroom. But now that he entered it and saw that it was decorated like a suite at a fashionable hotel, he was struck by its contrast with
the rest of her house.

He went back and checked the living room again, as well as the spare
bedroom, the kitchen and the bathroom. The bathroom had curtains, one
bath and one hand towel, a used bar of soap and a full roll of toilet paper.
But there was no linen in the drawers, no toiletry in the medicine cabinet,
no reading material, nothing more you'd find than at a public restroom.
The kitchen had service for two in one cupboard. The refrigerator had a
few cans of soda pop and a six-pack of bottled water in it. That was all.

It appeared to Cedar that Rachel was in the process of moving, and that
all of the rooms except her bedroom had been emptied of items that could
fit in boxes; only big furniture remained. That her bedroom was fully fur-
nished was a mystery. If you're going to pack your home in boxes, why
leave the master bedroom intact?

There was no time to think about an answer. He returned to Rachel's
bedroom and saw that the crystal tray contained Marty's watch, wedding
ring and pocket change, but no key ring. He was sure that Rachel had
taken it. He looked in her desk drawers, dresser drawers, pockets of coats
and dresses, and everywhere he thought one could hide keys. He found
nothing.

Where did Rachel keep her own set? He took the sofa apart and felt
inside its cushions. He looked behind picture frames. He looked for
bulges in carpets, flipped through books, turned vases and tables upside
down, checked the closets, even clawed through the soil in the living room

plants. When he finished, he was sweaty and frustrated. He hated her again.

"And to think I asked her to share the rest of our lives together," he said.

He wondered if he should wait for her to return. No, she would want that money as much as he did. He made a quick decision. If Rachel would not help him get the money, at least he could keep her from getting it.

~ ~

Joey pulled into the mall near Marty's. He went to the video store and borrowed a quarter from a clerk there, then walked to a bank of pay-phones outside Ralph's. There he saw Rachel. She was using a phone. Her back was to him. She had the receiver pressed to her ear and was looking down, as if hiding from passersby. Her body trembled and she was crying.

Joey wondered why the Mercedes was at Marty's while she was here on the phone. He also wondered to whom she was pouring her heart out. There had been rumors that Marty was jealous and possessive of Rachel, and that some of their biggest fights early on had come not so much from her drinking but from her desire to see other men. The most persistent rumor was that she and Marty had broken up for almost a year. Rachel's friends had reported not seeing her for months. Bernice was one of them. She had talked to Rachel on the phone, but Rachel had declined invitations to visit her. The reasons were always vague and inconsistent.

This was on Joey's mind as he wondered if Rachel was seeing guys on the side, if one of them perhaps was on the phone with her. After all, Uncle Marty was at the club every day and night, and she was beautiful and unmarried and had lots of time on her hands. And there was her reputation for promiscuity that his mother and Aunt Gloria had kept alive. He cursed himself for thinking about all this when his uncle's body was still warm and he had not yet called his mother—I'm jealous of guys I don't even know exist just because she got naked in front of me.

He went to the payphone farthest from the one Rachel was using and called the school where his mother taught. The principal's office told him that Freda had gotten an urgent call and that she'd just left for a family emergency. She's probably on her way to Aunt Gloria's, thought Joey. He wondered if he should be with them during their grief. He really wanted to, but Rachel had tapped something in him that he couldn't set aside.

Rachel finished her call, turned and saw Joey staring at her from two payphones away. He spoke first, before she had a chance. He indicated the bulge under his shirt. "I got the money here. Don't worry, I'll give it to my aunt, like you said."

Rachel quickly ascertained that he was too innocent to lie. "What are you doing here?" she said, drying her tears.

Joey couldn't get past her incredible beauty—those big round eyes and that perfect face and those candy lips. "Just thought I'd call my mom," he said, still holding the receiver.

"Here?" she said.

He hung up the receiver. "I needed a phone. What are *you* doing here?"

"I needed a phone," she said.

"Who were you talking to?" said Joey.

"That's personal," said Rachel. "How'd she take it?"

"Who?" said Joey.

"Your *mother*," said Rachel.

"Oh," said Joey. "I don't know. She wasn't there."

"You just said you called her."

"Yeah but they said she already left."

"So you *didn't* tell her?"

"No, she already left."

"Joey, does your mother know her brother's dead or not?"

"I'm telling you, they said she left for a family emergency, so I guess so."

"These are *not* difficult questions," said Rachel.

"Aunt Gloria must've called her just before I did."

"Oh, I forgot about her," said Rachel. "We've got to go to the club. I want to take up a collection to get her flowers. Will you help me?"

Help her? thought Joey. Is she *kidding?* For her I'd stand in diarrhea up to my neck. I'd trade spit with a snake. "Sure," he said.

"Where's my car?" said Rachel.

Joey pointed to it, some forty yards away.

"Give me my keys," said Rachel.

Joey gave her the keys.

"Stay here," she said. Then she walked to her Corolla. On the way she looked around, as if ducking someone. Joey watched as she unlocked the driver's door, got inside, and leaned down out of sight for a few seconds. Then she exited the car, locked it, and returned to Joey. What Joey *didn't* see was Rachel reaching for her robe at the foot of the passenger seat, getting Marty's key ring from a pocket in it, and putting the key ring in her purse.

"I'm leaving my car here," she said. "Walk with me."

She indicated for Joey to follow. He did. At the sidewalk on Arrow, Rachel turned north. Before them lay the residential area of Hillside Park. Beyond that was the hill and the street she lived on. Ahead was Vista Madera.

"Where are we going?" said Joey.

"Do you know Cedar Roach?" said Rachel.

"I've seen him a few times."

"We're going to stay away from him, that's where we're going."

"No, I mean I thought you wanted to go to Marty's. It's that way," said Joey, pointing over his right shoulder.

"I know where Marty's is," said Rachel. "I was working there before you were born. I just want to walk around a little first."

Taking this as a sign that she didn't want to be bothered, Joey walked alongside her without speaking. It turned out to be a good thing, because he could hold back a little and scope her out. Her slender arms and delicate fingers excited him. He saw muscle tone in her legs. And he thought her neck was thin as a wine bottle. When they reached Vista Madera, Rachel stopped at the curb. "Okay, I'm done," she said. "Let's go to Marty's."

She crossed Arrow. Her abruptness confused Joey. As they stepped off the curb, Rachel surreptitiously reached into her purse and threw Marty's key ring into a rain-collection gutter they just stepped over. She coughed once at the same time. The cough sounded fake and forced. Despite the cough, Joey heard the keys hit the asphalt and slide before dropping to the bottom of the dry duct with an echoing "clink." He looked back to see what had made the noise. Rachel saw this.

"She knew his real mistress was the club," said Rachel. "No wife should have to put up with that. There aren't enough flowers in this state for something like that."

"I thought you and Aunt Gloria never met each other," said Joey.

"We didn't," said Rachel.

"Then how'd you know that?"

Rachel waved off his question as one he could answer himself if he thought about it long enough.

"D'you just throw some keys away?" said Joey.

"No."

"I just heard some keys drop."

"What do you want me to do about it?" said Rachel.

Joey stopped in the middle of the street. Rachel stopped, too. "What's the matter?" she said, turning around to face him.

"I know what I heard."

Rachel give him an impatient look, then found her car keys in her purse and raised them up to his eyes. "Does it look like I threw these in the gutter?"

She continued walking. Joey caught up to her. "Sorry," he said. "Just sounded like some keys fell down."

They walked in quiet again. After some silence, Joey spoke. "How come you left your car back there?"

"Joey, your uncle loved you but he thought you had a little energy crisis between the ears. Maybe you shouldn't prove him right by asking so many questions."

"How come you used a payphone when you could've called from his club, or even your house?"

"I could ask you the same thing."

"Those guys might think I was there with the money," said Joey.

"Where is it, by the way?"

"I just told you." He indicated the bulge under his shirt. "And I didn't go to the club 'cause I'm a minor, and Uncle Marty's not there to let me in anymore."

"I left my car there for a reason," said Rachel. "I just don't think you need to know it."

"Why can't I? I want to know all kinds of stuff…about you."

Rachel saw a familiar, hungry look in Joey's eyes. "Oh God," she said under her breath.

Joey tried to backtrack. "He was my uncle. I just want to know what happened."

"That's not what you want," she said.

"How do you know what I want?"

Rachel shook her head. It signaled to Joey that she regarded him as less than a serious contender for her affections. He wanted to get under her skin. "I was wondering," he said. "Are you really a prostitute?"

"No," said Rachel.

"But you used to be? Didn't Uncle Marty pay you for sex?"

"Look, kid," said Rachel. "Your uncle—"

"It's 'Joey.'"

"Your uncle and I had an arrangement. He'd give me money and I'd shake him up over it. He'd say, 'Take this,' and I'd say, 'No, we're lovers, you shouldn't have to pay for it,' and he'd give it to me anyway. It's nature—you want respect, you've got to shake them up, make them work harder, not take you for granted. Now, did I answer your inappropriate question?"

"Could you sleep with *me?*" said Joey.

Rachel shook her head and looked away. "So he asks another one," she said.

"Well, how come?" asked Joey.

"Look, you want to know what's going on? Can I trust you?"

"That's what *I* should be asking *you*," said Joey. "You're the one that lied to me."

"How'd I lie to you?"

"The only reason we walked up to Vista Madera's so you could throw some keys in that storm drain. There's not another one like it till you get to the other side of Hector, and you know it. This is not a *big-huge* town, and I know you grew up here."

"I'm an expert on our flood control system," said Rachel.

"Besides, we could've walked to Marty's straight through the alley."

"I *showed* you my keys," said Rachel. "You want to see them again?"

"It was *keys*," said Joey. "*I heard keys.*"

Rachel stopped walking and faced Joey. "All right, listen. I did throw some keys away, keys Cedar's going to be looking for. He's probably at my house right now looking for them. Joey, Cedar Roach is a very bad man. Marty trusted him way too long. I left my car back there so he'd see it and maybe look inside for the keys."

"What makes you think he's going to be looking for it?"

"He's looking for *me*. He knows I drive a car. So I've got to make sure he thinks those keys don't exist. If he can't find them in my house or my car—and he's already searched *me*—then maybe he'll realize there *are* no keys. Now, if it's all right with you, I don't want to say anything more about this."

"Why not?"

"Marty never saw this in you, this persistence. And I thought he was perceptive. Anyway, listen. Cedar is a scary man, and now, without your uncle to keep a leash on him, he's a scary, *desperate* man."

"No, I meant why you won't sleep with me," said Joey,

Rachel sagged demonstratively.

"Just tell me why not," he said.

"For one thing, you'd be in love before you went limp," said Rachel. "Virgins do that. Joey, that was an attempt on your uncle's life. While you were sitting in his car out front, they were in the back getting ready to shoot him. I'm not sure about the details, but I know his heart attack thwarted them. Now I hope you get the seriousness of this."

Joey waited a moment before saying, "How'd you know I was a virgin?"

"When it comes to sex, every guy reads like a children's book."

"We can't all be like that."

"The bad part is, I don't think they can be charged with a crime. What proof of a conspiracy is there without opening a can of worms? So what if some transient overheard them at two o'clock in the morning outside a seedy bar? He has no credibility. Who's going to depose him, the D.A.?"

"What's wrong if virgins fall in love with prostitutes?" said Joey.

"Did I say I was a prostitute?" she said. "That's what men call you when you won't give them what they want."

"But what's wrong with it?" said Joey. "If you tell me I'll cook you the best Italian food you ever ate."

"He's already scheming," said Rachel.

"No, I'm just saying—"

"I *know* what you're saying. You're saying you're scared of girls so you cook. It's a cover. It's nature, it keeps your mind busy so you don't have to think about it. Nobody likes to deal with their insecurities."

Joey was astonished at her powers of observation. Everything she said heightened her appeal.

"Figures," said Rachel. "No father."

"Uncle Marty told you that?"

"Yes, but just don't go Dr. Phil on me over it," said Rachel. "There's bastards everywhere. Me, I didn't have a mother from four on. And don't give me that victim crap, either. I don't like it. Neither did your uncle."

After passing two blocks on Vista Madera, they turned south to go to Marty's, one short block away.

Joey exclaimed, "Hey," then pointed to an herb garden in large clay pots on the porch of a nearby house. "*Ocimum basilicum,*" he said.

Rachel looked. "What?"

"*Ocimum basilicum,*" repeated Joey.

"What's that?"

"German for basil," said Joey.

"'German'."

"Nothing smells better than fresh basil," said Joey. "You add it to tomatoes, little olive oil, chopped garlic, dash of salt…*magnifico.*"

"How can you think of food after what happened?" asked Rachel.

"Food helps, is all," said Joey. "Good food, that is."

"Maybe Marty was right," said Rachel above a whisper.

They continued to walk in silence. All in all, Joey felt pretty good about their rapport, though he had to admit it was strained.

~ SEVENTEEN ~

When Kenny boarded a bus to get back to his car, he took a seat next to an occupied one so that Cammy, who boarded at the same time, could not sit next to him. Kenny chose to sit next to a stranger because he did not want to talk; if he even opened his mouth, he knew his rage at Rachel and Cedar and Dom would be unleashed.

When the bus let them off at Arrow and Vista Madera, Kenny got in his car before Cammy had an opportunity to speak to him. What Kenny didn't realize was that Cammy did not want to speak to him either. The reason was that the bus ride had allowed Cammy a moment of solitude to think about what had happened in Rachel's house, and what followed was a profound change in his view of life.

As Kenny scurried back to his bar, Cammy unlocked his hot, stuffy car and sat in the driver's seat. He rested his forehead on the steering wheel and closed his eyes. Soon, two words crept into his mind, "safe" and "God." Though still agitated from his ordeal at Rachel's and being chased on Hector Street and getting shoved by Cedar, he felt tranquility washing over him. He'd been seconds away from killing a human being, two even, but an intervention had occurred. And if Kenny's theory about Rachel's refusal to call the police was correct, Cammy, for the first time in his life, could call himself the luckiest man alive. But even though he could, with simple reasoning, call himself the luckiest man alive, that didn't mean he was the luckiest man alive, or lucky at all. He'd *never* been lucky, never won anything, never gotten a break. No, this was divine intervention.

Cammy raised his head from the steering wheel and looked heavenward. Then, as if a torturous baptism designed to test his wobbly faith had cleansed his body and soul, he said, "I am reborn." He closed his eyes again and said, "I was tempted to sin, but you rescued me. You have sent me a sign."

He turned from his heavenward gaze and saw a shocking sight. There, at the window of his car, stood Jesus. His clothes were soiled and tattered. He hadn't shaved in weeks. His face was wrinkled from years in the sun and covered with grime. At His side was a grocery cart filled with scavenged items. Jesus mumbled something and stretched His palm out to Cammy.

Cammy heard Him say, "Behold, I stand at thy door and knock; if any one hears My voice and opens the door, I will come to him." He was about to open his car door and kneel at Jesus' feet when a car stopped in the lane Jesus and his cart occupied. Its driver honked for him to get out of the way. Cammy watched as Jesus graciously apologized to the motorist, then pushed His cart to the curb so the motorist could pass.

Cammy put his head back, closed his eyes, and cried tears of joy.

~ ~

Curly, filling in for Kenny, had answered the phone when Charlie, Dom's day bartender, called around to spread the news about Marty. Curly, in turn, apprised Kenny's three customers of it. A solemn silence followed before two of them remarked that Marty was younger than they were. Taking the news of his death as a wake-up call to clean up their act, they soon finished their drinks and left separately. With no one left to talk to—Curly was hardly worth talking to—the third customer soon left, too.

The impact of Charlie's news hit Curly belatedly, as did most things. He moved to the middle booth, sat down, and stared at the opposite seat for a long time. When Kenny returned and saw that his bar was empty, he barked at Curly. "What'd you do? Run everybody out?"

Curly didn't answer.

"Don't tell me you're tired from sitting on your *ass*," said Kenny.

Curly knew Kenny was looking for trouble. "Can you just leave me alone, Kenny?" he said without looking up.

"What are *you* so pissed off for?" said Kenny.

"I'm not," said Curly. "I just heard about Marty's all."

"Christ, is that all I'm going to be getting from now on?" said Kenny. "What'd he ever do for you? Nothing, just like with me. He had his own friends and customers and nobody else got a damn thing out of him 'cept misery. That's how come he died—greed drove a stake through that cheap heart of his."

Kenny moved behind his bar and looked in his cash register.

"Nothing!" he said. "You didn't do shit! I should've just closed up." He slammed the cash register shut. "I should've gotten somebody else to relieve me—nobody wants a *bum* for a bartender. Just go on, if you're going to cry in your beer over that dead wop, I got no use for you. What am I doing even *talking* to a guy 'barely knows how to tie his shoelaces."

Curly slid off the seat of the booth and headed straight for the front door.

"Where are you going?" said Kenny.

"To see Bernice," said Curly.

"Oh, I get it. That's why I came back to no customers. You and that hog spent the whole time on the phone, didn't you? Instead of paying attention to my customers, you yakked like a schoolgirl on the phone the whole time. No wonder they left. Customers want a bartender *they can talk to.*"

"She didn't call," said Curly. "I'm going up there on my own."

This surprised Kenny. "Since *when*?"

"I just feel like being with somebody that likes me and cares about me."

"What a pussy," said Kenny. "How many Blue Sevens did you steal off me? This is a *business,* Curly. I leave to go run some errands and *you* chase off my customers. What gross incompetence! You're a disgrace!"

Curly spoke slowly. "All's I know how to say's I hope you do better now, what with one less place people can drink at."

"Is that a brush-off?" said Kenny. "Are you trying to say you're giving *me* the brush-off after all I've done for you? Well here's what I think of *that*!"

Kenny poured himself a double shot of bourbon over ice, raised the glass in front of Curly, and took a big sip. "*This* is my friend," he said. "*This* is not an ingrate. *This* is there when I need a friend, not you or anybody else I can't depend on. So go on, get out of here, go see Moby Dick. You make a good pair, you two."

Curly turned and left. Kenny was miserable and agitated. He lit a cigarette, topped off his drink, sat on a stool and proceeded to get shit-faced.

~ ~

When Cammy had asked Leon O'Connor to tend bar for him, he'd said he'd be back by one. It was now after one and Cammy hadn't returned. Leon's seventy-two year old legs weren't used to standing so long. He'd had six customers during lunch hour, and they'd kept him busy. Now he sat on a stool next to Earl Zell, the only one left, and complained that Cammy was taking advantage of him.

"See if he's home," said Earl.

"What would he be home for if he told me he'd be here by now?" said Leon.

"Maybe he fell asleep by accident," said Earl.

"He's not home," averred Leon.

"How do *you* know?" said Earl.

Leon didn't like Earl's tone. "He's not home, I said."

"He's home—he's *never* anywhere else," said Earl.

"He's on the way," said Leon.

"'On the way,'" Earl said mockingly. "If he was on the way he'd be here by now. What's it, two seconds away? He's home, I tell you."

Leon was impatient enough to argue with Earl, but the argument was stupid. He reluctantly got off his stool, went behind the bar and phoned Cammy's apartment. He was surprised to hear Cammy answer.

"Cammy, it's me, Leon," he said. "What're you doing there? I'm tired. I want to go home. Did you forget about me?"

Cammy was sitting in his recliner with his bible open on his lap. "I'm sorry," he said. "It slipped my mind. If you want to go home, go."

Cammy's blithe tone worried Leon. "What do mean 'go home?' Earl's here. You want me to just leave with the doors open?"

"Earl?" said Cammy. "Well, um, just take money out of the till for the time you put in and leave."

It didn't sound like Cammy, thought Leon. "What are you doing that's so important?" he said.

"Me?" said Cammy. "What? I'm just reading Psalms."

"What did you say?"

"'Everything God does reveals His glory and majesty,'" said Cammy.

Leon thought, "I must be losing my marbles." "Cammy," he said. "You sound like you just got religion or something like that."

"I've always had it," said Cammy. "It's in all of us. Praise the Lord."

"Oh, you're praying for Marty," said Leon. "You heard he died, right?"

"He's gone to his final reward, yes. Go home, Leon."

Cammy hung up. Leon hung up but kept his hand on the receiver while he thought about the strange call.

"You look like you swallowed a turd," said Earl.

Leon was confused. "He said he's reading the Bible."

"What about coming back? Isn't he coming back?"

"He said go home if I want, just close up."

"Cammy din' say that," said Earl. "You din' hear him right."

"I'm telling you what he just told me," said Leon.

"You got it wrong," said Earl. "No way Cammy closes up 'middle of the day."

"Shit-for-brains, I know what I heard!" said Leon.

Earl snapped. "I'm a customer, you can't talk to me like that."

"What are you going to do? Get me fired? He said close up and go home so that's what I'm doing," said Leon. "So leave. My legs hurt."

"I'm not leaving," said Earl.

"Get the hell out of here!"

"What's eating *your* sorry mick-ass all of a sudden?" said Earl.

"God damnit, Earl, get out!"

"*Make me*!" said Earl.

Leon walked to the end of the bar, where Cammy kept a baseball bat, grabbed it, and raised it over his shoulder on his way back to where Earl sat.

"Now, just stop that right now!" said Earl.

"I'll hurt you," said Leon.

"I'm not leaving till I get a buzz on," said Earl. "I only just got here. I can't stand Marge when I'm sober."

Leon swung. Earl was quick enough to raise his arm as a guard against the bat, but the bat hit him on his elbow. "You hit me, you son of a bitch! I'd *never* turn on a friend like that!"

"That's 'cause you don't have any," screamed Leon.

Earl threw his glass at Leon. It drenched his shirt. Leon reached under the bar for Cammy's gun. Earl knew what Leon was reaching for, so he ran out of the front door. Leon was sorry that he'd offered to help his friend Cammy, and he was angry that Cammy didn't make sense when he talked to him. He locked the front door and then went out the back door, which locked by itself when it closed.

The blistering sun hurt Earl's eyes. He did not want to go home. He was pretty sure he wasn't welcome at Marty's, and Dom's was too far in the other direction. So he walked to Kenny's. When he entered, Kenny figured something was wrong; Earl hadn't been in his bar for three years.

"Hey, Earl," said Kenny. "Long time no see."

"Same here," said Earl. He took a stool. The bar was empty. It hadn't changed since Earl was in the last time. "Place looks nice."

"Thanks," said Kenny. "What can I get you?"

"You know me," said Earl. "I never change."

"Brandy-water?" said Kenny.

"That's putting points on the board," said Earl, reaching for his wallet. "Hey, is that what I think it is?" He indicated Kenny's drink. "You getting a toot on?"

"Yep," said Kenny.

"Ain't that something," said Earl. "They say things come in threes. I guess that proves it."

Kenny mixed Earl's drink. "What proves what?"

"Marty kicks the bucket, Cammy sees the light, and you fall off the wagon," said Earl. "Something funny's going on."

"Cammy what?" said Kenny.

"The fool's home reading the Bible instead of working," said Earl. "Leon filled in for him a couple hours, then the asshole eighty-sixes me. Them short guys, I swear, they're all nasty little pricks."

"Who eighty-sixed you?" said Kenny.

"Leon," said Earl. "He says Cammy tol' him close up, so he took it on hisself to clear the place. I'm gonna give Cammy a piece of my mind."

"Cammy told Leon to close up?"

Earl nodded. Kenny placed Earl's drink on a cocktail napkin in front of him. "On the house, Earl."

Earl smiled gratefully. Kenny knew the free drink was an investment. Earl drank so much that after his fifth or sixth, he was easy to rip off. When he used to come in before becoming a regular at Cammy's, Kenny would clip him an extra dollar for each drink, each with less and less brandy until it was all water and ice and Earl couldn't tell. But Kenny wasn't thinking about that now. He phoned Cammy at his apartment. Cammy answered.

"What're you doing?" said Kenny. "I heard you closed up your bar."

"That's right, Kenny," said Cammy. "Jesus said, 'I am the light of the world. If you follow me, you won't be stumbling through the darkness, because you will have the light that leads to life.'"

"Where'd all this come from?" said Kenny.

"I was at the brink of sin, but I was rescued. Kenny, I can feel my life changing as we speak."

"Naw, you got lucky, just like me," said Kenny.

"No, that's not it at all. This was divine. I'm going to spread the word, Kenny. I saw Jesus right after we got off that bus. He came to me. He held His hand out to me right outside my car. He asked me to join Him. He'll come to you, too. All you have to do is open your arms to Him."

"Yeah, soon as he wears a skirt and grows tits."

"That's blasphemous," said Cammy.

"What happened with Marty you could call a miracle, I'll give you that, Cammy. But for chrissakes, don't go over the edge 'cause of it. It was just a coincidence."

"Oh no," said Cammy. "It was Jesus showing me the way."

"Cammy, *I* got off that bus, too. *I* didn't see nothing but messicans."

"I must make my witness. Good-bye, Kenny."

Cammy hung up. Kenny turned around and saw Earl looking at him with a smug grin.

"Told you he went off his rocker," said Earl. "All them people are like that. 'Minute they find Jesus, God help the rest of us."

"I didn't know it could happen that fast," said Kenny.

"Small minds it can," said Earl.

"He'll get over it."

"I wouldn't be so sure on that. I moved some furniture for these bible-pounders once, and all they did was preach the whole time we were there. Me and the other driver, we're laughing inside. I almost asked 'em if they got a commission on saving souls. Only thing was, the wife was a real looker. Young, big tits. I wanted to say 'you could convert *my* ass *any* time, honey bunch,' but I din', 'cause I'd'a gotten fired. Her husband was this little dip shit with a high voice. Sounded like Tinker Bell. Reminded me of a little rodent. What a waste. They're all losers."

~ ~

Joey and Rachel turned the next corner at Vista Madera. A dozen houses separated them from the alley to Marty's parking lot. Beyond that, on Hector Street, cross traffic was heavy and noisy. A few cars were turning into the alley from both directions. Rachel recognized some of the motorists as Marty's longtime day customers. She was not surprised that after hearing about Marty's death they wanted to be with other customers at the club. Most were retired, and Marty's, from when it opened at noon until late afternoon, was their second home.

"How come you're afraid of Cedar?" asked Joey.

"I already told you," said Rachel. "He's scary."

"Lotta guys are scary."

"Look, can I still trust you to keep what I say confidential?"

"I'll keep it all confidential, sure."

"First, I need you to do me a favor. I'll give you money if you'll help."

"You don't have to do that."

"No, you can buy a car with it," said Rachel.

"I use my mom's."

"So then a new wardrobe."

"Mine fits good."

"Then bus fare out of this place."

"I'm okay here."

"Kid, don't tell me you can't use anything."

Joey grinned pointedly. "Oh, I can use something."

Rachel showed hopelessness.

"Well what's the matter?" said Joey. "I already saw you part naked. It's just like the next step, right?"

"There *are* no steps," said Rachel. "There is no rule book. Your first time ought to be with someone special."

"But you're, like, *totally* special," said Joey. "You're fantastic."

"See this is what I meant," she said. "You've got your clutches in me now. Imagine if I gave you sex?"

"I'm trying to," said Joey.

"Not funny," said Rachel. "Clever, but not funny."

"No, really," said Joey. He used his hands and arms to help express himself. "What happened today, with those close calls we had and all, I feel like, I don't know, I feel like maybe, like, we bonded in some, you know, some sort of spiritual way."

"Bullshit, you saw my tits," said Rachel.

Joey couldn't deny it and couldn't conceal an impish grin.

"Don't be a pig about sex," said Rachel. "Most men are pigs about sex."

"All right, all right," said Joey. "So what do you want me to do?"

"I've got to get some documents out of the club and I can't be real open about it."

"Sure they're there?"

Rachel nodded. "There's no way Marty would've kept them at his house, not with the Housekeeping Queen of North America there."

"You got that right," said Joey. "Stand still and she vacuums you. So what are they, like, secret documents?"

"They're personal," said Rachel. "And if Cedar gets them, I'll be wiped out."

"Gets them first, you mean?" said Joey. "Well, like, whose are they?"

"Joey, you need to listen better. You need to hear what people mean but don't exactly say. Sometimes people don't like to spell out everything. 'Personal' is a code word meaning 'none of your business.' You should know that by now. You *have* passed puberty, I assume."

"Right," said Joey. "Big-huge mistake, all right?"

"They're mine, but Cedar wants them."

"How come he wants them?"

"Did I just waste my breath?"

"No I'm just curious is all."

"You've got the astuteness of a tennis shoe, you know that?"

"Just asking."

"But even after I explain, you still don't get it," said Rachel. "Maybe you should just go your way and I'll go mine."

"No look, can I, like, be *really* open about something?" he asked.

"I know what you're going to say," said Rachel. "I've heard it a thousand times."

"You won't even listen?" asked Joey.

"That's right," said Rachel.

Joey stopped walking. "Then why should I bother helping you?"

Rachel stopped walking and glared at him. "Joey, if you're trying to bribe me for what I already said is out of the question, I'm going to get pissed off. I've got a lot on my mind. How am I even going to go to the funeral without his wife making a scene? Don't you think I want to pay him his last respects? I can't even mourn him because of this *thing* with Cedar. He threatened me. He threatened my life."

"He can't do that," said Joey.

"He can do whatever he wants," said Rachel. "He's got a reputation. That's what's on *my* mind, and all *you* can think about is getting laid."

"Well why don't you just call the cops?"

"That's my business."

"So you'd let him kill you instead of calling the cops?" asked Joey.

"Just go home to mommy," said Rachel. "I can handle myself."

Rachel resumed walking, now at a faster pace. Joey stayed behind. She'd gone the length of two houses when he called out. "All right, I'll help," he said. He rejoined her. "Just tell me what you want me to do."

Rachel took a breath. "Cedar's going to try to stop me from getting into the Kitchen at the club—you know, that's your uncle's storage room?"

"Sure," said Joey.

"He thinks I have a key for the lock and a key for the alarm. But I don't. As you know, I just threw away the only set there is."

"Then how are you going to get in?" said Joey.

"There's a spare alarm key in Marty's office, not his personal office, his hallway office."

"Yeah, I was there this morning," said Joey. "I really liked the pictures of you on the walls. How come you threw them away?"

"I told you. He wants those keys. I know he's already gone to my house, and I'm sure he found out they're not there."

"So he thinks you've got them," said Joey.

"No, he frisked me," said Rachel.

"Wish *I* could."

Rachel frowned at him.

"Well when did he do that?" said Joey.

"Just before I went to use the payphone. But he's smart enough to know there's a spare set somewhere. Marty was a careful man. And if it's not at Marty's house and it's not in mine and it's not on me and it's not in my purse, then it's got to be in the club. Don't you think that's how he'd see it?"

"I guess," said Joey.

"I'm trying to put myself in his devious mind."

"But why wouldn't he think you've got it in a safe deposit box or some-place safe like that?" said Joey.

"Banks aren't open twenty-four hours. When Marty couldn't close up because he was sick or incapacitated, he'd call me at all hours to do it for him. Cedar knows all this."

"Then he's got to know *you've* got the keys somewhere," said Joey.

"I *don't,* I'm telling you. I lost them and just never got around to telling Marty. I didn't think he'd die like this. Sixty-six is not that old. He may not have exercised like I asked him to fifty thousand times, but at least he watched what he ate. Who knew something like this would happen? Damnit, he *wanted* me to have those documents. If he knew his health was bad he wouldn't have left all this to chance." She turned away from Joey to hide tears. "Anyway, I just don't have it."

"Where's the spare set?"

"In his office. He hid it for emergencies."

"Won't Cedar look there himself?"

"He will if he thinks they're there. He'll take every brick apart."

"Where are they at?"

"In the pencil sharpener, the part where the shavings collect," said Rachel. "You need to get in there and get it. It's a ring with two keys on it. Just put it in your pocket and don't get any publicity in the process."

"How am I getting in?" said Joey. "I'm still a minor."

"Damn, I forgot, I'm babysitting. No, don't worry, the bar's closed anyway."

"'Babysitting'," said Joey. "Nice."

"Toughen up, kid," said Rachel. "Nobody likes bleeders."

"Wait," said Joey.

"Now what? Don't tell me you're scared."

He held out his arms, grinned invitingly, and waited for Rachel to hug him. Then she did, perfunctorily. But Joey wouldn't let go.

"That's enough," she said.

He released her and said, "Wow."

"Cool your engines," said Rachel.

"I'll try," said Joey.

They continued on to the alley. Joey stopped and got Rachel's attention. "Now what?" she said.

"I just want to say, um, I'm like a hundred-percent infatuated with you. We can be honest about that, right? I mean, I know I should be feeling bad about Uncle Marty. And I do, really. But it's, what I'm really trying to say is it's not like a really bad thing is it if, like, enjoying you right now is, like, keeping me from thinking about Uncle Marty? I mean should I feel bad about that? In your opinion?"

Before Rachel could think of an answer, Joey saved her the trouble. "Never mind, really, you don't have to answer. Because I'm feeling a connection right now with Uncle Marty—and he's telling me, it's like he's winking 'Way to go, Joey. Way to go.' Like he understands what I'm going through. Isn't that weird? I never really felt a connection with him before. I mean I liked him—loved him, really—but right now he's smiling at me like he never did before."

Joey continued walking. Rachel watched him walk ahead for fifteen or so steps, then caught up with him. They didn't speak again until they entered Marty's from the rear.

~ EIGHTEEN ~

Bernice was pruning rose bushes in her back yard when she heard the doorbell ring. She removed her gloves and put them and a clipper on a counter in the kitchen on the way to the front door. She looked through her peephole and saw Curly, looking like a lost puppy, standing on her porch. Never had he come to her house unannounced or uninvited. She excitedly swung open her door.

"Curly," she said in big-eyed surprise. Before she could imagine why he'd come, she saw sadness in his face. "What the matter, honey?"

He stood impassively, as if he'd been banished from class.

"What's the matter?" she said.

"You know Marty Bagliamente?" he said.

"Of course I know him," said Bernice. "Oh wait, did they do something bad, those three creeps?"

Curly shook his head. "Heart attack. Natural causes."

"Oh my," she said, putting her hand to her mouth.

"He's dead."

"Oh my, oh my," said Bernice. "Poor Rachel. And his widow, too, oh my. First your only child, then your husband. How'd you find out?"

"Charlie, Dom's day bartender, he's calling all over, y'know, spreading the news. I was subbing for Kenny when he called and told me to tell anybody that came in. Kenny had to go to the D.M.V., so he asked me to fill in for him. Remember the other day I told you?"

"This is horrible." Bernice opened her door wider. "Come in, Curly. Every time I hear something like this it reminds me when my parents

215

died. It's so awful. I'm glad you came over. I wouldn't want to be alone now."

Curly spoke as if he were dazed. "Charlie didn't like Marty too much, on account of bad blood between Dom and him, but even he was acting like kinda the end of the world's here."

"I should say so," said Bernice. "Come on in, will you?"

Curly stepped into the living room. "Sorry I came over without an invite."

"Don't be silly. You don't need an invite."

"I just thought you'd want to know, what with Rachel being your friend and how close her and Marty were with each other and stuff."

Bernice escorted Curly to the sofa. He sat on the edge of it with his eyes aimed ahead. In a heavy, dispirited tone, he said, "I just think nothing's going to be the same around here anymore, just like Charlie."

She saw his red eyes. "Honey, are you crying?"

When Curly didn't answer, Bernice put her arms around him. "Did somebody hurt you, Curly? Did Kenny hit you or something like that?"

Curly shook his head as if he had no more to say. Bernice removed his shoes and helped him lie down, then went into her bedroom for pillows and to a hallway closet for a sheet to cover him. "What can I get you?" she asked. "Can I get you anything?"

"No," said Curly. He reached for her hand. She took his in hers. He was shaking. "Just stay with me, Bee."

"Of course I'll stay with you. Curly, you're scaring me, though. Are you sure you're not sick. Is something else wrong?"

"Just don't let me go, Bee," said Curly. "Just hold me."

"I'd never let my baby go if that's what he needs." She knelt at the side of the sofa and put her head sideways on his chest while squeezing him with her arms. "You're shaking. You're so sensitive, so caring."

Curly cried harder. He covered his face with his hands.

"Let it come out, my baby," said Bernice. "You're safe now. Nobody's ever going to hurt you again."

"No, I did it myself."

"You haven't done anything wrong, you just take too much guilt on for other people's problems." She looked into Curly's eyes. "You know what? It's sad, but nothing good lasts forever. That's just life. Marty had to die some time, and I agree Hillside Park probably won't be the same without him, but that's not your concern. The truth is, everything changes with time. But you know what doesn't? Love, love between two people. I love you and I'm sorry you're so hurt about this, but you have me and I have you and nobody can take that away from us. In fact, I was going to call you anyway. I wanted you to know I've been floating on air since Saturday night. What you said was so sweet. I'll never forget it."

Curly didn't remember what he'd said on Saturday night, but he was glad Bernice liked it.

"I love you, Curly," said Bernice. "Try to rest. There's nothing you can do about what happened. We'll talk about it later, okay? I'm going to call Rachel. She's going to need somebody to talk to."

Bernice kissed Curly's cheek and patted his forehead, then went to her phone. She called Rachel but got no answer. She left a message.

～～

Cammy closed his bible, tucked it under his arm, and drove to his bar. He parked in back, unlocked the rear door, and entered the building. He walked to the front door to unlock it, but realized he was doing this only out of habit. So he stopped, stood in the middle of his empty bar and thought: "This is Monday, anyway, the slowest night of the week, unless football's on. So why should I open up?"

He went to the back room and fetched a short table lamp with a seventy-five watt bulb in it. He plugged it into a wall next to the middle booth and put the lamp on top of the table. He turned the lamp on, sat and studied his bible. The light wasn't good, but it was better than the ceiling lights.

He occasionally used the lamp when he did paperwork at his bar. For the first time since he got them, he was glad he'd bought reading glasses. He remembered having to strain his eyes before; now he didn't have to. He looked up from his bible and thought: "I got glasses because I'm getting old, and I don't care anymore. The older I get, the closer I'll be to eternal life."

~ ~

Kenny poured himself another drink. The first had worked its magic. Fuzziness entered his vision, consonants softened, motor movements began to lag behind his brain commands, and everything narrowed, including his attention to Earl. When Earl used to come in, Kenny paid him the kind of attention you pay a zoo animal: look once and move to the next cage. But now they talked like old army buddies. They laughed and recalled anecdotes that weren't funny when they happened but which were now uproarious. When the subject of Kenny's ex-wife came up, Earl said, "Tell you the truth, I never liked her."

"Me either," said Kenny.

They laughed.

"You know what I hated most about her?" said Kenny.

"Her face?"

They laughed again.

"She never cared shit about me," said Kenny.

"They're all like that," said Earl.

"You know when you get depressed and want to talk about it?"

"Forget it."

"I'd try to talk to her—shit—she couldn't care less. They don't care, women. It's all about how much you bring home so they can sit on their lazy asses and booze it up all day."

"Same with Marge," said Earl. "You want company, get a dog. Dogs don't care about your moods. Even when you kick 'em around, they'll still come back, 'long as you pet 'em once in a while."

"Yeah but you can't fuck a dog," said Kenny.

Earl grinned. "Says who?"

They exploded in laughter. When it died, Kenny got thoughtful. "'You believe Cammy getting religion?" he said.

"What a loser," said Earl. "Never said a thing?"

"Not a word."

Earl got reflective. "Member when that fat broad across the street from him went nuts one day?"

"One with the push lawn mower?" said Kenny.

"Yeah, they saw her mowing her front lawn with nothing on but sunglasses and high heel shoes? Cammy leaves work to go see if he could get a date out of it—only a loser like that'd think he could get a piece of her."

Kenny laughed.

"Them's the ones that get Jesus," said Earl. "They don't ask nothing, they're afraid to hurt people's feelings. Nothings, you know, Kenny?" Earl pushed his glass forward, "Gimme another one. My glass got a hole in it."

Kenny made another brandy and water.

"I'm glad I came, Kenny."

"Me too," said Kenny, already short-pouring Earl while eyeing his cash.

"Cammy's no fun," said Earl. "I can't remember 'last time he told a joke. You gotta make people laugh—that's a bartender's job."

Kenny put the drink in front of Earl and took an extra dollar from his change for its cost. "He don't know how to laugh."

Earl pushed forward two dollars. "That's yours," he said.

Kenny put the two dollars in his tip jar. "Thanks, pal."

"Don't mention it," said Earl. "Probably good times ahead for you and Cammy, huh? Dom too? People gotta drink *some*wheres in Hillside Park."

"I haven't given it much thought," said Kenny.

"If I was you, I'd hook up with Cammy, open a big place, wipe that
Dom outta business. If it wasn't for that soup, he wouldn't have *no* business. Nobody likes hearing, 'keep it down, you're bothering my diners.'
He always tol' me that. Fuck his diners. I din' go in there to watch a bunch
a' fat asses eat garlic bread and drip red sauce all over 'em. I went in there
to *drink*. And my money's as good as the next fella's."

"You're absolutely right," said Kenny.

"Damn right I am," said Earl. "My money's as good as the next fella's."

~~

Rachel and Joey turned into the alley behind Marty's. They were about
thirty seconds from the parking lot when Rachel indicated the other end
of the alley. There, after turning recklessly off of Arrow Avenue, was
Cedar, racing his Cherokee toward them.

"Who's that?" said Joey.

"Cedar Roach," said Rachel. "Keeping walking, act normal."

"Think he sees us?" asked Joey.

"Of course," said Rachel. "I'll try to distract him while you get the keys.
If you get them, just leave, and we'll meet up later."

They watched Cedar turn into the parking lot and stop. He kept his
eyes on Rachel as he shut off his motor.

"There's time to run," whispered Joey.

"Run where?" said Rachel.

Cedar got out of his Cherokee, locked it with a remote, and waited for
Rachel and Joey to approach. His demeanor was threatening, his expression neutral. As they got closer, he moved to block their entrance to the
club. "I told you," he said to Rachel. "Club's closed."

"Doesn't look like it to me," said Rachel. She indicated the other cars.
"These are Marty's friends. You can't tell them to leave."

"Closed to you," said Cedar.

Joey cleared his throat. "I'm Marty's nephew. She can go in."

Neither Cedar nor Rachel acknowledged that Joey had spoken. Rachel stepped around Cedar and headed for the entrance. As he reluctantly moved aside, Joey sneaked around his other side. Cedar followed them. Rachel didn't know if he was going to grab her from behind or let her go. He followed her down the hallway to the Main Room. She wanted to try the door to Marty's hallway office, but his shadowing prevented it. The three entered the Main Room.

Bartenders were leaning against the back counter with their arms folded and eyes down. Gino Cardona was alone at a table with his legs crossed and hands folded in his lap. All looked shell-shocked. Customers sitting glumly on bar stools and at tables had nothing to say to each other. The only sound was the water fountain. Gino had honored Marty's request to close the bar upon his death; the drinks being nursed were soft drinks, juices or water.

Rachel turned everyone's head. Her red, puffy eyes connected to what the others were feeling. Several of the men came to her with outstretched arms. Hugs abounded. No one but Gino noticed Joey. Gino gave him a sympathetic nod, which Joey appreciated, as he was nervous about Cedar.

The few times Joey had seen him, Cedar was always in a suit. He looked like any businessman, but with muscles. Today, in his sweats, he reminded Joey of a heavyweight boxer, with a bad attitude, ready to enter the ring.

None of the customers spoke to Cedar. Soon Rachel got a cocktail napkin from the bar, dabbed at her eyes and addressed the customers. They'd returned to their seats.

"Marty would have been proud to know you came here to say goodbye. This was his life. He used to tell me he was born to be a nightclub owner. But it never had anything to do with money. It was always about making people happy. It's impossible to think about him without thinking about this club. For this reason, and because it was his wish, the club must close its doors."

Groans of disappointment followed. Rachel spoke over them.

"I'm going to send his nephew here across the street for a sympathy card for you to sign for his widow. I'd also like to take up a collection for flowers. As a lot of you know, Mrs. Bagliamente did not hold this club in very high regard, and as far as I know she doesn't know any of you by name or face. But I don't think that means she won't be moved by your thoughtfulness. I hope you feel the same." She turned to the bartenders. "Can you put your shaker glasses up?"

The bartenders set two mixing glasses atop the bar and, to prompt the others, put bills in them. The customers did the same.

Rachel turned to Joey. "Go get a card, will you?" Then, to Cedar, she said, "Can he get out the front door?"

Cedar nodded. He looked at Joey. "You'll have to come around to get back in. The front door doesn't open from the outside."

"Get a few," said Rachel. "We want lots of signatures."

Then she gave Joey a look to convey that this was his opportunity to do what she'd asked of him. Joey nodded and headed for the front door. Cedar watched him go, then sidled next to Rachel. "You're not leaving my sight," he whispered.

"You're not leaving mine, either."

Joey bolted through traffic and ran to Cooper's. He plucked six cards from a display without reading them. The cashier, Meg Szymczak, a woman in her forties who knew Joey's mother, offered condolences. Joey said thanks, reached into his pocket to pay for the cards, then realized he still had the thousand dollars Marty had given him to hold. He sprinted down Hector Street to the first side street and took the alley to Marty's parking lot. The whole time he was praying he could get into Marty's hallway office. The door was unlocked. Joey entered, went to the pencil sharpener, jostled loose the casing, and found at the bottom of it a set of keys. He put them in his pocket, then went to the Main Room.

Heads turned to Joey when he entered the Main Room and handed the cards to Rachel. "Got it," he whispered. Then, in his normal voice, said, "I better go. My mom's probably been looking for me."

Rachel nodded, and Joey left through the front door. Rachel hid her relief at Joey's news by putting the cards, open-faced, on the bar. A line started to form. As the first customer took a pen from the bartender and prepared to sign his name, Rachel felt a grip on her arm.

"May I have a word with you?" said Cedar.

Rachel went with him to Marty's office. When they got inside and Cedar closed the door, Rachel saw that Joey had spilled some of the contents of the pencil sharpener. She feigned a sneeze to blow it away. Cedar didn't notice. He stood in front of her and started to speak, but Rachel cut him off.

"I don't give a damn about that money, Cedar. It's something Marty wanted for me."

"Sure," he said. "Where's the alarm key? It's not at your house."

"I told you, I don't have it. I lost it."

"You told me you didn't have it. 'Marty never gave them to me,' you said. Now you're saying you lost it. Which is it?"

"I lost it a couple of months ago," said Rachel. "I just kept forgetting to tell Marty. That's the truth."

"I know what Marty meant to you. I know this is tough on you. But there's something you're not taking into consideration, and that's that I deserve something, too. I worked for him longer than you two even knew each other. You spread your legs for him a couple times a week, but I was here twelve plus hours a day, every day."

"We already talked about this, Cedar. I want you out of my life. Can you just respect that?"

"That's not going to happen. See, there isn't a fiber in my body that believes Marty left you bereft."

"The Grim Reaper doesn't always come with a fanfare."

Cedar shook his head. "That doesn't mean Marty didn't plan for his death. He had everything figured out, including spare keys. And don't tell me I'm wrong."

"Maybe they're at his house," said Rachel.

"Gloria could've thrown him out any time she felt like it, and he knew it. That would've left him stranded if he lost his own keys. So he had to trust *you* with them. So where's the spare set?"

"I can see we're going to go back and forth on this. Look, Cedar, I don't fancy myself a rat in a maze, so I'll make a deal with you. If the money's there, we'll split it, we'll say goodbye and that'll end it, once and for all."

"So there *is* a spare set," said Cedar.

"As far as I know," said Rachel. "I never had to use it."

"So you're a liar," said Cedar.

"Go to hell! If he never told me he was going to take care of me, I never would have known. But he insisted. So don't call me a liar just because I want what *he* wanted for me."

"I'm torn up over your outrage," said Cedar. "Where's the key?"

"Is it fifty-fifty?" said Rachel.

"Isn't that obvious?" said Cedar. "Where is it?"

"In my car, in one of those metallic key holders you attach under the hood or someplace like that. He got one for me a long time ago. I never even looked. I'm just assuming it's there."

Cedar reached for the door. "Where's your car?"

"In front of Ralphs."

"What's it doing there?"

"I felt like walking," said Rachel. "I wanted to mourn him. He may have been a boss to you, but he was everything to me."

"Yeah, yeah. Let's go," said Cedar. He opened the door and they walked down the hallway to the exit. "What was that stupid kid doing with you?"

Rachel showed dismissive irritation. "Believe it or not, he wants me—in the biblical sense, that is."

Cedar smirked while unabashedly undressing her with his eyes. "Least he's not a fag."

They exited the building and got in Cedar's Cherokee. He started the motor and backed out. In the sixty-some seconds it took him to drive to the mall a short block away, Rachel saw her life flash by. There was no key holder and no set of spare keys in her car. She'd told him this only to stall. Now she regretted it. Maybe she should have had a final confrontation with him in Marty's when there were witnesses. But she could not have allowed a public spectacle of her and Cedar fighting over what was in the Kitchen.

Rachel looked out the passenger window and wondered: "What if I did give him sex? How bad is that compared to the harm he could do? Then I *would* be a whore." She clutched her purse as if it were a life raft. Just in case, she always had the pepper spray.

Cedar found an empty space next to her Corolla. He kept his motor running, grabbed his door handle, and said, "Give me the key."

"It's not locked," said Rachel. "Who'd steal it?"

Cedar opened the driver's door on her car and found the hood-latch lever. He popped open the hood, looked under it, felt where he couldn't see, cursed under his breath, then slammed it shut. Then he looked inside the car: he checked the glove compartment, inspected the headliner, felt under the seats, searched the trunk, everywhere. He re-entered his Cherokee, sat with ostensible calmness, and looked ahead.

"I can see your tombstone now," he said. "'Here Lies a Master of Wild Goose Chases.' You want to stiff me again, Rachel? Go ahead. Lead me around by my nose again. I like it."

"I don't have anything left to say," said Rachel. "Why don't you just kill me? You wouldn't believe anything I said anyway."

"That's what you want?" he said. "You want me to kill you?"

"Of course not," said Rachel.

"You surrender?" he said.

"It's my only option."

Cedar did not think about his next question. It just came out. "Does that mean you'll sleep with me?"

"That's your ultimate control, isn't it?"

"I prefer to think it's renewing an old relationship, one that never should have ended."

"What if I do sleep with you?" said Rachel. "What then?"

"I don't know," he said. "To tell you the truth, I didn't think you would. But now that you might, I'm at a loss." He looked pensively through his windshield for a moment. "I believe I could leave it all. If we became lovers, I could drive away and never think about this place again. See, I've been imbued with a power that only a handful of mortals get. Even so, I don't want to control women. I couldn't be with a woman who didn't give herself to me voluntarily. That's what love is. So, if you gave yourself to me and we left Hillside Park, you would get a devoted man and I would get the only thing I've ever wanted—you. Can you live with that?"

"Just hours ago you threatened to kill me," said Rachel. "Now you're saying if I give you sex, all that changes?"

"I couldn't kill my lover."

"And the money in the Kitchen? You'd forget about that, too?"

"If you will," said Cedar. "Are you willing to make that sacrifice?"

"God must have a sense of humor, you know that, Cedar?"

An edge entered his voice. "You think what I said is funny?"

"Hilarious," said Rachel. "Here I lose a man I depended on with no warning, next minute this dork wants to sleep with me, *you* want to sleep with me, and I'm asking myself, 'What the hell do *I* get out of it?'"

"I *told* you what you'd get out of it."

"That's what you *think* I'd get out of it. *I* think you'll get your fill just like every other guy and then you'll kill me. Because what you can't control you destroy. Whatever you feel now, that million bucks will start working on you like a cancer, then pretty soon it's 'Rachel *who*?'"

"How could you make love to me when we were young and innocent, and now it's out of the question?"

"That wasn't me," said Rachel.

"No, I'm asking how you can doubt my sincerity."

"Something only a narcissist would ask."

"I'll ask again," he said with emphasis. "How could you doubt my sincerity?"

"I'm not doubting it. I'm saying it's your dick talking."

Cedar's eyes exploded. "*God damn you!*"

Behind her back, Rachel wiggled her fingers into her purse and found the pepper spray. Cedar flipped a switch on his dashboard that locked all doors and windows. He grabbed her collar and ripped the buttons off her blouse. She aimed the canister it at him with her finger on the spray button.

"You don't want to use in that a closed environment," said Cedar.

Neither he nor Rachel would know if his warning deterred her, because he saw that Joey had come from a hiding place and was looking inside the Cherokee through Rachel's window. Seeing Cedar's gaze move away from her, Rachel turned and saw Joey. When Joey recognized terror in her face, he tried to open the door, then banged on the window.

"Open up," he yelled.

Cedar smashed his fist through the passenger window, grabbed Joey by his collar, and pulled his head through the window up to his shoulders. Shattered glass spilled on Rachel. Cedar's hands squeezed Joey's neck. Joey kicked at the side of the Cherokee for leverage and tried to push away. Rachel pounded on Cedar's massive arms, but it was futile. She tried to pry his fingers from Joey's neck, but it was also futile. Joey was turning blue. When he started to lose consciousness, Rachel took her gun from her purse and shot Cedar in his left thigh, about two inches above his knee. He let go of Joey and grabbed his leg with a full-throated wail. It was ninety-percent pain and ten-percent surprise. Joey, gagging and choking, fell prostrate on the pavement. Rachel reached through the window and opened her door from the outside. She got out and helped Joey to his feet.

Cedar shouted, "You're going to die for this."

Rachel half-carried the limp Joey to the passenger side of her car, opened the door, and pushed him in. She looked at Cedar. His features contorted as he tried to stop the bleeding in his leg. She got in her car and drove away. As she left the mall, she saw that a few people, including nearby merchants and shoppers, were looking on with curiosity after hearing the gunshot.

Cedar pulled his sweatshirt off and fashioned a tourniquet from his undershirt. He wrapped it north of the bullet wound and pulled tight until it knotted into his skin. He cursed not only the pain but Rachel's audacity. For a man who prided himself on maintaining control over his own behavior, setting himself up for getting shot by a woman in his own vehicle was utterly sickening. He heard a voice.

"Need some help, buddy?" asked a middle-aged, heavyset Latino cook with an apron skirt over jeans. He'd come from a café next to the video store.

"Aw man, my gun misfired," said Cedar. He tried to sound more like a disappointed, self-castigating, half-hapless gun owner than a repelled assailant. "It's just a flesh wound, but thanks anyway," he said.

Cedar always saw himself as a man who, through self-application, was above others. Where pain would undo them, it challenged him. He so despised weaklings that he loved imagining he could pass any test designed to measure thresholds of pain. Because of this, he now found himself saying to no one, "Raise the bar, bastards! *Raise it*!" He ground his teeth and thought that if he could get home, he not only would recover but he would be stronger. "Slapper put me on the canvas," he said to himself. "But the fight's not over. Indeed, this is a rite of passage. I will prevail. So let it be written, so let it be done."

~ NINETEEN ~

Helen was worried. Cedar had said he was going out for supplies and would be right back. That was hours ago. Since then, she'd hammered and drilled holes in their living room wall, and she wanted to surprise him with the result. As it was, she rarely got to impress him. Everything he paid her to do was routine. But this bookcase-bracing job was outside her duties, and she wanted praise for it.

Maybe it was time to confront Cedar about his lateness. If she'd kept *him* waiting, he'd punish her. What harm would a little confrontation do? He'd raised a hand at *her* when she threw a snit the other day.

Helen was used to temperamental men. Her father, Roberto, a convicted rapist, hated when Helen or her mother questioned his authority. But her mother never understood that. Helen did. Her rules were to stay in the background and not criticize. Take care of Roberto instead of fighting him on every little thing, she used to tell her mother. But her mother would not be mistreated in her own home, and she didn't like Helen opposing her. So when Roberto went to prison, her mother moved to El Paso to live with her sister, and Helen became homeless in the dead of winter.

She vowed that if she ever got her own man, she would treat him like a king. She later wondered if this vow was evident in her eyes, because it's what Cedar responded to when they met. It happened on a deserted Sonoma Boulevard one night when Cedar, driving home from work, saw a crazed drunk harassing Helen near the bed of discarded clothes she'd called home. Cedar jumped out of his Cherokee and disabled the attacker. Helen mixed her show of gratitude with a plea for shelter. Cedar thought, why not? He took her home and made her take a hot shower while he listened to talk radio in the living room. That's when Helen decided, if she was ever going to get off the streets, she needed to go for broke.

After showering, she knocked on the bathroom door to ask Cedar for a towel. A little slow on the uptake that night, Cedar told her through the closed door that there were towels in the bathroom. When Helen asked him *again*, he figured out what she was doing and opened the door. He saw her wrapping her nude body in a towel with exaggerated slowness. She gave him an eyeful. Though he was privately amused at the awkward, naive way she teased him, he did not shy away from looking at what she wanted him to see. Her boldness contained a little-girl modesty, which aroused him more than her body did. It was a green light to get real friendly. They went to bed, and the next morning, after screwing again, Cedar knew he had a sex robot for the taking. His only demand was that she use contraceptives, which was fine with her. That was five months ago.

Helen's worry over Cedar's lateness vanished when she heard his Cherokee pulling into the driveway. She went to the wall she'd drilled and hammered, turned around and, like a fashion model at a car show, smiled in anticipation of his entrance. But when he hopped in on one leg and she saw his blood-soaked pants and bullet wound, she screamed. Cedar slapped her until she stopped. She assisted him to the bathroom, where he sat on the toilet-seat lid and took his pants off. He told Helen to fetch a first-aid kit, hydrogen peroxide and cough syrup from the medicine cabinet, a sewing kit from the washroom, and a liter of vodka from the pantry. She gathered all items. When she returned, Cedar was pouring peroxide into his wound. Helen flinched at the sight of the chemicals foaming when they met blood and torn flesh.

Cedar told her to thread a needle. It took several tries because she was shaking. While he was waiting, he gulped vodka. When Helen asked what had happened, he told her he had an accident with his gun. When she asked why he didn't go to the hospital, he told her to shut up. He took the needle and thread with both hands, tilted his head back, and had Helen pour vodka into his mouth. What he didn't swallow spilled onto his chest. As he started stitching the wound, he said, "Upon the king! Let us our lives, our souls, Our children, and our sins lay on the king!"

Helen used a washcloth to wipe away blood so Cedar could see what he was doing. With each stitch, he swallowed more vodka. "Command the health of it?" he continued. "No, thou proud dream, That play'st so subtly with a king's repose." He finally closed the entry wound.

Helen positioned a hand mirror on the floor so he could see the exit wound on the underside of his leg in the reflection. "O God of battles!" he continued. "Steel my soldier's hearts; Possess them not with fear; take from them now…"

Helen was too slow to clear blood away, so Cedar yanked the bottle from her and poured vodka over his leg until it rinsed the area clean. He resumed stitching. "…The sense of reckoning, if the opposed numbers pluck their hearts from them."

Soon Cedar could feel the booze, but his face showed the same intensity as always. Nor were his motor skills impaired. "God's will! I pray thee, wish not one man more." He closed the exit wound. As he wrapped his leg with gauze, he said, "By Jove, I am not covetous for gold, Nor care I who doth feed upon my cost."

He untied the tourniquet. Helen assisted him to their bedroom and onto the bed. Then Cedar did something even he thought was weird. He told Helen to get naked and to sit on his stomach. She did. He was in too much discomfort to get an erection, but her warm thighs against his body and her breasts in his eyes excited him. He soon felt a feeling for Helen that was unfamiliar to him. He knew why: he was seriously injured and, for once, he wanted to be nursed and babied. Also, he was unconsciously reacting to her maternal impulses, which were brought out by his neediness.

Helen was equally moved. That she could comfort her man merely by pressing her flesh against his gave her a new sense of power, particularly in view of his weakened condition. She purred soothing words in his ear and caressed his face and neck while ensuring that her nipples teased his chest.

Cedar showed appreciation. Gone was his frenetic rush for quick gratification. His feelings had never been realized the way they were at that moment. She wished she could express in English what a contradiction he was to her: a cold exterior hiding a wellspring of emotion. That it took five months and a gunshot wound for this to come out just added to the contradiction.

While Cedar drank cough syrup a few bitter sips at a time, he gave Helen instructions on what to do after it and the vodka knocked him out. She was to take a bus to Marty's and watch for anyone who tried to get in the unmarked door next to the rear entrance. If she saw anyone try, she was to call immediately from a payphone at Ralph's. He told her Marty had died and that people were trying to rob the club.

Helen nodded that she understood. Cedar was drowsy but in too much pain to fall asleep. Helen wanted this new depth of feeling between them to last. Another opportunity like this, where he was the sick infant and she was the caretaker, would not come again. She whispered, "Joo wan to may loff?"

On the dizzy side of woozy, Cedar managed a grin for the generous thought, but said he was too out of it for sex. The grin, however, was all Helen needed. She reached behind and fondled him, but he stayed flaccid. Then she knelt at the side of the bed and used all her powers to arouse him. Soon it happened. With his eyes closed and his head on its side, Cedar murmured quiet pleasure.

For a man who normally took one or two minutes to satisfy himself when Helen was on her back, Cedar stayed aroused for so long that she was pleased and concerned at the same time. She was pleased because he enjoyed it but concerned because she didn't know why he was not coming to orgasm. She'd never seen him drink cough syrup and alcohol together, so maybe that was it, because he hadn't indicated pain from the gunshot since she started to pleasure him.

When she stopped to see what would happen, he moaned, "Don't stop."

She continued with renewed eagerness. Soon she wondered if it would help for him to be inside her. She got back on the bed, boarded him, guided him between her legs, and moved up and down. That did it. When his dreamy moaning increased, Helen was happy; she knew he was on track to climax. In the interim, though, something unexpected happened: Helen got aroused. It was a new experience, because Cedar was always so quick to finish sex with her. Yet here she was, experiencing a brand new sensation.

My God, she thought, this is great.

In his delirium, Cedar had drifted back to high school, to when Rachel made love to him the same way that Helen was doing. It didn't matter that Rachel shot him an hour earlier, or that she had emasculated him, or that they would tangle again over the money in the Kitchen. All that mattered was that Rachel had given him the greatest sex ever, and that with Helen making love to him he was able to imagine Rachel atop him and trying, with great determination, to drive him wild. When the moment came, he indeed went wild. Seconds later, he passed out.

He didn't hear Helen whisper that it was great for her, too, and that she loved him.

~ ~

Rachel drove into the hills near her home and parked on a small street with tall trees on both sides. She turned off her motor and closed her eyes with her head back. She was still shaking. A dry breeze blew through her car windows and helped to cool perspiration she'd worked up at the mall. She was far enough away from Sonoma Boulevard and Hector Street that all was quiet around her, except for the chirping of pet birds from a nearby house.

Joey was in the passenger seat. He'd gotten his breathing back to normal and his excitement level down. When he spoke, it was more of an exhalation than a coherent thought. "Thank God the cops'll do something now."

"Who's calling the cops?" said Rachel.

"Paramedics, when they show up. Someone had to have called when they heard the gun go off."

"Joey, I said no cops."

"*I'm* not calling them," said Joey.

Rachel didn't respond. Something else was on her mind. "Joey, there are no documents in the Kitchen. It's money your uncle left me, so stop worrying about the cops and help me get it, and then I'll be gone from Hillside Park for good."

"You'd leave just like that?" he said.

"No, faster."

This disappointed Joey. "Well how much is it?"

"A lot," said Rachel.

"Couldn't be more than *this*," he said, patting the pouch under his shirt.

"That's your aunt's. Give it to your mother to give to her."

"Hey, Uncle Marty's dead. Why don't you just take *this*?"

"It's not what he wanted," said Rachel.

"Yeah but—"

"Joey, stop talking and listen. I was a bad girl before I met your uncle. People don't think you can change, but I did. He always said, don't fall back on old habits; don't get stuck in ugliness. I still have a temper, but I'm grown up now. But these men here, in Hillside Park, the way they look at you, they see the old me and it makes me sick. It's never a friendly hello. It's always this lecherous look. They're such children."

"Can't you just move somewhere else but still, you know, close?"

"Joey, don't you understand? I can't think with Cedar all over me. You saw what he's capable of. He was going to rape me back there. Of all the men I was every with, no one ever tried that. Still though, I shot him. Marty wanted me armed so he made Cedar get me a gun and here I turn around and shoot him with it. It's incredible what we're capable of. I still can't believe I actually did it. But I did and that's that. I had to. But now he'll kill me."

"Then *I'll* call the cops," said Joey.

"No, I said. With cops everything gets exposed. Innocent lives get dragged out in the open. Joey, will you help me and not hinder me?"

"Well, I don't want you to leave," he said. "I've been hearing about you my whole life. You've been like a *dream*. And now I meet you and I can't believe how perfect you are. I swear, I'm in love with you."

"Pathetic."

"No, the thing is, you're nothing like I expected. Yeah, I saw your pictures in Uncle Marty's office, but you can't really tell from pictures. Now though, you're a babe *and* smart *and* cool and, and you really kicked ass back there. I can't believe it. Look, let me help you. I'll help you get that money, *whatever* you need, whatever I can do, just ask me—or tell me. I'll do anything. *Anything*!"

"Joey, I can't predict the future."

Joey lit up. "You mean there's a chance—"

"There's no chance. I only said I can't predict the future."

"Yeah, but—"

"No 'yeah-buts,'" said Rachel. "I'm not going to lead you on."

"Okay, I'll help you. We'll see what happens. But I'm keeping these." He held up the spare keys. "Till you're ready for them."

Rachel thought a moment, then nodded.

"You'll go along with that?" said Joey.

"I trust you," she said.

"*Another* surprise. You were practically ready to get killed over these, and now you'll let me keep them? This is like a roller coaster, being with you. I bet Uncle Marty *never* got bored around you."

Rachel was looking away and thinking.

"Maybe you'll let me cook for you," said Joey. "My cooking's *so* cool, everything's fresh."

"Yummy," said Rachel without enthusiasm. Looking for a distraction, she turned on the radio. The station played Radiohead.

"You listen to *that?*" Joey said with disapproval.

"Why? What do you listen to?"

"Opera."

Rachel shrugged.

"Other kinds of music too," he added quickly. "Mostly songs from my mom's generation, but I know what's happening now, too."

"You don't have to get defensive about it," said Rachel. "It's legal to listen to lots of different kinds of music in this country."

"I'm not," said Joey. "It's just I didn't think someone your age would listen to Radiohead. I mean—not that you're old or anything."

Rachel shrugged again. That ended the discussion of music.

"They say opposites attract," said Joey.

"They say all kinds of stuff."

"Maybe you'll help *me*," said Joey.

"Help you what?"

"You know," he said. "Show me the first steps and all."

Rachel sighed. "That didn't take long." She looked in Joey's eyes. "You want your first lesson now?"

"You're kidding."

"No, not what you're thinking. This would be *advice*. You need it. Believe me, right now you're in Benny Hill territory."

"Who's Benny Hill?" said Joey.

"Never mind. Here's your first lesson. Ready?"

"Absolutely."

"Seduction begins at the dinner table."

Joey had expected more. "Yeah, I think I know what you mean."

"Good," said Rachel. "Now I have to say good-bye."

"Don't you want me to help you anymore?"

"I think it's safe to say Cedar doesn't have any keys, and he sure can't break into the Kitchen with one leg."

"Well, what're *you* going to do?"

"You're badgering me, Joey."

"I can't believe you're just going to take me home after all this."

"I'm not. You're walking."

Joey frowned.

"I'll call you," said Rachel.

"You don't know my number," said Joey.

"I have it. Marty insisted, just in case."

"I got my own phone. It's one thing my mom keeps her nose out of."

He looked in her glove compartment for something to write with, found a stubby pencil, wrote his number on the back of an ATM receipt and handed it to her. She put it in her purse.

"I've even got private access to my room," said Joey. "It's in the back, so she doesn't have to know when I come and go."

"That's real interesting," said Rachel.

She gave him a friendly kiss. He opened his door. "Seduction begins at dinner, right?" said Joey.

"Dinner *table*. We like to be taken someplace, not just pizza and beer over ESPN in a smelly apartment."

"Gotcha," said Joey. He got out of the car and closed the door. "Oh wait," he said. "I forgot. Can I have your phone number?"

Rachel gave him her phone number, which he memorized.

"Don't come by," said Rachel. "Cedar might be staking it out."

"Then where are you going to stay?"

"You're doing it again."

"Sorry," said Joey. "Oh, I forgot." He took the rest of the thousand dollars from his pocket. "What do I do with this? Uncle Marty gave it to me to hold."

Rachel stared at the money and thought about Marty. Joey, sensing she might cry again, put it back in his pocket. He walked away from her car. Rachel started the motor and drove off.

~ ~

Helen took a bus to Arrow and Hector Street, then walked to Marty's parking lot. When she got there a little before dusk, one car was left. She sat beside a utility pole and kept her eye on the door Cedar had asked her to watch. She'd been there twenty minutes when the last person to exit Marty's came out. It was Gino. He had a poster rolled under his arm, strips of masking tape on his forearm, and a bag of items. When the door locked behind him, he taped the poster to the door. It read "Closed Due to Death in Family."

There was a similar sign in the Kitchen that Marty had made for his son's funeral, but, like Cedar, Gino did not have keys to get in. Earlier, he had gotten a call from Marty's lawyer, Lou Carini, who told him that Gloria wanted immediate cessation of all business at Marty's and that after the funeral she would prepare severance packages for everyone on the payroll, right down to the cleaning and parking crews.

Through the night, Helen saw people drive into the alley, then leave when they saw that the lights that normally lit up the alley like Monday Night Football were dark, and that no parking attendants came to greet them. A few read the death notice first.

Helen didn't mind staking out the place for Cedar. She knew he owed a lot to Marty. Hiding in an alley reminded her of when she was homeless, but she couldn't hold that against Cedar, because that's how they had met.

~ ~

Bernice and Curly had their first fight. It was a simple communication problem, but neither one could see through their emotions to discern this. The deeper problem was something else altogether. Bernice had been on edge; this was manifest the other night when she nagged Curly about moving in with her and about saying he loved her. All she knew was if the wrong person said the wrong thing, she could chomp his head off like T-Rex, growls and all.

The fight started when clashing pans from the kitchen woke Curly from a nap. Bernice had been doing light housework and otherwise trying to keep noise down so as not to wake him. But when she looked for her colander in a cabinet full of cookware over her refrigerator, and two saucepans in front fell on the floor, she swore out loud. Curly heard a tone in her outburst that worried him. In his paranoia, he thought that by coming over without an invitation he had disrupted her domestic tranquility. Not knowing what to do, he put his shoes on, sat up and waited. He wanted to leave without telling her, but that would have been rude.

Bernice put the pans back in the cabinet, then peeked around the corner to see if she had awakened him. When she saw that he was awake, she said, "How long have you been up?"

"Not long," mumbled Curly.

"Why didn't you tell me?"

"Well I just…I don't know," he said. "Guess I didn't have a chance."

"I told you we could talk when you woke up. Didn't you want to?"

"Not really," said Curly.

"I thought that's why you came over"

"I don't know," he said. "Like I said, I just wanted to be with you."

"I don't understand you, Curly. You come over practically traumatized, but it's not like you ever even *went* to Marty's. Is there something you're not telling me?"

"No," said Curly.

"But you act like Marty was a close friend, like Kenny, or that guy, that Nick that owns the hardware store."

Curly shrugged. "What's wrong with them guys?"

"*Nothing's* wrong with them."

"Why can't I just be sad someone I knew about died?"

"You can."

"Are you mad 'cause I came over without you asking me to?"

"What kind of question is that? Curly, I practically *beg* you to move in all the time. Do you realize how preposterous that sounds?"

"Well how am I supposed to know? 'One thing, it's the first time you never asked me to take a shower when I got here."

"That's because I normally know when you're coming, so dinner's prepared. Don't I always have everything ready when you get here?"

"That's what I mean," said Curly. "This time I just showed up."

"You're being ridiculous. I don't know what you're thinking anymore."

"I'm not thinking *anything*, Bee. I'm the same I always was."

"You're so defensive."

That did it. Curly stood up and walked to the door.

"Where are you going?" said Bernice.

"This was a bad idea," said Curly. "I'm gonna leave now."

"You can't leave. I'm starting dinner."

Curly walked onto the porch, turned and faced her. "It was a bad idea. I shouldn't of come over without an invite. I'll see you later."

"Don't you dare leave me," she said.

Curly marched off. Bernice stood on the porch and called out, "Curly, come back. We have to talk. It's important."

Curly didn't believe there was anything to talk about except his coming over, which turned out to be a disaster. He continued walking away from the house. Bernice had half-a-mind to haul him back physically. The only thing that stopped her was the incredulity of the moment. She cupped her hands and yelled.

"You come back here, Curly Peetz!"

Curly shook his head without turning around.

"I mean it!" shouted Bernice. "Don't you leave me mad like this!"

Curly soon was out of hearing range. Bernice was fit to be tied.

～～

In all the time Cammy read his bible, only once did someone try to come into his bar. But the door was locked, so the person left. Curly wasn't even curious about who it was. Around eight, he got hungry. Tired of hot dogs and bar snacks, he drove to Ralphs and bought vegetables and cooked, sliced ham. He made a sandwich and green beans with butter. He usually ate at his kitchen table while reading *Reader's Digest.* Tonight, he took his meal into the living room and channel-surfed until he found a fire-and-brimstone preacher. The preacher's speech rhythms and dynamics inspired Cammy. I need to learn all I can, he thought. Around nine-thirty, he drove to Kenny's.

Kenny was alone except for Earl, who was comatose but still upright on his stool. This didn't surprise Cammy. What surprised him was seeing Kenny drunk. When Kenny drank, he went through three stages. Stage one was giddiness. Stage two was bellicosity; he could pick a fight with Mary Poppins and make it look as if *she* started it. The third stage was stiff-legged ambulation under immobility from the waist up, and speech that sounded as if his jaw were wired and marbles filled his mouth. His eyes got hollow and his mouth stayed open. Drool dangled from his chin like live worms. When he used to go on binges, toward the end he would say, "Why can't I just pass out like normal drunks?"

"Look at you," said Cammy. "You're a mess."

Kenny was a standing zombie. "I been drinkin'," he said. His limbs were loose, like clothes drying in the sun. He tried with great effort to distinguish blurred *single* vision from blurred *double* vision. "You know the *reason* why I been drinkin'?" he said.

Earl looked up but didn't register who Cammy was. His head bobbed back and forth like those pirates in that ride at Disneyland. When Cammy went around the bar to make coffee, Kenny addressed the spot where Cammy stood a moment earlier. "I was expectin' some kind of 'phoria or something," he said.

"*Eu*phoria?" said Cammy.

"Instead I got nothin'. Jail or something, *killed*, but not *nothin'*."

Cammy emptied a half-inch of mud from Kenny's coffee pot. He filled it with water, put fresh grounds in a filter, and turned it on. "You might be premature about that, Kenny. I'll sell you my inventory for seventy-five cents on the dollar, lock, stock, and barrel. You can't beat that."

Kenny hadn't heard. He hadn't even realized that Cammy was no longer in front of him. "Somethin' like this," he said, "you gotta talk about it. But I got nobody to talk to. Never did, still don't. Judy, forget it. No family, no friends, nobody."

"You've got Jesus," said Cammy.

"You'd think one person would wanna listen, jes' one. But you find me one and I guarantee you they won't care, either. 'Yeah Kenny, thas' terrible, yeah Kenny, thas' really bad. Yeah, Kenny, your hard life sucks.' I can hear it now. Jes' more bullshit."

"You've got Jesus," said Cammy. He rifled through his bible. Until he found what he was looking for, he said, "He died for you, so He cares. You just have to open up to Him. You know what He did, Kenny? After He was crucified He walked into a room full of people and instead of talking about Himself He talked about them. I just read about it." Cammy found what he was looking for. "Here it is," he said. "Listen. It's John, Nineteen. Jesus walked in the room and said, 'Peace be with you.' Then here, in twenty-two, it says, 'He breathed on them and said to them to receive the Holy Spirit.' Kenny, that's proof right there, proof He cares about you and what you have to say." Cammy scrambled to find another page he'd marked. "Here's another one, Kenny. 'I took my troubles to the Lord; I cried out to Him and He answered my prayer.' What do you think of that, Kenny?"

Kenny wasn't listening, but he finally registered that Cammy was beside him. Moving as if in a trance, he faced him. "'I ever tell you what happened when I was little?"

Cammy shook his head. "I can't bear to hear it again, Kenny."

"No, really, it's important. She wakes me up, says 'come help me.' This is a six-year-old kid! She's waking a six-year-old kid up out of a sound sleep…a kid, the stupid woman!"

"You shouldn't talk about your mother like that," said Cammy.

"Says 'come help me,'" said Kenny. He stumbled but stabilized himself by holding onto the counter. "Six years old. No kid ought to have to see that. She should've known, the stupid woman. Moms are supposed to know shit like that. She never thought what that would do to me. No, it was jes', 'come help me.' The ignorant, stupid woman."

"I'm making coffee," said Cammy. "You're going to drink some fresh hot coffee. Where's your aspirin?"

Kenny jerked his head toward Cammy. "What?"

"Where's your aspirins, I said."

"I don't have any," said Kenny. "Can't afford 'um."

Cammy escorted Kenny to the closest booth. Earl's eyes followed them until his neck craned and he almost fell.

Cammy sat across from Kenny. "Did you hear what I said about buying my inventory for seventy-five cents on the dollar or not?"

It took a moment for Kenny to answer. "'You selling out?"

"Yes. And if you're not interested, I need that man's name you said was looking at bars here, the Arab fellow."

"You're not selling out," said Kenny. "'You selling out?"

"I won't contribute to sin anymore."

"*What* sin?" said Kenny. "There's no sin here."

Cammy got up and poured a cup of coffee and brought it back. Kenny took a sip. It burned his lips. "Shit, thas' hot."

"Where's Curly?" said Cammy.

"Probably with that tub o' lard he's bangin'," said Kenny.

"Somebody's got to help Earl home. Shucks. Do you know Marge's work number to call her at? Oh well, I'll take him home."

"Let him walk," said Kenny. "Maybe he'll get hit by a car."

"Try to sober up, Kenny. I want to talk about getting rid of sin in Hillside Park, and I'm going to start by exposing Marty and Rachel."

"'Got something against the good old in-and-out, do ya'?"

"The adultery's over now," said Cammy. "No, the other thing."

Kenny was blowing on his coffee. "Whatever," he said.

~ ~

Cedar woke up near midnight. He was groggy. His head felt thick, like a bowling ball. Though the cough syrup and vodka had put him under as he'd planned, the sleep it induced was fitful. His leg was sore but not on fire. He turned on his bedside light. Bleeding was visible through the gauze bandage, but it wasn't much. He hopped to a chest of drawers for clean sweatpants. He put a T-shirt on, and socks on both feet, but only one shoe; if the pain didn't remind him not to walk on his leg, his shoeless foot would.

He knew he could drive—his Cherokee was an automatic—and if he had to get around outside the truck, he could hop. After all, he was in great physical shape. He washed down four ibuprofen tablets with orange juice, drenched his face with cold water, and found his car keys. He knew Rachel was out there. He was going to find her.

~ ~

When Joey got home, he checked the answering machine. He knew instinctively that his mother had left messages. She was neurotic anyway, and hearing that her only sibling had died was sure to have ruptured her.

Their house had two bedrooms, one bathroom, a living room that included a dining room, and a kitchen that included laundry facilities. French windows lined two walls in the living room. Freda complained that they took up wall space and made decorating impossible. She couldn't put furniture against the windows or they wouldn't open, nor did they leave room for pictures. To redecorate, she had to change curtains, which cost a fortune. Despite this, she redecorated every year. And when she changed curtains, she had to repaint and sometimes get new furniture and carpeting. She was never satisfied with any new look for very long.

A door in the rear gave Joey access to his bedroom from outside. When he brought friends over, they remarked unfavorably about Freda's artwork, which included peace signs and psychedelic album covers from her flower child days, posters of Gandhi, Ché, Iron Eyes Cody, and prints by Robbie Conal.

Joey and Freda didn't hate each other, but they had nothing in common. He spent most of his time cooking with a CD player blaring opera. But to Freda, who was overweight, their kitchen was a torture chamber. She usually had breakfast at Starbucks on her way to work. For lunch she went out with other teachers and had salad. For dinner, with her whirlwind social life, meals were eaten on the fly. When she didn't go out, she drank Slim Fast or a concoction blended from ingredients she bought at a health-food store in South Pasadena, which Joey thought should be bombed off the planet, except for its produce section. He couldn't stand what his mother ate, bridled at her political fulminations and couldn't find one woman among her friends he would ask out if he were older. They all complained about how worthless men were while secretly wishing they had one. They belittled fashion models for being too thin while secretly wishing they were even thinner. They were always *against* something—tobacco companies, violence on TV, the N.R.A., Howard Stern, saturated fat—and never mildly, like most people. If envy could burn calories, thought Joey, they'd fizzle into skeletons. And *then* they'd complain about not having any clothes that fit.

Joey was right about the answering machine. His mother had left four messages. He listened to them while emptying his pockets of the paring knife, cutting board and sliced garlic. He took the money pouch from inside his shirt and the remaining hundred-dollar bills from his pocket.

The first phone message was, "This is Mom. I have bad news. Uncle Marty had a heart attack. Call me on my cell phone."

The second was, "Call me on my cell phone immediately."

The third: "Where the hell are you, Joseph? Did you get my last two messages? Are you all right? Call me on my cell phone or at Aunt Gloria's. It's urgent."

The fourth message said, "Goddamnit, what the hell's the matter with you? You should have called me by now. I know you know what happened because you were driving Uncle Marty's car and they told me it's back at his bar and you were there with that *trash*. You're the man of the family now. You should be more responsible than this. Call me on my cell phone *right now*."

Joey wondered what to do. At first he didn't want to call his mother for fear of having to defend Rachel. But when he heard his mother's voice, he felt bad that he'd put his concern for Rachel above his mother's concern for him at such a sad time for the family. She may be a fruitcake, he thought, but she's still my mother. He lifted the receiver to call her when the doorbell rang. He saw through the peephole that it was Gino Cardona.

"Hey, Joey," said Gino with a sober expression.

Joey opened the door. "Hey, Gino."

"I've got some stuff here for your mom to give Marty's wife." Gino handed him a plastic bag. "It's the cards you got for her. We got about fifty signatures. That was real considerate of Rachel."

Joey looked through the bag. "Yeah."

"I got the cash from the registers. I put it in Marty's office in a bag under his desk. Five hundred, thirty-four dollars and change. We only sold a couple of drinks before the news hit. The club's all closed up, so nobody's got to worry. Stuff's in the refrigerators, but it's good for a couple of days. Otherwise, the place can stay closed up till the funeral's over. One thing, though. Marty always brought back cash from the bank. Would you know where that is?"

Joey pointed to the dining room. "I'm going to take it to my Aunt Gloria, that's what Rachel said to do."

"Then that fills out the grocery list."

"Is it safe, the club I mean?" said Joey.

"From what?"

"I don't know. Burglary, I guess."

"Well, I wouldn't put the word out on the street the alarm's not set," said Gino. "Marty had the key with him when he went to Rachel's. She's supposed to have one, but she left before I could ask her about it, and there's no answer at her home. I left her a message. All she needs to do is come by and set it. Otherwise, somebody could get in by jimmying the locks—except they're pretty thick and all the locks are double-bolted."

"Do you trust Cedar?" asked Joey.

"Trust him how?"

"I don't know," said Joey. "I'm not sure what I mean, just curious."

"He's a tough one," said Gino. "Always keeps his distance. Nobody knows what he's thinking. But nothing would surprise me. We thought he'd do whatever Marty wanted, but now Marty's gone."

"'Cause like, I don't understand how come Uncle Marty didn't let him have spare keys if he trusted him with everything else."

"Cedar's got spare keys," said Gino.

"To the Kitchen?" said Joey.

Gino studied Joey's eyes for a moment. "There was one thing about Marty," he said. "He'd tell you anything you wanted to know and he'd give you anything you needed. But something he never talked about was what's in that room. If you asked more than once, you got pink-slipped. It's been that way for years. So in that sense, Cedar was just like the rest of us, with the keys, that is. Rachel's the only one with spare keys."

"Thanks," said Joey.

"Your uncle was one in a million," said Gino. "I'm sorry."

"Thanks," said Joey. "I'll make sure my aunt gets this stuff."

"I know you will," said Gino. "Marty always told everybody you were a good kid."

They said good-bye. Joey put the money pouch and cash in the bag of sympathy cards, then called his aunt. His mother answered. "Where've you been?" she barked. "Why haven't you called me before this?"

"I was busy, Mom. I'll tell you when I see you."

"You ought to be ashamed of yourself," said Freda. "Well, I can't come get you. Aunt Gloria's too upset to be left alone. She told me I could leave to pick you up, but I said you could take a cab."

"Yeah, I'll take a cab."

"Get one now," said Freda. "We'll pay him when he gets here. You know your aunt's exact address?"

"I'll tell him, Mom," said Joey.

"Don't waste any time, Joseph. And bring my sleeping pills. Aunt Gloria won't be able to sleep tonight. Don't forget."

"I'll bring 'em, Mom. See you when I get there."

"Wait a minute," said Freda. "Aunt Gloria wants you to try on your cousin's suit for the funeral."

"She just got me one for my birthday. Besides, I don't want to wear something that belonged to him. I never even knew him."

"Don't be disrespectful," said Freda. "She wants you to."

"Well what's wrong with the one she gave me last night?"

"I'm not going to argue with her about it. She's saved everything Paulie ever owned, and now she thinks it's appropriate for you to wear one of his suits."

"But I thought he was a big guy, some jock or something."

"Not *always*. Joey, if she wants this, why are you arguing with me? This is an emotional time for her. I'm not going to make it worse by telling her you're being stubborn."

"All right, Mom, I'll do what she wants. Let me call a cab now."

"Don't waste any more time."

Freda hung up. Joey called a cab and then changed into jeans, tennis shoes, and a T-shirt. He phoned Rachel's number. There was no answer. He didn't want to leave a message so soon after seeing her, as he didn't think it was a good idea to sound so eager this early on in their relationship.

~ TWENTY ~

Cammy spent three hours and a pot of coffee talking to Kenny about Jesus. All he did was get him sober. During that time, Kenny went to the bathroom every half-hour, and Bernice called every hour for Curly. The third time, Kenny said, "You guys having a beef?" Instead of answering, Bernice hung up on him.

At eleven-thirty, Cammy drove to the coffee shop at Hector and Sonoma and got Kenny a tuna salad sandwich. Kenny never drank after meals, and Cammy wanted to make sure he didn't drink again. When Cammy left, Kenny dragged the comatose Earl off his stool and threw him into the second booth like a bag of potatoes. He went through his pockets and took forty dollars for himself. When Cammy returned, he and Kenny sat across from each other in the first booth and Kenny nibbled on the sandwich. But when Cammy read aloud from his bible again, Kenny shouted, "I'm sick of that shit."

"You're being blasphemous," said Cammy.

"And you're a hypocrite. You were *this* close to murdering two people, and now you want to purify the world."

"I never said I'd actually do it, so…"

"*Two* days you'll go back the way you were. I thought you said this was tuna salad. It tastes like snake meat. Watch me get ptomaine poisoning."

"Cynicism's the opposite of faith, Kenny."

"Whatever that means."

"Faith, hope and love are all related," said Cammy.

"Fine. I'll invent a drink called 'Faith, hope and love.' Anybody 'drinks it's gonna get the same charge you get out of Jesus."

"It hurts me to hear you talk like this."

"I *always* talk like this."

"You don't really believe what you're saying."

"No, I like flapping my lips."

"Do you know what I found out before I saw Jesus? I realized all I really wanted was to be loved. I just wanted a woman to love me with her heart and soul. That would have made me the happiest man in the world."

"So now Jesus does all that instead."

"As a matter of fact, that's right."

"But your dick's still going to fall off from lack of use."

"Kenny, fulfillment comes in ways you'd never expect."

"I'll take the old fashion ways."

"You're a lost soul, Kenny."

"Yeah? Ask yourself what you'd be doing right now if you actually *shot* them two."

"I know now that I never could have done that."

"You had the gun," said Kenny. "You were right there."

"I couldn't have done it, I said. Kenny, I know this in my heart."

"Bullshit!"

Cammy raised his voice. "I'm telling you once and for all I could not have done that evil deed. Jesus was in me then, I just didn't know it. He came to me afterward to reward me for not doing it."

"You're trying to tell me if Marty didn't have a heart attack you would've gone in that room and what, dropped your pants?"

"I said I know I could not have gone through with it."

"See, that's why you bible-types make the rest of us sick. You see the light, you got Jesus, instant sainthood, and it's all crap."

"I *was* saved at the last minute."

"The guy had a *heart attack*. If Jesus was there why didn't *He* save Marty's life?"

"Kenny."

"Why didn't *He* give us more customers so we didn't even have to be there in the first place?"

"Kenny."

"Why didn't He clone Rachel for us? Why didn't He stop my old man from hanging himself in the shower with his belt and having my ignorant mother wake me up to help her cut him down when I'm *six fucking years old* and *sound asleep*? What God would do that to a six-year-old kid? What God would even make a stupid woman like my mother in the first place?"

"He sees things, but that doesn't mean—"

"How come He waited *your* whole miserable life to save *your* loser ass *now*? You want me to go on, Cammy? 'Cause I could go on till hell freezes over why I don't buy this shit. No, there is one thing about it I buy, and that's we're on this earth to get tested, but for what I don't know. I don't think we're *supposed* to know till after we keel over."

"Kenny—"

"Let me finish! If we had any *real* answers, what would we need to go on for? What'd He even create us in the first place for? We're no better off than animals. They get killed by predators or die of old age *just like us*. Life and death, that's all it's about, the whole animal kingdom, us included. Tell me why that's all there is."

Cammy started to answer but Kenny cut him off.

"You can't. If I knew I was going to win the Lottery when I'm fifty, why wouldn't I just go live in the streets till then, like Curly? Or, if I knew I was going to die when I'm fifty, why wouldn't I just end it all now? You can't tell me that, 'cause *you don't know*! And there's nothing in that bible of yours that's got any answers either. Just 'cause you *think* you got 'em don't make 'em any more truthful than *mine*. In fact, I'm *smarter* than you and I'm *better* than you 'cause I don't *presume* to have them answers. *But you do!*" Kenny pointed to Earl. "Are you telling me God's smiling on *that* worthless pile of shit over there? And something else. If you're going to spread what Cedar said about Marty and Rachel around, good luck. 'Cause if it gets back to Cedar, he'll kill you. Maybe you *want* to be a martyr. *I* don't. So do all that on your own."

Cammy had been rifling through his bible.

Kenny said, "No! I don't want to hear any more of that."

"Just let me read you something out of Samuel, twenty-two—"

"—I said, I don't want to—"

"—just a little—"

"—I don't *want* to hear it, Cammy. I'm warning you."

"—just two sentences. Listen—"

"—not two *words*. I'm serious here—"

"—no, Kenny, right here it says, 'God is my strong fortress; he has made my way—'"

"—*I'm* my own fortress—"

"—let me finish…'He has made my way safe. He makes—'"

"—I'm gonna smack you, Cammy!"

"—He makes me as surefooted as a deer, leading me safely along the mountain heights.'"

Angry as Kenny was, he could not smack Cammy. Instead, he threw his sandwich on the table, grabbed Cammy's arm, and pulled up until he was forced to stand. "You're eighty-sixed!"

Cammy resisted. "You can't do that. I'm not drunk."

"It's my bar and I can do whatever I want."

"Well forget it!" said Cammy. "I can leave on my own. I know when I'm not wanted."

"Are you *sure*, Cammy? 'Cause I sure hope I didn't *offend* you."

"I just don't know what your problem is."

"You *don't know* what my problem is?" shouted Kenny. "After all that. You know what? If Cedar *did* put a bullet through your head, all you'd do is go 'ouch,' 'cause it wouldn't hit any vital organs."

Cammy headed for the door. "I'm going to pray for your soul."

"Fuck the soul! Pray I win the Lotto!"

~ ~

Curly had walked all over Hillside Park since he left Bernice's house. He was numb from fatigue and the double jolt of her inexplicable testiness and Marty's death. He wanted to collapse and sleep for the night, but something about Kenny's beckoned him. Maybe he wanted to be miserable in the company of Kenny, Mr. Misery himself. Maybe he wanted a Blue Seven. Maybe he wanted to hear from Bernice, who knew to call him there. He drifted into Kenny's a little after midnight. He didn't say hello or acknowledge the ill treatment Kenny had shown him earlier in the day. He sat in his favorite booth. So wrapped up in himself was he that he didn't notice Earl Zell asleep in the second booth.

"'Cat dragged in," muttered Kenny.

"I thought you'd be drunk."

"I was. Cammy stopped by and forced me to drink a couple gallons of coffee. I feel like I took the longest nap in the world and I can't wake up out of it all the way."

"Can I have a Blue Seven?" asked Curly. "You owe me from today anyway."

"It's on the house," said Kenny. He made the drink. "Your sweetheart's been calling every five minutes."

"She's mad at me," said Curly.

Kenny put the drink in front of him. "Probably on the rag. Judy got like that too. Everything's coasting then, pow, right out of nowhere, they show them fangs. Nothing you can say works anyway so you might as well get out."

Curly sipped his Blue Seven. It was refreshing as always, but it didn't transport him. "That's about how it was," he said. "Just how you just said. I guess she was kind of that way the other night, but not this bad. What'd you tell her?"

"I said you weren't here," said Kenny. "She'll probably call again 'fore the night's over. You want to talk to her? Tell me now."

"Should I?"

"Nah, make her work for it. Let her worry. Let her think you got run over by a garbage truck somewhere."

"I guess," said Curly. He sipped his drink again, then heard a grunt from Earl. He turned around and saw him slumped over the next booth. "Hey, what's Earl doing in here?"

"Cammy closed up, so he didn't have nowhere else to go," said Kenny.

"Cammy closed up his bar?" said Curly. "What for?"

"He's nuts, why else?"

"Just tonight or for good?"

"I don't know, he's into Jesus now," said Kenny. "Got the cure. Thing is, if he's serious I get more business, and that means more work if you want it. I can pay you regular sort of, so much a week."

"I think my time's up here," said Curly.

"Cause of your girlfriend? She'll come crawling back, they always do."

"Judy didn't," said Curly.

"Any day Judy she could walk through that door. That's the thing, they're unpredictable."

Curly was whispering. "I really thought she didn't want me over there at all today, like I was some leech or something."

"What happened? D'you take a dump on her carpet?"

"I just went up 'cause I was sad about Marty," said Curly. "I think maybe she wanted me to call first."

"Bullshit," said Kenny. "The way she calls all excited and cooks up a feast? I'm no Romeo, but even I could see that."

"I guess."

"And what's with Marty?" said Kenny. "He wouldn't even let you through his frigging door."

"Yeah, I tried a couple times. He said get some deodorant."

Earl sputtered awake and pulled himself into a sitting position with his legs over the side of the seat and his big square head hanging in his lap. "Where am I?" he said.

Kenny thought he'd have fun. "Marge is waiting for you, Earl! Better hurry up, she's mad."

"Yeah, yeah," said Earl with sudden panic. He scrambled to his feet. "I'm coming. Just tell her wait, I'll be right there." Earl walked to the door as if he could tilt over with each step.

"I'll tell her," said Kenny.

"Yeah, thanks," said Earl as he opened the door. "Good seeing you again." Earl lost his balance but recovered before falling down.

Kenny said, "Another graduate of the William Holden School of Equilibrium."

Though Curly didn't take his reference, he showed concern for Earl. "His wife's not going to be there till two o'clock, Kenny. How come you did that?"

"The fresh air will do him good. 'Sides, if he barfed in here, I'd have to kill him."

The phone rang.

"You want to talk to her or not?" said Kenny.

Curly showed indecision. The phone rang again.

"What's it going to be?" said Kenny.

"I don't know. Should I or not?"

Kenny picked up the receiver. "Kenny's? No, he's not. No, he didn't. I don't know. Hey, it's not like he's got a ball and chain around his ass, y'know." He listened for one second, then hung up and looked at Curly. "That is *not* a happy girl."

"Why, what'd she say?"

"Forget it. Give it a day or so, then go on back up there. She'll probably drop right to her knees and give you a big-league Lewinsky."

Curly didn't like that kind of talk about Bernice. He ignored the comment and sipped his Blue Seven.

~ ~

Joey's cab ride to Glendale made him anxious. He feared having to lie to his mother and aunt about the day's events. He knew he couldn't lie anyway. Marty used to tell him at Sunday dinners that lies never got you anywhere except deeper in the hole you were digging, and that most people would just as soon stand back and watch you bury yourself than confront you. This did not draw charges of hypocrisy from Gloria or Freda because Marty never denied his relationship with Rachel; he just wasn't vocal about it.

Another thing Marty said when he got Joey alone: "Honesty's the best policy, but full disclosure's not always the best way to go." Joey didn't get it. Marty explained. "If somebody's trying to get inside your head and you don't want them there, you can fudge. You have that right. This is America."

Joey thought he could answer all questions his mother and aunt asked about the day, except specific ones about Rachel. He did not need to say he saw her breasts. He didn't need to mention the alarm key, the money Uncle Marty stashed away for her, that Rachel shot Cedar, or that Cedar nearly strangled him to death. Everything else was okay. Once he reached this mindset, he was able to think about Rachel. He was a dreamer anyway. Most of his youth was spent fantasizing. At any given time, four big fantasies swirled in his head.

1) What would happen if his mother were rich?

2) What if she lost seventy pounds and got facial reconstruction and met a cool guy he could hang out with?

3) What if the head cheerleader showed up outside his window and begged him to let her in so he could rescue her from the rotten guys at school that kept hitting on her like she was a piece of meat?

4) What if the Big One hit and everything west of his house fell into the ocean and he ended up with beachfront property, and then bikini-clad goddesses asked him for a spot in front of his house to sunbathe on and would he put lotion all over their bodies?

Joey was still entertaining fantasies right up to that day, when Rachel ran to him in Uncle Marty's car and inadvertently revealed her naked breasts. But since then, he had resolved that wealth, step-dads, cheerleaders and sunbathing beauties could go to hell. He'd met his own fantasy, and he was going to see her again soon.

His daydreaming had caused disruptions in his life anyway. He'd gotten summer jobs from which he was fired for not concentrating. He flunked classes for the same reason. Conversation and other social situations were hard for him. Freda eventually had to send him to therapy to see if he had a mental disorder. The therapist she'd chosen, Dr. Holly Knox, who had an office on Brand Boulevard in Glendale, was an attractive and wise woman in her fifties. Joey liked how she carried herself. She had an elegance that women in Hillside Park didn't. She wore tasteful dresses, nice jewelry, and just enough makeup to highlight her probing but non-threatening eyes.

Holly always sat on a straight-backed, armless chair with her hands folded in her lap and her eyes fixed on Joey's. Her questions came from a genuine curiosity about him, rather than the process of therapy. He felt this because she never showed a hint of boredom when he spoke. She made him feel important. Another thing about Holly that Joey never forgot: when she sat, her crossed legs always faced him. They had a nice shape but, like Holly herself, weren't what he considered hot. She was like Aunt Gloria. Joey always thought Aunt Gloria must have been a babe when Uncle Marty married her. Back then, when Joey was seeing Holly, his definition of "hot" meant wanting the girl in question to get naked. That wasn't what he had in mind for Holly. What he liked about her and Aunt Gloria was their easy way of making him say things he thought should be private, things no one else, his mother included, could get out of him. Their caring eyes and soothing voices melted his defenses.

Joey fell in love with Holly but never acted on it. He never even told her. He thought she knew anyway, probably because he mentioned how much she reminded him of Aunt Gloria, whom he had identified as a woman he wished his mother had been like.

One day, after Joey revealed a secret, Holly called Freda to say that a personal crisis had entered her life and that she would have to refer her newer patients, including Joey, to another therapist. When Freda told Joey he couldn't see Holly again, he was sad but, on the other hand, he didn't feel he had much more to say to her. In a way, Holly was like the secret he had revealed to her.

The secret Joey revealed was that from his earliest memories, he always daydreamed. Holly had said, "Dreamers may become great thinkers, writers, artists and such. But there's always danger of blurring the line between reality and fantasy."

When Joey responded that he *still* didn't think there was anything wrong with daydreaming, Holly smiled bemusedly. While some of his comments were peculiar, and most reflected his immaturity, he nonetheless had an irresistible charm, one aspect of which, thought Holly, was an utter lack of vanity for a young man with such an infectious warmth. Holly wanted to tell him how adorable he was, and that if he played his cards right he could have girls in the palm of his hands when he got older. But she feared that the opposite would happen, that if she told him he might get conceited and vain.

His daydreaming started as an escape from his mother's insufferable whining at the breakfast table when he was little. Freda would go on and on about her lousy salary, her students' laziness, their uncaring parents, the school's wimpy administrators, the disastrous lack of funding from a miserly Republican governor, and everything else about public education except its health and vacation benefits. Then she'd rant about life *outside* teaching, which included every topic known to mankind. She never asked Joey what he thought and she never stopped talking except to put food in her mouth, and even then she could still spew venom.

Through it all, Joey was forced to sit there and listen. One thing that distracted him, however, was a tall jar of honey his mother kept on the table before she cut sugar from her diet. She'd used it in herbal tea at each meal.

The way some kids read cereal boxes at breakfast, Joey studied the honey's movements. He would turn the jar upside down. From the bottom would rise a round shiny golden bubble as wide as the jar. He marveled at its unspoiled shape and how it dissolved against the top of the closed container with the same slow perfection with which it formed at the bottom. Sometimes it took seven or eight seconds to reach the top. Other times, when the kitchen was warmer, it took half that time. But through its journey, Joey imagined a fantasy world inside that bubble.

Nobody else could claim that bubble. Nobody else had the imagination to think of a world inside it. The instant the bubble formed, Joey's world took shape. If he were a king inside it, he would be a great king, and his queen would be the most beautiful anywhere. If he were a slave inside it, he would lead the other slaves to freedom, and his reward would be the pretty water girl. If the bubble housed a coliseum, Joey would get the greatest cheers. Holly had asked Joey if he'd ever felt bad that the worlds he created in the bubbles ended so quickly after he created them. He said no, that when he turned the jar over again he was blessed with yet another opportunity to create yet another world in which he got to be a hero.

"Joey," said Holly. "Can you stand back from those breakfasts and see another little boy watching the bubbles?"

"I guess."

"Let's call him Tommy."

"Okay."

"What do you feel when you see Tommy staring at these bubbles while the whole world around him sort of passes by?"

Joey didn't know how to answer.

"Is Tommy a lonely child?" said Holly.

Joey got instant tears.

"It's okay," said Holly. "Is Tommy a lonely child?"

"I guess," said Joey.

"But he enjoys these worlds in the bubbles."

"Yeah."

"When breakfast ends, is he sad he can't create more worlds?"

"No," said Joey.

"Why not?"

"'Cause it's time to go to school."

"He's not disappointed his fantasies end so fast?"

"No," said Joey. "He can just do another one."

"See, Joey, that's what I'm having trouble with," said Holly. "One of the neat things about fantasies is you get to set your own rules. You can alter physics, you can go anywhere, you can do anything you want. So why would Tommy create a whole world in which he can do heroic things when that world vanishes seconds later?"

"'Cause the bubble vanishes seconds later," said Joey.

"Perhaps Tommy believes nothing good lasts forever."

"Well not me," said Joey.

"We were talking about Tommy."

This made Joey think.

"Joey, have you ever heard the expression, 'burst your bubble?'"

"Yeah, sure."

"What does that mean to you? You, not Tommy."

Joey shrugged. "Nothing."

"Why not?"

"'Cause mine didn't burst," said Joey.

"What happened to them?"

"They just sort of went away. I had to turn the jar over to get a new one. They smoothed out, real slow, no ripples or anything."

Holly opened her arms as if illustrating a mushrooming cloud. "But Joey, they're fantasies. They don't *have* to end until you *want* them to. You ended them before they could expand into something really wonderful."

"The *jar* did."

"You *let* it end."

"No I didn't, I said. The jar did."

"The bubble in the jar stimulated your imagination. But when the bubble squished or dissolved, or whatever you call it, your imagination ended too. Why, Joey?"

"It just did, I don't know."

"You just said the jar made it end. The physical limitations of the jar ended your imagination. But imagination knows no boundary."

Joey was fidgety.

"Is it possible you didn't *know* how to enjoy fantasies?"

Joey didn't answer.

"And therefore you *welcomed* a quick end to them?"

Joey didn't answer.

"An end you could have controlled if you'd wanted to?"

"I don't know," said Joey.

"I think you know you're *afraid* to enjoy *any*thing for very long."

Joey started to cry.

"You don't feel entitled to enjoy anything for very long so you allowed yourself a limited indulgence, in this case the brevity of the life of the honey bubble."

Joey fought back tears.

"Perhaps these honey bubbles represented limitations you put on yourself, not on the bubbles. Limitations based on fear."

Joey turned away.

Holly's voice was gently imploring. "Why don't you feel entitled to enjoy what other kids your age feel? Are you afraid someone is going to take it away or tell you to stop?"

Unable to contain his emotions, Joey left his chair and moved to Holly with his arms open. She rose with her arms open, too. They hugged for a long time, during which Joey cried on her shoulder. It was the first time they'd had physical contact.

As the cab wound its way to the hillside home of Joey's aunt, he recalled that final day with Holly some three years earlier. He wondered if something he did during the embrace made her terminate their therapy instead of the personal crisis Holly had cited to his mother as the cause. Here was a woman in his arms he admired for her intelligence, grace, professional accomplishments and concern for his emotional health, and she was hugging him back, and their cheeks touched, and he could smell her perfume, and his lips were next to her ear, and if he wanted to he could whisper right into it, and her hair tickled the back of his neck.

The sensation was brand new to Joey. This was a *woman*, a doctor, in an industrial complex in the best part of Glendale. And here was Joey Bagliamente of Hillside Park, where no building was over two stories, holding *her* in *his* arms. And the strange thing was, Holly did not try to dislodge from him. He felt flattered and needed. He knew if therapists got seriously involved with their patients they could get sued. Yet here she was, hugging him two, three minutes, with nary a word spoken.

Later, when Joey thought about that moment with Holly, he took pleasure in imagining that she was succumbing to him, that his lips on her neck had weakened her. But he could never be sure. Maybe her legs were just getting tired.

When Joey and Holly separated from their hug, they locked eyes for fifteen seconds, then she took his hand. "You're entitled to happiness, Joey. Just go get it. Don't let anyone or anything, especially your own fears, keep you from it." She walked to the door and said, "Time's up for now." Then she smiled as if acknowledging that a breakthrough had happened. Joey would never know if it was in his therapy or something personal between them. He stood there looking into her eyes, then walked out and never saw her again.

As Joey's memory of that last day with Holly ended, the cab turned off of Chevy Chase Drive and headed for Aunt Gloria's house. Joey prepared himself to meet what was left of his grieving family.

~ TWENTY-ONE ~

Cedar hopped to his Cherokee and sat gingerly in the driver's seat. He drove to Rachel's and stopped in front. Her car was not there, nor were lights on in the house. He took a gun from under his seat, a nine-millimeter Browning, and went to the front door. It was unlocked, just as he'd left it. He went inside and determined that Rachel had not been home since he was there earlier. The mess he'd made looking for keys was untouched. An answering machine in her bedroom flashed five messages. Cedar played them.

One was from Bernice; she'd heard about Marty, offered condolences, and asked Rachel to call to talk about it.

The next message was from Gino, who had detailed the status of the club upon its closing and had asked Rachel to stop by and set the alarm. He had added that cash from the three registers, totaling five hundred and thirty-four dollars, was in Marty's hallway office.

The next was Bernice again, this one urging Rachel to call, as she'd had a terrible misunderstanding with Curly, who'd fled in a fit, a first for them.

The next was a wrong number from a girl to her mother saying she'd left a message on some other number but was leaving one on this machine too, just in case. She'd scheduled a flight and would be coming into LAX on Thursday at such and such time and such and such flight number on United.

The last was from Bernice, who, more distraught than the last time, begged Rachel to call when she got in, regardless of the time.

Cedar rewound the messages then drove to Freda's house. No cars were in front. He parked half a block away and waited. All houses within sight were dark. An hour later, Freda pulled into the driveway with Joey. They entered the house as if part of a death procession. He carried garment bags over his shoulder.

Where was Rachel? wondered Cedar. He knew that she and Bernice were friends, but, from Bernice's phone messages, that Rachel was not with her. He wasn't about to check motels, and he couldn't think of anywhere else Rachel might be. He drove to Marty's to see if Helen had seen anything. When he arrived, she got to her feet slowly to compensate for tightness in her legs and back. Dirt and gravel stuck to her pants. She showed concern that Cedar was not convalescing at home.

"I've got things to do," he said. "Have you seen anyone at that door?"

"I yess see alotta peebles in their cars," said Helen. "They dun' stop, they have yess kep' on goeen."

"All right," said Cedar. "I'm going back. I'll pick you up in the morning. Do you want something to eat?"

Helen nodded. Cedar said he'd bring back food. He drove to Cammy's. As soon as he turned onto Hector Street, he looked to where it veered south toward downtown, about a mile and a quarter way. In between, nothing moved. No cars, no pedestrians, no stray animals. Traffic signals tapered into the horizon like runway lights. Everything he passed by was either dull black or bright and electrical. Traveling through this tableau reminded him of his high school years, when he and his pals cruised the street. It was just as lifeless back then, he thought.

There, up ahead, he saw a figure in front of Cammy's, a large man with his hands in his pockets and hunched over as if chilled by frost, when in fact the night was warm. It was Earl Zell. Earl stood erect when he saw Cedar pull up and stop. Cedar yelled through the passenger window, "What are you doing, Earl?"

"'That you, Cedar?"

"What are you doing outside?"

"Waiting for Marge." Earl nodded behind him. "Place is closed."

"What do you mean it's closed?"

"Door's locked. Marge don't get off work till two, so I'm waiting."

"How long's it been closed?"

"This afternoon," said Earl. "I got eighty-sixed."

"Cammy eighty-sixed *you?*"

"No. Leon, his back-up. I haven't seen Cammy since last night."

Cedar couldn't figure this out. Without saying another word to Earl, he drove to Kenny's. He parked in front and walked awkwardly into the bar. His one-legged, teetering transit put beads of sweat on his forehead. They made him feel dirty, as if the vodka and cough syrup were toxins weakening a temple of purity.

Kenny froze when he saw Cedar enter. Cedar approached the bar without a look of greeting or need. Though his face showed the discomfort of walking with a crutch, he could have been hobbling from his front door to pick up the morning newspaper. "What the hell are *you* doing here?" said Kenny.

Curly was surprised, too. Why would Cedar deign to come to Kenny's? he asked himself. "Hey, Cedar," he said. "Long time no see."

Cedar didn't answer. Curly shrugged and turned back to his Blue Seven. Cedar moved behind Curly, vise-gripped his chin with one hand and the back of his head with the other, then jerked the head in a three-quarter turn until Curly's eyes faced the rear of the bar and his shoulders had barely moved. The maneuver forced Cedar to put weight on his bad leg for an instant, and he winced. Meanwhile, Curly went limp instantly. When Cedar let go of him, Curly fell into a lifeless heap on the floor.

"*Jesus Christ, man!*" screamed Kenny. "*What'd you do that for? He was harmless. What the fuck d'you do it for, man?*"

Cedar went around the bar, whirled Kenny around by his shirt, and pushed him until the back of his head lay on the bar. "That was for you," he said. "Now sit down and have a cigarette."

Cedar let him go. Kenny, white-faced and gasping, tried to catch his breath, but Curly's death had terrorized him. He moved from behind the bar, in the process holding onto it like a side rail on a capsizing ship. He was unable to look at Curly, then was unable not to. Curly had landed sideways with his arms and legs in front of him. His Blue Seven fell along with him and soaked his shirt. The empty glass, still intact, lay by his back with its two straws still inside.

Kenny sat on the stool closest to Cedar and reached for a cigarette. His fingers shook too much to extract one from the package, so Cedar did it for him. Kenny took a lighter from his pocket but couldn't flick the friction wheel. Cedar did that for him, too. Kenny took a long drag and exhaled. He felt the harsh smoke, but his nerves still rattled like tracks under a train.

"I'm launching a new offensive," said Cedar. He said it calmly, they way you'd say you're thinking of ordering banking checks with a new design on them.

Kenny studied Cedar's now-calm exterior, then said with a strained voice: "You said after Marty and Rachel you'd be gone."

"That went bust. I'm still getting out of here, but I may need to return periodically. When I do, you'll be my contact. For that you can't be doing time. And with Curly still alive, you'd be doing time."

"So you killed him for me. I feel blessed. What new offensive?"

"It's a job for you and Cammy. I don't know where he is, his bar's closed."

"We lost him," said Kenny.

"What do you mean by that?"

"After we left Dom's, when he got in his car, he saw Jesus outside his window. 'Ask me, he's a goner."

Cedar processed this information. "Just as well. He's soft. So you'll recruit Dominick instead. Do it tonight. I don't want to talk to him. He makes me nauseous."

"How come you're limping?" asked Kenny.

Cedar hated the question's impertinence. "Bunionectomy," he said. "You and Dom are going to guard Marty's while I tie up some loose ends inside. This is tomorrow night. I want you both packing."

"Guard it from what?" asked Kenny.

"Somebody else interested in tying up the loose ends."

"Who're you going to kill after that?"

"Curly knew about the plan."

"How'd *that* happen?"

"Your big mouth in Dom's parking lot the other night. He was sleeping there."

"Jesus. How'd *you* find out?"

"He told Bernice Horl and she told Rachel. Rachel called me to look into it."

"When was all this?" said Kenny.

"Sunday. I never got back to her."

"'You going to kill them too?" said Kenny.

"Don't have to. Curly's dead. You can't convict on hearsay."

"Well, Mr. Foresight," said Kenny. "I'm impressed."

"I want you and Dom at my house tomorrow night at eight-thirty sharp," said Cedar. "You know where I live?"

"Two houses off Colorado on that street near the donut shop," said Kenny. "White with green trim?"

Cedar nodded. "If you're not there on time or somebody else shows up, don't ever let me see you again."

"What the hell am I supposed to do with Curly?" said Kenny.

"Figure it out," said Cedar. "The homeless die all the time."

"Look, I've got to know what loose ends you're talking about. I got *nothing* out of today. I'm right back where I was before we even talked about it. We didn't even get that check-cashing money."

"Whose fault is that?" said Cedar.

"She had a gun on us."

"You're going to blame a woman?"

"She had a gun on us, I said."

"You're going to blame a woman and a skinny little kid?"

"Cedar, she had a gun on us."

"A woman and a little kid out-smarted you and Cammy. Is that the story you're going with?"

"She had a gun!"

"So did you," said Cedar. "That made you even. So now you're left with a skinny little kid. Is that the story you're going with?"

"What're you, Johnny Cochran?"

"You coughed up that hundred grand. Are you blaming Marty's nephew for that?"

"What do you want out of me, Cedar? I'm telling you what happened. Her and that kid had us by the balls."

"Let me tell you about that kid. His old man took his mother's cherry one night, and when he found out what a nightmare she was, he went and joined a flaky little circus doing a two-day stint over by the Santa Monica Pier. Next day he slipped on elephant feces and got impaled in the neck by the ringleader's baton. He died with runny feces on his face and a hole in his throat. That's the kind of brains that kid inherited, and *he* out-smarted you and Cammy. Now tell me again that's the story you're going with."

Kenny avoided Cedar's imposing stare and didn't speak.

"That's what I thought," said Cedar.

"Did you expect us to shoot it out with Rachel right there in the open like Dodge City, for God's sake?"

"I expected you to do what was necessary."

"*Cammy* had the gun," said Kenny.

"I told *you* to take it."

"Well I didn't have it then. Maybe you know where there's a time machine so we can go back and do it again different."

"All right, drop it."

"I was ready to, then *this*," said Kenny. "Christ, I still can't believe you killed Curly like that, right in front of me."

"Don't bring it up again," said Cedar. "Some things have to be done. Now listen. I can get that money back for you."

Kenny brightened. "The hundred grand?"

Cedar nodded. "If you do your job like I know you can."

"Your dirty work, you mean."

"Socrates said, 'Be of good hope in the face of danger.'" The actual quote said "death," not "danger," but Cedar didn't think the literal quote reflected good salesmanship.

"Dom will say he's blind," said Kenny.

"He can guard a door," said Cedar.

"So can a dog. You know that stubborn bastard."

Cedar straightened up and prepared to leave. "Show up with Dom and do this one last thing."

"How do I know I'll get that hundred if we do?"

"Gino told me he put it in a bag under Marty's desk. Would I tell you that if I didn't think I could get it for you?"

It sounded workable to Kenny. "Why don't *you* want it?"

"Just be there," said Cedar. He hobbled to the front door, turned and indicated Curly. "Get rid of him."

"No, I think I'll keep him there for a conversation piece."

"Put him behind Nick's Hardware," said Cedar. "Run over him. It'll look like he went to sleep too far out from the building."

"You want *me* to do that?" said Kenny.

"I snapped the C-3 vertebrae in his upper spinal cord. His brain suffocated from paralysis of the respiratory muscles near the fracture. That's going to be the official cause of death. They're not going to look for who did it because homeless drunks always put themselves in harm's way when they crash. Do it before anyone comes in."

Cedar left. It was a quarter to one. Kenny looked at Curly. "Poor bastard," he said. "What do I do with you?"

The phone rang. Kenny knew who it was. "Kenny's," he said.

It was Bernice. Her voice was shaky. "Did Curly ever come in?"

"No," said Kenny, then hung up. He dragged Curly by his feet into the back room and out the rear door to his thirteen-year-old Nova, whose odometer had turned over twice and whose trunk, roof and hood were rusted. He put Curly in the trunk and closed the lid. "I can't cry for you, pal," he said. "You're doing better than the rest of us now. But I will say 'so long.'"

No one came into Kenny's the rest of the night. At ten minutes to two, Kenny locked up and drove to the alley behind Nick's. It had thick, high hedges on the other side so residents south of the alley didn't have to see all the traffic coming and going. Kenny stopped at the alley's entrance, tossed the cigarette he was smoking out the window, then lit another to help him through the task ahead. He turned off his headlights and drove toward the parking lot behind Nick's. When he was almost there, he cut off his engine and coasted the rest of the way with his headlights off.

Nick's had two dumpsters against the south wall of the building and an open space between them where Curly often slept. The dumpsters always contained collapsed cardboard that he'd used for bedding. The owner, Nick Foto, didn't mind that Curly slept there occasionally. If anything, his presence could deter vandals.

When Kenny got to the open space, he touched his brakes to stop the car. His taillights cast a red glow on the wall, dumpsters, and hedges. He kept the driver's door open, popped up the trunk lid and put Curly's body on the ground so that his head was in the middle of the alley. He returned to his car and pushed it forward. When he came to the end of the alley, he jumped in, started the motor, and turned on his headlights.

He was sure he'd made no noise. He drove around the block and returned to the alley's entrance. This time he ran over the body. He felt Curly's head under both left wheels.

"Yuck," he said to himself. He kept on going, turned onto Hector Street, and drove to Dom's. Dom never closed before two, so Kenny knew he had time to get there and tell him what had happened.

~ ~

Cedar refused to patronize the coffee shop at Sonoma and Hector Streets. Its food was inedible, and even though it was not for him, he wanted something tasty and filling for Helen. The closest all-night coffee shop that served decent food was where the Pasadena Freeway turned into Orange Grove Boulevard. It took half an hour to get there, go inside, order take-out, and get back to Helen. Her reaction upon seeing the cheeseburger, fries, Coke and apple pie was worth the extra effort to Cedar. He went home and tried to get some recuperative sleep. But he couldn't sleep. He got out of bed and thought about what to pack for his new life in the wilderness. He went to his beloved books and sat by them on the floor. They were still in boxes waiting to be put back in the bookcases after the bolting job he and Helen started earlier was finished. The job was a ruse, of course, but its half-completed state symbolized his efforts to get out of Hillside Park.

If Marty and Rachel had been killed, Cedar would have obtained the alarm key from Marty's effects at the death scene, gotten into the Kitchen, found the cash, and been gone forever. But that was "if," and he did not like to dwell in what might have happened, unless it involved Rachel. *She* occupied his mind every time her name came up. And now, even after she'd shot him, he still had lust for her. He didn't know if he could ever get her out of his mind. No, maybe there was a way. If they both grew old in Hillside Park and he saw her getting white-haired, shriveled, shapeless and slow, maybe he'd lose interest. But even that might not do it, he had to confess. More than her beauty and sexuality, her intelligence and passion put her levels above other women.

Cedar went through his books to choose which ones to take. He'd read them all, but his Cherokee would not hold them all. He decided to take Shakespeare's complete works, six biographies of Thomas Jefferson, and the Federalist Papers. As he thumbed through the Shakespeare book, he asked himself, "Am I like Hamlet? Deceiving myself and others?"

He closed the book, lay down and asked himself whether he was crazy or just determined. Let's do a Q&A session, he thought.

Q) If I get that million dollars then go live alone in the middle of nowhere, what good will the money do me?

A) Some day I'll leave the middle of nowhere, and I'll need the cash.

Q) Am I running from something or running to something?

A) I've never run from anything or anyone in my life. My time here is spent. New challenges await me. Therefore, I am running to something.

Q) Will I miss human contact?

A) I have very little now, and it does not enrich my life one iota. The answer, therefore, is no.

Q) Am I secretly hoping someone will stop me and make me see what I don't see right in front of me?

A) The one individual capable of that is Rachel Ellis, and she's made herself my enemy.

Q) What if I removed the door to the Kitchen, found the money, and just *gave* it to Rachel?

"Damn," he said aloud. "Every question involves her." He caught another whiff of his neighbor's jasmine. It was a pure fragrance. Nature is pure, he thought. It is all that is pure. Mankind is a scourge on nature. Mankind is evil. I am a part of mankind. I therefore will retire to nature at its most bountiful and let its purity cleanse me. Nature will determine if I am crazy. It is bigger than Rachel. It is even bigger than Slapper. To survive in nature at its most bountiful is therefore the greatest challenge of all. And I, as a man of character, must accept that challenge.

~ ~

Kenny pulled into Dom's empty parking lot the same time another car did. He knew the driver, Red Kennedy, a skilled craftsman and degenerate drunk in his sixties with no teeth and a beer gut the size of a TV. When he didn't have the shakes, Red did respectable tile work all over Hillside Park. He used to be a regular at Kenny's until he was evicted from the apartment he rented on the other end of Hector

Street. Now he lived around the corner from Dom's. Kenny didn't hold it against Red that he stopped patronizing him in favor of The Sonoma Inn. He was a good tipper when he did come into Kenny's. Kenny called to him. "Hey Red."

"How's it going, Kenny?" said Red.

"Can't complain," said Kenny. "You taking Dom home?'

"Yeah, he called me a little while ago."

"Well I'll do it. Him and me need to talk."

Red shrugged okay and then drove off. Kenny went into Dom's. He found him finishing up paperwork spread out across his bar. Dom looked up and saw a figure. "Is that you, Red?"

"It's Kenny. We've got to talk."

"I told you to stay away from me," said Dom.

"Something came up," said Kenny. His tone was non-combative, so Dom didn't push it. "Bad news. Our fire-breathing friend said we're back in business, you and me."

"What are you talking about?" said Dom.

"Cedar's got a job for us."

"Cedar can fuck himself."

"Think so? He just killed Curly Peetz, just like that, right in front of me."

"What'd you say?"

"Curly's sitting there, Cedar comes in, snaps his neck like a pretzel. Left it up to me to get rid of the body."

"What do you mean he killed Curly?"

"What part of that don't you get? Guy takes them big hands of his and snaps Curly's neck right off. Curly didn't stand a chance. Dead 'fore he even hits the floor."

"Holy Jesus."

"And I have no doubt he will come in here and do you too if you tell him 'take a hike. You got kids, Dom. You got grandkids. Want 'em burying you? Your wife crying over your casket? This place going to some towel-head? Do *not* say no to this guy. Dom, he didn't even flinch, just goes from killing Curly to telling me what he wants out of us, like breaking that bastard's neck's no different than pulling out a stool. That's a psychopath, man. That's the definition of one."

Dom glared at Kenny. "Cedar *murdered* Curly tonight?"

"Am I talking to you or Cammy? Go look if you don't believe me. I just dumped him off behind Nick's so's it looks like he got run over by accident. What the hell else was I supposed to do? He left that smelly bastard right there on my floor. Can you imagine if a customer came in just then?"

"Christ," said Dom. "I knew that kid thirty years. He knew this town like the back of his hand. Used to raise all kinds of hell. D'you ever know his aunt?"

"Before my time."

"Cora Wiley," said Dom. "Worked for Sam Cooper till he fired her. She'd sleep with anybody, male or female, anywhere, anytime. Loud, foul mouth. Her kid got killed in Vietnam. She changed her hair color every ten minutes, red, green, purple. A lot of these guys here lost their virginity on her. She drank White Russians. One night she climbed on one of the tables out there, dances naked, everybody's whooping and hollering—some night, I'll tell you that."

"A slob like her?" asked Kenny.

"This was *way* back," said Dom. "She started off a looker, nice body, kind of like Rachel, only shorter."

"D'you nail her?" asked Kenny.

"We all did. Then some jailbird biker she was shacking up with knocked out all her teeth. After that's when she went to the dogs. Hung around another ten, fifteen years. Somebody said she hit the skids. Nobody saw her again."

"Let's move off memory lane," said Kenny. "What about now?"

"What's Cedar want?"

"He's got something to do in Marty's tomorrow night. He wants us guarding outside. When he's done it's 'so long Hillside Park.'"

"Guarding for what?" said Dom.

"You think he's going to tell *me*? All's I know's we're supposed to be at his house eight-thirty sharp and packing."

"How long's it supposed to take?" said Dom.

"He didn't say."

"Why me? Who knocked shit-for-brains out of the loop?" asked Dom.

"Oh, forget *him*. He had a vision of Jesus, says he's through with his bar. He closed his doors in the middle of the day."

"How come only morons get to see Jesus?" said Dom. "I've been a good Catholic all my life, I never saw Jesus." He shook his head. "What a waste, that guy."

"Cammy?"

"No, Jesus."

Kenny felt the sting of Dom's sarcasm. Dom didn't regret his jab, but he also didn't want Kenny to stew long enough to turn sarcastic himself. "I wouldn't be surprised if he never got laid…ever."

"No question about it," said Kenny. He needed to defend himself against the same charge. "Speaking of that, I nailed this nurse the other night, just like that, ba-*doop*. Comes in, instant chemistry."

"No."

"Oh yeah, needs a place to wait till Triple-A comes for her car."

"Good-looking?"

Kenny made an "iffy" sign with his hand. "Right there on my pool table. It was great, man. No strings attached, nothing."

"Well a man needs to dip his wick once in a while, that's for sure. Anyway, there's something's wrong here. Why's Cedar need us outside? It's got to be money. The safe maybe?"

"Why not? He blows the safe, grabs the cash, he says 'thanks fellas,' and the game's over. You see it any different?"

"Yeah, I see it different," said Dom. "He blows the safe, he grabs the cash, he splits, then Gino finds out what happened and *we* get locked up. *That's* what he wants—*us* holding the bag."

"He doesn't have to know where we're at, Dom. We can drive around or something. Hide out, something like that."

Dom got an idea. "Did he say anything like this to you and Cammy before today?"

"Nope."

"So whatever Cedar wanted after Marty and Rachel got whacked he can't get now, right?"

"Right."

"'Cause Rachel's still alive."

"Yeah. That must mean *she* can get in."

"So why doesn't he go after *her*? What's *she* want that *he* wants inside that club?"

"It's got to be dough," said Kenny.

Dom paused a moment. "Two people Marty had closest to him, his body-guard and his mistress. Now they're scrapping over what's left. The maggots. If I didn't hate that dead bastard, I could almost feel sorry for him."

"That's some legacy," said Kenny.

"Did he say anything about the check-cashing money?"

"Nothing," said Kenny. "I get the impression that's a sayonara. Me and Cammy heard Rachel tell that nephew to turn it over to the missus. It's hers now, the club's hers now, everything. Hey, you got any of that soup left?"

"It's cold now," said Dom.

"Can I take some home?"

"Go ahead," said Dom. He indicated a kitchen entryway behind him. "There's paper containers back there."

Kenny headed in that direction. "I didn't think I could eat after what happened to Curly, but that soup's too good to pass up."

Dom gathered his paperwork. Kenny shouted from the kitchen. "'Least *you* can get away. I don't have anybody to cover for me anymore. Hey, even cold this ain't half-bad."

~ ~

The walls of Joey's bedroom were covered with unframed opera posters. He had classical CD's stacked on the floor, atop his dresser, and in his closet. A queen-size bed, flush against one wall, was his only piece of furniture. Against the other wall stood a four-tier bookshelf he'd made of long boards on three rows of cinderblocks. A computer, printer, speakers, TV, and CD player occupied the top shelf. Hardcover cookbooks sandwiched a VCR on the next. The second tier had all CD's on it, and the bottom shelf was filled with videos, an aquarium, and junk. His phone was on the floor.

Rachel called at eight o'clock the next morning. Joey was asleep. On the first ring, he scrambled to pick up the receiver. He cleared his throat before speaking. "'Morning, Rachel," he said with sudden spryness.

"How'd you know it was me?" she said.

"'Cause of a Chinese saying this therapist I had told me once. Do you want to hear it?"

"Go ahead."

Joey affected an accent. "'When the student is ready, the teacher will come.'"

"Don't start making plans with me, Joey. You're going to be disappointed."

"No *way*. Let me pinch myself." He feigned a pinch. "Ouch. No, I'm talking to the most beautiful babe in the world."

"What have you heard about the funeral?"

"It's on Thursday. There's a mass, too. My uncle's at Harper's. Where are you calling from?"

"Do you want to meet today?"

"Absolutely," said Joey.

"My place, eight tonight. We'll go eat."

"No, I want to cook," said Joey. "Can't we come over here? My mom's out Tuesday nights."

"Sure, whatever," said Rachel. "I'll see you then."

"Wait, *wait!*" said Joey. "What's the hurry? Can't we talk? And how come we have to wait till tonight?"

"What do you want to talk about, the history of England? I'm busy."

Joey was offended by her entire tone. "What's the matter?"

"I spent all night crying, that's what. There's only one way to grieve, I don't care what they say. Talking about it, medication, keeping busy— none of that works. You have to cry and cry hard until you can't cry any- more, and that's what I did, and I'm exhausted and I've got lots of stuff to do. Does that answer your question?"

"Sorry."

"See you tonight, Joey."

"Wait, will you?" said Joey. "Will you please *wait?*"

"*Now* what?"

Joey got whiny. "You don't sound like you want to do this."

"What do you want from me, Joey? I'm too tired for handstands."

"I'm just saying it doesn't sound like you really want to."

"I suffered a big loss yesterday, Joey. You might think about that a little. Do you have a heart or just a penis?"

"Guess you're right," said Joey. "But promise about tonight?"

"I'll be there," she said. "I'll need to shower before we go out anyway, so I've got to be there. You want me to write it in blood?"

"Can you say it like you really mean it?"

Rachel scoffed. "You're *nothing* like Marty described. Are you sure you don't have a twin?"

"C'mon, please?"

Rachel took a breath and tried to sound perky. "I promise we'll get together at eight at my place, okay? Then we'll go to yours."

Joey was satisfied. "I'll have a feast ready, you'll see."

"Bye," Rachel said, then hung up.

"She probably just wants those keys back and she's buttering me up till I give 'em to her," Joey thought. Despite the disappointing aftertaste of the phone call, he went to his cookbooks for ideas. He knew what entrée he was going to make, but for a side dish he wanted to be creative.

Rachel had called Joey from Burbank where she'd spent the night at a house doing what she told Joey she'd done. She'd cried her eyes out. Throughout the night, she moped from room to room, then every few hours walked through the quiet neighborhood and thought about Marty. She used half a box of tissues. The total sleep, intermittent that it was, didn't amount to two hours.

The house in Burbank was Rachel's residence. The house on Golding Circle in Hillside Park was a front. She and Marty bought the Burbank house when they committed themselves to each other. At the time, they made a private pact that no one would learn about the Burbank residence.

The effort to convince everyone that Rachel lived in Hillside Park was worth the trouble to her. Whenever she and Marty agreed to meet, she drove to Hillside Park and he visited her there. It's where he picked her up for evenings out and where he dropped her off afterward. If Gino or Cedar needed to contact him and he wasn't at Sunday dinners with his family, he could be reached at the Golding Circle number. It's where Rachel got mail and phone calls from people who thought she lived there. If she wanted the latter forwarded to her Burbank residence, she programmed her phone thusly. If she didn't, her answering machine there kicked in and she checked for messages by remote. Even her Corolla was a front. Her real car was a Lexus GS 430.

The Spanish-style Burbank house was built in the early thirties and was well preserved by its owners. It had an elegant courtyard of tiled walkways with fountains and statuary in the corners and tree ferns and gardenias in between. New Guinea impatiens in Mexican clay pots hung from two walls. Bird feeders made it feel like an aviary. The back yard had a swimming pool and a covered patio with piped-in music. If you sat in the patio, all you could see beyond the kidney-shaped pool were rows of roses of all colors.

The house opened to an entry with a Tibetan rug on the wall next to a wooden mirror between polished-brass candleholders. The step-down living room had dark-wood floors and raw ceiling beams. Artwork featured impressionistic seaside villas. A russet-and-green chenille sofa and loveseat combination sat between a high-arched window and an oval Persian rug in the center. Opposite a glass-hooded, stone fireplace was a nineteenth-century handcrafted, walnut gun cabinet with beveled glass doors, sans the guns. It contained books, crystal, fine-polished pottery and hammered-copper vases. Three captain's chairs circled a ceramic bistro table with candle pots on top. The dining room had rustic Spanish decor, with wood-and-leather chairs and a black-wood trestle table. Where the dark-red walls met the ceiling, Rachel had lain in a row of checkered, green-on-white ceramic tiles. Her kitchen had apricot walls with canary trim and plain-wood cabinets over clay-colored floor tiles. The bedrooms were Early American.

Rachel spent the night at her Burbank house for two reasons: she lived there, and she knew she wouldn't be safe at Golding Circle. Her plan that morning was to drive to Marty's and arm the security system so that while she tended to other matters arising from Marty's death, Cedar could not get in without setting off the alarm. The plan was aborted, however, when she checked her answering machine at the Golding Circle house. It had one message left by a distraught Bernice at four twenty-two that morning. The message said, "This doesn't sound like you, Rachel, not returning my calls. We've always been there for each other."

"What calls?" wondered Rachel. She phoned Bernice.

Bernice had barely slept. She ached all over from non-stop worry over Curly. She picked up the phone with a start.

"It's me," said Rachel. "I just got your last message. I don't know what happened to the others you referred to. What's the matter?"

Bernice was already crying. "It's horrible, Rache. Curly and I broke up I think. He left really mad yesterday and I tried all night to reach him at Kenny's, but he never went there, or he did and he didn't want to talk to me. Please come over. I'll never make it through the day if I can't talk about it. I know you're grieving about Marty but I'm nev—hang on, I've got another call. It could be him, you never know." Bernice clicked her reset button and said, "Hello?"

"Hello. Is this Miss Horl?" said the caller, an elderly man.

Bernice got a lump in her throat. "Yes," she said.

"Miss Horl, this is Nick Foto, I have a hardware store down on Hector Street here in Hillside Park."

"Yes, I know where it is."

"We still have a card in our files for Eddie Perez with your number on it," said Nick.

"Eddie was my gardener," said Bernice. "He passed away."

"I thought so," said Nick. "He was a good customer, then all of a sudden we never—"

"What are you calling me for?" said Bernice. Her heart raced.

"Well I'm not sure if you're the right person to talk to about this, but...are you a friend of Curly's? He often made mention of you."

Bernice felt a chill. "Yes. Why do you ask?"

Nick cleared his throat. "I got a phone call early this morning at home from the police. It appears that Curly—you know he slept behind me here on occasion?—I'm sorry to say he was run over by a car last night sometime during his sleep."

"My God," said Bernice. "Is he all right?"

Nick paused. "He's been taken to the Coroner's office."

Bernice dropped the receiver, collapsed onto her bed, and wailed like an animal caught in a trap. Nick heard her as clearly as if he'd been in the same room. Rachel, still on hold, knew something was wrong. She was unsure whether to hang up. Finally, she hung up the phone and drove to Eagle Rock to comfort Bernice in person. Nick also wondered how long he should stay on the line. He continued to listen to Bernice's agonizing cries. Soon, she used the sleeve of her nightgown to wipe off her tears, her crying subsided, and she picked the receiver up off the floor.

"Nick?" she asked through sobs.

"I'm still here, Ms. Horl."

"Did the police say if I can claim the body?" asked Bernice.

"No, but I can tell you what they did say. They're treating this as a hit-and-run accident, so they had to do tests for what they called trace elements around the body. The coroner's investigator I talked to is going to run fingerprints for a positive identification and see if he had any relatives to contact. They'll do an autopsy to confirm there was no foul play. This is all routine."

"He doesn't have any relatives," said Bernice.

"That's what I thought, too," said Nick. "I mentioned his aunt that used to work at Cooper's, oh, I don't know, twenty-five, thirty years ago at least, Cora Wiley."

"Curly always called her his crazy aunt."

"Yes," said Nick. "I would assume she's passed on. She would have to be in her late eighties and I don't think she lived a very healthy lifestyle. I'm Christian myself."

"They won't find anything," said Bernice. "She wasn't a blood relation anyway."

Nick was running out of things to say. "I would venture to guess they'd let you claim the body if you wanted to, Miss Horl."

"I hope so," said Bernice. "I want him to have a proper burial."

"Of course," said Nick. "Harper's does a good job."

"They did my parents," said Bernice.

"If there's anything I can do, Miss Horl, please let me know. I arranged for coffee and donuts this morning. There was quite a crowd by the time the police got here."

"Who found him?" said Bernice.

"A sanitation crew," said Nick.

Bernice started crying again. "We had a big fight. It was our first one, after nine years. Now he's gone, and there's no way I can say I'm sorry. It was a terrible misunderstanding. He was so easily hurt, you know. That poor man had absolutely no ego."

Bernice broke down further. She kept the receiver to her ear. Nick vaguely remembered her father. Budd Horl had shopped at Nick's seven or eight times a year for gardening supplies and other items. Then one day Nick read in the paper about the head-on collision that killed Budd and Doris. Bernice stopped crying long enough to thank Nick, then hung up the phone. She put her robe on and went to the phonebook to find the number for the Coroner's office. She wanted them to know that Curly didn't have an enemy in the world and that it was foolish to suspect foul play.

But most of all, she did not want them cutting him open. The very thought of autopsies made her skin crawl. Before finding the number, however, she broke down under a second wave of emotion. She had forgotten that she'd left Rachel on the line.

~ TWENTY-TWO ~

Rachel was on her way to Eagle Rock when she realized she could be making a mistake by getting entangled with Bernice when she had her own crisis to deal with, which was to keep Cedar from Marty's. It was time to be bold. She stopped at a payphone on Glendale Boulevard, found Cedar's phone number in her purse, and phoned him. He was in his bathroom tending to his leg when the call came. He hopped to the living room and picked up the receiver.

"Hello?" he said.

"This is Rachel. I armed Marty's security system last night, so don't try anything funny."

"You must think I'm an idiot," said Cedar.

"If I thought about it."

"You haven't been anywhere near Marty's."

"Cedar, sometimes you push that know-it-all attitude too far."

"I know one thing. I had it guarded all night and you never stepped one foot near it."

"You must think *I'm* the idiot," said Rachel.

"Why do you say that?"

Rachel thought fast. All she was looking for was a stall anyway, but she had to sound convincing in her ruse. "Your guard took a siesta."

"What's that supposed to mean?"

"It means nobody stopped me. You know what they say, Cedar: if you want something done right, do it yourself."

Cedar was furious, but he did not want Rachel to know. "You told me you lost the keys."

"Lost and found," said Rachel. She hung up.

Cedar felt screwed and let down at the same time. He had trusted Helen to be vigilant last night. Now he had doubts. When she moved in with him, she often made stupid mistakes, like pulling out electrical cords to important appliances so that she could plug in the vacuum cleaner. He'd get home and find out that his VCR hadn't taped "Andy Griffith" or "Jeopardy!" Or that his alarm clock was off. He explained to Helen what she'd done wrong, then reset the VCR and alarm clock, only to find that she'd repeated the mistake the next time she vacuumed. But when he threatened to smack her if she did it again, she learned to use other wall outlets. Within a few weeks, she was efficient. Thus, he'd had confidence that she could guard Marty's.

At the same time, he knew that Rachel was clever and gutsy. If she told him the truth about arming Marty's, she'd figured a way around Helen. If she lied, it was a masterful lie, because he had no way of knowing if the alarm was set without opening the door. Cedar grumbled to himself, then left to confront Helen about what really happened last night.

~ ~

Kenny didn't sleep well. Three things kept him awake. One was his imagination. It conjured up all kinds of ideas about what Cedar and Rachel were after in Marty's. It had to be really big. Now, finally, it was obvious: Cedar had joined him and Cammy and Dom because he wanted that really big thing, and whatever it was, he couldn't get it when Marty was alive. So that added to the intrigue. And if it were anything other than money, why would Rachel want it too?

The second thing that kept him awake was the loss of Curly. His bar was open from six in the morning until two at night. No human being could work those hours seven days a week. The only way he'd managed before was by having Curly fill in while he napped. But with Curly gone, he would die from sleep deprivation.

The third thing was Dom's spicy-sausage soup. When he'd gotten home he'd heated it on his hot plate and ended up eating half-a-gallon. On top of that, he'd added Tabasco. His stomach felt like it was hosting a hockey game.

~ ~

Cammy had a long, sound sleep, one of his best in months. He'd been liberated from material worries and was now doing the Lord's work. For breakfast he ate buttered toast, a banana and cottage cheese, then washed it down with orange juice. Also, he had a nice bowel movement, which to him was the only way to start the day. Rachel was on his list of things to do. He was going to her house on Golding Circle later on to make her confront her sins.

~ ~

When Rachel got to Bernice's house, she knocked on the front door but got no response. She went to the side of the house, where she had to wade through a patch of shin-high ivy until she came to the master bedroom's windows. They were halfway open to collect the breeze that cooled Eagle Rock when the sun went down. She called Bernice's name. A low murmur followed, the kind people make when they're seconds away from much-needed sleep and you're bothering them. Rachel shielded the sun from her eyes to see through the window screen. There she saw Bernice lying on the floor with blood flowing from a deep cut above her left wrist.

~ ~

Cedar drove to the alley behind Marty's. From his window as he pulled up beside Helen, he asked if she'd fallen asleep during her watch. The rabid look in his eyes scared her. She not only denied falling asleep, but insisted she hadn't moved from her spot.

"Did somebody go to that door with a key?" said Cedar.

Helen shook her head. "I wash all night lon. Peebles come in their cars and they have see the sign but nobody try to get in."

Cedar didn't know whom to believe. He looked away to try to clear his head. For seven short blocks east of where he sat in his Cherokee until the alley forked with Hector Street, he saw employees arriving for work at stores that faced Hector Street. They parked their old cars in designated areas of the alley that didn't encroach on parking spaces for businesses on either side. His rearview mirror showed the same activity in the other direction. It seemed almost quaint, the normal, everyday, back-street life of small businesses eking out enough profits to keep their doors open. He heard buses, honking cars, hydraulic brakes on delivery trucks, even the bell on the door of Cooper's Drug Store signaling an entering customer.

All he looked at and listened to made Cedar wonder if his perceptions were off. He'd spent most of his adult life either in bed sleeping or at Marty's working. How did he really know anything? Santayana said that a fanatic is one who redoubles his effort when he has forgotten his aim. Is that me? he wondered. Here I am, about to smack Helen for letting Rachel sneak by her last night, but how do I know Rachel's telling the truth? Blaming Slapper for futzing with his synapses was too easy. Real men blame themselves. But Cedar's self-doubt went deeper than culpability. It went to whether he was in a psychosis.

He got out of his Cherokee and limped to the heavy, steel-plated door to the Kitchen. He examined the keyhole for the alarm key. There was no way to know by looking at it whether the system was armed. Before Rachel shot him the previous day, he was going to spend the night dismantling the Kitchen door from inside. No one would have known because no one would have heard. But now, if Rachel had set the alarm as she said, he couldn't even get *in* the building, much less the Kitchen.

Was it worth the risk to unlock the building? If the alarm went off and police showed up, he could say he was there to shut the place down at the late owner's request. Would they believe him? Word would get to Gloria and she might call Marty's attorney, Lou Carini, and tell him to get professionals to guard the building until its contents were removed and the business sold. If that happened, Cedar had no chance to get what he wanted from inside the Kitchen.

He determined that it wasn't worth the risk. His focus should be on Rachel, not the building. He returned to his Cherokee, nodded for Helen to get in, and drove home. She asked what he was thinking. He told her to shut up. The same thing happened when she asked if his leg was better.

Helen was hurt. One, Cedar hadn't thanked her for the arduous vigil she'd kept the whole night in an alley. Two, he wouldn't tell her what his plans were now that his boss was dead. And three, the great sex they'd had—the first time they climaxed together and her first time, period— might as well have never happened. It confirmed what her mother had said about men: once they wet their whistles, they treat you like a dog.

~ ~

Joey decided what to make for his dinner with Rachel. As he prepared a shopping list, Freda entered his room in bathrobe and slippers. She had just showered and washed her hair, what little there was of it; she kept it short because when she let it grow it made her look like a fat Dutch boy.

"What's that?" she said while swabbing her ear with a Q-tip.

"Stuff to cook," said Joey without looking up. "If I cook it'll take my mind off Uncle Marty, y'know."

"Well, that's not very respectful," said Freda.

Freda was five-four and weighed one-sixty. She was round all over, like Cammy, from her fat cheeks to her football-size ankles. Her dark-brown eyes were set close together over a flat nose, and her eyebrows were all but gone. Like Marty, her forehead had deep lateral wrinkles, only on him they added to a look of wisdom, as if trial-by-fire thinking had put them there. With Freda, they looked as if she'd walked into a tree. She had a double chin, stubby neck and small lips—the lower one sticking out farther than the upper one. Her breasts lay flat against her sloping chest, and she was bow-legged.

"Did you try the suits on?" she said, scratching her stomach.

"No, but I will."

"The blue one looks like it'll fit. Aunt Gloria thinks so too."

Joey was on item four of his shopping list and thinking about getting to the grocery store. "I'll try it on first."

"We're going to see the body at five," said Freda. "It's an open casket."

"Want me to go with you?" asked Joey. He hoped she'd say no.

"Well, *don't* you?"

"Yeah, that's why I asked, Mom."

"We'll probably stay there for a while. We need to make sure the guest book gets signed and the flowers are properly displayed. Some of these funeral directors are retards. You just can't trust them. I don't know how long we'll be there. It depends on how many friends come. The notice should be in the paper this morning. With all his customers there could be a big turnout."

Joey tried to make his next question sound motiveless. "What're you doing after that?"

"We thought we'd go to dinner," said Freda. "She knows a place that'll give us a private room. There's a lot of grief yet to share."

"Then maybe I better not go with you."

Freda sounded indignant. "Why not?"

"Mom, we all got our own ways of grieving."

Freda stifled an involuntary belch. "What do *you* know about grieving?"

"Don't start, okay? I loved Uncle Marty but I don't want to talk to you and Aunt Gloria about it all night long. Last night was bad enough."

"That's a *terrible* thing to say."

"I just meant seeing her cry. It makes me uncomfortable. I don't know what to say anymore. Besides, cooking's my way of handling things. When did you say they start showing the body?"

"Ten this morning," said Freda. "Aunt Gloria's got preparations to make for Thursday and I've got two classes to teach, so we'll meet there at five. She may get there earlier."

"Then I'll see him before then. Can I have money for groceries?"

"How much?"

"I dunno. Sixty maybe."

"*Sixty dollars?*"

"Mom, we need meat and vegetables. We're out of olive oil, tomatoes are expensive, lots of stuff."

"I'll leave it on the table," said Freda grudgingly. She turned to leave but remembered something. "I wanted you to know I thought that was kind of you to get those cards for Aunt Gloria. She was touched by it."

Joey was close to saying whose idea it was. "Yeah, well I like her. She's a really nice lady. He was lucky to marry her, I think."

Freda waited a moment. "You've never done anything like that on your own. I didn't think you had it in you."

"Yeah, well I never lost my only uncle before."

Freda left. Joey wondered if he could have Rachel over for dinner and out the door before his mother got back from dinner with his aunt. The logistics were formidable.

~ ~

Cedar took Helen home so she could clean up. He was obsessed with cleanliness, even for people around him; it was a reason he couldn't stand Kenny, to whom deodorant was Agent Orange. When they got home, Helen saw that Cedar had placed several books next to the kitchen door that led to the driveway. She asked about them.

Cedar said, "Never mind. Go shower." He had every intention of driving her back to Marty's to guard the building until he figured out how to find Rachel. If Rachel beat him to the Kitchen, he would not know how to handle his rage, which was already starting to brew. He had set his eyes on that money from the start. Each time Marty took two thousand from his weekly deposit and gave half to Rachel and hid the other half in the Kitchen, Cedar added to the total in his mind. He knew taking it was unethical, but it was not criminal. For one thing, Marty could do with his profits what he wanted. For another, his wife had her own money, from her father, a rich banker and country club drunk. And last, if Rachel never got the money, she could still rebound. All she'd have to do is hang out at some tony gym on the west side and wait for a rich Hollywood type to hit on her.

But now, after all the years of seeing that money in his hands one day and having no conscience about taking it, Cedar felt Rachel's encroachment on his long-time dream. Just as he was about to put his fist through a wall from frustration, he got an idea: if *he* couldn't get into Marty's without the alarm key, he could fix it so *she,* even *with* it, couldn't either. He'd jam the keyhole.

While Helen showered, Cedar used wire cutters and a chisel to grind bits of scrap metal from his garage into a pea-sized pile. Then he fetched a hammer and plumber's cement and drove to Marty's. He used a pencil to mix metal and glue into a paste, then forced it inside the keyhole's chambers. He hammered it until the gap the key went into was banged closed on one side. After inspecting his work, he knew that no one with a key could get in.

"Now we're even," he said.

On the way home, Cedar imagined Rachel's expression when she found out her alarm key wouldn't fit. She'd know who jammed it. That gave him satisfaction. The worst that could happen after that was that they might have to put their heads together to bypass the alarm. Until then, the race to see who got the money first was off.

~~

When Joey wasn't using the bus to get around Hillside Park, he rode a ten-speed bike. After breakfast and before going to the grocery store, he rode it to Rachel's on the slim chance that he might find her there. Plus, he wanted exercise. He put *Don Giovanni* in his portable CD player to listen to on the way. It wasn't the liveliest of operas, but, in deference to Marty, he chose it because it was somber.

Instead of finding Rachel home, Joey found Cammy parked in front of her house and reading something in his lap. Joey, despite his immaturity, had ascertained that Cammy was a dunce, mostly because he looked like one. He looked even more like one today. He wore a short-sleeve white shirt with a narrow black tie that even Joey, who knew nothing about fashion, hadn't seen except in videos of old movies, the ones whose stars were long dead.

Joey coasted to the driver's side of Cammy's car and stopped. "What're you doing here?" he said.

Cammy offered a welcoming grin and got out of his car. Joey saw a bible in his hands. "Allow me to apologize for my craven act yesterday," he said, stretching his hand out. "Friends call me Cammy."

Joey wouldn't shake his hand. "You got a lot of nerve," he said.

"No, my son, for you are ignorant. Listen here." Cammy read from a page in his bible he had dog-eared. "'Lord, if you kept a record of our sins, who, oh Lord, could ever survive? But you offer forgiveness that we might learn to fear you. I am counting on the Lord; yes, I am counting on Him. I have put my hope in His word.'" He looked at Joey. "Hear the scriptures, for we are all sinners, myself included. But I am repenting, for I have found Jesus the Savior."

"What're you doing here?" asked Joey.

"Atoning for my part in what happened yesterday. What's your name?"

Joey wouldn't answer.

"You're Marty's nephew. Listen, nephew. I was wrong. I tried to kill Marty and Rachel here because they're evil. But today I seek a different path. I seek a path of reconciliation with Jesus Christ."

"What are you talking about 'evil?'"

"They sinned," said Cammy. "You won't find a record of it, but the seeds of their godless deeds fill our television sets with shocking crimes every day." His speech patterns had started to emulate the speech patterns of evangelists he'd been watching on TV.

"What are you talking about?" said Joey.

"They sold drugs to black youth. And Marty supplied illegal weapons to police to help them roust out gangs."

"Sure."

"The proof's in the Kitchen. Nobody has a record of those guns. You can see for yourself. You can't trace bullets back to cops if you know the cops didn't use the guns."

Joey just stared at Cammy.

"I got this from the horse's mouth," said Cammy. "Rachel and your uncle, they worked with the police and the politicians to keep inner-city youth paralyzed from gutter depravity. Open your eyes. Mine are, and now I'm spreading the word." He rifled through his bible looking for a specific verse. He glanced at one he'd underlined, dismissed it, went to another on a dog-eared page, dismissed it, searched again, was unsuccessful, but then found the right one. "Here-it-is," he said. "The Lord is kind and merciful, slow to get angry, full of unfailing love. The Lord is good to everyone. He showers compassion on all his creation.' *That's* why I'm spreading the word. Let the great light of sunshine shine on Rachel's deeds. You'll see, you'll all see. Then we'll all lay down and praise the lord!"

"Shut up," said Joey.

"Of course you don't want to hear it. I didn't either. But why didn't she call the police yesterday? She *knew* we stole that car. Why didn't she report it? Why not *indeed*! It would have been a very sticky situation, that's why."

"Crack and drive-bys and all that? Are you trying to tell me that they helped pull off all that shit?"

"Heavens to Betsy, yes."

Joey angrily raised his anchoring foot from the pavement and pedaled his bike down Golding Circle. Cammy called after him. "You tell Rachel Cammy's waiting for her. He'll stay here. He brings the gospel. If she repents, she'll be saved!"

Joey kept on pedaling.

~ TWENTY-THREE ~

Paramedics took Bernice to the E.R. at Glendale Adventist, where she received transfusions, treatment for her arm, and was sedated. Doctors evaluated her to see if she was a danger to herself or others. With no previous suicide attempts and Rachel's promise of support over the next seventy-two hours, they said she could go home later that day.

While Bernice was being treated, Rachel called Nick Foto for specifics. Nick, an inquisitive and meticulous man, told her what he knew from talking to a coroner's investigator. Tire tracks on Curly's body matched tracks on the alley's pavement, where separated asphalt exposed impressionable dirt. Being run over when asleep was not an uncommon way for transients to die. The way Curly's head was turned flat on its side, he'd probably died from a broken neck, which could result, he was told, in permanent paralysis. Curly could have ended up a quad, or, depending on where the damage in his spinal column occurred, it could have caused asphyxia.

"What about toxicology results?" asked Rachel.

"They're going to take a few days," said Nick. "But Curly's shirt was soaked with alcohol. He drank that fruity brandy, you know."

"Blue Sevens," said Rachel. "That means he was at Kenny's."

"I suppose," answered Nick.

"It's about the only place he drank at anyway."

"The odor was strong."

"So they're thinking Curly was drunk," said Rachel. "Even though he never got drunk."

"No, I never saw him drunk."

295

"He never had more than one Blue Seven per sitting, sometimes the whole day," said Rachel. "Thanks for your help, Nick. I hope to see you at Marty's funeral. Curly's, too, now that I think of it."

"Marty's wife called me last night to ask if I'd be a pallbearer. Stop by some time, I haven't seen you in a while."

Rachel said okay. During Bernice's psychological evaluation, when Rachel was outside the E.R., Bernice's doctors told her she was pregnant. She wasn't surprised, not after her mood swings the last several days. Still heavily medicated, she asked for Rachel to come in and for her doctors to leave the room. When they did, she looked sadly at Rachel and spoke slowly, as if she were somnambulant. "How could I tell Curly I might be pregnant?" she confessed. "After all these years, I still didn't know how he'd take it. He was afraid of his own shadow. He might've skipped town for good. You know, Rachel, I think he wanted to die."

"What gives you that idea?"

"My last conversation with him, it was like he was running a tape over and over in his mind. I can't explain it."

"A tape of what?"

"I don't know but he sounded guilty about throwing his life away. He was fatalistic. I didn't hear it then, but now it's so clear."

"He couldn't be fatalistic and devoted to you at the same time."

"Oh, he liked me, I know that." She smiled wistfully. "He loved the sex. He was always sooo grateful afterward. And I certainly don't mean because of the money I gave him."

"No, you were just looking out for him."

"Somebody had to. But isn't it funny how he'd never take more than forty dollars? And you couldn't tell he spent any of it, either."

"Why do you think he was fatalistic?" said Rachel.

"He told me he got Kenny angry that night he saw him and Cammy together. He thought *he* started their scheme to stop Marty from getting all the drinking business in Hillside Park."

"Because of what he said to Kenny?"

"That's what he thought."

"What did he say to Kenny?"

"Something about his crazy aunt."

"Cora Wiley."

Bernice nodded. "He said he pissed off Kenny and that's why he called Cammy and that's why they went to the Sonoma Inn later on."

"Kenny's always been irascible."

"But why was Curly so bothered by it that night? He used to laugh off Kenny's outbursts. I know, because they offended me, especially when Kenny ridiculed him. But that night, Curly took it harder. He cried, you know."

"You didn't tell me that."

"He told me about a time in his youth, a time he was completely relaxed…sort of like I am now, I guess. It was so vivid to him. I was thinking, how did he go from feeling guilty about pissing off Kenny to thinking about some serene time in his past? It sounded like he was evaluating his life. I'll never know, anyway. Maybe it'll just be a mystery, just like why he wouldn't move in with me, like why he had to die at such a young age."

Rachel didn't believe Curly died accidentally. The police report would explain everything. But now, such suspicion wouldn't change Bernice's loss or how to deal with her pregnancy, so she didn't bring it up. "What are you going to do?" she asked.

"I want the baby," said Bernice.

Rachel held her hand for a long time. Bernice asked if they could pick up Curly's effects from the Coroner after she was discharged. "They're all I'll ever have of his," she said.

"Of course," said Rachel. "I'll see when they'll be ready."

Rachel left to make the call. Instead of calling from the E.R., she went to the hospital cafeteria. Bernice needed to rest before she was to be released anyway, and Rachel was hungry. She didn't call the Coroner's office right away. Instead she called the Northeast Division of the L.A.P.D. to ask who was assigned to Curly's death. She was given the name of a lead

detective who was there when she phoned. Calling herself, as an anonymous tipster, Rachel told him whose tires he could check to see if they
matched the tracks where Curly died.

"It's a hunch," she said. "But you could look at a Kenny Grimmet and
a Cedar Roach. Kenny Grimmet has a bar on Hector Street called
Kenny's, and Cedar Roach lives in Eagle Rock just off Colorado
Boulevard." She'd ruled out Cammy as being too weak to kill Curly and
Dom as too vision-impaired.

When Rachel finished, she said good luck to the detective in such a way
as to signal the end of her offer of free advice. The detective thanked her,
and she hung up. She then spent a moment wondering what made her
violate her vow not to get cops involved. The answer was obvious: Curly
was murdered. She had admonished Joey—and before him, Bernice—to
realize that when cops investigate a situation, innocent people can be
dragged into the spotlight. But by insisting that cops not be brought in,
Rachel unintentionally paved the way for an innocent person to be
harmed, in this case, Curly.

What had eluded Bernice in her trance-like analysis of what led to
Curly's death was the glaring fact that he'd lived in streets and alleys his
whole adult life. Unlike transients who pass out from drugs and alcohol,
often where automobiles pass, Curly was attuned to the dangers of street
life. He would spend hours on a single Blue Seven, far too long for a
watered-down shot of Kenny's blueberry-flavored brandy to affect his
judgment. And he'd slept in the same spots that he'd always slept in, none
of which was dangerous.

Rachel called the Coroner's office to see if she could get Curly's effects.
She was told yes, but that it was an on-going investigation and that they
might have to hold on to his effects without further notice. She explained
Curly's relationship to Bernice, that Bernice was the closest relation he had
to a family, and that after today she could be reached at home to take cus-
tody of his body. She left her cell phone number, bought a muffin and a

bottle of cranberry juice, sat at a table in the cafeteria and thought about what to do next.

She had planned to visit Marty's widow that morning, a daring and bold move, to plead for Gloria to postpone the funeral another day. To make her case, she would disclose her reason and at the same time risk secrets about her relationship with Marty. But that plan had to wait because of Bernice's suicide attempt. She also had to get in the Kitchen. For all she knew, Cedar had ignored her bluff and was already inside. Nor did she know the extent of his injury. But even if she'd shot his leg clean off, he would still find a way to get that money. She felt powerless sitting in a hospital cafeteria.

Her biggest fear was what would happen if Cedar got her alone in the Kitchen. If he trapped her in the house at Golding Circle, she could scream and the neighbors might hear. Also, two doors and countless windows were possible escape routes. But in the Kitchen, no one could hear her scream. There were no windows, only doors heavy as steel and slow to open.

Worse still, Rachel didn't know what to look for. A box? A suitcase? Coffee cans? Marty never told her how he'd hidden the money, just that, God forbid, if he died without warning, all she needed to do was get in the Kitchen and look, that she'd know when she saw it.

~ TWENTY-FOUR ~

Kenny made a killing in his bar that day. As word of Curly's death spread, people came because they knew Curly was a fixture there. After lunch hour, Kenny had counted eighteen customers, a record. He clipped every one of them: short-pouring, over-charging, sweeping their loose change up in his towel. The eighteen consisted of his morning and lunchtime regulars, Curly's acquaintances, and regulars from Cammy's and Marty's. Recollections of Curly were only part of bigger discussions at the bar. In one day, Marty died, Cammy closed his bar without notice, and a homeless man people knew seemingly forever was dead in a freak accident.

When Kenny turned around to ring up a sale on his register, he thought, "Cedar ought to kill more bums around here, ba-*doop*."

~ ~

Dom also benefited. Six men, all retirees, came in, four separately and two together. All sheepishly greeted him and his bartender, Charlie. Their demeanor of "let bygones be bygones" was received by Dom with equanimity. He didn't even mention Marty's long-time threat of banishment if they patronized his bar. Instead, he picked up their first round and served each one his famous soup. Soon Marty's former customers were mingling with Dom's regulars as if Marty's never existed. Dom knew he could count on their continued business, and he was sure more of Marty's regulars would soon be his. Rather than whistling "Jimmy Cracked Corn," he whistled "Happy Days Are Here Again."

~ ~

Now that Cedar no longer needed Helen to watch over Marty's, he told her to sleep. She was tired anyway. His leg was sore and he had lots of work ahead: load the Cherokee with supplies, track down Rachel and get into the Kitchen. He drove to a medical supply store in Glendale and bought crutches. Next stop was Golding Circle, where he intended to wait for Rachel. There he saw Cammy in his car. Rather than curse the pesky Cammy, Cedar got creative. He nudged his bumper with Cammy's car. This brought Cammy's eyes up from his bible.

Cammy walked to the Cherokee with his bible held high, as if to signal that some things even *Cedar* had to respect.

"What are you doing?" asked Cedar.

"I came to talk to Rachel," said Cammy. "I've seen Jesus, Cedar. I'm not the Cammy Waller you knew before yesterday. I've been born again. I came here to get her to see the error of her ways."

Cedar was out of his Cherokee and leaning on his crutches. "You're wasting your time on Rachel. She's always been wild."

"Jesus loves everyone," said Cammy.

"Let's go inside and talk about it," said Cedar.

Cammy was skeptical.

"Come on," insisted Cedar. "I've never talked to anyone who's seen Jesus. I know of a power not quite as great as His, but it's close. Let me share it with you and see what you think."

"A power close to the Lord's?" asked Cammy.

"A different kind," said Cedar. "You're working on faith. Mine's synaptic variances. Do you know what those are?"

"I've never heard of them, so…" said Cammy. "Are they in the Bible? They don't sound familiar."

"We'll see if there's a connection."

Cammy moved with Cedar to Rachel's front door.

"Are you surprised I believe in God?" asked Cedar.

"Not really," said Cammy.

"Fingerprints," said Cedar.

Cammy opened the door for Cedar. "Fingerprints?"

"Name a biological justification for human fingerprints."

"Well," thought Cammy. "They help us grip things, so…"

"I'm talking about their uniqueness to each individual."

Cammy thought about it. "Identification?"

They entered Rachel's house and stood in the barren living room. "That's not biological," said Cedar. "I'm asking what the *function* of *fingerprints* is in *nature*."

"Oh, I see. Gosh, I don't know," said Cammy. "It's not my field, so…"

"You can't name one," said Cedar. "They were designed millions of years before the technology to exploit them for non-biological reasons was developed. Only God would have had the foresight for that."

As Cammy put his head down to think about this, Cedar lifted his left crutch like a club and hammered it into Cammy's forehead. Cammy fell backward and landed on the floor with a thud. His bible and glasses fell, too. He was out cold. Cedar drove Cammy's car around the block, returned to his Cherokee, and took a roll of duct tape from his toolbox. He returned to the house and bound Cammy's ankles and wrists behind his back with it. He taped his mouth shut after putting a balled-up pair of Rachel's panties in it. With her bedspread, he wrapped Cammy up, tamale style, tied the ends with clothesline, dragged him to the garage out back and threw him in. He was going to douse the package with gasoline and do a controlled burn with a garden hose at the ready in case it made too much smoke, but he was sure Cammy could stay alive for a few days. After that, Cedar would be gone.

Cedar parked his Cherokee one street south so it was out of sight, went back in Rachel's house, and rested on her bed with a pillow under his leg. It was throbbing but not enough to waylay Cedar. He did not intend to sleep anyway, just rest. When Rachel returned, he wanted to catch her by surprise.

But the longer Cedar lay there thinking, the more something started to bother him. It was like a vague memory, or a thought that didn't connect when it first came to him. Soon he sat up with a start.

"Jesus Christ!" he exclaimed.

He went to the bedroom and played back the messages on Rachel's answering machine he'd heard last night. There it was, the girl with flight information for her mother. Cedar originally thought it was a wrong number. Now he had a different opinion.

Could Rachel Ellis have a daughter? he wondered.

Has Rachel led a life *outside* Hillside Park?

Does that explain the *other* number the girl mentioned?

Is that why this house has such sparse furnishings, because it's a front?

Cedar wrote down the information in the message, then phoned L.A.X. To a customer service rep, he said, "I'm calling to confirm a reservation my daughter made on flight 27 arriving Thursday at eight-thirty p.m., last name Ellis."

He heard computer keys being punched. "That's confirmed, sir," said the customer rep. "Ms. Dina Ellis, arriving from New York."

A stunned Cedar hung up without saying good-bye or thank you. That Rachel could hide such a fact all these years made his respect for her soar. His disbelief turned to belief when he started running questions and answers through his mind:

A daughter would explain the phone call Rachel started in Marty's office yesterday, for which she wanted privacy.

A daughter would explain why she told him he could never understand non-ephemeral love, surely a description of parental love.

A daughter would explain why she was seen so *in*frequently around Hillside Park. Maybe she spent most of her time away, or in New York. Was she even *here* for the Monday Nooners Cedar chauffeured Marty to each week? Was he, Cedar, a fool to sit in Marty's car outside her house while Marty was alone inside giggling because he was pulling a fast one on Cedar and everyone else in Hillside Park?

But what was the daughter doing in New York? Could this "Dina Ellis" have predated Rachel? Could Marty and *another* woman have conceived the child when he and Rachel were on the outs over her drinking early on in their relationship? Cedar never saw her pregnant, nor had anyone else. Therefore, could *Marty* have paid Rachel to raise *his* illegitimate child outside of Hillside Park as her own? Marty would do anything to keep his wife in the dark about an illegitimate child fathered by him.

The scenarios were wild. One thing was sure, though: a young woman dear to Rachel was coming in by plane two nights from now, and Cedar knew when and where she would arrive. Still marveling at one of the great surprises of his life, Cedar returned to his Cherokee and drove home without rushing. According to plans he was developing, there was no need to rush.

~ ~

On the way back from Rachel's house, Joey bought groceries with which to make a memorable meal, but when he started preparations, his heart wasn't in it. Instead of light Italian opera to cook by, he put on *Boris Godunov*. His mood change came from what Cammy had told him about Marty and Rachel. Some of Joey's classmates had died of drug overdoses and gang warfare. His mother had gone to countless symposiums about the human destruction drug use had wrought on communities in Los Angeles. A congresswoman had publicly condemned local and federal policing organizations for secretly participating in the distribution of crack cocaine to the inner cites. Uncle Marty had exhorted his customers to take on civic responsibilities; it made sense he'd help the cops in their war on drugs and gangs in his own way, by supplying arms the city couldn't trace back to them. But, thought Joey, that was *illegal*.

The biggest thing on Joey's mind, however, was Rachel's staunch refusal to call the cops when she confronted Kenny and Cammy yesterday and when Cedar tried to rape her. Anyone would have reported what she knew. She'd admitted men had plotted to murder her and Uncle Marty. Only a person with something to hide wouldn't call the cops.

By midday, after stewing veal and braising vegetables for the meal he'd planned for that night, Joey was rapidly losing interest in Rachel. If his mother and uncle and aunt had taught him anything, it was not to consort with bad people.

~~

Helen was asleep when Cedar got home. He knew Kenny and Dom were coming over that night, but he wasn't sure he needed them anymore. Just the same, he'd keep the meeting open.

The phone rang minutes later. It was Gloria Bagliamente.

"Mrs. Bagliamente," said Cedar. "I'm sorry for your loss. Marty was like a father to me."

"Thank you, Cedar," said the soft-voiced widow. "Martin thought very highly of you, too. I'm calling to ask if you would be a pallbearer. The funeral's Thursday morning. There'll be a mass, followed by a motorcade to the cemetery, then a reception at my house. I've selected you, Gino, our nephew, our lawyer, Nick Foto, and a friend of the family here in Glendale. May I count on you?"

"Of course," said Cedar. "But I'm on crutches. Doc said it'll be a week before I can lift anything."

"How unfortunate. I'm using a cane from hip surgery myself."

Cedar didn't want to disappoint her. "If it doesn't breech protocol, I'll be glad to walk alongside the other pallbearers."

"I think that would be fine," said Gloria. "I'll check with the church and get back to you just to be sure."

"If I'm not here, leave a message. Again, I'm sorry, Mrs. Bagliamente. I'll see you Thursday, if not before, at Harper's."

"Thank you, Cedar. Bye now."

Cedar said good-bye. He saw that Helen had awakened and was rub-bing sleep from her eyes as she entered the room. She wore a see-though nightgown with nothing on underneath, just how Cedar liked it. Her plump breasts, with brownish nipples and even darker areolae, swayed from her lumbering gait. A heavy layer of flab around her waist didn't bother him, as long as he had a clear view of her breasts. She sat next to him and rested her head on his shoulder, puppy-like, then ran her hand up and down his forearm. "Who was that?" she asked casually.

Her breath was offensive, but Cedar didn't say anything. He couldn't afford to fight with her, as it would weaken his focus.

"They want me in the funeral," he said. He wanted to avoid follow-up questions, so he said the first thing that came to mind. "I'm taking a job in Sacramento, a top security firm up there's making me head of operations."

Helen looked hopefully into his eyes.

"We'll get a bigger house, a pool and everything," he added.

She kissed his cheek for including her in his plans. Cedar wanted more than a kiss, especially after seeing her breasts flop and sway. He slid down and untied the belt of his sweat pants. Helen, who knew when she paraded her naked chest in front of him that he would get aroused quickly, craftily placed her palm on his flat, muscled stomach with her fingers pointed toward his crotch. She wanted to keep her hand there as a tease until his penis, already stiffening, was a tent pole in his pants. But Cedar didn't have the patience. He nodded for her to do it. So she moved her fin-gers, spider-like, down his stomach until they went under his pants. That made him erect. Even then, he was impatient. So he did what he'd never done with Helen. He put his hand on the back of her head and pushed until her face was in his lap.

Helen was pleasantly surprised. With the exception of last night, when he was groggy from cough syrup and alcohol, the few times she'd tried to give him oral sex, he instead pushed her face away, boarded her and went for quick relief, and when he finished he was out of the mood for more sex. So now, after good news that they were going to get a big house with a pool, and especially after their unprecedented sex the night before, Helen eagerly gave him what he wanted.

Cedar threw his head back, relaxed every bone in his body, closed his eyes, and let Helen pleasure him orally with no urgency to get it over quick.

~ TWENTY-FIVE ~

When Rachel returned to the hospital to inquire about Bernice's discharge, a nurse told her that she was asleep. So Rachel went home to get her Lexus, which was bigger than her Corolla and had air-conditioning. On the way there, the Coroner's investigator in charge of Curly's case called her cell phone to say that his effects were still needed because detectives, acting on an anonymous tip, were broadening their investigation.

Rachel didn't know what to say to Bernice if Curly's death was ruled a homicide. That would indict her in Bernice's eyes for citing Curly as the source of the rumor she'd passed on to Cedar. It was an innocent mistake, she told herself, and she tried to put it out of her mind.

When Bernice was ready, Rachel pushed her in a wheelchair to the parking lot. Still medicated, Bernie said, "Whose Lexus is that?"

"Mine," said Rachel.

"When'd you get that?"

Rachel put the passenger seat back, pulled the seat belt out farther than she thought it could go, and stretched it around Bernice's zeppelin girth. Then she drove. "I'll tell you about it, and some other things, over dinner, okay?" Her tone was fatalistic.

Bernice looked at her. "You can tell me now."

"Let me get you home first," said Rachel. "We'll order in."

"What about Curly's things?"

"They're not ready," said Rachel. "Maybe tomorrow, they said."

Bernice looked out the window at the passing hospital landscape as Rachel headed for an exit off the hospital grounds. "What other things are you talking about, Rache? I've never kept anything from you."

Rachel headed to Colorado Boulevard. "I haven't told anyone this."

"Not more bad news," said Bernice.

"It's not about Curly."

Hearing fear in Rachel's voice, Bernice took her hand. It was if as she'd forgotten about Curly and now needed to be her friend's ears. Rachel couldn't start talking without getting a tissue. She wiped her eyes and spoke with difficulty. "The other day, someone told me no secret lives without guilt."

"Uh-oh," said Bernice.

"I think I'm going to cry."

"Is it that bad?"

"No, but we're not supposed to hurt people we love."

"Rachel, it's all right. I can take it. This medication's really working. I feel okay, really."

"Bee, I have a daughter. She's the most beautiful and loving child in the world, and she's my whole life." She had to stop talking to catch her breath from crying.

"Did you say you have a...*daughter?*" said Bernice.

Rachel nodded. Bernice blinked as if trying to figure out a punch line to a joke whose set-up was vague. "I think this medication's messing with my mind."

"You heard right. I said I have a child. I'm a mother."

"You *what?*"

Rachel kept her eyes on the road. "I love her so much, Bee. I've spent her whole life protecting her from my past. I refused to let her grow up in Hillside Park. She doesn't know I was a tramp, she doesn't know about all the guys I slept with, the drugs, the alcohol, waking up with strangers, public drunkenness...Marty worshipped her, too. Oh, she went to the club the few times I couldn't get a babysitter, that sort of thing. And he went to her school functions and other things. She knows about Marty and his family, but she doesn't know anything about my history in Hillside Park. I live in Burbank. Marty and I got a place there to make sure she was far away."

"Burbank," said Bernice. Her face was drained of color.

"I raised her there. She helped me turn my life around, just by being so innocent. I shielded her from my old haunts, my high school, even my father's grave. It's not so much that I was ashamed. I believe I've grown since then, but I worried that she'd emulate me, if not on purpose, then by unconscious design. The first thing you learn about parenting is how impressionable children are. The concept of role models has you by the throat. I never knew any of this before, but with A.A., Marty, and then becoming a mom, I changed. My whole outlook changed. I don't think that would have happened if I had stayed in Hillside Park."

"What's your…daughter's name?"

"Adina. We call her Dina. My mother was Italian—or is, I don't know if she's alive or what—but she wanted to name me Adina. It means 'delicate' in Italian. This is what my father told me anyway. But I was nine pounds, three ounces, so they passed on that. In Italian I'm Rachele."

"Adina's beautiful," said Bernice. "How old is she?"

"Eighteen. I just sent her to New York to go to school. She just got an apartment, and now she's looking for one for me."

"A double blow," said Bernice. "You're moving there?"

"To be with my daughter? Absolutely."

"But you've never lived anywhere else in your whole life."

"Dina may be a legal adult but she's still my baby."

"Did Marty know you were moving there?"

"He was in denial about it. Bee, she got a scholarship to N.Y.U. Can you imagine a product of Hillside Park going to a top East Coast university like that?"

"I can't believe you would've left Marty."

"It wasn't going to be easy."

"But you two—"

"He didn't need me. Dina does. Besides, we're not going to live together anymore, just close by."

"That sounds so drastic," said Bernice. "Moving to New York."

"Look what happened to *me* without a mother around."

"Yes but you got it together eventually."

"At what cost?" said Rachel. "Every guy in Hillside Park thinks I'm a slut."

"Rachel, these are guys that go to Kenny's. Who cares what they think?"

"I still didn't want Dina hearing from her classmates that their fathers slept with me."

Bernice put her fingers to her forehead. "I may pass out. I can't *process* all this."

"I'm sorry," said Rachel. She reached for another tissue. "I've been wanting to tell you for years."

"No, I'm glad you did. I'm just…in shock."

"I fought hard since I got sober not to sound like a victim, especially to myself. But now I probably sound like a classic victim."

"Are we friends or not?"

"I appreciate that," said Rachel. "It's not a coincidence you're the first person I told."

"Well, if you ask me, I think you've been too hard on yourself."

"Have you forgotten the reputation I had back then?"

"Forgotten? I was jealous of it."

"I was *this* close to ending up in a place like Kenny's the rest of my life. No, I have no regrets about how I raised Dina. Her head's screwed on straight."

"I hope I can meet her."

"Absolutely." Rachel wiped at the tears in her eyes. "But there's a problem. Marty was going to help with expenses. It takes a lot of money to live over there. I don't mind getting a job, but I don't have the slightest idea what I'd apply for. All I've ever done is tend bar."

Bernice affected a timid voice. "Can I ask…"

"What?"

"Is Dina's father…Is Marty her father?"

Rachel shook her head decisively. It was a clear signal that she wanted no follow-up questions. "She's coming in because of Marty, but she won't be here in time for the funeral. I want to ask Marty's wife if she'll postpone it a day, but I've never met her and I know she despises me."

"I don't want to be in your shoes for that."

"It's probably too late anyway. But I've got to ask."

Rachel had reached Colorado Boulevard. She was at a red light. "Bee, countless times I wanted to bring Dina over to show you, to have you hold her, to play with her, to let her call you 'Auntie.' And I think Curly would have enjoyed her."

"Aunt Bernice," said Bernice. "Uncle Curly."

"But with all the gossip…the things people say…I guess I just kept putting it off till I thought the time was right." The light changed. Rachel turned left to go to Eagle Rock. "I wanted you to see our house, too," she said. "We haven't touched the nursery since Dina was a baby. The things you regret at times like these…"

"You can say that again," said Bernice. "Why didn't I ever invite you over to meet Curly? What was I thinking?"

"One or two evenings a week, you needed time alone with him. I understand that. Marty and I never socialized either."

"Look at us, Rachel. Best friends since high school. Now I find out you're a single mom and your daughter's going off to college, and probably by her first spring break I'll be a mom, too. And my baby's father is dead before it's even going to happen."

"Bee, you're going to love being a mother."

Bernice didn't respond.

"Maybe there is something to what you said about Curly," said Rachel. "That he wanted to die."

"I still don't see it."

"Just telling you about Dina now, I can feel a spirituality about myself. I was asking Marty to get more spiritual, you know, to accept certain turns in life as inevitable, as part of a bigger meaning. Like my moving to New York was a bigger thing than our staying together as lovers, how being with my daughter while she grew accustomed to a big city like that was far more important than what we would've tried to keep together. I don't think Marty ever really got that. He wasn't spiritual. Logical, yes. But Curly was the opposite. Maybe he had a gift after all."

"I always thought he was smarter than people gave him credit for. I knew he was in touch with his feelings. He *was* spiritual."

Rachel took Bernice home so she could make plans for Curly's funeral. She wanted Harper's to do the service. Burial would follow at a cemetery in East Los Angeles on Whittier Boulevard.

~ ~

As a veal shank simmered in a covered pot and penne he just extruded from his own pasta machine dried on wax paper in the dining room, Joey put on the suit that had belonged to his cousin Paul, then he took the bus to Harper's Funeral Home. With stops along the way, the ride took twenty minutes. He stood out among other passengers; some wore baggy jeans and knee-long shirts and had tattoos.

Harper's was a colonial-style building fronted by a lush lawn and a crescent-shaped row of Greek statues. It had four, thirty-foot-high, ivy-covered columns all around it. Recessed between the center two in front were double wooden doors with stained-glass windows. Despite its proximity to a Burger King, the property projected an old-world dignity. A little ways down from the road was a single-story cinema with an art-house facade and a marquee of smutty titles suggesting anal intrusion.

As Joey approached the entrance gate, four men middle-aged and older entered the building. Though they were solemn, their attire was casual.

Joey wondered if he was too dressy for a funeral home in the middle of a muggy, hot July afternoon. He entered a darkened foyer that was almost too cold from refrigerated air. Soft organ music contrasted sharply with the noisy street. Yellow roses in white vases on waist-high pedestals added color to the otherwise low-keyed room. An attendant in a black suit, a slender, bald man in his fifties with a gray goatee, greeted Joey with a sober expression. His hands were joined in front.

"The name of the deceased, sir?" said the attendant.

Joey whispered, "Marty Bagliamente. He was my uncle."

The attendant indicated the second room on Joey's right where the foyer opened to a promenade whose arched ceiling was painted with murals of biblical settings. Its four viewing rooms were closed. Between each was a high-backed, plain wooden bench. Opposite the viewing rooms were two empty chapels with their doors open.

Joey entered the viewing room. A casket with gold handles and gray-velvet exterior lay open on a marble pedestal against the farthest wall. Marty's head was visible from where Joey stood. The four people who'd entered before him were talking quietly to Gloria. It appeared to Joey that they were introducing themselves. After each man said a few words of sympathy, he moved to the casket, bowed, then moved to the side and waited for the others.

Joey stayed in the back. Marty didn't look natural to him. His hair was combed to the side instead of back, the way Marty combed it. He had too much makeup on. But he looked comfortable.

Gloria brightened at seeing Joey. "You came," she whispered as she walked to him, using a cane.

"'Course," said Joey.

Gloria was five-foot five and frail. Her handsome features, highlighted by striking, blue-gray eyes, projected an indomitable strength that was undercut only by her narrow shoulders, which hunched forward as if they'd given in to the weight of heavy crosses over the years. She had firmly poised lips, a straight nose, and eyebrows that rose by dint of curiosity at all times, as if she were attuned to and interested in your thoughts. She wore a black dress, diamond necklace, and matching earrings. Her hair was fashionably short, gray-and-white, and cut to the contour of her head.

"I'm glad you chose that suit," said Gloria. "It fits you. But why'd you wear it now in all this heat?"

"I told my mom I'd try it on and it fit, so I wore it," said Joey.

"You could've waited until the funeral, but it's sweet you wore it to come here."

Joey kissed her on the cheek. "You look nice, Aunt Gloria."

"Thank you. You didn't ride your bike, did you?"

Joey shook his head. "The bus."

"We need to get you a car. I'll see to that. In fact, I'd like to give you Uncle Marty's car."

"Aunt Gloria, can we go somewhere and talk for a little bit?"

Gloria was surprised that Joey had no reaction to getting a car, his first, and an expensive one at that. "Of course," she said.

Gloria indicated the promenade. Joey opened the door for her, and they stepped out of the viewing room and sat on the bench facing each other. She searched Joey's eyes and waited for him to speak. The organ music was bugging him. Music was supposed to lift one's spirits.

"It's a weird time to ask," said Joey, "but I was wondering. Did Uncle Marty ever talk about crime, y'know, like, violent crime? I mean enough to do something about it?"

"What a curious question," said Gloria.

Joey held his tongue. When Gloria saw that he wasn't going to comment, she answered respectfully. "He didn't like it, if that's what you mean. We had to sell our restaurant in Cleveland because of street crime. He spent a fortune for security around the club, lighting, parking personnel, insurance. We donated to the L.A.P.D. and the Sheriff's Department, and we went to their social functions. He felt good about that. Does any of this answer your question?"

"I'm not sure," said Joey. "It's kind of hard, y'know. Did he ever, like, donate money to, like, secret organizations to fight crime?"

"Secret organizations, Joey?"

"No, I just always heard the C.I.A. sold crack to gangs and stuff, y'know, like you drug animals. Did you ever hear that?"

"Those are allegations," said Gloria. "But what's it got to do with Uncle Marty?"

"I don't know. I just heard a lot of rich people want African Americans to stay in South Central, the violent ones. They don't want 'em going out of the hood. In fact, they don't care if they kill each other over drug deals and all that stuff. In fact, some of them get illegal guns and stuff like that, y'know, to help out cops, and some of 'em even give money to secret organizations that make sure bad stuff happens down there and it stays down there."

"Did you hear that Uncle Marty did any of that?" asked Gloria.

"Not really."

"Yes you did or you wouldn't be asking me about it."

Joey looked away. "Well, can you just tell me if he did?"

"He didn't have a prejudiced bone in his body."

"No, I know, but…what about his attitude toward criminals, the ones that ruin it for everybody else?"

"One of the things Martin used to say was that laws are like trees. If you run into them, you get knocked out, and if you keep running into them you get hurt bad, and that's how it's supposed to be, because enough trees are supposed to keep a certain element from running amok. But if the trees are cut down, there won't be anything to stop those who would run through a civilized society taking whatever they want. He hated reading in the newspaper about violent, senseless crime. He thought it was so destructive."

Joey blew out a breath of air. "This is going to sound weird, Aunt Gloria. You know how you and him sort of, like, you were almost, like, just living under the same roof? I mean married but—"

"Yes," said Gloria. Her interruption was to stop Joey's struggle to find euphemisms.

"And, like, wasn't that 'cause of how Paulie got killed? That you sort of blamed Uncle Marty? Not him personally but, like—"

"Joey, what are you trying to say?"

"Well, like, in that same vein, could the fact that a drunk driver killed Paulie sort of make Uncle Marty do something, like, radical?"

"I'm not sure what you mean."

"Well you said Uncle Marty wouldn't break the law or condone anybody else breaking it, right? But what if what happened to Paulie made him go back on that in sort of the same way you went back on your marriage responsibilities?"

"Are you asking if our son's death subverted his principles?"

"Yeah, exactly."

"A drunk killed our son and Uncle Marty refused to get out of the business of turning drunks out onto the streets to kill other innocent people."

"But what I'm really asking…Did Uncle Marty take the law into his own hands because the drunk *got away with it?*"

"Now I see what you mean." She patted Joey's hands lovingly. "Joey, two things you need to understand. Three, actually. One, I *always* hated alcohol. My father abused it, not publicly, but at home he went from a sophisticate to a bumbling fool. Two, a country that lets drunks drive isn't a civilized or compassionate society. I should have been fighting that all these years, but instead I internalized it, and I suppose that didn't make me a very good wife. But the divide between Martin and me started before that. At one time he and another man wanted to open a fancy Italian restaurant in Beverly Hills. The lure of movie stars put big dollar signs in their eyes. Well, I didn't trust the other man. For one thing, he flirted with me when Martin wasn't looking. And sure enough, I found out he cheated on his wife. He'd done other disreputable things, too. They needed my money for financing, so when I refused it fell through. Martin's ego wouldn't let him tell the other man I was to blame, so they had heated words. Each blamed the other and so forth. It wasn't long after that that Paulie was killed. Martin was so devastated, he looked for a scapegoat, and that man became his scapegoat."

"That guy was the guy that owns the Sonoma Inn?"

Gloria nodded. "Dominick Catina."

"Wow," said Joey. "I heard it was 'cause Uncle Marty thought the drunk came from Dom's that night."

"You can't rule that out, not when you look at the geography between the two bars. But the bigger point, what Martin wouldn't recognize, was that a drunk from his *own* bar could have done the same thing. No, a brand new green pickup truck was reported stolen the next day. The description by witnesses was verified by the dealer on North Figueroa Street who sold it, but it was never recovered and we'll never know if Dominick was a party to it."

After all this sunk in, Joey said, "What's the third thing?"

Gloria's voice turned chilly. "As you know—I've spoken of it often—Martin had a mistress. I don't know much about her and I wish to know even less. But any woman who would carry on with a married man all that time has to have an empty life and cannot possibly have any morals. So whatever you wanted to ask me about Martin and his views on crime, or if he combated it in his own illegal way, I can't say. But she can, I'm sure. They had to talk about *something*."

"I appreciate all that, Aunt Gloria. But, like, from your gut, what do you think?"

"Martin would never do anything criminal."

Joey sighed with relief. "Then it's her," he said.

"Martin was a good man, Joey, but we couldn't get past what happened to Paulie. I held him responsible, yet the whole time I knew it was irrational. He knew having a mistress was wrong but he wouldn't come to me instead of her. So we both held firm against our better judgments, and that's the way it stayed."

"The honey bubble," thought Joey. "Classic case." He said it more to himself than for Gloria.

"Do you want to see him now?" said Gloria.

"Yeah," said Joey.

He helped Gloria to her feet, and they walked back into the viewing room.

~ TWENTY-SIX ~

Rachel wanted to look nice for her so-called date with Joey. He'd done a lot for her already, and she might yet need his help to get in the Kitchen. After spending time with Bernice in Eagle Rock, she drove home to Burbank and put on a light blue, knee-high, sleeveless shift dress with a deep, open square neck. She'd bought the dress the day before her last dinner at Mama Funelli's with Marty. Her intent was to distract Marty from episodes of melancholy that had become frequent near the anniversary of his son's death. But before he'd picked her up that night, she'd decided her intent was wrong, that Marty needed to talk about his melancholy instead of getting distracted by what she wore. So she put something else on that night.

For Joey, however, she thought she'd show off. God willing, her body wasn't ready to be put out to pasture. She added a small-beaded bracelet that matched the dress. Her stiletto thong sandals were brown, a shade darker than her tanned legs. She put lotion on her neck so it gleamed against her coal-black hair and silver earrings. Into a small leather handbag she put her wallet, makeup case, cell phone, pepper spray, spare keys and her gun.

An hour earlier, Rachel had left Bernice after assuring her she'd return within a few hours. Bernice said fine, particularly after she'd taken more medication and she'd lain down on her sofa to rest in front of the television. Rachel ordered pizzas and Italian ice cream and had it delivered for her. She also rented new video releases.

For the first time ever, Rachel drove her Lexus to Hillside Park. She knew Cedar would spot her Corolla because he'd seen it every week in her driveway for years. She parked near the Golding Circle house just before eight o'clock. No car was in the driveway and no strange cars were in front. She went inside the house and saw the damage done by Cedar. He'd thrown the contents of her bedroom bookcase on the floor, emptied drawers and ransacked her closet. And her bedspread was gone. The answering machine had no new messages.

She returned to the living room and sat on the sofa that faced the windows to Golding Circle. With her gun in her lap, she waited for Joey to arrive and at the same time kept a lookout for Cedar.

Eight o'clock came and went. Her phone didn't ring. By eight-fifteen she was restless. When she stood up to walk around the room, her foot felt something. There by the sofa was Cammy's bible. She thumbed through it. Selected text was underscored, checks in margins denoted certain passages, and countless pages were dog-earred. It did not have Cammy's name on it.

She tried to recall if Marty ever said that Cedar quoted from the Bible among his other sources of inspiration. Thinking he hadn't, she concluded that either Cedar had turned to God since Marty died or that some other individual with a religious bent had invaded her home. Whatever the answer, the house was giving her the creeps. Maybe it was the simple fact that Marty had died there. At eight twenty-five, Rachel drove to Joey's house. In his eagerness to be with her, thought Rachel, Joey at least could be on time for their date. That he wasn't made her think that something had gone wrong.

~ ~

At the same time, Kenny picked Dom up in the parking lot of The Sonoma Inn for their meeting with Cedar. When Dom got in the car, he tilted his head back to look at Kenny through the lower part of his bifocals. He saw an angry man whose features seethed.

Wanting Dom to know he was furious, Kenny gripped his steering wheel with white knuckles and kept his back straight and uncomfortably rigid.

"You need a drink," said Dom.

Kenny shouted: "I'm not talking till we get to Cedar's, then somebody's going to pay."

Dom's dislike of Kenny exploded. "You got something to say, say it now!"

Kenny exploded too. "Shut up or I'll kill you, I swear it."

"No baboon gets to talk to me like that!"

"I got a *right* to talk to you like that. Only *two* assholes knew about Curly, and *one* of 'em told the cops."

This surprised Dom. "How'd you find that out?"

"They came by a little while ago with a million questions. I *am not* going down alone! You hear me? I *am not* going down alone!"

"You think I'd rat on you, you sorry son-of-a-bitch?"

"We'll just see!" shouted Kenny. "*We'll just see!*"

Kenny cleared the intersection of Sonoma and Hector. Two miles ahead was Colorado Boulevard, then it was a half-mile to the street Cedar lived on. Traffic was light.

"I told you it was a set-up, but you wouldn't listen," said Dom.

"He *threatened* me," said Kenny. "What was I *supposed* to do? He kills a guy right in front of me. What was I *supposed* to do?"

"That was you and Cedar," said Dom. "You had no cause bringing me into it."

"He didn't give me a lot of options. I just told you he killed a guy right in front of me! That's a hard thing to get out of your mind when the guy doing the killing's giving orders!"

"Well now it's a two-way street," said Dom. "*We're* giving *him* the deal: *no* options! I've hated that Nazi prick as long as I hated his boss, so I got no problem getting tough with him."

"Wait a minute," said Kenny. "*We're* telling Cedar what's up? How the hell are we going to do that?"

"Figure it out. There's two of us and we got guns."

"Yeah but—"

"This guy's a loose canon," said Dom. "This shows how much control Marty had over him. There's no telling how bad this can get. He'll bring us all down. I was in business when he was still getting snot wiped off his nose. Marty and I were making money when he was still in high school. So if he thinks he can shove me around, we'll see who's capable of shoving him around."

"So how are we going to do it?" Kenny sounded a bit hopeful.

"First off, we're not guarding Marty's. Second, speak your piece. Third, we're out of there. If he gets rough, we shoot him. He's got to be stopped now. This circus stops tonight. The longer he's got the upper hand the longer we're in serious trouble."

Kenny felt a little better. He even relaxed his posture at the steering wheel.

～～

When Rachel reached Joey's house, she saw no cars in the driveway or in front. She parked on the street. The sun had set half-an-hour earlier, but it still wasn't dark out. Even so, a few porch lights up and down the street were on, kids played in front yards and on sidewalks, and people walked their dogs, jogged, or returned from Ralphs on foot with grocery bags.

Rather than risk knocking on the door and having Freda answer it, Rachel called Joey from her cellphone in her car.

He picked up on the first ring. "Hello?" he said.

"What happened to our date?" said Rachel.

Joey hung up. Okay, thought Rachel, something *is* wrong. She turned off her cell phone and walked to the front door of the house. When she reached it, Joey, as if he knew she was outside, opened the door and stood in the doorway with one hand holding open the screen door. His expression was sullen. He wore an apron over a long undershirt, baggy gym shorts and running shoes. Rachel stayed where she was, about eight feet from him.

A porch light above Joey's head lit Rachel against the murky twilight enveloping the neighborhood. Joey could not have had a better view of the sexy look Rachel had put together just for him. Her dress revealed a perfect hourglass figure. The light cast only the roundest of teasing shadows across her ample cleavage. Her chin and jaw were so cleanly pronounced that the effect made her neck appear even longer and thinner than it already was. Her features, freed from yesterday's teary eyes and smudged mascara, glowed freshly in the light. Rachel knew the preparation she put into her appearance had paid off; it was clear in Joey's eyes. She felt vindicated for buying the dress, but at the same time realized that he was troubled by something about her.

"Mmmm," she said, referring to kitchen smells wafting out the door. It was a subtle attempt to divine his thoughts without setting off his defenses.

After being momentarily blinded by her beauty, Joey looked coldly into her eyes but said nothing.

"Now that's enough," said Rachel. "You made me promise. I was there at eight. Now you hang up on me and you look at me with hate in your eyes.

Joey nodded to her car. "What kind of money buys *that?*"

"What? My car?"

"Not too many people in Hillside Park can afford a Lexus…unless they got something going on the side."

"What are you getting at, Joey?"

He mocked her. "Innocent people could get hurt if we call the cops. *Some* innocence. What a hypocrite."

Rachel's voice rose. "What's the matter with you?"

"I heard about your little social engineering. That's *so* uncool. I still can't believe it. You wouldn't call the cops 'cause you're *in* with them. Don't act so innocent. It's bad enough my uncle was involved."

"Did your mother put that trash in your head?"

"She doesn't know, but she was right about you anyway—Aunt Gloria, too. I just want to know how involved my uncle was. I can see some people sick of the criminal justice system getting together and maybe *talking* about, like, *limited* vigilante justice. I could see Uncle Marty doing *that* much 'cause of what happened to Paulie. But what you're doing to African Americans is *totally* wrong. Or are you a *total* sociopath?"

Rachel stepped closer, put her hand on Joey's shoulder as if he were delirious, and searched his eyes. "What happened since I saw you last?"

Her penetrating eyes stared into his like his therapist's used to. Her body soap or perfume was intoxicating. Nonetheless, he removed her hand from his shoulder and let it drop.

"You piss ant," said Rachel. "I got all dressed up to have dinner with you because of what you went through yesterday and now you're pushing me away? If you don't want to see me again, just tell me. I'm moving away after the funeral anyway, but I thought we could get to know each other a little first. I wanted to tell you what Marty had in his heart for you. I'm not even sure your aunt knows. But why should I after this insulting behavior?"

"Right now, I'm not sure I want to hear what he thought about me."

"You make me sick," said Rachel. "You'll never know another man like that. You know what he did? He always said 'thank you' after we got together. This was after *thousands* of times. Even though he paid me after each one and I told him it was foolish to *pay* me *and* thank me—like *I* didn't enjoy it—he *still* thanked me. And it wasn't to keep up appearances because he didn't do that. It was simple words expressing how much it meant to him deep down, and he said it every time and he meant every time. That's what a pure, honest, rock-solid man he was. And now you're turning against him because of some hateful lie you heard?"

Approaching headlights made Joey blink. It was his mother pulling into their driveway. Gloria, following, parked on the street behind Rachel. Freda drove a two year-old Toyota Celica, Gloria a new Buick Park Avenue.

"Great," said Joey with dread.

Rachel turned to see the women exit their cars. Freda carried a doggie bag from where they'd dined earlier. Gloria used her cane. They joined each other on the way to the front porch, then stopped when they saw Joey and Rachel. Curiosity about her overwhelmed them. For all their scrutiny, she could have been a Martian. Each moved a bit to get a better light on this mysterious woman.

"Who's your friend, Joey?" said a smiling, courtly Freda. Her voice contained a hint of worry that Joey's answer might be painful to hear.

Joey cleared his throat. "Uh, Mom, Aunt Gloria, this is uh—"

Rachel stepped forward. "I'm Rachel Ellis," she said.

Freda turned away as if Rachel radiated poison. Gloria, taking full measure of Rachel, was disconcerted at her indisputable beauty. She'd had a vague idea of her age, but even that seemed off-kilter.

"What's this *puttana* doing here, Joseph?" said Freda.

Before Joey could answer, Rachel walked toward Gloria with an imploring expression and her hand outstretched. "Mrs. Bagliamente, will you accept my condolences? It would mean a lot to me."

Gloria looked into her eyes. "We just came from the mortuary. I came here to grieve with the only family I have left and I find you here. And you dare speak to me?"

"That was not my intent," said Rachel. She felt the chill. "Please excuse me." She walked to her car without saying another word.

Freda spoke loudly so that Rachel could hear. "That woman's got no soul. She brought *shame* on this family."

Rachel drove away. She was crying. Joey tried to watch her, but Freda and Gloria briskly ushered him into the house.

~ ~

Kenny stopped in front of Cedar's duplex. Houses on both sides of the narrow street were modest. The street's grade increased from Colorado Boulevard into the foothills.

"Look at that," said Kenny, pointedly nodding to the driveway.

"I can't!" said Dom.

"Mr. Dependable's not even here," said Kenny. "His car's gone. Maybe he's late, I don't know."

"Let's scram," said Dom.

Kenny started to pull away, but Cedar drove into his driveway so suddenly that Kenny had to hit his brakes to avoid broad-siding him.

"What happened?" said Dom.

"He just showed up," said Kenny. "He was probably laying low."

Cedar kept his Cherokee half in the street to block Kenny from driving forward. With his crutches, he approached Kenny's car.

"This is my last day on earth," Kenny whispered to Dom.

Cedar leaned in. "Change of plans," he said to Kenny. "Take Dom back. I'll see you later at your bar."

"What change of plans?" said Kenny.

Cedar barked, "I'll explain when I see you."

Dom waited for Kenny to speak his piece. "*Tell* him, Kenny."

Kenny didn't say anything.

"Tell me what?" said Cedar.

"*Tell him!*" shouted Dom.

Kenny didn't know how to begin.

"Kenny," said Cedar.

"What?"

"Have you ever watched 'Jeopardy?'" said Cedar.

"Couple times," said Kenny. "What for?"

"That part after the first break where the host asks contestants about their interests and backgrounds?"

"What about it?" said Kenny.

"You're even more boring than that, so I don't care what you have to say."

Dom shouted: "Tell him what you told me, Kenny!"

"Back off and I will," shouted Kenny. He turned to Cedar and waited a moment before he spoke. "These two detectives showed up in my place tonight asking questions about Curly. They said they got an anonymous tip."

"What'd they ask?" said Cedar. His interest was suddenly high.

"So, you don't *care* about the anonymous tipper," said Kenny.

"You think it was me?" said Cedar. "*Do you think it was me?*"

Kenny was too scared to answer.

"Tell me what they asked," said Cedar.

"'Was Curly in last night.'"

"What'd you say?" said Cedar.

"I told 'em yes."

"There's that high I.Q. again."

"Two strangers in suits and ties come into my bar, *naturally* I'm not going to think straight!"

"Naturally," said Cedar.

"When I heard 'anonymous tip' I'm thinking one of you back-stabbers tried to cut my legs off."

"Who else knows?" said Cedar.

Kenny nodded toward Dom.

"Why didn't you just put out it on the Internet?" said Cedar.

"How *else* was I going to get him to come here, Cedar? I was trying to tell him how serious you were. Besides, Curly *was* in every night, except when he was with his girlfriend. I'm thinking they already asked around about that, so how *could* I say no? You think I want them guys hauling me away in handcuffs like some dog?"

"So what if you said Curly was in last night?"

"So *what*? Are you *kidding*? That fat snatch of his called a hundred times last night and every time I told her he *wasn't*. So right there, Johnny on the spot, these dicks got a discrepancy. That's how they know they got their guy. All they've got to do is ask a couple careful questions to mess me up and that's all she wrote for Kenny Grimmet."

"What else did they ask?" said Cedar.

"Was anybody else in that could confirm Curly was there.'"

"And?"

"I told 'em Earl Zell was. *Then* I thought, 'Earl can't remember *nothing,* he was so bombed.' So now if they go to Bernice *and* Earl, that's *two* people's words against mine."

"And none of you with the brains God gave a gopher," said Cedar. "What else did they ask?"

"'Is that your car out back.' They're saying it was a hit-and-run and whoever did it left tire tracks and they made a cast of them and they need to make a match and they're looking *right at me like I'm the one*! So now they can get me for lying about Curly *and* for running over him, and I didn't do anything wrong except cover *your* mess."

"They're not going to get you," said Cedar.

"They got me on all sides."

"They came here too," said Cedar.

It took Kenny three seconds for this to sink in. "What?" he said.

"They asked about me and my car too," said Cedar.

"What'd you tell 'em?" asked Kenny.

"I wasn't here," said Cedar. "I've been out keeping an eye on Marty's." A more thorough explanation would have included that he'd spent the entire day in a more-or-less continuous loop driving by Marty's, front and back, then to Rachel's house on Golding Circle, then to Bernice's house. He saw a Lexus in Bernice's driveway, but he dismissed it as not belonging to Rachel because he knew she drove a Corolla.

"Then how'd you know they came by?" asked Kenny.

"Someone's staying with me," said Cedar. "She told me. Her English is bad, so don't have any illusions about me tipping off the police."

Kenny believed him. He turned to Dom. A prolonged silence prompted Dom to speak. "Don't look at me," he said. "I don't know enough to tip bird shit off a fence."

"Then who did?" Kenny asked Cedar.

"That's not our worry right now," said Cedar. "Get Dom back to his rat hole before he molts."

"Not much to draw on now that Marty's dead, eh Cedar?" said Dom.

Cedar reached in and snatched Dom's glasses right off his face, then snapped them in half. "Don't speak to me again, Dominick."

Kenny laughed at Dom. "Now you look like Jiminy Cricket."

"Shove it up your ass, Kenny," said Dom.

Kenny turned to Cedar. "What about that cast, man?"

"Kenny, the D.A.'s going to ask himself why you would tell Bernice Curly wasn't there last night. Answer: he told you to. Same thing happens in every bar in every city when the other half calls. Then he's going to remind himself that Curly was a transient and that transients die from sleeping in the wrong places all the time. Then there's your car. He knows a lawyer can match your tires anywhere he wants to look. Then, unless it's a crime of passion, he can't make his case without a motive, and he'll know that running over a malodorous, expendable vagrant in a back alley at two in the morning in a nowhere town is not a crime of passion. But most of all, he's going to tell himself that Curly had no family, that his friends were bums, that he had no ties to high places. That's how the D.A.'s going to look at this."

"What about Rachel and Bernice?" said Kenny.

"Anything Bernice says is hearsay and Rachel has a whole other situation going on. The last thing she wants is attention."

"What do I say if they arrest me?" asked Kenny.

"Dom will bail you out," said Cedar. "If he doesn't, I'll make sure he's their prime suspect."

"You've got a lot of class, Cedar," said Dom.

Cedar straightened up. "If any of this gets out, I'll kill you both." He got in his Cherokee and cleared the way for Kenny to drive off. Kenny made a U-turn to Colorado Boulevard. On his way there, Dom shouted that he didn't want to hear any more about Cedar again.

~ TWENTY-SEVEN ~

As Rachel drove from Joey's house, she was hurt and bewildered. Was he a sexual nebbish or some lord of rectitude? She almost said it didn't matter, that she'd be gone soon and little Joey Bagliamente would have to work out his confusion alone. But she felt an obligation to Marty to give Joey a different perspective of his uncle than she was sure he'd gotten from his mother or aunt.

She wondered if getting the money from the Kitchen could be done before Bernice expected her back. Her bigger concern was not knowing where Cedar was or if he'd set a trap for her in the Kitchen. She decided to try.

Nobody was out front of Marty's or in back. She originally wanted Joey to drop her off, then leave when she went inside, then pick her up after she'd gotten the money. That way, Cedar wouldn't see her car and wouldn't suspect anything. But Joey was out of the picture now.

She parked on Vista Madera and walked to Arrow. Two guys in a carpet-cleaning van driving by made catcalls in Spanish suggesting she lift her dress and adjoin part of her anatomy with their faces. Soon she reached the door to the Kitchen, where she saw that the alarm lock had been bashed in and jammed up with hardened paste.

"My bluff worked," she said. Grinning in private admiration of Cedar's resourcefulness, she unlocked both deadbolts. She had apprehension about entering. She'd never been in the Kitchen without Marty except to lock up when he was sick. There they made love countless times, ordered in, and stayed up watching old movies and talking until dawn. But now the Kitchen was nothing more than a suffocating collection of junk, useless paperwork and bar supplies. And its quiet, which before meant cozy and secure, was now eerie.

Rachel entered, locked the door behind her, felt for the light switch and turned it on.

~ ~

Freda fell into her chair, kicked off her shoes, and screamed at Joey while removing her hose and massaging her feet. Over dinner earlier in the evening, Gloria told her about her son's questions regarding Marty at the funeral home. From the kitchen, where she was making tea, Gloria could hear Freda's merciless yelling. Joey stood in full-assault mode between the living room and kitchen, the farthest he could get from his mother and still remain in vision.

"Where'd you get those lies about your uncle?" said Freda. "*The Sopranos?*"

"No!" said Joey.

"We're Italian so we deal drugs, is that it? Whoever told you that is a big liar. Was it that *whore?*"

"Stop saying that," said Joey.

"She's a *nun* now? Excuse me, but she doesn't *look* like one. Maybe it's me."

"You never even talked to Uncle Marty. How do you know *what* he did? All you ever did was complain about him."

"Yes, I guess I'm just a tad old-fashioned when it comes to my brother destroying his marriage over *that woman.*"

"You don't even know how he treated *that woman*," said Joey.

"You mean if he was good to her it's supposed to make everything else super deluxe? Is that how I brought you up?"

"I didn't say that," said Joey.

"Then what *are* you saying?"

"I'm saying it wasn't what you made it out to be."

"*You* know this? What'd you do, *spy* on them?"

"He told me she's a good person and that was enough for me. But you don't know her and all you can do is call her names."

"*Now* embarrass his widow," said Freda. "Keep defending your new best friend before my brother's *even buried*."

Gloria returned from the kitchen. "Let's settle down," she said. She put her cane by a chair, sat at the table and faced her nephew. "Joey, why are you taking this woman's side if you think she and Uncle Marty were in on this illegal business together?"

"I'm not, Aunt Gloria. It's just I believed him when he told me she's a good person. But then I heard this other stuff, so I wanted to talk to her about it, but before I could you two got here."

"What'd she come over here for anyway?" said Freda.

"We were just going to talk," said Joey. "I made dinner."

"With *my* money?" said Freda.

"Easy, Freda," said Gloria.

"Oh it's nauseating," said Freda. "My own son."

"Joey," said Gloria. "Do you believe what you heard?"

"All I can say is the guy that told me knows what's going on."

Gloria looked at Freda. "Dominick."

"That's what it sounds like," said Freda. "He badmouthed Marty right up to the end, I know that."

"And he has reason to badmouth her," said Gloria. "They have a past."

"Find a penis, she has a past with it," said Freda.

"There you go again, Mom."

"There *you* go again, taking her side," said Freda.

Gloria raised her voice. "I don't want this lie hanging over the funeral."

"What am I supposed to do about it?" asked Joey.

"*Was* it Dominick Catina?" said Gloria.

"No," said Joey.

"Then who else is spreading these lies?"

"Aunt Gloria, today you acted like you couldn't care less."

"Today I was wrong. I've been thinking about myself throughout this when I should have been thinking about Martin. He was a proud man. If what you heard is a vicious rumor started by one of his competitors, then I want that known, and I want the rumor obliterated before it spreads any further."

"What if it's true?" said Joey.

"All the more reason to find out," said Gloria. "Martin didn't need the money and I can't imagine any other reason he'd do what this rumor implies. Joey, I want you—you're an adult now and you carry his name, our name—I want you to be able to hold your head high. This is an honorable family, despite its flaws. I want to know how this started."

"And why now?" said Freda. "Why didn't we hear about it before now? You know that floozy at Cooper's?"

"Meg Szymczak?" said Gloria.

"Yes, her. She's been going to happy hour at Dom's with her husband for years. He manages the health food store I go to. We talk all the time. This would have come out before now, the way they gossip over there. He would've told me. Meg would've told me. Sam's wife would've told you, Nick or Adele. *Somebody* would've heard."

"There's one way to find out," said Joey.

Freda sat forward and glared at Joey. "I don't want you talking to that *filth* anymore. I don't ever want to see her again. I should call an exterminator."

"I care about our name too," said Joey. "Just let me find out my own way."

"I don't want you getting hurt," said Freda, now choking up. "Is that such a bad thing for a mother?" Her features crinkled into a self-pitying grimace. "This family's endured too much pain. I don't want anymore of it. I don't want you involved with bad people. I couldn't live with more pain. I don't have anything left in me that isn't dead from all the pain. I always hoped, in spite of my self-image, that I was a good mother. I tried to raise you with values. But now I hear the same things out of your mouth that came out of your uncle's mouth. You both *like* that bunch, you're drawn to that drinking, that whoring around. It's not what I wanted out of you, Joey. And if it's true what you heard and you go snooping around the likes of Dominick Catina and Kenny Grimmet and that *leech bitch*, you're going to get hurt. You're naïve. My brother was tough and smart and he had a bodyguard. Tell him, Gloria. Tell him I don't want to lose him."

Gloria spoke to Freda with sympathy and understanding. "Joey can handle himself."

"Now *you?*" said Freda.

"Freda," said Gloria. "Martin was worried Joey didn't have much fire inside him. He'd be proud to know he's ready to protect our honor."

"He'll get caught up in it if he tries," said Freda.

"He won't become one of them," said Gloria.

"You know what they say about sleeping with dogs," said Freda.

"Mom, you're way off on this."

"Freda, it would be better if you gave Joey your blessing," said Gloria. "Let him do what he has to. You'll find out you did a good job with him."

Freda put her head down. "Joey's right," she said. "I never talked to Marty. All I did was complain about him. And he helped me and he was a good provider. He just never recovered from losing that adorable boy. You have to be happy to make others happy, and I just never was."

"Mom, please."

"Please what?" said Freda.

"Uncle Marty wouldn't like hearing that. The last thing he told me was how he liked seeing people have a good time. He'd hate us sitting around all gloomy and pissed off and stuff."

Freda studied Joey. "When did you get so smart?"

"Mom, we'll still have Sunday dinners."

"Of course," said Gloria. "Nothing breaks this family apart."

~ ~

After dismissing Kenny and Dominick, Cedar went into his house with confidence that his plans were falling into place. A conversation with Kenny tonight, a few busy things tomorrow, an appearance at Marty's funeral, and a big finish that night were all that was left before the second half of his life got underway. He counted the hours. Helen was watching television when he tossed his crutches in a corner and sat beside her. "We're going to Sacramento tonight," he said. "Tomorrow we'll look for a house."

"Joo haff to talk to the policemens, don you?"

"Later," said Cedar. "I have a meeting in a minute. After that, we'll go."

"Joo wan for me to bring clothes?"

"Enough for a day. Don't answer the telephone when I'm gone."

"Okay."

"Clean up. It's a long drive."

Helen reached for Cedar's hand, pulled him close, and kissed him on his lips. He returned it, then stood up and got his crutches. On the way to his car, he wiped the kiss from his lips.

~~

After things settled down at Joey's house and Gloria went home, he rode his bike to Golding Circle. It was a clear night. He could see the downtown skyline. A breeze cooled the air. Aside from TV's heard here and there, the neighborhood was quiet, like an empty mountain campground. He was disappointed not to see Rachel's Corolla or Lexus. Nonetheless, he parked his bike and approached the front door, which was ajar, and went in.

Looking through the house, Joey was surprised at how little furniture it had outside of the main bedroom. The barrenness of the bathroom surprised him, too. Towels, washcloth, shower mat, its walls, all dry as sun-baked cardboard, that was all. Rachel told him that morning that she was going to shower before they met at eight, so where was evidence she had? Where was that luscious soap he'd smelled on her a little while ago?

The thought struck him that nobody lived there. He went into the bedroom. He found Rachel's high school senior yearbook. He took it for future reference, sat down, and ran his fingers through his hair. "If she doesn't live here," he asked himself, "where does she live? And how much more about her is phony?"

He heard a sound out back, a muffled voice. He sat up and cocked his ears to discover whence it came. He walked through the living room to the kitchen and turned on a light. The only counter appliance was a coffee maker. He opened a back door and listened again. The voice came from the ramshackle garage. Its doors, old, splintered and hanging from rusted hinges, opened accordion-style. Joey heard whole sentences coming from within, even though he couldn't make out the words. The speaker sounded as if his mouth were full of marbles. He opened the doors quietly. He didn't see anything, though he located the voice on the floor. He felt for a light switch. There was one inside, behind spider webs, on a center post where latches to the folding doors poked out of both sides. He turned the light on. There before him was Rachel's bedspread, rolled up, with a person inside.

"Hey," said Joey.

The voice stopped.

"Hey!" said Joey.

Cammy said excitedly, "Hel ee! Hel ee!"

Joey untied the bedspread. During this, Cammy rejoiced. "Ah ank-oo, ank-oo, ank-oo."

Joey saw Cammy bound, gagged, and blindfolded. He took the blindfold off, then the gag. Cammy blinked to adjust to the light. He had a goose egg on his forehead and was crying uncontrollably while also repeating what he was saying before Joey took off the gag.

"Oh Lord, hear my prayers, pay attention to my groaning, listen to my cry for help, for I will never pray to anyone but you."

When Joey peeled the tape off Cammy's wrists, Cammy pushed him aside so he could remove tape from his ankles himself. "Oh Lord, hear my prayers, pay attention to my groaning, listen to my cry for help, for I will never pray to anyone but you." When he got his ankles apart, he fell back and rotated his legs and arms as if exercising upside down on a stationary bike. He stopped every few seconds to rub his sore wrists. "Oh Lord, hear my prayers, pay attention to my groaning, listen to my cry for help, for I will never pray to anyone but you."

"Who did this to you?" said Joey.

"My bible!" said Cammy. "Where's my bible? Where am I?"

"You're in Rachel's garage," said Joey.

"I couldn't have survived without Jesus. I need to give thanks. Oh what a headache—but I wouldn't die—Jesus never left me. He summoned you. Go get me my bible."

"Where is it?"

"I had it in her house. Oh Lord, hear my prayers, pay attention to my groaning, listen to my cry for help, for I will never pray to anyone but you."

"Who did this to you?"

"Cedar Roach. He could have killed me. I never hurt him. I prayed for him even while I was suffering in here. See if she's got aspirins, will you? The pain's excruciating. It's God's punishment for my sins, but I still want aspirins. Does it look like I've been bleeding? Maybe I got brain damage." He felt his forehead. When he felt the goose-egg lump, he winced. "Maybe it's just on the outside."

Joey helped him off the floor. With his arm on Joey's shoulder, Cammy limped toward the house.

"Where'd you hear about that stuff you told me about Rachel and my uncle?" said Joey.

"Cedar, same guy."

"When'd he tell you?"

"A few days ago."

"*Why'd* he tell you?"

"Social injustice."

"You believed him?"

"Yes, he's an honorable man. Well, now I don't know. But so did Kenny Grimmet, the other man from yesterday. Is it still Tuesday?"

"It's Tuesday night."

"Kenny knew about it before Cedar told me. They wouldn't have told me if Cedar didn't think it was necessary. You know what? They don't trust me. They never did. They think I'm stupid. At least Cedar treated me with respect—till this anyway."

Cammy let go of Joey's shoulder and got himself a glass of tap water in Rachel's kitchen. He drank it in one gulp, which left him breathless. "I'm afraid to look at my forehead. Is it bruised? Hey, where's my glasses?"

Cammy went to the living room. Joey followed.

"They all knew it?" asked Joey. "Is there any proof?"

Cammy found his bible. He held it close to his chest, then looked around for his glasses. "What'd you say?" he asked distractedly.

"Did you just take their word for it?" said Joey.

Cammy got on his knees and looked under the sofa. His glasses were under it. He put them on and looked through them. "What do you know, they still fit."

"*Answer me!*" said Joey.

"What'd you say?"

"I said was there any proof what they told you?"

"It's in Marty's Kitchen. Oh it's great to be alive. I could have died in there. I kept rolling over, one side then the next, it was hard, but I managed. That kept my blooding circulating. But still, I could've died out there."

Joey left without saying good-bye.

~ TWENTY-EIGHT ~

On his way to Kenny's, Cedar drove by Marty's once again and looked at the alarm lock. It was still jammed. "She can't be blasé about that money," he thought. "Where's she been all day?"

He got back in his Cherokee and sat without starting the car. He had to figure how to reclaim his position of command and credibility in Kenny's eyes. He'd lost it when two big things he'd sold Kenny on had backfired. One was getting Marty's check-cashing money when they were supposed to shoot him. Two was disposing of Curly safely without repercussion. What he needed Kenny for now was bigger than all the rest. "This is what happens when you're dependent on people," he grumbled to himself. "The toughest individual depends on no one and needs only food and water. All else is desire, and therefore unnecessary for survival. I hate depending on the likes of Kenny, but there are exceptions to every rule."

Finally resigned to taking his lumps like everyone else, at least one last time, Cedar decided that instead of bullying Kenny, he would appeal to his pocketbook. He drove to an A.T.M.

~ ~

Kenny was smoking and pacing behind his bar. The irony that he'd planned to murder a prominent businessman and his mistress, when now the cops were on him for disposing of an *already* dead man, and a bum at that, was eating at him. Plus, he didn't have that bum to talk to anymore, he didn't have Cammy to commiserate with, Dom had shut him out, and on this rotten night, he had no customers. Why should he? He'd posted a

notice on his door saying "back soon" when he left to pick up Dom.
Naturally his customers weren't going to come back after seeing that. They
were feeble; it was all they could do to get out *once*, much less return after
getting blanked.

When Cedar entered Kenny's, he was smiling. "You'll like this, Kenny,"
he said as he leaned his crutches on a stool.

Kenny was skeptical. Cedar *never* smiled. "I'll like what?"

"We're going to do a little cloak-and-dagger."

No sale, thought Kenny. The son-of-a-bitch is buttering me up like
some wormy salesman. The son-of-a-bitch has always talked *down* to me.
Now he's Will Rogers?

"Cloak and dagger, huh?"

"Here's the story," said Cedar. "It's simpler than it sounds. By the way,
if somebody comes in, we need to be alone."

"Yeah, why would I want to make a nickel 'fore the night's over?"

"I found out something about Rachel," said Cedar. "I'm being honest
with you, I hope you appreciate it."

"Go ahead."

"I need you to help me find out where she lives," said Cedar. "Then I'll
be out of your hair. That's a promise I won't break."

"We know where she lives," said Kenny.

"She doesn't live on Golding Circle. That was for trysts."

"Very interesting," said Kenny.

"She's picking someone up at L.A.X. Thursday night. You and I will go
there in separate cars. You'll park across from the passenger terminal and
wait to hear from me. I'll go in but not in plain sight."

"You'll be hiding."

"I'll be hiding. I'll follow her back to her car. I'll call you and identify
what exit she'll take so you can tail her to where she really lives."

"Why don't you tail her yourself?"

"I could be parked too far away in time to get my car before she drives
away."

"That makes sense," said Kenny. "How are you going to call me?"

"I'm getting two cell phones tomorrow, one for each of us."

"I've never used one before."

"Neither have I, but I'm sure they're simple. Once I get in my car, you'll guide me to her. If she's leaving an attendant's booth, if she's already on Century Boulevard, it doesn't matter. If her car converts into a helicopter, you'll tell me that too."

"Then what?"

"Then I'll take over." Cedar grinned. "By the way, you can keep the cell phone."

That did it for Kenny. Cedar was trying too hard to be ingratiating. This was the set-up Dom had warned about. It was insulting, too. He didn't even *ask* Kenny to help; it was just a given he would. Nor did he even say what Kenny would get out of it. He just tried so hard to sound like a Regular Joe that he forgot Kenny was also a conniver. Kenny wanted the old Cedar, the one who'd threaten, not this namby-pamby, suck-ass imitation.

Kenny knew his biggest enemy was his own mouth. Even when he *knew* he was shooting his mouth off, he couldn't stop. It had cost him business, friends, a wife, God knows what else. But now, facing a sneaky and transparent manipulator, a deadly one at that, he vowed to keep his mouth absolutely shut so that Cedar had no idea what he was thinking. Like them Sphinxes, he thought.

"Any questions?" asked Cedar.

Just a million. "Nope," said Kenny. "It's simple, like you said."

"I'll be in Thursday with the cell phone. Give me a few minutes to set it up in your car. You should leave by six. The plane gets in later, but there's always traffic on the four-oh-five." He reached into his pocket and put twenty-five twenties on the bar.

"What's this?" said Kenny. He counted silently. "You're giving me half-a-grand?"

"For lost business," said Cedar.

"Ba-*doop*," said Kenny.

"You'll be out at least four hours. That should more than cover."

Kenny rubbed his palms together. "It does indeed."

"I don't have to tell you this is all private," said Cedar.

"Absolutely not. Especially if there's more of *this*."

"That I can't promise, but I won't rule it out either."

Kenny bit his tongue. "Your word's always been good, Cedar. If you can give me more, fine. If not, I'll know you couldn't."

Cedar had to laugh inside. Kenny was playing him just like he was playing Kenny. He took his crutches and left. Kenny was glad to have the cash. It certainly made holding his tongue worthwhile.

~ ~

Rachel spent an hour looking through the Kitchen but found nothing. She'd gone through coffee cans, old lard containers, brittle produce crates, wire baskets, plastic tubs, anything that could hold a growing supply of cash. Hundreds of cardboard boxes in three rows of shelves were left. Some came apart at the touch. Some required a stepladder to reach. Her hands were dirty, dust carpeted her hair and dress, and she was hungry. Two additional rows of shelves housed hardware, tools, bar supplies, and electrical and plumbing fixtures in trays, buckets and other containers rammed into place like pieces of a mosaic. The last row had fans, picture frames, books, lamps, display signs, car batteries, a folded baby carriage, juice blenders, foot warmers and anything else that wouldn't fit in containers.

The one wall free of storage shelves had Marty's desk against it with file cabinets on either side. Rachel found nothing in the desk or file cabinets except current invoices, payroll data and personal items Marty kept from his wife. She found nothing in his living quarters beyond furniture, clothes, toiletries, a TV and a table radio. Searching one row of boxes alone could take two hours, she'd calculated. And if she didn't put everything back, which would consume even more time, the clutter would prevent further navigation through the aisles.

She dragged the stepladder to the first row of boxes, put her shoes on Marty's desk, and climbed up. As she lifted the lid from a box on top, she heard a noise outside. It sounded like keys, followed by scratching and poking at the door. She climbed off the stepladder, leaned against the desk—which had a clear view to the rear door—and aimed her gun at it. She heard pecking at the doorframe. This told her the alarm lock was under assault.

Was Cedar trying to *un*jam it?

Rachel thought about running out the other door, through the club, and to the safety of Hector Street. That might save her life. But then what? She'd had an unwritten agreement with Marty that for all the time they were together he would build a nest egg for her. That egg represented over half of her life. Could she let Cedar get it merely because he was strong enough to fight her for it? No. If she had to stop him with a gun, so be it.

The sound stopped for agonizing seconds. A key inserted into the deadbolt unlocked it. Another key inserted into a second deadbolt unlocked it. That someone unlocked *both* frightened Rachel. Remembering the lights, she leapt to turn them off at the switch beside the door. Then, in total darkness, she felt her way back to the desk, turned and aimed the gun at the door. It opened slowly. A figure walked around it and stood in the doorway. It was Joey.

"Close the door," shouted Rachel.

Joey closed the door. Rachel turned on the lights. "What are you doing here?" she said.

"You're filthy," said Joey.

"You've got some explaining to do."

"What about you? You said you didn't have an extra alarm key."

"I didn't need it. It wasn't set."

"Then you've got one."

"Of course I've got one. Marty depended on me."

"Then you lied."

"That was to protect you. If you knew I had an extra set, Cedar would have beaten it out of you."

Joey held up his own set. "Then why'd you let me keep these?"

"That was after I shot him. From that point on we were dead no matter what. And we still are if he gets his hands on us. Now, what happened tonight?"

Rather than answer her, Joey did what he'd come here to do. He moved from row to row of shelves with deepening curiosity, both at the sheer volume of junk and at not seeing what he'd expected to see. He reached the last row, glanced into Marty's living quarters, then turned back to Rachel.

"There's no guns," he said. "It was a lie."

"What was a lie?" said Rachel.

"That fat guy told me Uncle Marty kept guns in here."

"Guns for what?"

"For bad cops," said Joey. "To get their kicks."

"Bad cops? What fat guy?"

"The Knothole guy."

"Cammy told you that? Who told *him*?"

"Cedar Roach. He said you drove around the city all day getting money from rich guys for some secret fund to keep African Americans on drugs and killing each other in gangs."

"I did that?"

Joey nodded. "You and Uncle Marty supplied gangs with crack and everything else to keep them drugged so they wouldn't go into white neighborhoods and do their crime there."

Rachel marveled privately at Cedar's twisted and self-serving imagination. "And you believed him?"

"Well it sort of sounded…"

"Cedar told an idiot lies and that idiot passed them on to you. I'll be. My hat's off to Cedar for exploiting the weakest link, and I guess I'd have to say the same thing about Cammy."

"Well, nobody ever saw in here before and nobody ever knew what you did all day..."

"If you wanted to know what I did all day, why didn't you ask me?"

"Well, I didn't—"

"Ask me now!"

Her tone scared Joey.

"I'll *tell* you what I did," said Rachel. "I raised a child. It took about thirty hours a day for the first few years, and after that, all the energy I had. I did it alone. It's the toughest job in the world. And you know why I did it outside of Hillside Park? Because of the exact kind of gossip here that makes *you* think your own uncle gave guns to cops and I sold drugs to gangs. Shame on you, Joey. Now get out of here."

Joey froze. Rachel took him by his arm and escorted him to the door. She pushed him out, then locked the deadbolts.

~ ~

Cedar got home from Kenny's to find Helen packing for their phantom trip to Sacramento. She was in their bedroom putting her slippers and folded nightgown on the bed next to a fresh set of underwear and a day's clothing. Next to her things she put Cedar's underwear and sweatpants and shirt. She turned to see him in the doorway. There was something odd about his expression.

"Was' wrong?" she said.

"I'm just not used to having this much free time," said Cedar.

"Joo like et?"

Cedar shrugged. Helen hoped he'd said yes, that spending time with her was more enjoyable than working seven nights a week.

"I'm going to take a shower," said Cedar. "Then we'll leave."

"Joo wan to may loff firs'?" said Helen.

"After I shower," he said. "Get ready."

Helen took off her clothes. Cedar went into the bathroom and locked the door. He took his clothes off, then the bandage on his leg. The wound was healing. He turned on the shower and stepped inside.

As hot water sprayed over him, Cedar thought about Slapper. What an episode it had caused in Hillside Park. It had zapped Kenny, Cammy and Dom into planning murder. Marty hadn't died from their plan, but, indirectly, thought Cedar, his death may have come from their negative energy. Curly died from their plan, but also indirectly; Slapper had sucked him into its vortex by placing him in Dom's parking lot to overhear the plan.

As for his own part, Cedar had been brought in to ensure that the evil wrought by Slapper did not get out of control. He knew, therefore, that whatever happened after he was brought in was justified, because Slapper had more power than any force on earth, and nothing so irresistible could be rejected by whomever it targeted for synaptic disruption. His analogy was this: if you're on the beach when a tidal wave comes and you kill someone trying to escape its path, that death is not your fault. It's the tidal wave's fault. Curly's death, therefore, was a consequence of Slapper's arrival in Hillside Park. Likewise, Rachel's fate was in Cedar's hands, because she, too, was inexorably connected to the evil planned by Kenny, Cammy and Dom.

He stepped out of the shower and dried off. With a bath towel around his waist, he went into his gym and closed the door. He liked to look at himself naked. He dropped the towel, spread his legs apart, put his hands on his hips and looked at himself at the wall of mirrors. Aside from the wound above his left knee, his body was flawless. He marveled at it. The exercise, the diet, the discipline all worked to make him a specimen to be admired.

The longer he stared at his body, however, the more he saw what wasn't there before. Indeed, something was happening. He blinked to make sure he wasn't hallucinating. There in the mirror, his body had started to glow from the inside. Veins, arteries, and muscles lit up as if plugged into an electrical circuit. The room went dim. His body stood out even more. Looking in the mirror was now a surreal experience. Everything but his body's reflection went black. He saw waves of light emanating from his form and dissipating in the darkness. Then his skeleton appeared by itself. His vascular system pulsated red. It was like an illustration of a transparent human body in a textbook, only everything was in neon.

His body now was the only thing in the mirror. Its shape stayed intact, but it floated a little to the right, a little to the left. Then a bolt of lighting, without sound, streaked across the mirror from right to left. Its blinding light exploded in Cedar's eyes. He had to turn away. When he returned his eyes to the mirror, the fading light showed that the room was gone. He was in another dimension.

The lightning came again, soundless like before, only this time it streaked from the other direction. Then it came again, this time from above, and this time it struck him on top of his skull and lit up his entire nervous system.

Then the lightning disappeared. In its wake, Cedar saw all the synapses in his body crackling like sparklers on a black night. They were taking over his motor movements. They took over his sight. He was lost. No mirror, no floor, no feel to the touch. An ungodly power had taken him over. His body floated. A network of neuro-connections hissed and buzzed from limb to limb.

When he could see again, he was standing over his bed. His breathing was unsteady, his forearms sore, his fingers clutched into Helen's pillow. They'd been pushing hard against pressure beneath it. He let go, stood back and lifted the pillow. Helen's face was under it. She lay motionless. Her features were still, though terror in them remained.

Cedar was still naked, his body dry, and no bath towel in sight. Helen was also naked. The clothes she'd gotten ready to pack were still on the bed. The clothes she was in before he took his shower were in a neat pile on the dresser. She didn't have a pulse.

Cedar dropped the pillow. "Holy God," he whispered.

He put his hand on Helen's and lay his head across her chest. Slapper came back, he thought. He'd invented Slapper, at least the Slapper Theory, and now it targeted him for evil? It made him kill Helen? How was that possible?

He said with sadness, "You didn't have anything to do with Marty and Rachel. I was going to let you stay here after I left. You were good to me and you never complained and you never asked for anything. This did not need to happen."

He crawled onto the bed to lie beside her. He turned her on her side with her back facing him so that they were joined with his arms around her.

"You can hear me," he said. "I've got this theory about human consciousness. It keeps going after we die until we meet our maker, then the good get separated from the bad. The bad go to hell but the good live on in some way, so let me tell you this so you'll remember it. It wasn't me, Helen. Curly was me, but not this. If you know anything about me you know I don't blame others for my actions. But this was out of my control. This was Slapper. We'll meet up again when I die. Maybe then we'll know why this happened. Until then I'm sorry. It must have been frightening for you. Only God knows what was going through your mind. I hope you didn't suffer long."

He pulled the top sheet over her body, including her head, then got up and knelt next to her.

"The innocent die young," he said. "But there's a reason for everything. It just takes a long time to figure it out."

He reached under the sheet to find her hand. He took it out and lay his head on it and held it for a long time. Sadness moved him. He'd already justified Marty's death before Marty died, and had done the same with Curly. But Helen's death shocked and mortified him. Questions swirled in his mind as he held her hand.

He didn't move until the phone rang forty minutes later. He was going to ignore it until he thought it could be the detectives. If so, and he didn't forestall them with a lie, they might come over to look around after thinking they were being stiffed. The last thing he needed was for the L.A.P.D. to find Helen dead. He walked to the living room and answered the phone.

"Hello?" he said.

"This is Cammy," said the caller. His tone was cold. "Where's my car? If you don't tell me I'm going to file a complaint for what you did to me."

Cedar was not prepared to deal with Cammy, whom he'd forgotten about anyway. "You're bothering me about that *now?*" said Cedar.

His voice scared Cammy.

"One street south of Rachel's!" said Cedar. "Don't call me again."

He hung up, returned to his bedroom and knelt beside Helen. He stayed there for a long time.

~ ~

Rachel had turned everything over in the Kitchen that wasn't boxed. It was after one o'clock in the morning. Scores of boxes remained to be examined. She hadn't eaten or called Bernice. Her efforts had kicked up so much dust that she had to hang her dress in Marty's closet to keep it clean. In its place, she found a three-button nightshirt and boxer shorts in his dresser. She put on two pairs of dress socks to protect her feet from the coarse, dirty floor. She felt irresponsible for not calling Bernice, at least to check in. But she knew if she didn't find the money, *she* would be the basket case and Bernice would have to protect *her* from herself. Also, it was too late to phone without waking her.

"How could you, Marty?" she said with grave disappointment.

A noise outside took her attention. She found her gun and aimed it at the door. She heard keys on the other side unlock both deadbolts.

"It's me," said Joey as he opened the door. Rachel sighed with relief.

At his feet he'd set a large, cumbersome cardboard box. He put the keys in his pocket and picked up the box. "I was wrong, okay?" he said. "I believed a *big-huge* lie."

Rachel put the gun down. "How could you even—"

"Hey, can we just put it behind us?" He added a smile to his plea. "I came back to get along."

He put the box on Marty's desk. Rachel locked the door.

"Is there another chair here?" he said. "No, it's okay, I don't need one."

From the box he took silverware and linen napkins for two place settings, a bottle of Chianti, corkscrew, two bowls of mixed greens in plastic wrap, and homemade vinaigrette in a jar. Then came two French rolls and two plates of food, each wrapped with tin foil, two wine glasses, each with a red-ribbon bow, and a portable stereo with a CD player.

"You like Mozart?" he said. "I brought *The Magic Flute.*"

He plugged in the stereo, put the CD in, and set the volume low. He uncorked the wine with flare and poured a glass. He removed the plastic from one of the bowls, tossed the salad in it, took a candle from the box and lit it with a lighter from his pocket. He removed the foil on one plate and put a roll on a bread plate.

"Voila," he said. He indicated the chair. "*Bon appetit.* It's osso buco. I made it today. I had to wait till my Mom went to bed so I could use her car."

Rachel looked at the braised veal with rice, garlic spinach, and mushrooms, and on the side, penne covered with marinara sauce.

"Why osso buco?" said Rachel.

"Don't you like it?" said Joey.

"It was Marty's favorite."

"I know. You like it too, don't you?"

Rachel nodded.

"You've got to be hungry," said Joey. "Why don't you eat?"

He held out the chair for her. She sat in it, and he pushed it into the desk. He put a napkin in her lap and handed her the wine.

"No fire water," she said.

"Aw man," said Joey. "I wanted you to relax. Oh, I know."

"What?" said Rachel.

"No just eat."

As Rachel started on the salad, Joey moved into position to provide his substitute for the wine: a shoulder rub.

Rachel responded immediately. "Just what the doctor ordered," she said. "I am sooo sore."

Joey loved her reaction.

"Aren't you going to eat?" said Rachel.

"I'd rather do this," he said. "I may never get the chance again. I want to enjoy it."

"You're so much like Marty it's scary."

"How?"

She took a bite of the roll and followed with a forkful of salad. "He knew just what to say, too—especially on our Friday nights."

"That's when you guys went to dinner?"

Rachel nodded. "Mama Funelli's. You know it?"

"Yeah, it's so-so."

"It's better than so-so. This is their Friday special. Marty said theirs was as good as his own."

"Wait till you try mine."

Rachel was melting in his hands. "Whatever you do, don't stop."

"Whatever I do, I won't. Go ahead, try the meat."

Rachel cut a piece of veal and tasted it. "Perfect," she said.

"Told you," said Joey. "Am I rubbing too hard?"

"God, no," said Rachel. "That's one thing Marty didn't do."

"Give you massages?"

Rachel nodded. "There wasn't time." She ate another piece of veal. "It's funny how it takes time for even the simplest things."

"You guys really loved each other, huh?"

"Yes and no," said Rachel. "I wanted to get married but he couldn't, so there was always that."

"You didn't love him 'cause he wouldn't marry you?"

"Loving's giving, Joey. It's not a convenience, it's not an outlet, it's not part-time. Anyway, I don't want to talk about it now."

"No, 'course not. Is that your daughter?"

He indicated a framed photo on the desk. It was of a pretty teenage girl smiling with soulful eyes. Rachel turned it face down. "I don't want to talk about that either," she said.

"How come it's in here?"

"What'd I just say, Joey?"

"Okay, okay." He pressed harder on her sore muscles.

"You're going to make some girl a wonderful wife, kid."

"'Long as she doesn't mind me cooking, 'cause if she gets in my way we'll have to get divorced. Unless we've got a *big-huge* kitchen."

"Don't worry," said Rachel. "We like being taken care of."

Rachel tasted the rice. "I haven't had a massage like this since junior high."

"Who gave it to you?"

"Some jerk. He came over when my dad was out. He schemed a massage, then…Well I was dumb those days. He was my first."

"Guy got a home run, huh?" said Joey. "How was it?"

"Eight, nine seconds."

"So he was a pig."

"Let me tell you, Joey. Women need time."

"Then what happened?"

"He got rough. Some guys hate you when they finish."

"What'd you do?"

"I ran," said Rachel. "He stole my baby-sitting money. I had over sixty bucks saved up."

"I would've kicked his butt."

"You weren't born yet."

"So what happened to him?"

"He died in Dom's parking lot one night. He threw his stomach up in little pieces all over the place."

"I'm glad I don't have much taste for alcohol. Beer's good on a hot day, though."

"Be glad. Go visit my father's grave. It's the one with a bulge in the ground where they couldn't tap down his bloated liver. Joey, let me ask you something. How come no girls your age?"

"Think I'm a loser?" said Joey.

Rachel didn't answer.

"I like cooking, that's all. I've got friends that like baseball and nobody calls them losers. Letterman was a loser when he was my age—"

"Still is."

"—but now he entertains America."

"Who does your cooking entertain?"

"These girls I know, they're just empty—in the head, you know. They don't know anything. You make them a dinner like this…they'd rather have a rice snap. They can't tell a piano sonata from *Louie, Louie*. They think if you like opera you're from West Hollywood."

"Cooking isn't everything, Joey."

"Like I said, 'when the student is ready, the teacher will come.'"

Rachel knew he was being evasive. She let it go for the moment. "I always felt so safe here," she said. "Can you imagine the two of us in here, me and Marty? Like a couple of college kids staying at the folks' house. Well, I guess it's time to grow up."

"It's hard for me to feel real bad about Uncle Marty now."

"What do you mean?"

"He had everything. I bet if you could bring him back and ask him the one thing he could have more of, he'd say time."

"He'd want his boy to outlive him."

"No, I meant now, this time of his life. He loved Aunt Gloria and she loved him, it just didn't work out the way they wanted. And he loved his club. That's two *big-huge* things right there. On top of that, he had you. What more could any man want?"

"I'll never lack for flattery with you around."

"Sometimes I wish I could just shut up. You know Al Pacino in the first *Godfather*? Do you know from the time he laid eyes on that girl in Italy until after they got married, he never said *one word* to her. Even on their wedding night when she took her dress off for him, he didn't say one word. I wish I could be the silent type. I guess girls kind of like that. But it's not me. I can't stop saying how cool you are. I can hold some things in, but not that."

"Do you flatter girls your age?"

"No."

"Why not?"

"I dunno, they're different."

"I'm not looking for obvious answers, Joey. You're smarter than you let on."

He shrugged. "I don't know why. They're just different."

"Are you afraid they'll reject you?"

"Like I'm not afraid *you* won't."

"I don't think you are."

"Yes I am. I've got feelings, y'know."

"You think I'm a prostitute, that's what drives you."

"That's *so* wrong," said Joey.

"It's all you ever knew about me. It's not going to go away just because I told you I'm not."

"How can you say that, Rachel? You told me you weren't, so I believed you."

"Joey, you came onto me like gangbusters, but you won't even approach girls your own age. You expect I'll reject you because I'm old enough to be your mother. So if I reject you it's nothing ventured, nothing gained. But if you were rejected by a girl your own age, one you had high hopes for, you'd be devastated."

"I didn't mean to come onto you like that. Really, Rachel."

"Don't apologize. I've heard it a million times. But I want you to understand what drives your behavior."

"I already went to therapy."

"Don't get defensive."

"I'm not."

"Joey, you've got so much to offer a girl—"

"I'm sick of hearing that. That's all my mother ever says."

"Look, you asked for pointers, so let's talk about it. We can talk about things she wouldn't feel comfortable talking about with you."

"What about things you're not comfortable talking about?"

"Like what?"

"Like your daughter."

"This is about you, Joey."

"So there's places you don't want to go to, either."

"If I don't want to talk about them, I don't have to."

"Yeah, that's controlling."

"*I'm* controlling?

"Yeah. You can't just let things happen instead of taking them all apart and analyzing them."

Rachel thought he had a point. Silence followed. As she ate more of her meal, Joey put more concentration into the massage. "'Relaxed yet?"

"Very," said Rachel. "I hope your hands aren't getting sore."

His hands were very sore. "Not at all," he said.

Rachel got a thought. "What am I saying? This is no time to be self-indulgent. I've got work to do. I haven't found the money."

"We'll find it together."

"I appreciate that, but we're wasting time."

"No, really," said Joey. "We'll find it. Finish your meal. You'll hurt my feelings if you don't."

"Your uncle sure misread you, Joey. If he could see how persistent you are when you know what you want…"

"That's 'cause I never wanted much," said Joey.

"Then why now?"

Joey didn't answer.

"Joey, if it's because of me, that's wrong."

"You already said that. See, that's you being controlling again. You've got to put a comment on everything."

"I like my opinions. They haven't come easily. I never used to make judgments because I never thought about things before. I just did them. I just reacted to other things. It takes awhile to get a sense of yourself. When that happens, you get a perspective on life. If you're clear-headed, that's the kind of perspective you get. If not, you see things the way they aren't, and sometimes you can't hear others when they tell you you're not seeing things correctly."

"Why can't you just let something happen without putting it in this box or that box? I mean, what's the big deal?"

Rachel had a mouthful, so she didn't respond. Joey indicated the other end of the Kitchen. "Uncle Marty stayed overnight sometimes? Is it clean over there?"

"Yeah, he did laundry at my house."

"I didn't see a washer and dryer there."

"I don't live there. I never did. You're the second person today I've told that to—the second person ever."

"That's why it's empty?"

"That place was for getting together with Marty. It's empty now. We didn't spend *all* our time in bed. We'd sit in the living room and talk, too, you know. The furniture in it is being shipped to New York as we speak. My daughter just found an apartment there. She's starting college there this fall."

"How come you're telling me this now?"

"We kept it secret. But I'm leaving soon, so it won't matter."

"That's how come this place was so secret too?"

"Marty was very fond of my daughter. He'd call her from here and they'd talk for hours. He's got mementos of her in here, the kind you keep at home. But he couldn't keep them in his for obvious reasons. We wanted to protect her from my past, and the only way was to keep my past from her."

"Can I say something that's going to embarrass me again?"

"Just say it."

"I don't want you to move away."

Rachel put her utensils down, stood up and faced Joey. "I can't deal with that right now. I need to look for the money."

"Just say it doesn't matter if I don't want you to leave."

"It does, but I can't talk about it now. Cedar's still out there. I've got to find that money."

"Okay look, go lay down," said Joey. "I'll find it. I swear I'll find it. The second I do I'll wake you up, I promise."

"I'm too dirty to lie in that bed."

"No you're not, Rachel. You just ate. Take a little nap."

"There's no—"

"This is what I was talking about. You never just go with the flow."

"But I—"

Joey pulled her by the hand toward the living quarters, an area separated from the rest of the room by a sliding curtain. It had a closet, drawers, a queen-size bed, a TV set and a hot plate. Unlike the rest of the Kitchen, it was carpeted. A door next to the closet connected a bathroom with a shower. On the chest of drawers were photos of Marty, Rachel and Dina.

When they reached the bed, Rachel sat on the edge of it and looked sadly at the floor. "I'm starting to think it's not even here."

"If he promised you, it's here," said Joey.

"I looked, Joey. All those boxes, all that junk..."

"I said I'll find it."

"It's got to be right in front of our eyes. He wouldn't make me go through this."

Joey put his hands on Rachel's shoulders and gently pressed so that she fell back on the bed. "Wait one second," he said. He went to the bathroom and returned with a washrag he'd moistened with hot water. Rachel was staring morosely at the ceiling.

"Don't freak out," said Joey. "I'm just going to wipe off the dirt."

Rachel didn't object. Joey gently wiped away dust and smudges from one of Rachel's arms, then rinsed the washcloth and started on the other one. After rinsing the washcloth again, he started on her legs. He took his time. His ministering was a relief. Rachel didn't say anything, didn't even move. Her eyes were closed. Joey took her socks off and washed her feet with hot, soapy water. Every part got special attention, even between her toes. He made several trips to the bathroom to keep the washcloth hot and soapy. Each trip was made with haste. The next time he rinsed the washcloth, he returned with a tube of skin lotion he'd found in the bathroom. He applied it to her arms, legs and feet. He rubbed all over with great attention to knots in her muscles.

Every once in a while, Rachel murmured how good it felt. Joey didn't stop until the first CD stopped. When he got up to put the second one in, he rose so carefully that Rachel didn't notice. When he returned, he continued rubbing her legs and arms and shoulders. He couldn't tell if she was asleep. Soon, he leaned into her ear and whispered, "I need to do your back."

Rachel grunted what sounded like: "I'm too tired to move."

He gently lifted her arm and leg on one side, and she did the rest. She turned over on her stomach, at the same time reaching behind and lifting the back of the nightshirt so that her back was exposed.

Joey looked up and silently thanked God. He put lotion on his hands and rubbed Rachel's shoulders and upper arms. Soon he did the same with her back, then behind her thighs, knees and calves.

By the time the second CD ended, Joey had used up the lotion. It was after three o'clock in the morning. He was tired but far too excited to think about sleep. He had washed, rinsed and rubbed lotion into every square inch of her exposed body. Next he wanted to touch his lips to her skin. Would she let him? he wondered.

Then he remembered his therapist's admonition that he tended to limit himself where others would not and that he had every right to go after what he wanted. This recollection, plus knowing Rachel would be leaving soon and probably would never return, prompted him to take his therapist's advice.

Cautiously, he unhooked Rachel's bra. She didn't move. He pushed the ends of the straps aside and touched his lips to the middle of her back. He puckered them and kissed the spot. He was sure he hadn't awakened her. Then he kissed another part of her back, then another. With each kiss, he felt less inhibited.

"God, don't let this end," he said to himself.

Then something unbelievable happened. Rachel found Joey's hand with hers and squeezed it affectionately. At first, he thought she was going to push him away. But then he knew she was showing approval, the kind that encouraged him to continue what he was doing.

Joey's kissing went on for twenty minutes. He pulled her boxer shorts down a little and kissed the lowest part of her back. She squeezed his hand harder.

"Unbelievable," he thought. So this is how it works.

He kissed her legs, up and down and all around, slower than a drowsy snail. Never did the kisses become anything more than delicate. Then he kissed the back of her neck and behind her ears.

The second CD stopped, but he was not going to leave to put in the third disk. The only sound in the room was the "ppf-ppf" of his kisses. This continued for a long time.

Then a lazy, drawn-out whisper came from Rachel. Her face was flat against a pillow. "Now you can ask me about my daughter."

"Does she like Radiohead?"

"Cute. Now you know."

"Why'd you keep your past from her?" said Joey.

Under the drug-like spell of his caressing and kissing, Rachel's speech took effort. "I didn't want her to be like me when I was her age. Marty didn't want her ridiculed. 'Bastard baby' and all that."

Joey moved his mouth and nose up and down her back, like the ebb and flow of waves on sand. "The honey bubble," he said between kisses.

"What's that?"

"This therapist I had once named Holly, she made me talk about it when I was a kid. See my mom always complained. She's like a broken CD. At breakfast I couldn't stand it so I used to turn this big tall jar of honey she had over and over and I'd watch these big bubbles go to the top one at a time real slow. Holly said I was tuning my mom out with it. Anyway, I'd imagine all kinds of cool stuff going on inside each one where I was a hero, like they were little movies sort of. Holly said I was limiting myself by cutting them off when the bubbles dissolved 'cause deep down I didn't think I deserved being a hero too long. She'd go, 'You're making sure nothing good lasts forever.' So she said the honey bubbles sort of represented my 'self-imposed limitations based on fear.' Her words."

Rachel thought about this for a moment. "I'm imposing limitations on my daughter because of *my* fears?"

"Well, like, putting myself in Holly's mind, I'd say, yeah and, y'know, most fears are irrational."

"So I'm stunting her growth," said Rachel. "Is that what you're saying?"

"I'm saying what you're trying to keep from her probably wouldn't hurt her like you think it would."

Rachel was silent. Joey didn't know what she was thinking. After a few minutes, she spoke. "I never told anybody this."

Joey already felt privileged. Whatever he was doing was working.

"After my father died," said Rachel, "I found an envelope he'd stuffed in one of his dresser drawers. It had been there for, I don't know, twenty years or so, just shoved back behind his underwear or socks or t-shirts, I forget which. Anyway, I opened it and read it. It was a little note written on a piece of paper from the tablet he used to figure out his roofing bids. I couldn't tell if he was sober when he wrote it or not, just that it was fairly legible, for him anyway. Usually you couldn't read anything he wrote, it was so scribbly. It said, 'Dear Rachel. There's only one thing I know for sure. That's the only times I feel total joy is when I go into your bedroom at night when you're asleep and I just stare at you. You're a little angel sleeping there, so pretty and sweet. Sometimes it's hard to believe you came from me, you're so innocent laying there. I just thought I would write this down so one day you would know about it.' That's all it said, word for word."

Joey didn't speak for a moment. Then he said, "Think he ever told your mom?"

"I have no idea," said Rachel. "For all I know, she'd left by then."

"You never even told Uncle Marty about it?"

"No."

"Why not?"

"Marty's cynical side used to piss me off sometimes," said Rachel. "I could see him saying something cynical about it. He hated my dad. I mean, it's a cherished memory. God knows there weren't many. I just did- n't want Marty spoiling it, you know?"

"So why'd you tell me?" said Joey.

"I don't know. Maybe I'm wrong, but I just think you can appreciate the sentiment in it."

"I do," said Joey.

"Cynicism doesn't honor anything but its own self-importance."

"Yeah," said Joey. "I know. I'm glad you told me."

"You've earned it," said Rachel. "I just wish he'd said more things like that to me, or written them, whatever. But he never did."

Joey didn't have anything else to say on the matter. It was just as well, he thought, because just then the Red Sea parted. Rachel rolled over and faced him. She may have wanted to say something, such was the dawning look in her eyes. But before she could speak, Joey responded to an impulse. Without thinking of the consequences, he kissed her lips. They were full and red anyway, just begging to be kissed. She put her hands on the back of his head so he couldn't pull away until she wanted him to.

When they broke, Rachel whispered, "Turn off the light, I don't want you to see my wrinkles."

"I want to see them," he said. "I want to see everything."

After a moment, Rachel unbuttoned her nightshirt. Joey helped her wiggle out of it. Her bra got caught up in it, so everything showed but what the boxer shorts covered. Tempted as he was, Joey couldn't look anywhere except in her eyes. He thought she was still trying to tell him something.

"What," he whispered.

Rachel grinned.

"What?" he repeated.

She whispered. "Who's teaching who here?"

Joey took it as a compliment. He moved his eyes down to her breasts. He didn't show any expression. Instead, he looked back into her eyes, kissed her again, pulled back and whispered, "Wow."

He kissed her again. This time she took him into her arms.

~ TWENTY-NINE ~

Rachel got to Bernice's house a little before seven the next morning. As a peace offering, she brought a box of fresh donuts. When Bernice opened the door and saw her decked out in her blue dress, she showed with a hurtful expression that she'd been snubbed. Rachel apologized, and Bernice, in pajamas and robe, opened the door, took the donuts, and told Rachel to join her in the kitchen, where coffee was brewing.

"How was your night?" asked Rachel.

Bernice bit into a donut. "Not as good as yours, I'm sure."

"Will you let me explain?"

"Why bother?"

"Bee, you know I wouldn't abandon you if I wasn't tied up."

"I'm sure to you he was just another homeless bum."

"We *both* lost someone," said Rachel.

Bernice swallowed what was in her mouth. "I'm sorry. Go ahead."

Rachel sat across from her. "When Dina started school, I wanted to work, at least part-time, to know what I was capable of, to contribute something, to earn a paycheck, whatever. But Marty wouldn't let me. He wanted the wife his wife couldn't be, which was being available when he could get away from the club. In return, he promised to take care of me. If anything happened, all I needed to do was to look in his storage room. Well last night I looked, and it's not there. I looked and looked and before I knew it the sun came up. I just left there now."

"You always dress like that when you look for money?"

"This was for Joey, Marty's nephew. Yesterday I promised him we'd have dinner. He went through hell with me the day Marty died. I was just trying to show some gratitude and have a little talk I knew Marty always wanted to have with him. Then I came over here and saw what you'd done to yourself. I didn't want to cancel on him, not after he stuck his neck out for me, so I kept the date. Besides, it's the first time I dressed up for anyone other than Marty since I can remember."

Bernice finished the first donut and reached for another.

"There's more," said Rachel. "Cedar wants that money. That's why I had to try to get it last night, before he beats me to it. It's all complicated with alarm keys and deadbolts and all that."

"But Marty promised it to you," said Bernice

"You think Cedar cares about that? To him it's just sitting there for the taking. Bee, he almost raped me yesterday."

Bernice stopped chewing. "You're kidding."

"He was strangling Joey. I had to shoot him or he would have killed him."

"You shot him? My God, you should've called the police."

"It's all falling apart. I'm scared Marty didn't leave me anything. I suppose I can take care of myself, tend bar again, whatever. But what about my daughter? She can't live back there without financial assistance."

"Your house must be worth something," said Bernice.

"I don't know who the deed belongs to."

"I mean your Burbank house."

"That too," said Rachel. "Marty did things his own way and he didn't like questions. I told you I'm thinking of going to his widow and begging for compensation."

"Forget it," said Bernice. "She'll throw you out."

"If she throws me out, she throws me out."

"Rachel, I want Curly's things. They're all I'll ever have of him."

"We'll go today. I'll drive."

"I hope so," said Bernice. "I'm so down." She reached for another donut and ate it in two bites.

"How's your medication holding up?" said Rachel.

"I don't want to take it anymore. I don't want chemicals in my system, not with a baby inside me."

"You need to make an appointment with an OB/GYN."

"I'm going to."

Rachel rose from her seat. "I'll be back, Bee. Don't do anything like you did yesterday."

She kissed Bernice on her cheek, then left. Bernice ate another donut and threw the rest away.

~~

Rachel cleaned up and changed clothes at her Burbank house before driving to Glendale. It took about ten minutes to reach the hillside home of Marty and Gloria Bagliamente. Marty's Mercedes was in the driveway next to Gloria's car. Rachel had never seen the house. After summoning courage, she walked up the long steps to the front door. She had not practiced what to say, nor was she going to sound like a victim. Her rule was "just say what comes out."

She'd put on soft-cotton twill chinos, a long-sleeve linen blouse that was cropped at the hip and thick-leather platform sandals. She knocked on the door. After a moment, Gloria answered. She wore a dark blue dress, diamond necklace and white high heels. Seeing Rachel took her aback.

"I'm sorry, Mrs. Bagliamente," said Rachel. "I need to talk to you."

"You shared your bed with my husband and now that he's gone you can't leave me in peace? You must want something. People like you always do."

"Please hear what I have to say."

When Gloria didn't answer, Rachel walked past her into the foyer and, seeing the living room, walked into it, then turned and waited for Gloria to join her. Gloria closed the front door, walked into the living room and stood in front of Rachel with her arms stiffly at her sides.

"You'll excuse me for not asking you to sit," said Gloria.

Rachel looked around the room. "That was your mother's," she said, indicating a portrait of an elderly woman. She pointed to an empty candy dish on a marble-top table stand. "That was an anniversary gift from Marty. It's usually got lemon drops in it."

"This is cruel," said Gloria.

"I don't want to be cruel, but Marty and I talked about you all the time. I feel I know you. He loved you but he couldn't share with you the one thing that gave him so much joy, his club and all the people there. He couldn't change your attitude about that. Bars were my life, too, when I met him. That's what brought us together. No one wanted to cheat on anybody. We just had that in common, and I'm sorry you disapproved of that so much."

"I don't need you to tell me about my husband."

"No you don't. I'll leave in a minute. But first I have to say this. Mrs. Bagliamente, Marty made a commitment to me, just like he did to you. Yours was at the altar, mine was at Mama Funelli's."

"What commitment?"

"To take care of me for the years I gave him."

"I was right," said Gloria. "She's come to ask for money."

"Mrs. Bagliamente, if I end up a pitiful old bag in the filthy streets of Hillside Park, I won't cry because I don't make excuses. But I'm responsible for someone, and she can't end up like me."

Gloria's disgust turned to mild curiosity.

"I want her to have an education," said Rachel. "You would too if you met her. She's a lovely, lovely child, and so innocent."

Gloria bowed her head and made the sign of the cross. "You're telling me you have a daughter?"

Rachel nodded.

"I may be sorry for her but not you," said Gloria. "Please leave."

"I need to know if I'm in your husband's will."

"His will? He's not even buried yet."

"He wanted me in it. Doesn't that matter to you?"

"I don't know if you're in Martin's will. His attorney is coming over in a little while. But if you are, I'll fight it."

"You'll fight it."

"I swear I'll fight it. And I'll win."

"He loved my little girl, and I know he would not have left her with nothing."

"Martin knew her?"

"She was the closest thing to a child he knew since Paulie."

Gloria bristled. "You mention them in the same breath? Who's the father?"

Rachel said in a shameful whisper, "I don't know."

Gloria processed this response, then said, "What's the girl's name?"

"Adina. My mother was Italian. I'm sure Marty didn't tell you."

An awkward silence followed.

"Ms. Ellis. We shared a man all these years. But all I got was a shell of that man. You got his passion. I have nothing more to say."

Gloria stepped aside for Rachel to have a clear path to the door. Rachel moved to the foyer, then faced Gloria. "Dina can't get here until after the funeral, so we'll stop at the cemetery later. But is it going to be a problem if I go to the funeral?"

Gloria waited a long time before answering. "It will not be a problem."

"Thank you for your time, Mrs. Bagliamente."

Rachel opened the door and left.

~ ~

Kenny's day customers were gone by ten o'clock. They normally stayed until the lunch crowd arrived, but since Cedar had left him the night before, Kenny was a wreck. His mood made his customers uncomfortable, so they didn't stay long. In addition, the new ones he'd had the previous day didn't return. At ten-fifteen, Cammy strolled in with his bible under his arm. He wore striped Bermuda shorts, thongs with over-the-calf socks, and a short-sleeve shirt. His chubby legs were a pasty white.

"You look like a stupid tourist," said Kenny.

"It's comfortable," said Cammy.

Kenny saw the bruise on his forehead and welts on his wrists. "What's with the bruises?"

"Cedar did it," said Cammy. "I could be dead because of him. He struck me with a crutch on my head and left me to die."

"Did you try to baptize him or something?"

"I was at Rachel's when he came over. He knocked me out and tied me up and threw me in her garage."

"What were you doing there?" said Kenny.

"I wanted her to accept Jesus."

"She'd jump at that."

"I was tied up like an animal the whole day, Kenny. He gagged my mouth, he blindfolded me, he tied my wrists and legs, everything."

"You don't look dead to me."

"Marty's nephew came there to find Rachel and he heard me shouting. Do you think I should call the police? I have a mind to. It would serve him right. He can't keep getting away with harming people like he's always done, so…"

"Then what?"

"What do you mean?"

"What if they arrest him and he gets out on bail? How safe will you be then? Did you hear about Curly?"

"What happened to him?" said Cammy.

"Cedar killed him."

Cammy gasped.

"Right here, right in my bar," said Kenny. "Snapped his neck then left it up to me to get rid of the body."

"He really killed Curly? You're not kidding me?"

"No, a piano fell on him. Could I make up something like that?"

"My God, what's the world come to."

"Guess what Curly's real name was?"

"I don't know."

"Gary," said Kenny. "Gary Peetz. The cops told me."

"We have to call the police," said Cammy.

"Not so fast. He's got me doing something with him tomorrow night, and I think when it's over he's going to kill me."

"What are you going to do?"

"I don't know. I got two things on my mind. One's Cedar, the other's this place. You know that camel-jockey I told you about? I'm thinking of calling him to see if he still wants to buy a bar here. I figure with Marty's and your place closed, if I low-ball him an offer, maybe he'd buy me out quick and I could high-tail it out of here before I even have to deal with Cedar anymore."

"Before tomorrow night? That's not possible, Kenny. The title transfer alone takes—"

"I don't mean *consummate* the sale, damnit! You know what else? After you left the other night, Cedar tried to get me and Dom to guard Marty's so he could get in the Kitchen and get a hold of something. Rachel's after it too. What in hell could it be? What's in that place?"

"I don't know, except illegal weapons."

"What the hell would Cedar *and* Rachel care about a bunch of guns for?" said Kenny. "Cedar's got a million of them anyway."

"As far as I know, nobody knows what's in there."

"He swore he was going to leave this town once he got whatever it was. Well he's still here, so *it's* still there. What if it's a gold mine?"

Cammy opened his bible. "Let me read you something."

"I don't want to hear that now," said Kenny.

"No really, just let me read from Romans for you. Listen, I marked it. 'And I am convinced that nothing can ever separate us from His love. Death can't, and life can't. The angels can't, and the demons can't. Our fears for today, our worries about tomorrow, and even the powers of hell can't keep God's love away. Whether we are high above the sky, or in the deepest ocean, nothing in all creation will ever be able to separate us from the love of God that is revealed in Christ Jesus our Lord.'" He looked up at Kenny. "What do you think of that?"

"Can we stick to the real world here? Can you help me out?"

"What do you want?"

"Can you help me get in the Kitchen?"

"I won't do any such thing."

"What if it's enough to start up a church or something? I'll split it with you."

"Start up a church on stolen money?"

"It's got to be a *fortune,* Cammy. You *know* it's the reason why Cedar joined us in the first place. What if it's six figures?"

"The Lord is my savior, not money."

Kenny was tightening. At this point in previous conversations with Cammy, he usually won him over, whatever the subject. He lit a cigarette. "Do you think Rachel would let me make a deal with her, say if I help her get it and I get a cut of it?"

"We tried to kill her Monday, I doubt it."

"I can't function here, Cammy. Can you fill in for me till I go somewhere and figure things out? This guy's crazy."

"The best thing I can do is call the police on him."

"You're too late. Somebody already did. They checked my car yesterday for tire tracks where I put Curly's body. Cammy, what am I going to do? Do you want to see me dead? *Do* you?"

"The police will protect you."

Kenny's voice rose. "Bullshit. Cedar will rat on us to clear his own ass."

"It's the responsible thing to do."

"Fine, call 'em. You'll get thrown in the joint so fast you won't know whose cock's up your ass."

Cammy covered his ears.

Kenny shouted. "I hate talking to you!" He didn't know if Cammy heard him. "*Try reading your bible to them animals in there, Cammy!*"

He still didn't know if Cammy heard him. He ran around his bar and violently ripped Cammy's hands from over his ears, then screamed in his face. "I had eighteen customers in here yesterday, Cammy! Eighteen! Now look what I got! I'm not a bartender, I never was. I don't know *how* to run a stupid bar. I've just been hanging on too long. You've got to help me do something to save myself, Cammy, *anything.*"

"You need to find Jesus—"

"They'll come arrest me, and I didn't even kill Curly. That'll be the end of me, Cammy. You've got to help!"

"Jesus is your best—"

Kenny hit Cammy in the mouth. It stunned Cammy but didn't knock him over. Kenny, now hysterical, swung again, but Cammy blocked the punch, and Kenny lost his balance and fell face-forward on the floor. Cammy ran out of the bar. Kenny didn't pick himself up for a long time. When he did, he went behind his bar and got his gun from beneath it. A lot of time passed before Kenny did anything other than stand behind his bar with the gun at his side. In the quiet, the start-up cycle of his refrigeration unit began with a snap-whiz, and then roared like a tractor. It always made these noises when it started up. Usually Kenny tuned them out. But now he listened. It was like a voice, albeit a mechanical voice, exhorting him to take charge, to get fired up, to put his life in gear and step on the gas. He looked at the gun, made sure it was loaded, then put it on top of the bar and covered it with a bar towel. In a moment, he pretended that Cedar just came in.

"Hi, Cedar," he said with a taut smile. He snatched the gun from under the towel and pretended to fire it at Cedar. "Pow!" he said.

He put the gun back and covered it again. "Oh, hello again, Detectives," he said with another phony smile. "You want to what? You want to arrest me?" Again he snatched the gun from under the towel and pretended to fire once into each detective.

"Pow! Pow!" he said.

Kenny then put the gun back on the bar and covered it with the same towel. He breathed easier, but felt no less anxiety.

~ THIRTY ~

Joey lay in his bedroom with his eyes staring morosely at the ceiling. He'd been awake for hours. The noon sun crept through the blinds on his window. He was too depressed to put music on, although he'd been tempted to stick a funeral march in his CD player.

What Rachel did was a crime, he thought. She gave herself to him, the most exciting and glorious experience of his life, then stealthily left him asleep with no means to reach her. He'd awakened in the Kitchen thinking he was dreaming. How often do you wake up with a smile? He turned over to say, "Good morning, cutie," only to find she'd gone. The nightshirt and boxer shorts she'd worn were next to the bed. Her half-eaten meal was still on the desk. He didn't even have time to absorb the meaning of being abandoned by her, as he had to get the car home before his mother found out it was gone. Since then, he lay awake with questions: "Why'd she even bother? I was just kissing her. *She* went to the next level." Then he added, "Not that I minded…"

He remembered when he'd crassly asked if she'd sleep with him, that she'd said no, that when virgins have sex with you they fall in love with you. She sure was right about that. But did she have to be so cold-blooded about it? He thought *guys* made the quick getaway after sex, *guys* never called again. *Girls* were supposed to get the short end of the stick. *Girls* were supposed to be the ones waiting hopelessly for that phone call thanking them for a wonderful time.

"Man, I hurt," he said aloud.

~~

Bernice flushed her medication down the toilet. When the last of her pills wore off, despair took over. Rachel returned from her futile visit to Gloria, and the two of them drove to the Coroner's office. Bernice wore non-denim overalls, sandals, and dark glasses to hide her swollen eyes. She cried and complained the whole way. "I got rid of the pills," she said. "Now it's just me and my emotions."

"I'm here," said Rachel.

"You know the irony, Rache? Of all the times we could have argued, the one time we didn't have to was the last time we got together. It was so pointless. He thought I was annoyed because he came over without being invited. And he left mad over it. Now I'll never know if he *jumped* in front of that car because of our fight. God, if he just moved in with me like I begged him to, this never would have happened."

"Bee, I'm no philosopher. But I just know in time we find things out that we didn't understand before…or we weren't listening to before…"

"I suppose. You know what I've been thinking about lately?"

"What."

"Remember when my mother used to always say 'I'm too pooped to pop?'"

This made Rachel smile. "She *always* said that."

"It's funny how you remember some things."

Rachel welcomed the momentary relief the fond memory brought. They arrived at the Coroner's office near downtown twenty-five minutes later. A coroner's investigator gave Bernice a plastic bag containing Curly's effects. She clung to it without crying the rest of the way back. Rachel drove to the Eagle Rock Plaza so Bernice could buy a suit for Curly to be buried in. She wanted him to look good for his viewing that night and for burial the next day. Finally, they took the suit to Harper's Funeral Home, where Bernice selected a casket while Rachel stayed in her car. She didn't say why she wanted to stay in the car. Bernice thought she just needed space. But Rachel had reasons. One was that Gloria's car was there, which meant she was inside. Another was that she did not want to see Marty in cosmetics. Her opinion was that death required dignity, not beauty aids. She also hated Harper's for the way it price-gouged her for the cost of her father's funeral years ago, an episode that had sent her into a public rage.

"I was a piece of work back then," she recalled.

It was neither a fond or hurtful memory; indeed, she saw merit in shooting her mouth off and saying exactly what she felt. Although she still spoke her mind, albeit now in a civil tongue, some of what needed airing since she got sober she'd kept secret, and those secrets, she worried, were coming back to haunt her. One was Marty's promise to provide for her future. Her instincts had made her ask for proof on many occasions, but Marty's insistence that she take his word had prevailed. Her instincts also told her to force an ultimatum of marriage or an end to their relationship, but Marty rejected ultimatums.

Running all this through her mind, Rachel wondered if Joey's observation was accurate when he said that a self-imposed limitation based on irrational fears can backfire. *Honey bubble*, he'd called it. One such fear, she thought, forced her to leave him that morning in the Kitchen while he was still asleep. She knew it would hurt his feelings, but if she didn't cut him off then, he could complicate the next few days.

"Besides," she privately complained, "the little shit seduced me."

Joey's world-class massage was like a drug, his pecking kisses an irresistible bonus. She remembered feeling anesthetized from head to toe. The ceiling could have collapsed and she would not have been able to move out of the way, even if it dangled an hour before falling. Then, when he talked about having to escape his mother's unrelenting disagreeableness by creating mini-fantasies in honey bubbles, Rachel felt a connection with him from her own difficult youth. He had tapped into what she had suppressed for years: an involuntary reflex to satisfy a man's needs without thinking of the consequences.

When Bernice returned to the car, she said Curly would be ready for viewing later in the afternoon. They went to Bernice's house to make an eight-by-ten notice of Curly's viewing and funeral times, then to Kinko's to make copies. They posted fliers on the doors of businesses up and down Hector Street, anywhere that people who knew Curly could see them.

~ ~

Cedar spent the morning preparing for his departure from Hillside Park. He bought two cell phones. He bought camping gear and supplies. He found a car to steal later that night so that federal agents wouldn't be looking for his Cherokee when they finally determined, after staking out his house, that he'd probably left the state.

The car belonged to one of Marty's long-time customers, a clothing broker who spent half his time in France and Italy buying women's fashions for his American clients. When abroad, he left his car, a new Taurus, in the garage of his San Marino home. Cedar figured he could drive the Taurus into the mountain states before the broker returned from his trip to report it stolen. By then, Cedar would have disposed of the car in a lake or a deep canyon.

When Cedar returned home for lunch, he heard a car drive up. It was the detectives who'd stopped by the previous day. He answered their questions with cooperation and a helpful attitude. When they said they'd gotten an anonymous tip that he might have information about Curly's death, Cedar showed puzzlement. "I heard he got run over in an alley," said Cedar. "Are you saying it was foul play?"

The detectives answered only by saying that they had to follow leads. One asked to look at the Cherokee. Cedar said okay but asked why. They said a similar vehicle was observed near the crime scene around the time the Coroner determined death occurred. When the detectives left, Cedar knew their interest in him was over.

~ ~

Joey moped around his house all day. Once he looked through Rachel's high school yearbook and stared at every photo of her. Guys had written racy stuff to her in it, but he didn't care. He didn't care if she'd slept with every guy on the planet. He thought several times about getting back in the Kitchen and perhaps finding Rachel's money, but then what? How could he get it to her? How could he even tell her he'd found it?

He slept on and off. He had no appetite. Finally, around two o'clock, with nothing to do and no energy to ride his bike, he walked to the house on Golding Circle. It was that kind of July day. A breeze had cleared away dirty air, and the heat was dry. He didn't expect to find anything that would help him locate Rachel. He knew by then she was too smart for that.

When he got to the house, he saw that nothing had changed. He went to the bedroom and looked through the vanity desk. The intoxicating smell on Rachel when they were together was not among her perfumes. Nonetheless, he sniffed each bottle many times over. He rubbed her dresses with his fingers, then against his cheek and lips. He even sniffed the inside of her shoes. He studied all her makeup paraphernalia. He wanted to hold her right then and there.

"I am sick," he said. "It's got to show. How do I avoid Mom? She'll know. She'll see it all over my face."

He lounged around the house two hours, most of it spent reclining on the sofa. It was peaceful atop the hill with the breeze blowing through the windows and doors. Soon he left. He took his time walking home. When he got there, he was disappointed but not surprised to find no messages on his answering machine from Rachel.

"You'd think she'd at least thank me for the meal I made her," he lamented.

~ ~

Early that evening, Rachel drove Bernice back to Harper's Funeral Home to see Curly on display, then went on to Burbank to get a change of clothes so she could spend the night with Bernice in Eagle Rock. Because it was rush hour, Bernice did not expect her back for a long time.

No one was in Curly's viewing room when Bernice entered. The lights were low and all was quiet. She walked straight for his casket and reflexively touched his hands, which rested on his chest. They were hard and cold. He looked odd in the suit she'd bought him. Now she regretted buying it. His normally unruly curls were combed back and matted down.

"Stupid mortician," she said to herself.

The gap where his front teeth used to be was hidden because his mouth was closed. "Oh my dear," she said sadly. "This just isn't you."

She looked into his face and squeezed his hands. She silently told him that she'd tried to kill herself, but that she'd recovered, that she was pregnant, that Rachel was going to help out until she left for New York, and, boy, wasn't that a surprise about her being a mom and living in Burbank all these years.

She was only intermittently aware that dozens of visitors passed through the promenade behind her to pay respects to Marty in another viewing room. No one came to Curly's room. Soon, however, Bernice felt the presence of another. She turned to see a woman about her age approaching cautiously, as if she'd rather be anywhere but in a funeral home. The woman spoke tentatively.

"Is this…where Curly Peetz is?"

"Yes," said Bernice.

Bernice realized she was blocking the woman's view, so she stepped aside. Seeing Curly, the woman put her trembling fingers to her mouth.

"I just don't like these places," she said. "Are you Bernice?"

"Yes. Who are you?"

The woman extended her hand. "Meg Szymczak. I work in Cooper's Drug Store down on Hector Street."

Bernice shook Meg's hand. "Curly talked about you."

"We were friends," said Meg. "I'm sorry to have to meet you under these circumstances."

"Me too," said Bernice. "But thanks for coming. I'm glad someone did."

Meg returned her eyes to Curly. "They did a good job, don't you think?"

Bernice lied. "His hair's wrong, but yes."

"Obviously you didn't know Curly before you met him," said Meg. "But I can tell you he changed a hundred percent after meeting you. You could always see him shuffling around Hector Street here and there with no purpose or anything. Then he met you and he was never the same again. He was so cute when he came in. He had that little boy thing going on there. I always knew like clockwork when he came back from a night in Eagle Rock. It was in his eyes."

Bernice thought it was borderline impudent for this strange woman to talk about intimate nights Curly had spent with her.

"He came in your store just to tell you about seeing me?"

"Oh no," said Meg. "Not at all. He came in to buy an envelope and a stamp. But at the same time he talked about how much fun he had at your place."

"He bought an envelope and stamp?"

Meg nodded. "I kept a box of plain envelopes under the counter just for him because he only wanted one. I had to charge him a dime apiece. He could have saved a lot of money buying a box, but he didn't want to carry a whole box around wherever he went."

Bernice didn't want Meg to know this was all a surprise to her.

"He was like a kid at Christmas," said Meg. "He'd tell me what great dinners you fixed for him—'the best cook in the world,' he said—what movies you watched together, that kind of stuff. He just loved visiting you."

Bernice could not resist asking: "Do you by any chance know who he was writing to?"

Meg said no. Bernice thought it was harmless for Meg, even as a stranger, to share endearing anecdotes about Curly with her, but this particular revelation was so disconcerting that, at the risk of appearing rude, she ignored Meg from then on. Meg chalked it up to realizing, perhaps too late, that Bernice was in no mood for comity.

After a long silence, Meg excused herself and left. When Rachel returned from getting her night things, Bernice was standing in the parking lot. She was visibly agitated.

"What now?" thought Rachel.

Rachel opened the passenger door, and Bernice backed into the seat. When she sat, the car dipped as if a wrecking ball had hit it. "I just found out Curly was corresponding with somebody on a regular basis," said Bernice. "Do you know Meg from Cooper's?"

"What about her?"

"She told me Curly mailed a letter out to somebody every single morning after he spent the night with me."

"How would Meg know that?"

"He bought an envelope and stamp from her. That's obviously why he wouldn't move in with me. He had another girlfriend."

"Curly didn't have another girlfriend," said Rachel. "He probably mailed the forty bucks you gave him to someone. That's why he never spent it."

"Who would he mail forty dollars cash to once or twice a week? You can't send cash through the mail."

"You can, they just advise against it," said Rachel.

"I knew he was holding back, I just knew it."

"Take it easy, Bee. Maybe it was a savings account."

"He'd have to get bank statements for that," said Bernice. "He didn't get any mail. He said he didn't have any connection to anybody anywhere. He lied to me."

"What about his crazy aunt?" said Rachel.

"Cora Wiley?" said Bernice. "What about her?"

"Maybe he sent her the money."

"He never knew what became of her." She hit the door with her fist. "He was a fraud. Our whole *relationship* was a fraud."

"Maybe he did know what became of her, Bee."

"Then why would he say he didn't?"

"People do fib."

"Why would he fib about that?"

"Maybe to protect her."

"From what?"

"Trouble with the law, anything" said Rachel. "She could be in a retirement home where you sign over your assets and she needed the cash. You shouldn't get all worked up over this, Bee."

"Why not? I have to find this out right after he dies, *and* from a total stranger? What *else* am I going to find out?"

"Curly loved you. You're making yourself crazy."

"It's all right for *you* to make *your*self crazy if Marty didn't leave you any money, but it's *not* all right for *me* to make *my*self crazy when I found out my boyfriend of nine years was doing something behind my back with money I gave him for his own use."

"It's not an easy time for either of us," said Rachel.

"I want some food," said Bernice. "Take me to Taco Bell."

"I'm not taking you there," said Rachel.

"Now I'm not allowed to get hungry?"

"You're not hungry, you're pissed off."

"It's my body and I want to eat."

"Did you forget you're pregnant?"

"Of course not. I'm eating for two now."

"That's a myth. You have to watch your weight now."

"Fine. I'll walk there myself."

Bernice put her hand on the door handle, but Rachel batted it away. "We're going to go home and talk about this," she said.

"I said I'm hungry and I want to eat *now*."

"You don't even know what you're angry about."

"Don't tell me I don't know what I'm angry about! Curly took advantage of me. He ate my food, he slept in my bed, he took my money, and the whole time he was deceiving me."

"I got one hour of sleep last night and the night before was just as bad. So the least you can do is stop giving me grief when I'm trying to help you."

"*You* help *me*? Before yesterday you never even told me you were a mother. You never invited me to your house. Before I met Curly, you never introduced me to *one* man, even your rejects. And last night, the very night of the day I tried to kill myself, when you promised you wouldn't leave my side, you got all prettied up and went out on the town. And now I feel terrible and you won't even let me *eat* to satisfy a craving. It's the only thing I have left and you're denying me *that*. So don't tell me you're helping me!"

Rachel turned on the motor and slammed the accelerator until she burned rubber out of the parking lot.

"What're you doing?" screamed Bernice.

Rachel didn't answer. Bernice kept quiet during the ride home. When they got there and went inside, Rachel said, "Where'd you put his stuff from the Coroner's office?"

"Why do you want to know that?" said Bernice.

"Just get it."

Bernice got Curly's effects from her bedroom and laid them out on her dining room table. She felt the pockets in his pants and found nothing. She opened his wallet and showed Rachel that it had no plastic holders for licenses or credit cards. "Empty," she said in a tone of vindication.

"Then why'd he have it?" said Rachel. "Give it to me."

Bernice handed her the wallet. Rachel opened the compartment for folding bills, then pulled loose a flimsy cardboard separator. There, folded over once, was a worn piece of paper the size of a matchbook cover. She showed Bernice. Bernice kept her surprise in check until she saw what was on the paper. It had been there so long that it needed to be peeled from the separator with extreme caution, lest it tear. She finally got it out and opened it. Written in longhand, yet barely legible, was a two-line address. She read it to herself then looked at Rachel.

"It's an address," said Bernice. "What's 'S.B.?'"

"Santa Barbara?" said Rachel.

"No wait," said Bernice. "San Bernardino. Curly said he spent time there—Pomona and San Bernardino, he always said."

"That's probably where Cora lives," said Rachel.

Bernice pulled out a chair and sat down to think about this. "I'm sorry, Rachel." There was relief in her tone.

"Forget it."

"If that's where Cora lives, I want to talk to her. She'd be his only relative. Would you drive me there?"

"Not tonight," said Rachel.

"No, I know. I can wait."

"Tomorrow, after the funerals," said Rachel. "I'd rather drive out there than sit around waiting for Dina's flight to come in."

"What if that's not it and Cora's dead or gone forever and I never find out where he sent his letters?"

"If she's alive she's probably the one. I doubt Curly was doing anything he was ashamed of."

"But why would he be ashamed of that with me?"

"Maybe Cora left Hillside Park owing money. Maybe she changed her name to collect government assistance. It could be anything."

"You're right," said Bernice. "We'll know tomorrow."

Bernice was relieved. Her spirits rose later in the evening when she and Rachel made dinner side by side while listening to songs that were popular when they were in high school. Rachel spent the night in a guest bedroom. A few times she woke up from hearing Bernice cry.

~ THIRTY-ONE ~

Marty's funeral mass was standing room only. Gloria, Joey and Freda sat alone in the first pew. Rachel sat in the last. Cedar had jettisoned his crutches. He limped through the procession with the other pallbearers. He made eye contact with Rachel once during the service; it lasted long enough for each to convey a refusal to be intimidated by the other.

Joey couldn't stop turning around every few minutes to find Rachel. He never did locate her. She saw him, however. She thought he looked precious in his dark blue suit. And by repeatedly gazing over his shoulder, he looked like a restless little boy.

Bernice was the only one at Curly's service. She knew that anyone likely to say goodbye to him would be at Marty's instead. When the service ended, she saw that Kenny and Cammy had crept in and seated themselves on opposite ends of the last pew. Cammy wore an old brown suit and a narrow black tie. Kenny was in his normal sloppy attire, though instead of a T-shirt he wore a short-sleeve plaid shirt that needed ironing.

Kenny avoided Bernice by sneaking out when she thanked the chaplain for the kind, albeit generic, words he spoke over Curly's casket. Cammy nodded to her as if to communicate condolences; he knew she didn't like him so he didn't attempt personal contact.

At Curly's gravesite, only Bernice, the chaplain, and two attendants from Harper's Funeral Home were present.

The procession from the church to Marty's burial site was miles long. Cars continued to arrive even as the graveside service ended. His plot, along with one for Gloria, was purchased when they buried their son twenty years earlier.

Joey sat with his mother and Gloria on folding chairs next to the grave. He kept looking for Rachel. He finally spotted her when she stepped out of the standing crowd and waved. She indicated with a nod that she would remain until he could join her.

When people headed for their cars, Joey slipped away to speak with Rachel. She looked fabulous in a black trim dress with a matching jacket and high heels. Like most of the others, she wore dark glasses. Just seeing her again stirred Joey. Rachel didn't know what to expect from him. He fixed his eyes on her as he moved through the dispersing crowd. When he reached her, they hugged briefly, then Joey stood back, at arm's length.

"Some funeral, huh?" he said.

"Hell of a turnout," said Rachel.

"You look nice."

"Thank you." She smiled. "The suit makes you look older."

"I *am* older."

Rachel smiled fondly.

"Did you go back there to find the money?" said Joey.

She shook her head. "It's not there."

"You're not giving up, are you?"

"I'm sure Marty meant well, but he didn't follow through. It's my fault. I should have gotten a job—sold Tupperware, robbed banks—anything to save money. But I can't cry about it now. They were good years. He helped me turn my life around, and that's worth more than a nest egg any day."

"Guess so," said Joey. "Could you believe Cedar was there?"

"He was a shoo-in for pallbearer."

"But what nerve, after what he did to us."

"That's why I'm glad I'm leaving," said Rachel. "You better watch out."

"No, he doesn't care about me," said Joey.

"Don't be so sure. Things are going to get ugly. There was a death the other night, a homeless guy, on the surface just another casualty of the streets. The cops are on it, though, and I think heads are going to roll when they dig deep. We'll see how Cedar toughs his way out of this one. I sure don't want to be here when that happens."

"When are you leaving?" said Joey.

"I'll talk it over with my daughter. She comes in tonight."

Joey looked at the people leaving, most with little to say to one another. Their drawn faces merely expressed acceptance that a friend had died. Rachel studied Joey's eyes. Nothing he looked at seemed to register. After some silence, he looked at her again.

"Can I ask you a favor?" he said.

Rachel's tone was kind. "Joey, let's just leave things the way they are. You caught me at a weak moment the other night, but it happened anyway. I think it's best just to walk away from it and get on with our lives."

"I was just going to ask if you'd take your sunglasses off."

Rachel showed awkward embarrassment. She happily removed her sunglasses.

Joey looked at her for a moment, then shook his head. "Could you put them back on?"

She was curious, not irritated. "What's this all about?"

Joey turned his head away as if not wanting her to see what he was thinking and feeling. She could tell he was near tears.

"Joey, what's the matter?" She put her hand on his chin and made him face her. "Tell me what's wrong."

Lumps in his throat made speaking difficult. "I just wanted to look in your eyes. You know they could make a movie about them? It would win an Oscar."

"Then why'd you ask me to put my sunglasses on again?"

"No, you're right again. You're always are, I found out. No, I tried to be cool, just now, y'know, but I blew it. I wanted to see if I could tell by your eyes how come you left me to wake up alone in the Kitchen. But I couldn't. They saw right through me. Laser beams got nothing on your eyes."

"What's so great about being cool?" she said.

"Why *did* you leave me alone? Wait, I know. It's 'cause you're older and wiser. Well I guess I can't be cool about it 'cause I can't get you out of my mind. I couldn't move all day yesterday. I stayed in bed almost all day. I never did that before, unless I was sick. But you know what? It's not really that bad, feeling like this, especially if you want to lose weight. But in case you haven't noticed I'm not exactly a *big-huge* fat guy."

"I'm sorry," said Rachel.

"What am I supposed to do with these feelings? I've got physical ones, I've got emotional ones, I've got some I didn't know I ever had before."

Rachel wanted Joey to answer his own question. But he didn't. He just looked at the people passing by on the way to their cars. Some saw that his eyes were teary.

He tried to speak with irony. "They probably think this is 'cause of Uncle Marty." He broke into a grin. "Free tears, right?"

"It's good you can smile about it. You know what that means?"

"What."

"It means you feel better already, getting it off your chest."

"Venting."

"Yes, venting," said Rachel.

"That's what Uncle Marty always said at Sunday dinners."

This surprised Rachel. "He what?"

"Yeah, he said it all the time, especially to my mom. I mean, he couldn't stand her complaining but he knew it was healthy for her."

"Marty said that?"

"Yeah, what's wrong with it?"

"I'll be damned," said Rachel. "He used to mock me for saying that. He said it was gobbledygook. That son-of-a-..." She stopped, then smiled.

Joey was glad he'd revealed something that pleased her.

"Now we're both relaxed," said Rachel.

"Yeah, it's better, huh?"

"Sure is. And there's something you were right about."

This perplexed Joey. "What was *I* right about?"

"How we think we're doing someone a favor by denying them the truth, but that it only makes things worse in the long run."

"I said that?"

She winked. "Perhaps you had something else on your mind at the time."

"All I know is I'm never going to have another night like that."

"Nonsense," said Rachel. "You'll be batting them away like flies. And not the kind that goes for 'cool,' either, the kind that goes for expressiveness. We're verbal, Joey, we like hearing what you think about us."

"Long as you keep giving me advice, I'll keep taking it."

"Then here's more. Stop putting your mother down."

"What?"

"You heard me. And if Marty were still alive, I'd tell him the same thing. I didn't like how she treated me last night, but that doesn't mean she hasn't been a good mom. You're a caring and sensitive young man, Joey. I know. I've seen it. And I also know you didn't get that from cooking tomatoes and basil. You got that from the only parent you've ever had. And from what I've seen my whole life, I can tell you you're *already* a stand-out kid in that department, and you can only get better with age. All right?"

"Okay," said Joey.

"Just don't quote me on it," said Rachel. "It'll be a cold day in hell till she buys anything *I* ever say. But you should know it. Believe me, the more you know about yourself, the better you are."

"You're right again."

"No, sometimes I'm wrong. But not about this, your mother I mean."

"I don't think you're wrong about anything."

"Now you're the one who's blind," said Rachel.

"Maybe a little," said Joey. "So what are you going to be doing now?"

"Look for a job, get the cobwebs out, join the working class."

"Well anyway," said Joey. "There's a reception at my aunt's. That's where everybody's going."

"I'm driving a friend to San Bernardino."

Joey waited a moment. "I was wondering if I could see you again."

"I can't say. I don't know. I'm sorry."

"No, that's all right," said Joey.

Rachel kissed him on his cheek. "Bye," she said.

"Thanks again, Rachel."

She headed for her car.

"Wait," said Joey.

Rachel turned back. Joey approached her and whispered. "I just wanted you to know...I really enjoyed that night."

Rachel grinned. "I kind of figured that out."

Joey appreciated her response. She continued to her car, then turned back on her own. "I forgot to tell you. The osso buco was fantastic."

"Glad you liked it. Oh, that reminds me. Did Uncle Marty ever make some for you like he said he would?"

"No, he never found the time."

Rachel continued on her way. Joey watched her walk to her car, then joined his mother and Aunt Gloria by the graveside, where they continued to receive condolences and good wishes.

~ ~

Cedar bought two cell phones at a store on State Street in Pasadena. And because he didn't trust Kenny not to drain the battery before his cell phone was needed that night, he also bought a charger adapter. He spent the rest of the day packing his Cherokee and making sure nothing in his home would provide leads to his destination after leaving Hillside Park.

The impression he wanted investigators to get was that he'd fled town in a panic to avoid getting caught for crimes committed the last few days and still to be committed. For this reason, he made sure his house looked not as if its resident were on vacation but as if he were out to buy a candy bar between TV commercials. Newspaper and mail deliveries would continue, lights would remain on, the sprinkler system would go on as programmed—even his VCR would continue to record "Andy Griffith" and "Jeopardy!" until the tape ran out.

He packed hand tools, matches, guns, a rod and reel, a hand mirror, a straight razor and enough food and water for a five-day journey on foot into an area with ample fishing and hunting, an area he could call his new home. Montana sounded good. With his tools he could build a small cabin using natural resources. He packed no radio or communication devices. The only cash he'd take was two hundred dollars, enough for gasoline and food on the way. He'd leave his credit cards. Into a garment bag with a heavy shoulder strap he packed jeans, underwear, shoes, boots, coats, gloves and blankets.

Throughout the day, he made a mental itinerary. Go to Kenny's at five and hand over the cell phone with last-minute instructions. Come back home and load his Cherokee with all he'd packed. Eat a big meal and leave the plates and cooking utensils on the table. Leave for L.A.X. by six. He expected to follow Rachel from the airport to where she lived no later than nine o'clock. Once there, he would take care of all business. He would leave her home with the money Marty had left her or Rachel would lose her daughter. Around eleven o'clock, he would drive to San Marino to get the Taurus he'd targeted for theft. He could transfer supplies to it from his Cherokee in seconds. Then he'd be off to the nearest freeway and a new life.

~ ~

Kenny kept his eyes on the clock the entire day. He knew tonight was going to be big, bigger than the planned execution of Marty and Rachel. For that he had Cammy as a partner and Cedar as de facto supervisor—even Dom as a distant accomplice. So if something had gone wrong, the four of them could've put their heads together and found a way out, or at least gotten busted as a foursome. But going into tonight, Kenny felt alone.

Deep down, he knew he was a coward. His big mouth and sarcasm were designed to deflect from that. But, as he kept telling himself all day, there comes a time when a man's got to stand up for what he believes in. Today would be that day. He psyched himself up for a confrontation with Cedar. He was going to make demands and not back down. He was prepared to suffer the consequences if Cedar refused.

His mindset came from two inescapable facts. One was the unrealized consequence of Marty's death. Today, when Marty was buried, he had expected to see his bar transformed into a nightclub by craftsmen paid with his share of Marty's check-cashing money. He had expected to be auditioning cover bands to draw younger, high-paying customers. He had expected to be interviewing bartenders and cocktail waitresses for the onslaught of new business. Instead, he saw the same dreariness, the empty stools, and the same terrorizing hopelessness. And Curly wasn't around to absorb his imprecations.

He had called Mike Shihadeh last night to ask if he wanted to talk again about buying his bar on the cheap. But he knew from Mike's hesitation that he wasn't interested. Then when he told him that Marty's had closed, as did another bar, Mike's interest shot up. So Kenny screamed into his receiver, "Go hump a camel, you date-eating, sand-crawling prick!"

The second inescapable fact was that the cops were bound to come in any minute with handcuffs out and singing the Miranda rights. By now they had to have matched his tires with the telltale tracks where they found Curly. What was he supposed to do then? And what was he supposed to demand of Cedar? To leave Hillside Park with him? Could they live as co-fugitives?

Kenny finally realized that money was the only thing to demand. That's what this whole thing was about anyway. He just wasn't sure how much. He knew what Cedar and Rachel wanted in the Kitchen was gigantic. He wanted some of it. Nothing else could save him. Marty's and Cammy's were gone, but Dom's wasn't. Dom would get extra business, and he'd figure a way to keep it. He'd badmouth Kenny. He'd deliver his spicy-sausage soup door-to-door to induce new customers to try his restaurant and bar.

Kenny said, "It's High Noon in Hillside Park and I'm Gary Kiss-My-Ass Cooper."

~~

Rachel went home to change clothes, do some miscellany and fill her car with gas before picking up Bernice for the drive to San Bernardino. Bernice had written directions to the address she'd found in Curly's wallet. Their destination, about eighty miles away, was northern San Bernardino, about halfway between the State University to the west and the highway to the east that led to mountain resorts like Lake Arrowhead and Big Bear.

They didn't talk much during the trip. Bernice ran what-ifs through her mind in the event that bad news lay ahead. She had no problem with Curly sending money to help an old relative. But if it was for any other reason, she would have to reevaluate her opinion of him and their whole relationship, and that altered judgment could affect her view of the child she carried.

Rachel was consumed with worry that one day Bernice would connect Curly's death to what he overheard in Dom's parking lot a week ago. How could Rachel explain that when she volunteered Curly's name to Cedar that Cedar was turning against Marty? She would be saying that she killed Curly by ignoring Bernice's warning to keep his name out of it.

Rachel had just praised Joey for opening her eyes to the danger of suppressing the truth, even when doing so for good intentions. And Cedar, of all people, had told her that no secret lives without guilt. Yet she was harboring a secret from Bernice and already feeling guilt from it. Even establishing a new life in New York would not purge the guilt.

And whenever she would think about Bernice's child growing up fatherless, the guilt would hurt more.

~~

The funeral reception bored Joey. He hardly knew anyone. Gloria had hired valets and an army of caterers, even a string quartet to keep the mood restrained. All Joey could think about was Rachel. He knew he'd embarrassed himself by choking back tears and admitting that he tried at first to project indifference to what became his rite of passage with her. He got Gino to drive him home before the reception ended. It was okay with Freda, who was lapping up attention that came from being the deceased's only sibling. When he got home and peeled off his suit, Joey found a surprise. A greeting card had been shoved through the window in his bedroom. Its envelope said "For Joey: Personal and Confidential."

He knew it was from Rachel. She must have come by when he was at the reception. In fact, she'd dropped it off on her way to San Bernardino. Joey sat on his bed with anticipation. She'd written on the inside of a friendship card. Her longhand was neat and legible.

"Dear Joey," it read. "I realized there was more to say after our talk at the funeral, so I got this card and am now writing my thoughts to you. I hope I don't stick it through the wrong window at your house!

"What happened the other night was very special for me, even though I had no intention of letting it happen. So put away any doubts you have of not being a ladies man!

"When I was young, I ended relationships without warning. Thank God I didn't with Marty, because he changed my life. But maybe not in some ways, because the old me surfaced with you. There is no other immediate explanation for my behavior. It disturbs me to know that I may be regressing, because the old me hurt a lot of people.

"Joey, you are the last person I would want to hurt. You must forgive me for any pain I caused with my abrupt exit. I fully intend to keep communication with you. Dina and I will come to visit our friends here, and you will be included. We can write as often as you wish, even when I'm old and you're out cavorting with ladies your own age.

"All I ask is your patience. I need to clear my head and establish a new life in a different city so I can be with my daughter. When that time comes, I will call you and we will spend a fortune on telephone bills, because there is much to talk about. The few days we were together only scratched the surface.

"Until then, do not shy away from your sensitivities. You may belittle them as <u>uncool</u>, but they are your strength.

"With much love, Rachel."

Joey read the note several times. It made him want her. He heard echoes of his therapist's exhortation to go for it. "Why shouldn't I?" he asked himself. "Holly would tell me I deserve more time with Rachel."

He put the greeting card in the top drawer where his clothes were, then tried to figure out how to find her before she left for New York.

~ THIRTY-TWO ~

Rachel took the Two-Fifteen East off the Ten, through San Bernardino proper, to an exit in a working class neighborhood. About a mile north of the exit, past a residential and commercial area, she went over a small hill, behind which was a long-withering unincorporated section of curbless streets and old, box-like houses with mailboxes on posts in front. It was a step down from Hillside Park. Bernice told Rachel to turn onto the third street after the pass through the hill. The road she turned on was a straight, decades-old concrete slab with power lines overhead and splintered phone poles on corners. Crooked streams of tar filled cracks in the pavement and gobs of asphalt filled potholes. There were no pedestrians. Rachel's was the only car on the street.

The neighborhood, despite its backwardness, seemed peaceful and lazy, if not a time warp back half-a-century. Many of the houses were small enough to make their lots ripe for subdivision if the properties were valuable. Some had garages converted to undemanding rental units. Others had fenced-in areas for horses. A mobile home with rusted siding, broken windows and weeds growing around its flat tires was at the end of one lot.

The address they sought was on the next street north, which ended the unincorporated section and gave way to a newer area of housing. It was hand-printed in block numbers on a tin mailbox with a red metal flag in the down position. Rachel pulled in front a few minutes after two o'clock.

"I don't want to deal with rush-hour going back," said Rachel.

"No," said Bernice. "We won't stay any longer than we have to."

They stretched their legs. The air was dry and hot, the sky hazy and gray. None of the houses would ever be the subject of a postcard. Neither unkempt nor adorned, one was adobe with a flat roof and a swamp cooler in a window, another an A-frame stucco with aluminum-frame windows and a zucchini garden in front. Another was a model for the little house on the prairie, except it had a lopsided picnic table in the yard and auto parts strewn on an oil-stained driveway in front. Some houses had porches, others didn't. Quiet was all around.

The house they looked at was a simple square structure behind a weedy lawn. From the street to the rear of the property ran a gravelly, sun-bleached asphalt driveway. A water heater was secured to the house with metal strips. To protect its pilot light, someone had fashioned a shield from a hammered-out coffee can and taped it over the light. A section of rain gutter hung precariously from a loosened screw at the edge of the roof in front.

They walked to the front porch, which was polished concrete under an overhang supported by two four-by-four beams. A swinging seat for two filled in the porch. On either side of the swing was as ashtray on a small table.

"I wonder if Curly ever came here," said Bernice.

"Not much to brag about if he did," said Rachel.

Bernice knocked on a screen door. They heard a noise around the house. When there was no answer to their knock, they moved to see what the noise was. Walking toward them from the driveway half-a-step at a time was a toothless old woman using a three-wheeled walker with rubber handgrips. Her eyes were down, as if she needed to concentrate on each step. She was five-six and plump, with deep wrinkles in her face and neck. She wore a long formless nightgown with a zipper down the front that was open to her navel but tied at the neck. It revealed a leathery, freckled chest. Her hair was in curlers. She wore slippers that made a swishing sound with each step. Rachel and Bernice waited for her to get close.

"Think it's Cora?" Bernice whispered to Rachel.

The woman looked up. She had small, round black eyes that sparkled. Bags under her eyes were puffy.

"It takes two?" said the woman. "Where's my groceries? I told that boy if he brings me warm beer again I'll skin him alive. Sixty-five cents I tip him, and last time he brought me warm beer. If you're here to defend him, you can go to hell and I'll find another store that delivers on time and appreciates my goddamn business."

"We didn't bring anything, ma'am," said Bernice. "We're looking for someone."

The woman stopped walking and studied Bernice. "Who are you looking for, darlin'?"

"Are you Cora Wiley?" said Bernice.

"I am," said Cora. "I haven't had a visitor in a coon's age. Where are you two ladies from?"

"My name is Bernice Horl and this is Rachel Ellis. We're from Los Angeles."

"I used to live in L.A.," said Cora. "Are you tired from driving? Would you like to sit down and cool off? I don't have much, but it's better than standing out here. I've got a trailer in back. If it wasn't for shade trees out there I'd cook to death. C'mon back."

Cora turned her walker around and moved toward the rear of the property. Rachel and Bernice walked on either side of her.

"I don't have a good feeling about this," said Cora. "There's only one way you'd know where I live at. Something happened to my nephew, I'm guessing. He wrote me every week, sometimes more. Sent me money every time. Oh I get Social Security but I can always use more." She turned to Rachel. "Cat got your tongue?"

Before Rachel could answer, Bernice interjected. "She just drove, Cora. I'm the one who wanted to talk to you."

"You're Curly's girlfriend, I'm guessing," said Cora.

"Yes," said Bernice.

"Is he dead?" said Cora.

Bernice glanced at Rachel, who nodded for her to answer.

"Yes," said Bernice. "His funeral was this morning."

"Poor boy," said Cora. "Used to get good grades, had dreams like every other school boy. Got a little wild for a while, but that's just boys. I had a son. He was wild too. Oh well, Curly knew it was coming. I hope for his sake he went fast. I saved his letters if you want to look at them. I know he kept them from you, all the letters. Held a lot in, that kid. Just like his mother. That's what killed her, nervous breakdown after nervous breakdown, too many drugs, all because she carried a hornet's nest inside." Cora pointed to the house. "These people here, they're Jim's son and his wife, Jim Junior and Marian. Junior likes to be called James. Jim left them the house on condition they let me stay here. They said okay so Jim bought me a trailer and put it out back. We don't talk much. They've got their own life, I've got my cable TV, my beer, my little Zippy—that's my dog. Oh, don't worry about me, I've got too much history in me to die. I did some acting in the movies, did makeup, costume design. Oh, I've got stories. Their son, Alan, that'd be Jim's grandson, he writes it all down, says he's going to put it in a book some day. Oh, I've got stories. He goes to the college up here, says he wants to write books."

The driveway curved behind the house and widened into a dilapidated, three-car garage. Each stall had it own door. All were closed. A side door was open. Rachel noticed a washer and dryer just inside. Cora's trailer had one door and two windows. It sat under tall shade trees. Thick, high oleander bushes insulated the property from neighbors on both sides and from the other side of the lot.

"There's home-sweet-home," said Cora. "I got a fan on and ice water in the fridge. If you need to use the bathroom, you can. I'm a generous woman, just never had all that much to be generous with. Help yourself if you're hungry, too."

The base of the door had a three-step, wooden stoop with hand railings. Cora rolled her walker to the side of the trailer, then lifted herself up the stoop by the handrails. Rachel and Bernice offered help, but she refused it. The trailer was clean and comfortable. A fat, small dog wagged its tail but didn't stand. Its eyes were glazed over.

"Say 'hello,' Zippy," said Cora. "He's blind. They say people get like their dogs. Well I'm old but I'm not blind yet. I suppose when Zippy goes, I'll go too."

Bernice went to the bathroom. Cora had framed pictures everywhere. "That's me and Jim," she said, pointing to a photo of her when she was younger. In it, she stood next to a lean, rugged man wearing a painter's cap and suspenders. Both were smiling.

"Jim passed in eighty-four…cancer," said Cora. "Curly never met him."

"Where'd you meet Jim?" said Rachel.

"He drove a truck for a living. He stopped at a filling station on his way back out of L.A. one day when I was looking for a ride out. My time there was long over. I already lived in every town west of there, so I thought I'd head east. Well Jim lost his wife awhile before then and he was still torn up about it, but I chased the blues out of him fast, I'll tell you that. I could always show a man a good time. Still had my shape then, too. He brought me here. We never did marry, but nobody knows. Hell, we didn't need a paper saying we're man and wife. It was nobody's business anyway, right?"

"Right," said Rachel.

"I knew I liked you when I saw you," said Cora. "Look here."

Cora pointed to a five-by-eight photo in a cheap frame on a wall over her television, an old Quasar. Bernice had come out and seen the framed picture. It was of Cora and Curly. "He's got teeth," said Bernice excitedly. "Rachel, did you see this?"

Rachel looked at the picture. "He was handsome."

Cora had opened a drawer in a desk. "Here's some of them letters I was telling you about, darlin'. I got more in the garage—pictures, too, some of Curly when he was a little boy with his mom." She held a stack of letters. "I got the first one he wrote about you, darlin'. Want to read it? He can't complain now if I let you."

Bernice looked at Rachel and blushed.

"Go ahead, Bee," said Rachel.

Bernice started to read them. In no time, she was tearing up. As Cora commented on various letters while Bernice read, Rachel got her cell phone from her purse and said, "I'm going to see if the flight's on time."

Bernice nodded. Rachel stepped out and called her answering machine and L.A.X. She had a message from Lou Carini, Marty's lawyer, asking her to call at the number he left. This surprised Rachel. He had never called her and she'd never met him. She returned the call, but Lou's secretary said he was taking a deposition. Rachel wondered how Lou got her home phone.

Cora stuck her head out the door. "Darlin'," she said. "Your friend wants to see the pictures. They're in the garage. Do you mind? Through that side door there, cabinet's on your left. My stuff's in a cardboard box."

Rachel went in the garage and turned on a light. Dust and rat droppings were everywhere. The first stall had a pickup truck in it with four flat tires and a rusted body. She found the cabinet and photos and carried the box out. Before she reached the trailer, however, she stopped suddenly, put the box down and returned to the garage. With each step, she grew more alarmed.

An old canvas tarp was draped over the front of the truck. It had lain atop the vehicle for so long that it could have been a layer of skin, such had it molded to the contours of the body. Rachel lifted it. The front end was dented into a v-shape. The hood was buckled. One headlight was out. Rachel rubbed her finger through dust on the body. The color was green. Its license plates were temporary. The dealership it was sold from was on North Figueroa in Highland Park, south of and contiguous to Hillside Park.

Rachel shuddered. My God, she thought, after all this time.

~ THIRTY-THREE ~

Around three o'clock, Joey entered The Sonoma Inn. Dom was standing at the hostess's table. He cocked his head to see through the upper half of his bifocals who it was.

"Are you Dominick?" Joey asked.

"Who's asking."

"I'm Joey Bagliamente, Marty's nephew. Can I talk to you?"

Dom hesitated. "We'll go to my office."

He walked to the hallway between his bar and restaurant lobby. Joey saw four patrons in the bar. Dom closed the door, indicated for Joey to sit, then took his seat behind his desk. "What do you want?"

"I'm trying to find out where my uncle might've bought a house for his mistress. I don't know who else—"

"She's a couple miles away."

"Turns out that's not really where she lives," said Joey.

"Then you're out of luck."

"I heard you and my uncle were going to go into business once."

"That was a long time ago."

"So you had to be friends at least. He didn't spend hardly any time at home, so you must've known where he went to do certain stuff. Maybe he bought a house for other girls back then. I'm just trying to find out."

"We went way back, but a woman come between us."

"Yeah, I heard she worked for you awhile and—"

"Did I say it was Rachel Ellis?"

"No."

"Then shut up and listen," said Dom. "It was his wife. Him and me were going to build a restaurant over on La Cienega near Wilshire. But she said over her dead body. We tried to tell her this would be a different class of people, but she was another do-gooder. Ask me, the world's got too many of them. Anyway, this was going to be real dago food, from the old country, where Marty's grandparents emigrated from. They brought a recipe book with them in this ornate-type handwriting. That's how we were going to advertise it, kind of a gimmick. I mean, the book was real and the recipes were real, but the idea was to hook them with this authenticity thing. Idiots in L.A. love that shit, phonies that they are. Well when his wife put the kibosh on the deal, I says, 'Marty, 'least give me the book. All that wop food, I could make a killing if you're not going to use it.' No, he wanted it kept in the family. I got pissed off and we never talked again. But before that I took a recipe for this spicy-sausage soup in there. That's all I got out of the whole deal. I serve that here. I got credit for that soup and it's helped my business. I've got to admire your uncle for that, him not telling anybody that wasn't my own, not that it would've made a spit of difference."

"What happened to the book?" said Joey.

"Didn't I say we never talked again?"

Joey stood up. "I can see why Uncle Marty hated you."

"You can, huh?" said Dom. "He cost me a lot of money with his big mouth. I hope he rots with all the other shit in the ground. Get out of here."

Joey left by himself. He returned to the Kitchen.

~ ~

Cora Wiley wondered what was taking Rachel so long. With Bernice reading Curly's letters, she left to find Rachel. Rachel heard the woman's walker rolling into the laundry room.

"Coming," said Rachel. She met Cora in the laundry room and stopped. She indicated the pickup truck. "Did Curly bring that here?"

Cora couldn't conceal her surprise. "I plumb forgot. You must be a cop or lawyer or a private investigator. Is that the real reason you came?"

"I drove Bernice here because she wanted to find out who Curly sent letters to. She doesn't know anything about this. I'd appreciate it if you don't tell her, either. It would serve no useful purpose."

"I won't if you won't," said Cora.

"What can you tell me about it?"

"Curly wanted to kill himself over it, I'll tell you that. He never was the same after that night. Last couple letters, he wrote how it was coming up to a special anniversary of that night, twenty years of torture and guilt over that poor boy. That's why he ended up homeless. He had no piss and vinegar left in him after that, after he stole that pickup to go joyriding. He's paid dearly for it. Curly had a heart, I'll tell you. His world ended that night."

"What happened after that?"

"He drove that thing all the way here, the whole night, had to take surface streets, said the front wheel was busted from the crash and he couldn't go over a certain speed. He got here at sunup. Lucky for him he never got stopped, even though only one headlight was working. Jim was already on the road. I told him my nephew wanted to store that till he got enough money to fix it up like new. Well, before long Jim just forgot about it. It just became another piece of storage in this dirty old place. Then when he died, I put it in the kids' mind it belonged to me, and one day I'd get it fixed and sell it and go to Vegas till the money ran out. Anyway, it never came up again."

"Did Curly tell you who he killed?"

"Somebody important's all he said. Was it your kin?"

Rachel shook her head. A car horn took their attention.

"That's my groceries," said Cora. "If my beer's warm, you'll see a death right here, and it won't be mine."

Cora turned her walker around and left the garage. Rachel followed. Cora met a teenage boy with a large sack of groceries. As Cora looked through the bag, Rachel picked up the box of photographs and carried it into the trailer. Bernice was halfway through one stack of Curly's letters.

"Rachel, listen to this," said Bernice. "Here's what he wrote a couple years ago. 'Most people roam about to learn what is in their own souls, for others will tell them if they are asked and have no reason to lie. I roam about to learn my fate, but no one can tell me what it is, for they don't know what I have done. But God will deliver my fate through another person, for He knows.' Rachel, what was he talking about? It sounds like he had a death wish."

"It's possible he was at peace when he died."

"Yeah, I'm starting to see that, I really am. But didn't he think a part of *me* would die, too?" She folded the letter and put it aside. "Do you think I should tell Cora I'm pregnant? I'd like to come back and visit her on my own. Then she might see me as part of the family."

"By then it'll be obvious to her you're pregnant," said Rachel. "When the time's right you can."

"I guess."

"I'm going to wait in my car," said Rachel. "You need to spend time alone with Cora."

"Rachel, tell me the truth. I'm going to be a single mom and you're moving away. Do you think it's premature to think of asking Cora to move in with me, you know, like Eddie Perez used to live in my guest house? It's just sitting there. I have no one else, and she's at least family to my baby."

"Bee, you lost your parents, you lost Eddie, you lost Curly. Cora's not going to live forever. Do you want that when you're trying to raise a child?"

"But she's all alone."

"She's content. I suspect when she finishes telling her story to Jim's grandson, her age will catch up to her."

"You mean that's when she'll die?"

"Did you hear her, Bee? She talks nonstop. What happens when she runs out of stories to tell?"

Bernice thought about this. "But I don't want to be alone."

"Cora does."

The delivery boy brought Cora's groceries into the trailer and sat them on a table in the kitchen area. Cora followed him in. "Beer's cold," she said. "That's a smart fella there. I told him once, that's all it took."

The delivery boy nodded shyly to Rachel and Bernice, then left.

"I brought the pictures in, Cora," said Rachel.

"Good girl."

Rachel extended her hand: "Enjoyed meeting you, Cora. I'm going to wait outside for Bernice."

As they shook hands, they reiterated via their eyes that the history of the pickup truck would remain secret.

"Give me just a few more minutes, Rachel," said Bernice.

"Just as well," said Cora. "I'll need my nap soon, what with this heat."

She put her groceries away. It took effort, as she needed to support herself with one hand on the table. During this time, Bernice returned to reading Curly's letters. With both occupied, Rachel went to her car.

~ ~

Cedar pulled into Kenny's parking lot a few minutes before four o'clock. He brought in the new cell phone. Kenny got dry-mouthed and visibly nervous, but this was unseen by Cedar, who was busy unwrapping the cell phone from its packing. Kenny wondered when to confront Cedar about being dumped on. When Cedar was ready to explain how to operate the cell phone, he looked up at Kenny and saw his anxiety.

"Don't sweat it," said Cedar.

"What."

"This," said Cedar. "It's easy to use. I read the instruction documentation on mine. So here's your phone."

Kenny took the cell phone and glanced at it without interest.

"I'll call you when I see Rachel leaving the terminal with her passenger," said Cedar. "When that rings, press the green button there and say hello. Don't hang up. Listen and talk and drive. If we get cut off—they tell me that happens—I'll call you right back. Press the green button again. Any questions?"

"No."

"I'll follow her on foot to where she parked. If we stop at baggage, I'll let you know that too."

"If you know what terminal her plane's coming in on, why don't you just tell me now and I'll park as close as I can to it."

"And risk her seeing you?"

"Yeah, okay."

"It's fully charged, but you never know with these things. I'm putting a charger-adapter in your car. Plug it in when you start your car. If I plug it in now, it will drain your car battery. The charger plug goes here."

He pointed to the bottom of the cell phone. Kenny looked.

Cedar opened his palm. "Give me your keys and I'll set it up now."

Kenny gave him his car keys. Cedar took the cell phone and left the bar. In his absence, Kenny paced. Cedar returned four minutes later.

"The phone's on now," he said. "There's no password. The manual's too technical for that. I put it in your glove box. As soon as you start your car, plug the charger in and set the phone next to you. Don't touch it until it rings."

"All right," said Kenny.

"When you park your car, turn off your motor and take the charger plug out of the cell phone. It will stay charged. When I call you, start your motor and plug the charger back in. That's all until I tell you where she's parked. Still no questions?"

"Nope."

"When I call, get ready to pull out and pay the parking attendant. I will identify Rachel's car, including her license plate."

"I know what her car looks like."

"We don't know what she'll be driving. I never understood why Marty let her drive a clunker like that dented Corolla. I suspect she has a nicer car. I will tell you where she'll be exiting the airport. Go there and let me know the second she's in sight. When I'm on her tail, you can come back here. Before you close I'll bring you Marty's check-cashing money. That's your reward for all this."

"Where is it?" said Kenny.

"In Marty's office."

"The hundred grand."

"Yes," said Cedar. "Gino left it there."

Kenny's tone was flat. "Is that right."

Cedar had anticipated a different reaction. "What's the matter?"

Kenny moved backward. His voice was tentative. "I uh...I don't like this, Cedar."

"You don't like what?" said Cedar.

"I've got to have money up front or you got no deal."

Cedar tensed. "Where'd this come from?"

"I'll tell you," said Kenny. "I think this is a set-up. You're going to get whatever's in Marty's Kitchen tonight, even if you have to kill Rachel to get it, or she's going to get it even if she has to kill you for it. And nobody's going to give Kenny a red cent. Nobody gives a shit about Kenny. And hell's going to break loose. You might think I'm as dumb as a tree, but I know what's going on here. Little old Kenny's going to help out Cedar, then Cedar's going to get rid of little old Kenny."

"You think you're going to be left holding the bag?"

"All's I know's this is one time I'm not getting screwed. And I'm definitely not taking the fall for Curly."

Cedar tried to focus on a positive outcome, lest he strangle Kenny on the spot. He got a quick idea. "So do what I'm going to do."

"What."

"Get out tonight."

"With what?" snapped Kenny. "My good looks? If you want my help, I want money now."

Cedar had a response before Kenny's demand left his mouth. "I'll be right back," he said. He left.

Kenny lit a cigarette. "Least he didn't kill me."

Cedar drove to The Sonoma Inn. It had four cars in front. The hostess' table was unattended. He glanced in the bar and did not see Dom. He went to the office and opened the door without knocking. Dom was napping with invoices in front of him. Cedar's entrance woke him. Cedar closed the door, went around Dom's desk, and put his gun to Dom's temple. "It's Cedar. Give me the cash in your safe. I'm going to count to three. At three, you get a hole in your head."

Dom stood up and moved a framed picture on a wall. He opened the safe under it, reached in, and handed stacks of bundled cash to Cedar. Cedar put the gun in Dom's ear, pulled the trigger, and left. By the time he reached the bar area, four customers and the bartender looked on with frantic curiosity after hearing Cedar's gun. He shot three times into the bar while running toward the exit. Everyone ducked. He got in his Cherokee and used side streets south of Hector Street to get back to Kenny's. Six minutes later, Cedar entered Kenny's. Kenny was surprised he'd come back so soon.

"That was fast," said Kenny.

"Now you can sleep better," said Cedar. He put the stacks of cash on the bar. "Dom's dead. That's from his safe. Stay here like nothing happened. Leave for L.A.X. at six. If you screw up, I'll find you and kill you."

Kenny's face was white. He could not speak. Cedar, knowing he'd made an impression, left through the back.

Sirens filled the air immediately. Kenny went outside in time to see emergency vehicles racing in the direction of Dom's.

~ THIRTY-FOUR ~

Rachel got to L.A.X. twenty minutes early. She needed the time to relax. The trip back from San Bernardino had drained her. The whole time, Bernice kept talking about Curly's letters, and the whole time Rachel feigned interest. She could not share Bernice's affection for Curly's thoughts while knowing that he had killed Paul Bagliamente.

Yes, Curly was a loser. Yes, Paul's death was an accident. Yes, it ate at Curly every day of his life afterward. But not knowing who killed their son had eaten at Marty and Gloria every day of their lives, too. Marty died with the mystery. Rachel now had the power to solve it for Gloria. But what kind of power was that? Was she supposed to gloat or feel impelled to tell? All she knew driving back to L.A. was that she had yet another burden to carry.

The waiting area at the arrival gate, on the second floor of the terminal, was crowded and filling up fast. Rachel looked one last time at a flight-schedule monitor and then sat in a long row of seats that faced the runways. Men and women noted her. She'd changed into an orange cotton tank top, a silk beige fringe skirt, and short-heeled sandals.

Cedar stood hiding just outside the waiting area. He wore a polo shirt, jeans, and loafers. Once he saw where Rachel sat, he went to a guest shop and bought a bottle of water. As he sipped it and watched passersby, he felt anxiety. He could not go home again after killing Dominick. Maybe it didn't matter, because the closest he would get to Hillside Park later on was San Marino, where he would change vehicles. He could approach from the south and avoid northeast L.A., which would be crawling with police.

He watched Rachel. She'd rested her head on the back of the chair, folded her hands around her purse strap and crossed her legs. How serene, he thought. He could pull up a chair and watch her for hours. Guys sitting across from her stared, too.

Rachel may have looked peaceful, but inside she was roiling. She'd had to get tough with Bernice when she dropped her off before going home to change clothes. With rush hour slowing traffic from West Covina on, Rachel had worried about even getting to the airport on time. So when she arrived at Bernice's house and Bernice wouldn't get out of the car, her frustration forced her to raise her voice. "I have to get going, Bee," she said.

"But I don't want to be alone," Bernice said. "I just buried him this morning. Can't you see how much I'm hurting?"

"I've got to get to the airport."

"Was I blind, Rachel? I feel like I never knew Curly after reading all that stuff. There was depth there. It makes me feel even *more* alone. I'm so scared."

"Bee, maybe you should go back to the hospital for a while."

"Is that what you want to do with me?" said Bernice. "Warehouse me so you can go off with your daughter?"

"She's coming in because she wants to say good-bye to Marty at his grave with her mother. We need to be together for this."

"Who do I get to be with?"

Before Rachel could respond, Bernice got out of the car and stormed angrily to her house. Halfway there, she turned around. "Don't worry about me, Rachel. I won't try to kill myself again. I wouldn't want to inconvenience you anymore. We're not friends, anyway. A friend would tell me who the father of her child was."

This painful goodbye was on Rachel's mind as she sat there looking so peaceful to Cedar and the others in the terminal at L.A.X. After staring at her a little longer, he called Kenny. Kenny answered after two rings. "Where are you?" said Cedar.

"Circling the airport," said Kenny. "You're in a shitload of trouble, man. They got cops going door-to-door. They got road blocks, helicopters. They described your car on the news."

"Standard procedure," said Cedar.

"I pretended to be pissed off at the cops for scaring my business away. That's what I told one of 'em anyway, like he gave a shit. But it gave me an excuse for closing up. Man, it's funny how things work out. You realize I've got the only bar left in Hillside Park? A week ago we planned to bump Marty off so's I could get more business. Now look. He's gone, Cammy's a religious nut, and Dom's room temperature. It's incredible, man."

"I'm going to give you some advice, Kenny."

"Yeah, what's that?"

"Spend money on your place and get somebody else to run it. You don't know how to make customers feel welcome."

"Yeah, prolly not."

"Rachel could beef up your business. She learned from Marty. And you can trust her with the books."

"What am *I* supposed to do?" said Kenny. "Sit on my ass?"

"Get a personality makeover," said Cedar. "You're too wired up."

"That's something, coming from a laid-back guy like yourself."

Cedar didn't respond.

"I'm kidding, all right, man?" said Kenny. "Yeah, I could probably take a back seat. But it's not going to be Rachel. She hates me. Anyway, what made you turn against Marty after all them years?"

"He was slipping," said Cedar. "I like being on a winning team."

"How's that?"

"Never mind. The point is there will be inquiries. You don't want to know too much. You'll break under the strain. Just leave it alone."

"You've got to tell me something, man. What's the big mystery about the Kitchen?"

"Marty wasn't protecting it from anything people could steal."

"Then what was he protecting?"

"His privacy."

"I don't get it."

"You will in time. The plane lands in fifteen minutes. I'll call you back then."

Cedar hung up. Kenny patted his cell phone as if it were his ticket to a kingdom of naked, horny women. Cedar had given him eleven thousand dollars from Dom's safe. If he were frugal, he could paint and carpet his bar, get new stools and lighting, and maybe even retile the bathrooms. He just had to get through this night.

~ ~

Joey found what he was looking for in the Kitchen. The last row of shelves before the living quarters contained assorted books, most old and worn. Subjects varied from self-help in emotional matters, principles of business management, labor-relations practices, and so forth. Many were novelty books, mostly humorous, given to Marty as gifts over the years.

One book, however, stood out. It was tall, thick and old. Its binding was loose and fragile. Joey opened it carefully. Its title was *Ricette*. He turned to the table of contents, all in Italian, and found a page number for *osso buco*. Hidden there was a sealed glassine envelope. A name and address showed through. The name was Adina Ellis. The address was a Burbank residence.

After looking at the envelope, Joey stared in awe at the book. "This belonged to my great grandparents, Rosa and Augusto Bagliamente. Wow."

He left for the back exit. On the way he saw the turned-down picture of Rachel's daughter on Marty's desk. He picked it up and studied it. Out of curiosity, he took it out of the frame. On the back was handwriting.

~ ~

Rachel got up from her seat when the plane came to a stop and the passenger ramp was put in place. Cedar stayed out of sight. He had the luxury of a wide, circular column between him and Rachel. She had her back to him. She lit up at the sight of her daughter. When they made eye contact, each got bubbly. Seconds later, the reason for their reunion surfaced, and sadness overcame them.

Cedar was stunned at Dina's beauty. At five-eight, she was thin and lithe, with straight black hair that touched her shoulders. Her eyes were exotic and wide. Her face was a little bony, as if baby fat had burned off overnight and her skin had yet to accommodate the loss. Her smile glowed with warmth and friendliness. She wore a white Gabardine jacket, a vest with a plunging V-neck and black pants. A carry-on bag was draped over her shoulder. She wasn't sexy like her mother, thought Cedar, but she was prettier. Rachel was full-bodied and voluptuous. With no effort, she could be a pouty vixen or she could strut a naughty-girl sexuality. Her daughter, though, could do neither. She was too model-like even to have a shape, although he couldn't tell her age. Maybe full womanhood was just around the corner. She had the clean, crisp California look you see in TV commercials for diet soft drinks.

The hug lasted so long that passengers had to walk around them. Finally Rachel pulled away and they headed out. Cedar moved around the column until mother and daughter were ahead of him and on their way to the concourse that would take them to the terminal's exit and onto parking structures. He followed at a safe distance.

~ ~

Joey got home and took a quick shower. During it, he wondered how to ask his mother for the car. They hadn't talked since the funeral reception. He heard the TV in the living room. His mother was watching live coverage of the aftermath of Dom's killing. Joey had heard sirens earlier when he was in the Kitchen. He knew that Cedar was at the center of the chaos.

Joey got dressed in clean jeans, T-shirt and sneakers. He made a quick decision not to tell his mother he was going to take her car. She would go berserk at seeing him, through the living room window, drive off in her car, but he would rather suffer being yelled at than fight with her if she refused to let him use it.

He left his great grandparents' recipe book in his bedroom, but he put the glassine envelope from it in Rachel's yearbook, the one he took from her Golding Circle house, and brought it with him. He took two other things, Marty's gun and a map to find the Burbank address.

~~

Rachel and Dina waded through crowds until they reached the curb at the street separating terminals from parking structures. There, as taxis, shuttles and other vehicles passed by, they waited for the pedestrian light to turn green. They'd gotten past their initial sorrow and, with so much to say, had started talking effusively. Cedar had never seen Rachel so vigorously engaged.

Though to Cedar the light took forever to change, Rachel and Dina were talking too much to care. Worried that Rachel would see him, he kept turning away. He was amid hordes of people. On one such turn, he felt dizzy. For a second, everything went black. This alarmed him until he rationalized a cause. He had not exercised since his leg injury, nor had he been on his feet twelve hours a day at Marty's. Then a scarier thought came. Was it a lack of work and exercise or a recurrence of the blackout in which he suffocated Helen without realizing it? He wondered: "Is Slapper following me?"

An oxygen fix was all he needed. Get blood to the brain, he said. Then came another dizzy spell and loss of sight. He breathed harder, but too many people and the exhaust from passing vehicles made him claustrophobic.

Rachel and Dina hadn't crossed the street yet. Cedar phoned Kenny.

"Yeah," said Kenny. "What's happening?"

"Where are you?" said Cedar.

"Same. Circling. I feel like a racehorse, only slower."

"We're outside the terminal," said Cedar. "Kenny, do I sound all right?"

What a weird question, thought Kenny. "Yeah, 'course," he said. "Why, what's the matter?"

That was all Cedar needed. It's in my head, he thought, so don't acknowledge anything or you'll appear weak. "Where are you exactly?"

"Rounding down here in front of the international flights, all the little foreigners with all their cameras and shit."

"We're outside the last building down the road from you," said Cedar. Try to hide between cars so she doesn't see you stopped at the light."

"My car's going to stick out, man. I haven't had it washed in ten years, I think."

"The light's changing," said Cedar. "They're heading for the building across from me. Pull over and stop first chance you get."

"Okay, I'm pulling over," said Kenny.

"It looks like she parked on street level," said Cedar. "Yes, they're going in about…four, five, six, there, seven cars in, first row, they reached her car. She's unlocking it. It's a Lexus, dark blue, shiny. License plate starts with three—jay—p as in Peter. Got that?"

"Three jay pee," said Kenny.

"Right," said Cedar. "They're in the car. She's pulling out. The exit's just around the corner. Start moving now. She'll be out of here in thirty seconds. There's no line at the parking booths. Are you moving yet?"

"I just took off."

Cedar stepped up his pace when he saw that Rachel was headed for the garage's exit.

"She left the building," said Cedar a moment later. "She's pulling up to the parking attendant. She's handing over her ticket."

"I'm almost there," said Kenny.

"Get to the main exit," said Cedar. "Tell me when you see her. She's driving, but *don't get close.* Just tell me when you see the car."

"I'm looking," said Kenny.

Cedar took the stairs to the upper level, where he'd parked. All the time he kept the cell phone welded to his ear.

"I'm turning to the main airport exit," said Kenny. "I got a stop sign here—no Lexus yet."

"Don't lose her!"

"No, I'm on top of it," said Kenny. "Where are you?"

"Don't worry about that. Keep watching."

"You would've made a shitty school teacher, you know that, Cedar? Nobody can ask you questions without—"

"Concentrate on what you're doing!" said Cedar. He reached the top of the structure. He had rushed up the stairs so quickly that he felt dizzy again. Then came a blackout. He involuntarily dropped his cell phone. He put his palms against his temples as if to hold his head steady. In the blackness, he saw a fragment of a lightning bolt flash long enough for him to realize he was losing his grip on reality.

"It *is* following me," he said. "Jesus almighty, I'm cracking up."

He reached down to retrieve his cell phone. When he stood up, the dizziness returned. He leaned against a car to stabilize himself. The car's alarm went off. He blinked to keep his vision from going away. Then he heard Kenny's voice.

"Are you there? Cedar, are you there? Where are you?"

Cedar put the cell phone to his ear and tried to sound reassuring. "I'm here."

"Where'd you go?" said Kenny. "I kept yelling for you."

"I'm right here. Where are you?"

"I'm on her, man. She don't have a clue. She's just yakking away to some girl—typical woman driver."

"Are you on Century or Sepulveda?" said Cedar.

"We already passed Sepulveda. We're going straight on Century. She's probably going to take the freeway north."

"I'm getting in my car now."

Cedar unlocked his Cherokee and rolled down all the windows. He sped to the exit, all the time breathing fast to get oxygen in his blood. "Where now?"

"Still heading east," said Kenny. He lit a cigarette. "I love this, man. I feel like a gumshoe. Yeah, it looks like she's heading for the freeway. She's going north on the four-oh-five. See me yet? Oh wait, there's a red light. She's slowing down."

"Get behind another car," said Cedar. "Don't let her see you in her mirror."

"That won't happen, man. She can't shut up. I'm surprised she can even drive with her mouth working like that. Judy was like that, too. Women shouldn't get driver's licenses, I swear. Women and chinks, they're a menace on the road."

Cedar tuned out Kenny's commentary. He handed the attendant his ticket. Three dollars, said the read-out. He paid, waited for the gate to rise, then sped off.

"We're on the freeway," said Kenny. "Where are you?"

"Still on Century, about a mile from the on-ramp," said Cedar. "I'll make the light."

"We're in the second right lane. Traffic's not bad. Man, this is like a ride at Disneyland. I could make a living doing this, tailing people."

Cedar was feeling better. He hadn't had a blackout in a few minutes. Maybe it was just anxiety. Too much time in Hillside Park, where he was a big fish. He would have to analyze all this when he could find the time. It was probably panic attacks. But panic attacks happened only to weaklings. Cedar knew he didn't fit that category.

Soon he was heading north on the four-oh-five and going faster than traffic. "Do you see me in your mirror?" he said. "I'm in the next lane to your left."

"Yeah!" shouted Kenny. "We did it, man. You see me yet?"

"No," said Cedar. "Give me a minute."

Cedar lied about not seeing Kenny's car. It was only four ahead of his in the next lane. Rachel's was two cars ahead of Kenny's.

"Hang back so I can overtake you," said Cedar. "Do it slowly."

"You want me to slow down?" said Kenny. "Okay, here goes."

Kenny lifted his foot off the gas pedal. The car behind him braked and changed lanes at the same time. The other three cars did the same.

"See me now?" said Kenny. "You better, we're almost parallel."

Cedar didn't answer. He had set aside his cell phone and taken a gun from his glove compartment.

Not hearing an answer, Kenny looked over his left shoulder. There he saw Cedar, two lengths behind.

"Cedar!" said Kenny. "You've got to see me now, man, I can almost touch you."

Cedar sped up until he was neck and neck with Kenny. Kenny kept looking at him. He wondered why Cedar didn't have his cell phone at his ear. And where was his *other* hand? On top of that, what's that look in his eyes?

Cedar's eyes locked on Kenny with purpose and determination. This kicked in Kenny's instincts. He hit his brakes and held his steering wheel to prevent swerving if his wheels locked. He saw Cedar pointing a gun at him.

Cedar fired. Kenny ducked. The bullet shattered Kenny's windshield. At the same time he got rear-ended, as did the car that rear-ended him. Cedar moved into the next lane over, behind a minivan and out of sight from Rachel. He saw in his rearview mirror that the pileup from Kenny's braking involved four other cars. Spurts of smoke from screeching tires on subsequent cars braking fast looked like a series of cherry bombs going off.

None of the cars in front of Kenny stopped or slowed, though Cedar saw the driver behind Rachel reach for his cell phone, punch three digits, then frantically yell into it.

In his rearview mirror, Cedar saw cars in the three left lanes beside the pile-up continue on after their drivers rubber-necked the accident.

Kenny got out of his car to see the damage. His rear bumper was smashed in and his trunk had popped open. At the same time he was outraged that Cedar tried to kill him, he was relieved to be alive.

A glance at the other four cars revealed that no one was injured. Their drivers were just getting out.

Kenny didn't know what to do. Cars in the other lanes were zipping by perilously close. Curious motorists were slowing southbound lanes. He wanted to call the cops on Cedar because it finally hit him, with maddening lateness, that Cedar not only was murderously nuts but suicidal. This wasn't road rage. This was a planned execution on one of the nation's busiest freeways. Yet he didn't have the courage to report Cedar for fear that he himself was too entangled in Cedar's crimes. Instead, he hung his head and waited for events to catch up to him.

The four other drivers met in a group just behind Kenny. He was barely aware of them. They were asking each other if everyone was all right. Then there was a sudden hush. Kenny felt it even above the din of speeding cars. He looked at the group. All were staring at him.

"What're you looking at me for?" he screamed. "I got shot at. What the hell was I supposed to do?"

He'd expected a show of sympathy, some sort of concern that although he had triggered the pileup, they were all somehow related as victims of a mishap that could have been much worse.

"What the hell are you looking at?" he shouted. "Say something!"

Then he saw one of them peer into the trunk of Kenny's car. Another did too. Their reactions were queasy and disturbing.

What the hell are they looking at? Kenny wondered. He walked to them and saw Helen's naked body in his trunk.

~ THIRTY-FIVE ~

Rachel continued north on the four-oh-five past the interchange with the Ten. This surprised Cedar. He'd expected her to live near Hillside Park, due east of the interchange. Later, when she passed the interchange with the Hollywood Freeway, he was more surprised. This meant she lived in the Valley, an even greater distance from where she grew up.

She took the Burbank Boulevard exit and drove west around a golf course to an area of well-kept older houses. When she headed north on an intersecting street, Cedar stopped at the corner. He waited until he saw which house was hers, then followed her there, parked a few doors away and waited until she and Dina went inside.

Dina put her bag on the dining room table as Rachel turned on lights. "It's stuffy," said Rachel. "Let me open some windows."

"I'll get the blinds in front," said Dina.

As Dina closed the blinds in the living room and turned on a lamp, Rachel went to the bedrooms and opened windows.

Cedar made it to the rear of the property. He watched Rachel through one of the windows just before she closed its blinds. He started to remove its screen with a pocketknife.

Dina was in a captain's chair in the living room when Rachel returned and sat across from her. Dina removed her shoes to rub her feet. She and Rachel were exhausted from the day's activities.

"Jet lag?" said Rachel.

"That or depletion," said Dina. "This guy next to me asked if I knew it was true jet lag only happens when you're flying east to west."

"That's some pick-up line."

"Actually, he was cute."

"Did he ask for your phone number?"

"Not after I told him I was coming to L.A. for a funeral."

"I hate that word," said Rachel. "It's hard to believe Marty won't be coming over here again."

"It makes me cherish the time we did have together."

Rachel hesitated, then said, "When we took you to the airport, he cried all the way back."

"The old softie," whispered Dina. She wiped a tear with the back of her hand. "Did it have anything to do with me leaving?"

"Absolutely not," said Rachel.

"People do die from broken hearts."

"For you he had a *swollen* heart. You should have heard him. 'A diploma from N.Y.U.,' he kept saying. No, he was proud of you."

"Nothing was bothering him?" said Dina.

Rachel shook her head. "He was a little down."

"About what?"

"It was twenty years almost to the day his son died."

"I forgot," said Dina.

"So this is what it's come to," said Rachel sadly. "The stigma it put on you, how I let myself be held down just because I loved him and he supported us, all the time pretending—"

"Mom, stop it," Dina said emphatically.

"What do you think has been going through my mind this week?"

"What."

"Guilt and shame."

"Over what? He wouldn't leave his wife—God knows you tried to get him to. I remember those fights. He worshipped the ground you walked on and I know he gave *me* all the love any father could give…and I couldn't imagine a better mother than you."

"I tried."

"Besides, look at what he taught us about getting past stuff that others get bogged down by. He'd want you to get on with it. If you've got to get a job, that's a good thing. You'll meet a lot of exciting people in New York. Already there's so many different people there. It's so amazing, Mom, really."

Rachel looked away and shrugged.

"You couldn't find *anything* in the Kitchen?" said Dina.

"I can't figure it out," said Rachel.

"You think he forgot?"

"I think he procrastinated. He was still young, you know."

"I know he always said it was hidden. But from you?"

Rachel shook her head. "He was scared Gloria would find out."

"Have you taken the time to *think* about where it might be? I know you looked."

"No, I haven't had time to think. I haven't slept. Plus I didn't tell you—I talked to his wife about the will yesterday."

"*That* took guts," said Dina.

"It was not my best moment. I felt like a beggar."

"What'd she say?"

"'Go to hell.'"

"She must have thought you were a real class act."

"It was me paying for my sins. I felt like a beggar *and* a whore."

"Mom, will you please stop it? What do you think *she* felt like? *She* stayed in a dead marriage, and *she's* the one who made it *dead* in the first place, the way she shut Marty off and all."

A noise spooked Dina. She lowered her voice. "Shhh."

"What?" said Rachel.

Dina gasped at a sight behind Rachel. Rachel turned and saw Cedar entering from the dining room with his gun drawn. Her surprise had a deep, eerie quality to it, as if she were being physically violated.

"What a pair to draw to," said Cedar.

Rachel moved to protect her daughter. Cedar rushed forward and grabbed Rachel from behind. He threw her violently against the fireplace. Dina screamed. Rachel crashed into the glass hood of the fireplace, then landed dazed on the floor.

Dina jumped on Cedar's back with an arm around his neck and her other hand pummeling him in the back of his head. He peeled her arm away, turned, and knocked her out with a punch to her face. She landed in front of the sofa at the other end of the room.

He picked Rachel off the floor and slapped her into alertness. "It's your Prince," he said.

Rachel saw that Dina, unconscious and lying on her side, had a bruise swelling on her cheek and a bleeding lip. She tried to beat Cedar's face with her fists, but he held her wrists firmly.

"How'd you get here?" said Rachel.

"Don't worry about it."

"I said, how'd you get here?"

"And I said don't—"

"How'd you get here, damnit?!"

The volume of her voice surprised him. "You got sloppy, that's how," he said. "Just like Marty."

"I said, how'd you get here?"

Cedar nodded toward Dina. "She left a message on the answering machine at your other domicile."

"If you harm her I'll kill you, Cedar."

"I *am* going to harm her. And I'll enjoy it."

Rachel tried to wrest free, but Cedar held her wrists harder. When she tried to kick him in his groin, he threw her against the other wall. She slammed into the gun cabinet with such force that its glass doors shattered and caved inward. She tried to extricate herself but was caught in splintered wood and shards of glass. When she moved, the pain from razor-like cuts in her flesh made her yelp and squirm.

Cedar used the butt of his gun to clear away the glass and wood fragments that held her back. When she pulled loose, two hinge screws ripped
a tear in her top and hung her up. Cedar pulled the tear apart with both
hands until her top fell in tatters from her body. He stared at her bra, then
pinned her shoulders against what remained of the cabinet.

"I came for the money," said Cedar.

"There isn't any," said Rachel. "Marty lied to me."

"He did not. I knew Marty. It's there. You're just not smart enough to
find it and I can't go look."

"Because you killed Curly?"

"*And* Dom."

Rachel closed her eyes. "Jesus," she whispered.

Cedar moved his eyes back to her bra as if lost in the pleasure he could
yet derive from them.

Rachel told herself: "If it will save Dina's life, let him have it."

"You're going to pay for shooting me," he said.

"Just get it over with."

"No," said Cedar. "No rush job. This is going to be good for both of
us."

"Cedar, I'm bleeding. I'm in pain."

"So was I. Only it wasn't little marks like a rabbit makes. You almost
crippled me." He affected a supplicating tone. "Rachel, it's been too long."

Rachel just glared at him.

"You knew when you dumped me I'd want more," said Cedar. "Just like
the other guys. Was it revenge because your dad was an asshole? Or were
you born cold-blooded?"

"Cedar, I had problems back then. You can understand that."

"I can, but a higher source can't. No one gets away with anything for
long."

"What do you *want*?" shouted Rachel.

"I want to pick up where we left off. And if it's not to my satisfaction,
I'll try *her*." He nodded at Dina.

"Don't do that, Cedar. Can you just go away, for God's sake?"

"I'm entitled, Rachel."

Rachel started crying.

"That's the wrong approach," said Cedar.

He stared into her eyes until she nodded agreement. "A smile's better," he said.

"I can't," said Rachel. "Don't make me."

He moved in to kiss her neck. She let him; it would stall him until she could think of something else. He moved down to her chest. At the same time, he reached around for the hook on her bra straps.

Rachel took the horror of the moment as payback for sins in her youth. Cedar was right. She'd used guys like toys. The booze, the drugs, the sex—she knew it was all wrong. Her father was proof. But since then, she'd apologized to everyone she'd hurt. It took years, but she made amends for wrongs she'd done people, mostly classmates from high school. The exception was Cedar, and that's because he was Marty's right-hand man. Even accessing him would have been dangerous. She'd done everything she could to atone, but Cedar's punishment was a repercussion that leapt over the cleansing, intervening years.

She wondered if she could overtake Cedar: a knee in his groin, a sprint to the bedroom, her gun in the credenza. But she could not afford to put her daughter in greater jeopardy.

As Cedar used both hands to unclasp her bra, Rachel turned her head. She saw Joey standing in the shadows of the dining room. He'd come from the same direction as Cedar. He had Marty's gun but was scared white.

He mouthed to Rachel: "I…saw…his…car…outside."

Rachel mouthed back: "Shoot him."

Cedar looked up and saw Rachel's eyes pointed away. When he turned and saw Joey, he took out his gun.

"Shoot him, Joey!" screamed Rachel.

Joey raised his gun to Cedar. Cedar aimed his at Joey. Cedar fired at the same time Rachel pushed him away. The bullet missed Joey. Cedar jumped behind a captain's chair nearest him.

"*Shoot him*!" screamed Rachel.

Joey ran into the living room with his gun aimed at the captain's chair. Cedar got to his knees. Rachel jumped on Dina to shield her. Cedar looked from behind the chair. He aimed and fired. Joey had been running with his gun pointed. In his panic, he did not see the step-down into the living room. It tripped him and he fell on his face. Cedar's bullet went over his head. Cedar stood up, put both hands on his gun, and aimed it at the prone Joey.

Joey raised his gun from the floor, closed his eyes, and fired. The bullet went through the back of the captain's chair and into Cedar's groin. It jolted him enough for Joey to fire again. This time he aimed higher. The bullet went into Cedar's chest. Cedar fell backward onto the hardwood floor. Joey scrambled to his feet. He was going to fire again, but Cedar did not move.

Rachel crawled quickly to Cedar on her hands and knees and looked at him. Color was draining from his face. He tried to speak. It took effort. He coughed, spit out blood, then said in a whisper: "The world will little note…nor long remember…what happened here tonight."

Rachel hit him with her fist. "*I* will!"

Cedar closed his eyes and died.

Rachel turned to Joey. "You little shit!" she said. She leapt at him with her arms open. The force knocked him on his back. She kissed him with feverish gratitude. He was unresponsive. She stopped.

"Did you get shot?" she said. "Joey! *Joey*!"

He was dazed and speechless. Rachel heard a booming pounding on her front door.

"I called the police!" said a male voice on the other side.

Rachel did not place the voice.

"I'm warning you," repeated the male. "I called the police!"

Rachel tried to cover herself with her torn top but realized it wouldn't work, so she ran into her bedroom to get a blouse. Joey sat up and looked around. He saw Cedar with his eyes closed and not breathing. He saw Dina unconscious. He saw the room partly destroyed. He saw that cuts on Rachel's back had left a trail of blood.

Then came sirens.

When Rachel returned, she was buttoning a blouse and out of breath. She opened the door and saw a man in a suit holding a cell phone. He was in his seventies. He'd been crouching near the door. He was tall, thin, and well groomed, with close-cropped white hair.

"Lou!" said Joey, who had joined Rachel in the foyer. "This is Mr. Carini," he said to her. "Uncle Marty's lawyer."

"What happened?" said Lou. "That *was* gunfire, wasn't it?"

Before anyone could answer, Dina shouted, "Mom!"

Rachel turned to see Dina rushing to her side. "I'm okay, sweetheart. Are you all right?"

"Yes, yes," said Dina. "What happened?"

Rachel guided her to the sofa, where they sat arm-in-arm.

Lou entered cautiously. "Joey, what happened here?"

"I killed a guy," said Joey. The statement contained a hint of self-praise.

~ ~

Paramedics patched up Rachel's cuts and determined that Dina's bruised face was her only injury. They left with Cedar's body. Burbank police set up a crime scene. Neighbors watched for hours. Rachel put the police in contact with Detectives from the Northeast Division, who came to her house when she connected Cedar to the deaths of Curly and Dominick. En route, they got word that Kenny had been arrested with the body of an unidentified adolescent girl in his car trunk.

Rachel and Joey told the police everything they knew. Lou stayed around to offer what assistance he could. Between interviews, Rachel and

Joey went to the kitchen for privacy. Lou said he'd wait to tell Rachel why he was trying to reach her until they could speak in private. Joey had been carrying Rachel's high school yearbook under his arm.

"Do you know how Cedar found me here?" she said.

"No," said Joey. "I saw his Cherokee out front and I figured something bad was happening, so I looked for a way to get in. I saw a window screen leaning against the side of the house and the window open."

"How'd *you* find me?" said Rachel.

"I think you can answer that yourself," said Joey.

Rachel looked at him quizzically.

"What did Uncle Marty tell you about his osso buco?"

Rachel thought about it for a moment, and then it dawned on her. "Oh no," she said.

"What."

"The cook book," she said.

"Yeah," said Joey with a grin.

Rachel demonstratively slapped her forehead. "The cook book."

Joey brought forward the yearbook he'd taken from her Golding Circle house. "I took this," he said. "Hope you don't mind."

"I don't mind," she said. "I think I'll show it to Dina. It's time."

Joey took the glassine envelope from the yearbook and handed it to her. "This was in the cook book on the page for osso buco. I don't know what's inside."

Rachel saw her daughter's name and the Burbank address. She opened the envelope. Inside was a policy document. She perused it and then looked at Joey. "It's for Dina," she said. "It's a living trust. It matures on Marty's death." She looked heavenward. "You kept your word."

Joey was relieved. "And we were looking for cash."

Rachel lowered her head and closed her eyes. Joey couldn't tell if she was praying or crying or both, or if she was embarrassed at whatever emotion poured from her. He wanted to comfort her by saying that anyone under the crisis she'd had to shoulder over the last few days could easily have overlooked what might have been obvious under different circum-stances, but words seemed futile at the moment. He would have reached out and touched her hand, but she curled the fingers of one hand into a fist and placed it under her nose as if to keep sniffling in check. With the other hand she grasped her arm above the elbow. The impression was that she'd braced herself to reduce trembling.

Finally, Joey reached for her wrist that was closest to him and gently pulled it from the tautness she'd forced upon herself. She didn't resist.

"I'm going to miss you," said Joey.

Rachel leaned in and kissed him lightly on his lips. When she finished, she smiled and said: "What do you think of my daughter?"

"Nice," said Joey. "But don't worry. I wouldn't date a cousin."

Rachel studies Joey's eyes for four seconds. "What'd you say?" she said.

"You heard me."

Joey removed from his pocket the photo of Dina he took from the Kitchen and showed Rachel the handwriting on back.

"'To Daddy, with love,' signed Dina," said Joey.

Rachel gripped his hands. "You cannot tell anyone. Marty knew it would break his wife's heart to know he fathered another child."

"I don't want to break her heart either."

"You're a good kid, Joey."

"You're a good grown-up, Rachel."

They grinned.

"Now what?" said Joey.

"I'll stop by the Kitchen tomorrow. There's more of this in Marty's desk. Once I clear all that out, I'll breathe easier."

"Like anybody in New York would even care," said Joey.

"To hell with New Yorkers, *I'm* tired of secrets."

"It's about time," said Joey.

"I'm a slow learner."

Joey folded his arms, sat back and gave her a sly look. "Let's see how good you are."

"What's this, a quiz?" she said.

"A short one. Only one question."

"Go ahead."

"Do you really think we should keep it from my aunt?"

"What? That Marty's her father?"

Joey nodded. Rachel thought about it for a long time. "I don't know," she conceded.

"What kind of answer's that?" said Joey. "You just said 'don't tell anyone,' now you don't know?"

"Well, I'm thinking you're the man of that family now. You can decide."

Joey blushed.

"What's that for?" said Rachel.

"That's what my Mom and Aunt Gloria have been telling me."

"They're right."

"I don't want to have to be the one to decide," said Joey.

"That's tough, isn't it?"

Joey shrugged.

"Besides, Joey. I think you'll be seeing more of your aunt now."

"How come?"

"You'll need her advice on running the club."

"What?"

"Take it over, Joey. Marty wanted you to, he just didn't want to fight his wife or your mother about it. That's what I wanted to tell you when we were supposed to have dinner at your house."

"They're not going to change their minds," said Joey.

"If you close the bars and restore the restaurant, they might. Serve wine only, and just off the menus. Let your aunt manage it, and you manage the kitchen. Call it 'Uncle Marty's.'"

Joey smiled and looked away. "Uncle Marty's. That's cool."

"You'd be the fourth generation to run an Italian family-owned kitchen."

"It's getting awesomer all the time."

A few minutes later, Joey left. Lou Carini took his place.

"How'd you know where I live?" said Rachel.

"I'm a lawyer," said Lou. "Certain confidences go with the job."

"I wonder what else Marty told you."

"First, let's get to my promise to him. There's a reading of his will at his house in Glendale tomorrow, but you're not part of it. You are, however, the beneficiary of the house and property on Golding Circle."

"Oh my," said Rachel.

"Marty felt this house here would be too extravagant to bequeath to you without his wife contesting the will. Therefore, she'll inherit it as part of the estate. But the property on Golding Circle is paid for and in your name. All you'll owe is property taxes. I'll mail the deed to that address and you can do with the house and property what you wish."

"What about the contents of this house?" said Rachel.

"All yours."

Rachel showed relief. "A nest egg after all."

"I'm sure he would rather have told you himself," said Lou.

"Of course. Mr. Carini, Marty put cash away once or twice a week he said was for me. Do you know anything about that?"

"Yes I do. He always put it in a plain envelope and dropped it through the mail slot at my house on his way home from the club. I in turn paid the premiums on an irrevocable trust he purchased for one Adina Ellis. He kept the paperwork at his club. I didn't know who she was, and Marty told me not to ask. But it's in her name and it matured upon his death. He told me it was in a secure place."

So, thought Rachel, Dina is taken care of and I'm a homeowner.

~ ~

Rachel and Dina visited Marty's grave the next day. Both cried for a long time as they said good-bye in their own way. Rachel folded her hands in front and silently conveyed her thoughts.

"I hope you can hear me, Marty. I'm sorry to say I know who killed Paul. It was Curly Peetz. If it's any consolation to you, he was racked by guilt from that day on. In a way, that led to his own death. From what Bernice told me, and from what Kenny's been telling the cops—he's in jail, by the way—Curly was aware of the anniversary of that night. In his anxiety about it, he picked a fight with Kenny and evidently Kenny responded by calling Cammy to plan your murder. Bernice told me Curly's anxiety pushed Kenny over the edge. Anyway, Dom was included in the plan.

"Don't worry, I won't tell anyone about Curly. There's no reason to re-open wounds Gloria still feels.

"One thing led to another and the next thing you know, Curly got killed, Dom got killed, and Cedar got killed, plus a girl living with him. I told you she was just a sex-bag.

"Cedar was so much worse than I warned you about. I wish I could say I told you so, but even I never thought he'd go off the deep end like he did. Suffice to say, his whole world collapsed when you told him Joey would be taking over his Monday driving. Talk about a desperate, fragile life…

"Anyway, I learned a bit about myself, too. You hide stuff, you lie a little, it really hurts later on. Guess who opened my eyes? Joey. He's a gem. I suggested he take over the club. He liked the idea. One thing you don't know about him: when he gets something in his mind, he doesn't let go. So I suspect you'll get your wish that the club stays in the family. Only it might not be a nightclub anymore, just a nice, quiet restaurant without the bars. With Dom's closed, Joey can probably do a good business, especially if he spreads that Bagliamente charm all over the place.

"Dina's fine. She came back here to say good-bye to you. Joey knows you're her father. I'm leaving it up to him whether he tells Gloria. I won't.

Don't worry. But it's interesting to speculate that if Gloria finds out, will she take to her husband's daughter? Of course, who wouldn't? She's the greatest kid in the world, right?

"Anyway, Joey's a man now, and he has strong feelings about carrying secrets around. That therapist your sister sent him to did a lot for him. He opened my eyes on that score. You'd be proud of him, Marty.

"Thanks for the house and thanks for the trust you got Dina.

"There's one loose end I'm dreading. That's Bernice. But it's not your problem, so I won't bore you with it.

"We have a terrific daughter, Marty. She'll be a professional some day. We did good, you and me.

"I'm going to go now. I'll see you again some day."

~ ~

Later, Rachel dropped Dina off at the house in Burbank while she went to the Kitchen. She emptied Marty's memorabilia of Dina from his desk. During this time, Dina studied Rachel's high school yearbook.

Around two o'clock that afternoon, Rachel drove to Bernice's house and knocked on the door. Bernice refused to let her in. Instead, she stood in the doorway and screamed insults at her. They were loud enough for the neighbors to hear. The Northeast Division Detectives had informed Bernice earlier in the day of the Coroner's autopsy results and what Kenny confessed to them, that Cedar killed Curly, not an automobile.

"You betrayed my confidence!" shouted Bernice. "You killed my baby's father!"

Rachel was forced to leave abjectly and without opportunity to explain her side of the circumstances. She knew it wouldn't do any good anyway, as Bernice was hysterical.

That evening, Rachel took Dina to Hillside Park. They drove all over, literally every street between Sonoma Boulevard and Hector Street. Pieces of Rachel's history were here and there. Rachel showed her the house on

Golding Circle, the apartment she shared with her father on Sonoma Boulevard, her high school, the closed-up bars, the house where Joey lived, and her old haunts. She even pointed out Cammy as he stood on the corner of Hector Street and Sonoma Boulevard with his bible over his head and tried to flag down sinners as they drove by.

They ended up at Marty's around eight o'clock that night. Rachel wanted to see it one last time. She turned on the lights to the Main Room and the power for the water fountain. They sat and listened to the running water. Rachel didn't talk for a long time. Dina knew something was on her mind, but she waited until Rachel spoke.

"I have a confession to make," said Rachel.

"What? Your boyfriends in high school?" said Dina. "I read your yearbook. You sure had a lot of them."

Rachel chuckled. "As you can see, some were literate enough to sign the book."

"You could've trusted me to judge you as my mother instead of who you were in high school."

"I know," said Rachel. "I don't think parents really ever know if the choices they made were good or bad until years, even decades later. So all I can say is, if you think I mishandled your upbringing, go screw yourself."

They had a good laugh.

When it got quiet again, Rachel said, "No, this is about the future, not the past."

"Go easy on yourself, Mom."

"No, I'm not being self-critical anymore," said Rachel. "I've just got a big job ahead of me and I can't do it if I move to New York. I'm staying here."

This took Dina aback. But she quickly recovered. "That's your confession?"

Rachel nodded.

"Is it Bernice?" said Dina.

"Yes. She needs me."

"Can you get through her resentment at you?"

"I just have to," said Rachel.

"Don't worry, Mom," said Dina. "I'm a big girl."

They squeezed each other's hands as Rachel looked over the Main Room and thought about the bittersweet memories she had of Marty's.

0-595-65064-3

LaVergne, TN USA
31 January 2010
171659LV00002B/38/A